BY THE LIGHT OF THE MOON

BY THE LIGHT OF THE MOON

Dean Koontz

LONDON NEW YORK SYDNEY TORONTO

This edition published 2002
by BCA
by arrangement with Headline Book Publishing
a division of Hodder Headline

CN 109411

Typeset by Palimpsest Book Production Limited,
Polmont, Stirlingshire
Printed and bound in Germany by
GGP Media, Pössneck

This book is dedicated to Linda Borland and Elaine Peterson for their hard work, their kindnesses, and their reliability. And, of course, for catching me in that once-a-year mistake that, if not drawn to my attention, would mar my record of perfection. And for discreetly concealing from me that the real reason they stay around is to ensure that Ms. Trixie receives all the belly rubs that she deserves.

And at his prow the pilot held within
his hands his freight of lives, eyes
wide open, full of moonlight.
   —*Night Flight*, Antoine de Saint-Exupery

Life has no meaning except in terms
of responsibility.
   —*Faith and History*, Reinhold Niebuhr

Now take my hand and hold it tight.
I will not fail you here tonight,
For failing you, I fail myself
And place my soul upon a shelf
In Hell's library without light.
I will not fail you here tonight.
   —*The Book of Counted Sorrows*

1

Shortly before being knocked unconscious and bound to a chair, before being injected with an unknown substance against his will, and before discovering that the world was *deeply* mysterious in ways he'd never before imagined, Dylan O'Conner left his motel room and walked across the highway to a brightly lighted fast-food franchise to buy cheeseburgers, French fries, pocket pies with apple filling, and a vanilla milkshake.

The expired day lay buried in the earth, in the asphalt. Unseen but felt, its ghost haunted the Arizona night: a hot spirit rising lazily from every inch of ground that Dylan crossed.

Here at the end of town that served travelers from the nearby interstate, formidable batteries of colorful electric signs warred for customers. In spite of this bright battle, however, an impressive sea of stars gleamed from horizon to horizon, for the air was clear and dry. A westbound moon, as round as a ship's wheel, plied the starry ocean.

The vastness above appeared clean and full of promise, but the world at ground level looked dusty, weary. Rather than being combed by a single wind, the night was plaited with many breezes, each with an individual quality of whispery speech and a unique scent. Redolent of desert grit, of cactus pollen, of diesel fumes, of hot blacktop, the air curdled as Dylan drew near to the restaurant, thickened with the aroma of long-used deep-fryer oil, with hamburger grease smoking on a griddle, with fried-onion vapors nearly as thick as blackdamp.

If he hadn't been in a town unfamiliar to him, if he hadn't been tired after a day on the road, and if his younger brother, Shepherd, hadn't been in a puzzling mood, Dylan would have sought a restaurant with healthier fare. Shep wasn't currently able to cope in public, however, and when in this condition, he refused to eat anything but comfort food with a high fat content.

The restaurant was brighter inside than out. Most surfaces were white, and in spite of the well-greased air, the establishment looked antiseptic.

Contemporary culture fit Dylan O'Conner only about as well as a three-fingered glove, and here was one more place where the tailoring pinched: He believed that a burger joint ought to look like a *joint*, not like a surgery, not like a nursery with pictures of clowns and funny animals on the walls, not like a bamboo pavilion on a tropical island, not like a glossy plastic replica of a 1950s diner that never actually existed. If you were going to eat charred cow smothered in cheese, with a side order of potato strips made as crisp as ancient papyrus by immersion in boiling oil, and if you were going to wash it all down with either satisfying quantities of icy beer or a milkshake containing the caloric equivalent of an entire roasted pig, then this fabulous consumption ought to occur in an ambience that virtually screamed *guilty pleasure*, if not *sin*. The lighting should be low and warm. Surfaces should be dark – preferably old mahogany, tarnished brass, wine-colored upholstery. Music should be provided to soothe the carnivore: not the music that made your gorge rise in an elevator because it was played by musicians steeped in Prozac, but tunes that were as sensuous as the food – perhaps early rock and roll or big-band swing, or good country music about temptation and remorse and beloved dogs.

Nevertheless, he crossed the ceramic-tile floor to a stainless-steel counter, where he placed his takeout order with a plump woman whose white hair, well-scrubbed look, and candy-striped uniform made her a dead ringer for Mrs. Santa Claus. He half expected to see an elf peek out of her shirt pocket.

In distant days, counters in fast-food outlets had been manned largely by teenagers. In recent years, however, a significant number of teens considered such work to be beneath them, which opened the door to retirees looking to supplement their social-security checks.

Mrs. Santa Claus called Dylan 'dear,' delivered his order in two white paper bags, and reached across the counter to pin a promotional button to his shirt. The button featured the slogan

FRIES NOT FLIES and the grinning green face of a cartoon toad whose conversion from the traditional diet of his warty species to such taste treats as half-pound bacon cheeseburgers was chronicled in the company's current advertising campaign.

Here was that three-fingered glove again: Dylan didn't understand why he should be expected to weigh the endorsement of a cartoon toad or a sports star – or a Nobel laureate, for that matter – when deciding what to eat for dinner. Furthermore, he didn't understand why an advertisement assuring him that the restaurant's French fries were tastier than house flies should charm him. Their fries better have a superior flavor to a bagful of insects.

He withheld his antitoad opinion also because lately he had begun to realize that he was allowing himself to be annoyed by too many inconsequential things. If he didn't mellow out, he would sour into a world-class curmudgeon by the age of thirty-five. He smiled at Mrs. Claus and thanked her, lest otherwise he ensure an anthracite Christmas.

Outside, under the fat moon, crossing the three-lane highway to the motel, carrying paper bags full of fragrant cholesterol in a variety of formats, Dylan reminded himself of some of the many things for which he should be thankful. Good health. Nice teeth. Great hair. Youth. He was twenty-nine. He possessed a measure of artistic talent and had work that he found both meaningful and enjoyable. Although he was in no danger of getting rich, he sold his paintings often enough to cover expenses and to bank a little money every month. He had no disfiguring facial scars, no persistent fungus problem, no troublesome evil twin, no spells of amnesia from which he awoke with bloody hands, no inflamed hangnails.

And he had Shepherd. Simultaneously a blessing and a curse, Shep in his best moments made Dylan glad to be alive and happy to be his brother.

Under a red neon MOTEL sign where Dylan's traveling shadow painted a purer black upon the neon-rouged blacktop, and then when he passed squat sago palms and spiky cactuses and other hardy desert landscaping, and also while he followed the concrete walkways that served the motel, and certainly when he passed the humming and softly clinking soda-vending machines, lost in thought, brooding about the soft chains of family commitment – he was stalked. So stealthy was the approach that the stalker must have matched him step for step, breath for breath. At the door to his room, clutching bags of food, fumbling with his key, he heard too late a betraying scrape of shoe leather. Dylan turned his head, rolled his eyes, glimpsed a looming moon-pale face, and sensed as much as saw the dark blur of something arcing down toward his skull.

Strangely, he didn't feel the blow and wasn't aware of falling. He heard the paper bags crackle, smelled onions, smelled warm cheese, smelled pickle chips, realized that he was facedown on the concrete, and hoped that he hadn't spilled Shep's milkshake. Then he dreamed a little dream of dancing French fries.

2

Jillian Jackson had a pet jade plant, and she treated it always with tender concern. She fed it a carefully calculated and measured mix of nutrients, watered it judiciously, and regularly misted its fleshy, oval-shaped, thumb-size leaves to wash off dust and maintain its glossy green beauty.

That Friday night, while traveling from Albuquerque, New Mexico, to Phoenix, Arizona, where she had a three-night gig the following week, Jilly did all the driving because Fred had neither a license to drive nor the necessary appendages to operate a motor vehicle. Fred was the jade plant.

Jilly's midnight-blue 1956 Cadillac Coupe DeVille was the love of her life, which Fred understood and graciously accepted, but her little *Crassula argentea* (Fred's birth name) remained a close second in her affections. She had purchased him when he'd been just a sprig with four stubby branches and sixteen thick rubbery leaves. Although he had been housed in a tacky three-inch-diameter black plastic pot and should have looked tiny and forlorn, he'd instead appeared plucky and determined from the moment that she'd first seen him. Under her loving care, he had grown into a beautiful specimen about a foot in height and eighteen inches in diameter. He thrived now in a twelve-inch glazed terra-cotta pot; including soil and container, he weighed twelve pounds.

Jilly had crafted a firm foam pillow, a ramped version of the doughnutlike seat provided to patients following hemorrhoid surgery, which prevented the bottom of the pot from scarring the passenger's-seat upholstery and which provided Fred with a level ride. The Coupe DeVille had not come with seat belts in 1956, and Jilly had not come with one, either, when she'd been born in 1977; but she'd had simple lap belts added to the car for herself and for

Fred. Snug in his custom pillow, with his pot belted to the seat, he was as safe as any jade plant could hope to be while hurtling across the New Mexico badlands at speeds in excess of eighty miles per hour.

Sitting below the windows, Fred couldn't appreciate the desert scenery, but Jilly painted word pictures for him when from time to time they encountered a stunning vista.

She enjoyed exercising her descriptive powers. If she failed to parlay the current series of bookings in seedy cocktail lounges and second-rate comedy clubs into a career as a star comedian, her backup plan was to become a best-selling novelist.

Even in dangerous times, most people dared to hope, but Jillian Jackson *insisted* upon hope, took as much sustenance from it as she took from food. Three years ago, when she'd been a waitress, sharing an apartment with three other young women to cut costs, eating only the two meals a day that she received gratis from the restaurant where she worked, before she landed her first job as a performer, her blood had been as rich with hope as with red cells, white cells, and platelets. Some people might have been daunted by such big dreams, but Jilly believed that hope and hard work could win everything she wanted.

Everything except the right man.

Now, through the waning afternoon, from Los Lunas to Socorro, to Las Cruces, during a long wait at the U.S. Customs Station east of Akela, where inspections of late were conducted with greater seriousness than they had been in more innocent days, Jilly thought about the men in her life. She'd had romantic relationships with only three, but those three were three too many. Onward to Lordsburg, north of the Pyramid Mountains, then to the town of Road Forks, New Mexico, and eventually across the state line, she brooded about the past, trying to understand where she'd gone wrong in each failed relationship.

Although prepared to accept the blame for the implosion of every romance, second-guessing herself with the intense critical analysis of a bomb-squad cop deciding which of several wires ought to be cut to save the day, she finally concluded, not for the first time, that the fault resided less in herself than in those feckless men she'd trusted. They were betrayers. Deceivers. Given every benefit of the doubt, viewed through the rosiest of rose-colored lenses, they were nonetheless swine, three little pigs who exhibited all the worst porcine traits and none of the good ones. If the big bad wolf showed up at the door of their straw house, the neighbors would cheer him when he blew it down and would offer him the proper wine to accompany a pork-chop dinner.

'I am a bitter, vengeful bitch,' Jilly declared.

In his quiet way, sweet little Fred disagreed with her.

'Will I ever meet a decent man?' she wondered.

Though he possessed numerous fine qualities – patience, serenity, a habit of never complaining, an exceptional talent for listening and for quietly commiserating, a healthy root structure – Fred made no claim to clairvoyance. He couldn't know if Jilly would one day meet a decent man. In most matters, Fred trusted in destiny. Like other passive species lacking any means of locomotion, he had little choice but to rely on fate and hope for the best.

'Of course I'll meet a decent man,' Jilly decided with a sudden resurgence of the hopefulness that usually characterized her. 'I'll meet dozens of decent men, scores of them, hundreds.' A melancholy sigh escaped her as she braked in response to a traffic backup in the westbound lanes of Interstate 10, immediately ahead of her. 'The question isn't whether I'll *meet* a truly decent man, but whether I'll recognize him if he doesn't arrive with a loud chorus of angels and a flashing halo that says GOOD GUY, GOOD GUY, GOOD GUY.'

Jillian couldn't see Fred's smile, but she could feel it, sure enough.

'Oh, face facts,' she groaned, 'when it comes to guys, I'm naive and easily misled.'

When he heard the truth, Fred knew it. Wise Fred. The quiet with which he greeted Jilly's admission was far different from the quiet disagreement that he had expressed when she'd called herself a bitter vengeful bitch.

Traffic came to a full stop.

Through a royal-purple twilight and past nightfall, they endured another long wait, this time at the Arizona Agricultural Inspection Station east of San Simon, which currently served state *and* federal law-enforcement agencies. In addition to Department of Agriculture officers, a few flinty-eyed plainclothes agents, on assignment from some less vegetable-oriented organization, evidently were searching for pests more destructive than fruit flies breeding in contraband oranges. In fact they grilled Jilly as if they believed a chador and a submachine gun were concealed under the car seat, and they studied Fred with wariness and skepticism, as though convinced that he was of Mideastern origin, held fanatical political views, and harbored evil intentions.

Even these tough-looking men, who had reason to regard every traveler with suspicion, could not long mistake Fred for a villain. They stepped back and waved the Coupe DeVille through the checkpoint.

As Jilly put up the power window and accelerated, she said, 'It's a good thing they didn't throw you in the slammer, Freddy. Our budget's too tight for bail money.'

They drove a mile in silence.

A ghost moon, like a faint ectoplasmic eye, had risen before sundown; and with the fall of night, its Cyclops stare brightened.

'Maybe talking to a plant isn't just an eccentricity,' Jilly brooded. 'Maybe I'm a little off my nut.'

North and south of the highway lay dark desolation. The cool lunar light could not burn away the stubborn gloom that befell the desert after sundown.

'I'm sorry, Fred. That was a mean thing to say.'

The little jade was proud but also forgiving. Of the three men with whom Jilly had explored the dysfunctional side of romance, none would have hesitated to turn even her most innocent expression of discontent against her; each would have used it to make her feel guilty and to portray himself as the long-suffering victim of her unreasonable expectations. Fred, bless him, never played those power games.

For a while they rode in companionable silence, conserving a flagon of fuel by traveling in the high-suction slipstream of a speeding Peterbilt that, judging by the advertisement on its rear doors, was hauling ice-cream treats to hungry snackers west of New Mexico.

When they came upon a town radiant with the signs of motels and service stations, Jilly exited the interstate. She tanked up from a self-serve pump at Union 76.

Farther along the street, she bought dinner at a burger place. A counter clerk as wholesome and cheerful as an idealized grandmother in a Disney film, circa 1960, insisted on fixing a smiling-toad pin to Jilly's blouse.

The restaurant appeared sufficiently clean to serve as an operating theater for a quadruple by-pass in the event that one of the customers at last achieved multiple artery blockages while consuming another double-patty cheeseburger. Of itself, however, mere cleanliness wasn't enough to induce Jilly to eat at one of the small Formica-topped tables under a glare of light intense enough to cause genetic mutations.

In the parking lot, in the Coupe DeVille, as Jilly ate a chicken sandwich and French fries, she and Fred listened to her favorite radio talk show, which focused on such things as UFO sightings, evil extraterrestrials eager to breed with human women, Big Foot (plus his recently sighted offspring, Little Big Foot), and time travelers from the far future who had built the pyramids for unknown malevolent purposes. This evening, the smoky-voiced host – Parish Lantern – and his callers were exploring the dire threat posed by brain leeches purported to be traveling to our world from an alternate reality.

None of the listeners who phoned the program had a word to say about fascistic Islamic radicals determined to destroy civilization in order to rule the world, which was a relief. After establishing residence in the occipital lobe, a brain leech supposedly took control of its human host, imprisoning the mind, using the body as its own; these creatures were apparently slimy and nasty, but Jilly was comforted as she listened to Parish and his audience discuss them. Even if brain leeches were real, which she didn't believe for a minute, at least she could *understand* them: their genetic imperative to conquer other species, their parasitic nature. On the other hand, human evil rarely, if ever, came with a simple biological rationale.

Fred lacked a brain that might serve as a leech condominium, so he could enjoy the program without any qualms whatsoever regarding his personal safety.

Jilly expected to be refreshed by the dinner stop, but when she finished eating, she was no less weary than when she had exited the interstate. She'd been looking forward to an additional four-hour drive across the desert to Phoenix, accompanied part of the way by Parish Lantern's soothing paranoid fantasies. In her current logy condition, however, she was a danger on the highway.

Through the windshield, she saw a motel across the street. 'If they don't allow pets,' she told Fred, 'I'll sneak you in.'

3

High-speed jigsaw is a pastime best undertaken by an individual who is suffering from subtle brain damage and who consequently is afflicted by intense and uncontrollable spells of obsession.

Shepherd's tragic mental condition usually gave him a surprising advantage whenever he turned his full attention to a picture puzzle. He was currently reconstructing a complex image of an ornate Shintu temple surrounded by cherry trees.

Although he'd started this twenty-five-hundred-piece project only shortly after he and Dylan checked into the motel, he had already completed perhaps a third of it. With all four borders locked in place, Shep worked diligently inward.

The boy – Dylan thought of his brother as a boy, even though Shep was twenty – sat at a desk, in the light of a tubular brass lamp. His left arm was half raised, and his left hand flapped continuously, as though he were waving at his reflection in the mirror that hung above the desk; but in fact he shifted his gaze only between the picture that he was assembling and the loose pieces of the puzzle piled in the open box. Most likely, he didn't realize that he was waving; and certainly, he couldn't control his hand.

Tics, rocking fits, and other bizarre repetitive motions were symptoms of Shep's condition. Sometimes he could be as still as cast bronze, as motionless as marble, forgetting even to blink, but more often than not, he flicked or twiddled his fingers for hours on end or jiggled his legs, or tapped his feet.

Dylan, on the other hand, had been so securely taped to a straight-backed chair that he couldn't easily wave, rock, or twiddle anything. Inch-wide strips of electrician's tape wound around and around his ankles, lashing them tightly to the chair legs; additional tape bound his wrists and his forearms to the arms of the chair. His right arm was taped with the palm facing down, but his left palm was upturned.

A cloth of some kind had been wadded in his mouth when he'd been unconscious. His lips had been taped shut.

Dylan had been conscious for two or three minutes, and he hadn't connected *any* pieces of the ominous puzzle that had been presented for his consideration. He remained clueless as to who had assaulted him and as to why.

Twice when he'd tried to turn in his chair to look toward the twin beds and the bathroom, which lay behind him, a rap alongside the head, delivered by his unknown enemy, had tempered his curiosity. The blows weren't hard, but they were aimed at the tender spot where earlier he had been struck more brutally, and each time he nearly passed out again.

If Dylan had called for help, his muffled shout wouldn't have carried beyond the motel room, but it would have reached his brother less than ten feet away. Unfortunately, Shep wouldn't respond either to a full-throated scream or to a whisper. Even on his best days, he seldom reacted to Dylan or to anyone, and when he became obsessed with a jigsaw puzzle, this world seemed less real to him than did the two-dimensional scene in the fractured picture.

With his calm right hand, Shep selected an ameba-shaped piece of pasteboard from the box, glanced at it, and set it aside. At once he plucked another fragment from the pile and immediately located the right spot for it, after which he placed a second and a third – all in half a minute. He appeared to believe that he sat alone in the room.

Dylan's heart knocked against his ribs as though testing the soundness of his construction. Every beat pushed a pulse of pain through his clubbed skull, and in sickening syncopation, the rag in his mouth seemed to throb like a living thing, triggering his gag reflex more than once.

Scared to a degree that big guys like him were never supposed to be scared, unashamed of his fear, entirely comfortable with being a big frightened guy, Dylan was as certain of this as he had ever been certain of anything: Twenty-nine was too young to die. If he'd been *ninety*-nine, he'd have argued that middle age began well past the century mark.

Death had never held any allure for him. He didn't understand those who reveled in the Goth subculture, their abiding romantic identification with the living dead; he didn't find vampires sexy. With its glorification of murder and its celebration of cruelty to women, gangsta-rap music didn't start his toes tapping, either. He didn't like movies in which evisceration and decapitation were the primary themes; if nothing else, they were certain popcorn spoilers. He supposed that he'd never be hip. His fate was to be as square as a saltine cracker. But the prospect of being eternally square didn't bother him a fraction as much as the prospect of being dead.

Although scared, he remained cautiously hopeful. For one thing, if the unknown assailant had intended to kill him, surely he would already have assumed room temperature. He had been bound and gagged because the attacker had some other use for him.

Torture came to mind. Dylan had never heard about people being tortured to death in the rooms of national-chain motels, at least not with regularity. Homicidal psychopaths tended to feel awkward about conducting their messy business in an establishment that might at the same time be hosting a Rotarian convention. During his years of traveling, his worst complaints involved poor house-keeping, unplaced wake-up calls, and lousy food in the coffee shop. Nevertheless, once torture opened a door and walked into his mind, it pulled up a chair and sat down and wouldn't leave.

Dylan also took some comfort from the fact that the sap-wielding assailant had left Shepherd untapped, untouched, and untaped. Surely this must mean that the evildoer, whoever he might be, recognized the extreme degree of Shep's detachment and realized that the afflicted boy posed no threat.

A genuine sociopath would have disposed of poor Shepherd anyway, either for the fun of it or to polish his homicidal image. Crazed killers were probably convinced, as were most modern Americans, that maintaining high self-esteem was a requirement of good mental health.

Locking each sinuous shape of pasteboard in place with a ritualistic nod and with the pressure of his right thumb, Shepherd continued to solve the puzzle at a prodigious pace, adding perhaps six or seven pieces per minute.

Dylan's blurry vision had cleared, and his urge to vomit had passed. Ordinarily, those developments would be reason to feel cheerful, but good cheer would continue to elude him until he knew who wanted a piece of him – and exactly which piece was wanted.

The internal timpani of his booming heart and the rush of blood circulating through his eardrums, which produced a sound reminiscent of a cymbal softly beaten with a drummer's brush, masked any small noises the intruder might be making. Maybe the guy was eating their takeout dinner – or performing preventive maintenance on a chain saw before firing it up.

Because Dylan sat at an angle to the mirror that hung above the desk, only a narrow wedge of the room behind him was presented in reflection. Watching his brother, the jigsaw juggernaut, he glimpsed movement peripherally in the mirror, but by the time he shifted his focus, the phantom glided out of sight.

When at last the assailant stepped into direct view, he looked no more menacing than any fifty-something choirmaster who took great and genuine pleasure in the sound of well-orchestrated voices raised in joyous hymns. Sloped shoulders. A comfortable paunch. Thinning white hair. Small, delicately sculpted ears. His pink and jowly face looked as benign as a loaf of white bread. His faded-blue eyes were watery, as though with sympathy, and seemed to reveal a soul too meek to harbor a hostile thought.

He appeared to be the antithesis of villainy, and he wore a gentle smile, but he carried a length of highly flexible rubber tubing. Like a snake. Two to three feet long. No inanimate object, whether a spoon or a meticulously stropped razor-edged switchblade, can be called evil; but while a switchblade might be used merely to peel an apple, it was difficult at this perilous moment to envision an equally harmless use for the half-inch-diameter rubber tubing.

The colorful imagination that served Dylan's art now afflicted him with absurd yet vivid images of being force-fed through the nose and of colon examinations most definitely *not* conducted through the nose.

His alarm didn't abate when he realized that the rubber tubing was a tourniquet. Now he knew why his left arm had been secured with the palm up.

When he protested through the saliva-saturated gag and the electrician's tape, his voice proved no clearer than might have been that of a prematurely buried man calling for help through a coffin lid and six feet of compacted earth.

'Easy, son. Easy now.' The intruder didn't have the hard voice of a snarly thug, but one as soft and sympathetic as that of a country doctor committed to relieving every distress of his patients. 'You'll be just fine.'

He was dressed like a country doctor, too, a relic from the lost age that Norman Rockwell had captured in cover illustrations for *The Saturday Evening Post*. His cordovan shoes gleamed from the benefit of brush and buffing cloth, and his wheat-brown suit pants depended upon a pair of suspenders. Having removed his coat, having rolled up the sleeves of his shirt, having loosened collar button and necktie, he needed only a dangling stethoscope to be the perfect picture of a comfortably rumpled rural physician nearing the end of a long day of house calls, a kindly healer known to everyone as Doc.

Dylan's short-sleeve shirt facilitated the application of the tourniquet. The rubber tube, when quickly knotted around his left biceps, caused a vein to swell visibly.

Gently tapping a fingertip against the revealed blood vessel, Doc murmured, 'Nice, nice.'

Forced by the gag to inhale and exhale only through his nose, Dylan could hear humiliating proof of his escalating fear as the wheeze and whistle of his breathing grew more urgent.

With a cotton ball soaked in rubbing alcohol, the doctor swabbed the target vein.

Every element of the moment – Shep waving to no one and blitzing through the jigsaw, the smiling intruder prepping his patient for an injection, the foul taste of the rag in Dylan's mouth, the astringent scent of alcohol, the restraining pressure of the electrician's tape – so completely engaged the five senses, it wasn't possible with any seriousness to entertain the thought that this was a dream. More than once, however, Dylan closed his eyes and mentally pinched himself . . . and upon taking another look, he breathed yet harder when nightmare proved to be reality.

The hypodermic syringe surely couldn't have been as huge as it appeared to be. This instrument looked less suitable for human beings than for elephants or rhinos. He assumed that its dimensions were magnified by his fear.

Right thumb firmly on the thumb rest, knuckles braced against the finger flange, Doc expelled air from the syringe, and a squirt of golden fluid caught the lamplight as it glimmered in an arc to the carpet.

With a muffled cry of protest, Dylan pulled at his restraints, causing the chair to rock from side to side.

'One way or another,' the doctor said affably, 'I'm determined to administer this.'

Dylan adamantly shook his head.

'This stuff won't kill you, son, but a struggle might.'

Stuff. Having at once rebelled at the prospect of being injected with a medication or an illegal drug – or a toxic chemical, a poison, a dose of blood serum contaminated with a hideous disease – Dylan now rebelled even more strenuously at the idea of *stuff* being squirted into his vein. That lazy word suggested carelessness, an offhanded villainy, as though this dough-faced, round-shouldered, potbellied example of the banality of evil could not be bothered, even after all the trouble he'd taken, to remember what vile substance he intended to administer to his victim. *Stuff!* In this instance, the word *stuff* also suggested that the golden fluid in the syringe might be more exotic than a mere drug or a poison, or a dose of disease-corrupted serum, that it must be unique and mysterious and not easily named. If all you knew was that a smiling, pink-cheeked, crazed physician had shot you full of *stuff*, then the good and concerned and *not*-crazy doctors in a hospital ER wouldn't know what antidote to apply or what antibiotic to prescribe, because in their pharmacy they didn't stock treatments for a bad case of *stuff*.

Watching Dylan wrench ineffectually at his bonds, the stuff-peddling maniac clucked his tongue and shook his head disapprovingly. 'If you struggle, I might tear your vein . . . or accidentally inject an air bubble, resulting in an embolism. An embolism *will* kill you or at least leave you a vegetable.' He indicated Shep at the nearby desk. 'Worse than him.'

At the burnt-out end of certain bad black days, overwhelmed by weariness and frustration, Dylan sometimes envied his brother's disconnection from the worries of the world; however, although Shep had no responsibilities, Dylan had plenty of them – including, not least of all, Shep himself – and oblivion, whether by choice or by embolism, could not be embraced.

Focusing on the shining needle, Dylan stopped resisting. A sour sweat lathered his face. Exhaling explosively, inhaling with force, he snorted like a well-run horse. His skull had begun to throb once more, particularly where he'd been struck, and also across the breadth of his forehead. Resistance was futile, debilitating, and just plain stupid. Since he couldn't avoid being injected, he might as well accept the malicious medicine man's claim that the substance in the syringe wasn't lethal, might as well endure the inevitable, remain alert for an advantage (assuming consciousness was an option after the injection), and seek help later.

'That's better, son. Smartest thing is just to get it over with. It won't even sting as much as a flu vaccination. You can trust me.'

You can trust me.

They were so far into surreal territory that Dylan half expected the room's furniture to soften and distort like objects in a painting by Salvador Dali.

Still wearing a dreamy smile, the stranger expertly guided the needle into the vein, at once slipped loose the knot in the rubber tubing, and kept the promise of a painless violation.

The tip of the thumb reddened as it put pressure on the plunger.

Stringing together as unlikely a series of words as Dylan had ever heard, Doc said, 'I'm injecting you with my life's work.'

In the transparent barrel of the syringe, the dark stopper began to move slowly from the top toward the tip, forcing the golden fluid into the needle.

'You probably wonder what this stuff will do to you.'

Stop calling it STUFF! Dylan would have demanded if his mouth hadn't been crammed full of unidentified laundry.

'Impossible to say what it'll do, exactly.'

Although the needle might have been of ordinary size, Dylan realized that at least regarding the dimensions of the syringe barrel, his imagination hadn't been playing tricks with him, after all. It was enormous. Fearsomely huge. On that clear plastic tube, the black scale markings indicated a capacity of 18 cc, a dosage more likely to be prescribed by a zoo veterinarian whose patients topped six hundred pounds.

'The stuff's psychotropic.'

That word was big – exotic, too – but Dylan suspected that if he could think clearly, he would know what it meant. His stretched jaws ached, however, and the soaked ball of cloth in his mouth leaked a sour stream of saliva that threatened to plunge him into fits of choking, and his lips burned under the tape, and greater fear flooded through him as he watched the mysterious fluid draining into his arm, and he was *seriously* annoyed by Shep's compulsive waving even though he remained aware of it only from the corner of one eye. Under these circumstances, clear thinking was not easily achieved. Ricocheting through his mind, the word *psychotropic* remained as smooth and shiny and impenetrable as a steel bearing caroming from peg to rail, to bumper, to flipper in the flashing maze of a pinball machine.

'It does something different to everyone.' A sharp but perverse scientific curiosity prickled Doc's voice, as disturbing to Dylan as finding shards of glass in honey. Although this man looked the part of a caring country physician, he had the bedside manner of Victor von Frankenstein. 'The effect is without exception interesting, frequently astonishing, and sometimes positive.'

Interesting, astonishing, *sometimes* positive: This didn't sound like a life's work equal to that of Jonas Salk. Doc seemed to belong more comfortably in the mad-malevolent-megalomaniacal-Nazi-scientist tradition.

The last cc of fluid disappeared from the barrel of the syringe into the needle, into Dylan.

He expected to feel a burning in the vein, a terrible chemical heat that would spread rapidly throughout his circulatory system, but the fire didn't come. Nor did a chill shiver through him. He expected to experience vivid hallucinations, to be driven mad by a crawling sensation that suggested spiders squirming across the tender surface of his brain, to hear phantom voices echoing inside his skull, to be afflicted by either convulsions or violent muscle spasms, or by painful cramps, or by incontinence, to be overcome by either nausea or giddiness, to grow hair on the palms of his hands, to watch the room reel as his eyes spun like pinwheels, but the injection had no noticeable effect – except perhaps to make his fevered imagination register a few degrees higher on the thermometer of the unlikely.

Doc withdrew the needle.

A single bead of blood appeared at the point of the puncture.

'One of two should pay the debt,' Doc muttered not to Dylan, but to himself, an observation that seemed to make no sense. He moved behind Dylan, out of sight.

The crimson pearl quivered in the crook of Dylan's left arm, as though pulsing in sympathy with the racing heart that had once harried it to the farthest capillary and from which it was now and forever estranged. He wished that he could reabsorb it, suck it back through the needle wound, because he feared that in the coming nasty struggle for survival, he would need every drop of healthy blood that he could muster if he hoped to prevail against whatever threat had been injected.

'But debt payment isn't perfume,' Doc said, reappearing with a Band-Aid from which he stripped the wrapper as he talked. 'It won't mask the stink of treachery, will it? Will anything?'

Although once more speaking directly to Dylan, the man seemed to talk in riddles. His solemn words required somber delivery, yet his tone remained light; the half-whimsical sleepwalker smile continued to play across his features, waxing and waning and waxing again, much as the glow of a candle might flux and flutter under the influence of every subtle current in the air.

'Remorse has gnawed at me so long that my heart's eaten away. I feel empty.'

Functioning remarkably well without a heart, the empty man peeled the two protective papers off the Band-Aid tape and applied the patch to the point of the injection.

'I want to be repentant for what I did. There's no real peace without repentance. Do you understand?'

Although Dylan didn't understand anything this lunatic said, he nodded out of a concern that failure to agree would trigger a psychotic outburst involving not a hypodermic needle but a hatchet.

The man's voice remained soft, but a bleach of anguish at last purged all the color from it, even as – eerily – the smile endured: 'I *want* to be repentant, to reject entirely the terrible thing I did, and I want to be able to honestly say that I wouldn't do it again if I had my life to live over. But remorse is as far as I'm able to go. I *would* do it again, given a second chance, do it again and spend *another* fifteen years racked by guilt.'

The single drop of blood soaked into the gauze, leaving a dark circle visible through the vented covering. This particular Band-Aid, marketed for children, came decorated with a capering and grinning cartoon dog that failed either to lift Dylan's spirits or to distract his attention from his booboo.

'I've got too much pride to be contrite. There's the problem. Oh, I know my flaws, I know them well, but that doesn't mean I can fix them. Too late for that. Too late, too late.'

After dropping the Band-Aid wrappings in the small waste can by the desk, Doc fished in a pants pocket and withdrew a knife.

Although ordinarily Dylan wouldn't have used the word *weapon* to describe a mere pocketknife, no less menacing noun would be adequate in this instance. You didn't need either a dagger or a machete to cut a throat and sever a carotid artery. A simple pocketknife would do the job.

Doc changed the subject from unspecified past sins to more urgent matters. 'They want to kill me and destroy all my work.'

With a thumbnail, he pried the stubby blade out of the handle.

The smile finally sank out of sight in the doughy pool of his face, and a frown slowly surfaced. 'A net is closing around me right this minute.'

Dylan figured that with the net would come a significant dose of Thorazine, a straitjacket, and cautious men in white uniforms.

Lamplight glinted off the polished-steel penknife blade.

'There's no way out for me, but damn if I'll let them destroy a life's work. Stealing it is one thing. I could accept that. I've done it myself, after all. But they want to *erase* everything that I've achieved. As if I never existed.'

Scowling, Doc wrapped his fist around the handle of the little knife and drove the blade into the arm of the chair, a fraction of an inch from his captive's left hand.

This didn't have a beneficial effect on Dylan. The shock of fright that jumped through him was of such high voltage that the resultant muscle spasm lifted at least three legs of the chair off the floor and might even have levitated it entirely for a fraction of a second.

'They'll be here in half an hour, maybe less,' Doc warned. 'I'm going to make a run for it, but there's no point kidding myself. The bastards will probably get me. And when they find even just one empty syringe, they'll seal off this town and test everybody in it, one by one, till they learn who's carrying the stuff. Which is you. You're a carrier.'

He bent down, lowering his face close to Dylan's. His breath smelled of beer and peanuts.

'You better take what I'm telling you to heart, son. If you're in the quarantine zone, they'll find you, all right, and when they find you, they'll kill you. A smart fella like you ought to be able to figure out how to use that pocketknife and get himself loose in ten minutes, which gives you a chance to save yourself and gives me a chance to be long gone before you can get your hands on me.'

Shreds of the red skins from peanuts and pale bits of nut meat mortared the spaces between Doc's teeth, but evidence of his madness could not be found as easily as could proof of his recent snack. His faded-denim eyes brimmed with nothing more identifiable than sorrow.

He stood erect once more, stared at the pocketknife stuck in the arm of the chair, and sighed. 'They really aren't bad people. In their position, I'd kill you, too. There's only one bad man in all this, and that's me. I've no illusions about myself.'

He stepped behind the chair, out of sight. Judging by the sounds he made, Doc was gathering up his mad-scientist gear, shrugging into his suit coat, getting ready to split.

So you're driving to an arts festival in Santa Fe, New Mexico, where in previous years you've sold enough paintings to pay expenses and to bank a profit, and you stop for the night at a clean and respectable motel, subsequent to which you purchase a bagged dinner of such high caloric content that it will knock you into sleep as effectively as an overdose of Nembutal, because all you want is to spend a quiet evening putting your brain cells at risk watching the usual idiotic TV programs in the company of your puzzle-working brother, and then spend a restful night disturbed by as little cheeseburger-induced flatulence as possible, but the modern world has fallen apart to such an extent that you wind up taped to a chair, gagged, injected with God knows what hideous disease, targeted by unknown assassins. . . . And yet your friends wonder why you're becoming a young curmudgeon.

From behind Dylan, as though he were as telepathic as he was crazy, Doc said, 'You're not infected. Not in the sense you think. No bacteria, no virus. What I've given to you . . . it can't be passed along to other people. Son, I assure you, if I wasn't such a coward, I'd inject myself.'

That qualified assurance didn't improve Dylan's mood.

'I'm ashamed to say cowardice is another of my character flaws. I'm a genius, certainly, but I'm not a fit role model for anyone.'

The man's self-justification through self-deprecation had lost what little fizz it might at first have possessed.

'As I explained, the stuff produces a different effect in each subject. If it doesn't obliterate your personality or totally disrupt your capacity for linear thinking, or reduce your IQ by sixty points, there's a chance it'll do something to greatly enhance your life.'

On further consideration, this guy didn't have the bedside manner of Dr. Frankenstein. He had the bedside manner of Dr. *Satan*.

'If it enhances your life, then I'll have paid some reparations for what I've done. Hell's got a bed waiting for me, sure enough, but a successful result here would compensate at least a little for the worst crimes I've committed.'

On the motel-room door, the security chain rattled and the dead-bolt lock scraped steel against steel as Doc disengaged them.

'My life's work depends on you. It now *is* you. So stay alive if you can.'

The door opened. The door closed.

With less violence than on arrival, the maniac had departed.

At the desk, Shep no longer waved. He worked the jigsaw puzzle with both hands. Like a blind man before a Braille book, he seemed to read each piece of pasteboard with his sensitive fingertips, never glancing at any scrap of the picture for longer than a second or two, occasionally not even bothering to use his eyes, and with uncanny speed, he either placed each fragment of the image in the rapidly infilling mosaic or discarded it as not yet being of use.

Foolishly hoping that recognition of the desperate danger would transmit by some miraculous psychic bond between brothers, Dylan tried to shout 'Shepherd.' The soggy gag filtered the cry, soaked up most of the sound, and let through only a stifled bleat that didn't resemble his brother's name. Nevertheless, he shouted again, and a third time, a fourth, a fifth, counting on repetition to gain the kid's attention.

When Shep was in a communicative mood – which was less often than the frequency of sunrise but not as rare as the periodic visitation of Halley's comet – he could be so hyperverbal that you felt as if you were being hosed down with words, and just listening to him could be exhausting. More reliably, Shep would pass most of any day without seeming to be aware of Dylan. Like today. Like here and now. In a puzzle-working passion, all but oblivious of the motel room, living instead in the shadow of the Shinto temple half formed on the desk before him, breathing the freshness of the blossoming cherry trees under a cornflower-blue Japanese sky, he was half a world removed in just ten feet, too far away to hear his brother or to see Dylan's red-faced frustration, his clenched neck muscles, his throbbing temples, his beseeching eyes.

They were here together, but each alone.

The pocketknife waited, point buried in the arm of the chair, posing as formidable a challenge as the magic sword Excalibur locked in its sheath of stone. Unfortunately, King Arthur was not likely to be resurrected and dispatched to Arizona to assist Dylan with this extraction.

Unknown *stuff* currently circulated through his body, and at any moment sixty points might drop off his IQ, and faceless killers were coming.

His travel clock was digital and therefore silent, but he could hear ticking nonetheless. A treacherous clock, from the sound of it: counting off the precious seconds in double time.

Accelerating the pace of resolution, Shep worked the jigsaw ambidextrously, keeping two pieces in play at all times. His right hand and his left swooped over and under each other, fluttered across the pile of loose pieces in the box, flew sparrow-quick to blue sky or cherry trees, or to unfinished corners of the temple roof, and back again to the box, as if in a frenzy of nest-building.

'Doodle-deedle-doodle,' Shep said.

Dylan groaned.

'Doodle-deedle-doodle.'

If past experience was a reliable guide, Shep would repeat this bit of nonsense hundreds or even thousands of times, for at least the next half-hour and perhaps until he fell asleep nearer to dawn than to midnight.

'Doodle-deedle-doodle.'

In less dangerous times – which fortunately included virtually all of his life to date, until he'd encountered the lunatic with the syringe – Dylan had occasionally endured these fits of repetition by playing a rhyming game with whatever concatenation of meaningless syllables currently obsessed his brother.

'Doodle-deedle-doodle.'

I'd like to eat a noodle, Dylan thought.

'Doodle-deedle-doodle.'

And not just one lonely noodle—

'Doodle-deedle-doodle.'

But the whole kit and caboodle.

Bound to a chair, full of stuff, sought by assassins: This was not the time for rhyme. This was a time for clear thinking. This was a time for an ingenious plan and effective action. The moment had come to seize the pocketknife somehow, some way, and to do amazing, wonderfully clever, knock-your-socks-off things with it.

'Doodle-deedle-doodle.'

Let's bake a noodle strudel.

4

In his inimitable green and silent way, Fred thanked Jillian for the plant food that she gave him and for the carefully measured drink with which she slaked his thirsty roots.

Secure in his handsome pot, the little guy spread his branches in the soft glow of the desk lamp. He brought a measure of grace to a motel room furnished in violently clashing colors that might have been interpreted as a furious interior designer's loud statement of rebellion against nature's harmonious palette. In the morning, she would move him into the bathroom while she showered; he reveled in the steam.

'I'm thinking of using a lot more of you in the act,' Jilly informed him. 'I've cooked up some new bits we can do together.'

During her performance, she usually brought Fred onstage for her final eight minutes, set him on a tall stool, and introduced him to the audience as her latest beau and as the only one she had ever dated who neither embarrassed her in public nor tried to make her feel inadequate about one aspect or another of her anatomy. Perching on a stool beside him, she discussed modern romance, and Fred made the perfect straight man. He gave new meaning to the term *deadpan reaction*, and the audience loved him.

'Don't worry,' Jilly said. 'I won't put you in goofy-looking pots or insult your dignity in any way.'

Whether cactus or sedum, no other succulent plant could have radiated trust more powerfully than did Fred.

With her significant other having been fed and watered and made to feel appreciated, Jilly slung her purse over her shoulder, grabbed the empty plastic ice bucket, and left the room to get ice and to feed quarters to the nearest soda-vending machine. Lately, she'd been in the grip of a root-beer jones. Although she preferred diet soda, she would drink regular when that was the only form of root beer that she could find: two bottles, sometimes three a night. If she had no choice but the fully sugared variety, then she would eat nothing but dry toast for breakfast, to compensate for the indulgence.

Fat asses plagued the women in her family, by which she wasn't referring to the men they married. Her mother, her mother's sisters, and her cousins all had fetchingly tight buns when they were in their teens, or even in their twenties, but sooner rather than later, each of them looked as if she had shoved a pair of pumpkins down the back of her pants. They rarely gained weight in the thighs or the stomach, only in the gluteus maximus, medius, and minimus, resulting in what her mother jokingly referred to as the gluteus *muchomega*. This curse was not passed down from generation to generation on the Jackson side of the family, but on the Armstrong side – the maternal side – along with male-pattern baldness and a sense of humor.

Only Aunt Gloria, now forty-eight, had escaped being afflicted with the Armstrong ass past thirty. Sometimes Gloria attributed her enduringly lean posterior to the fact that she had made a novena to the Blessed Virgin three times each year since the age of nine, when she'd first become aware that sudden colossal butt expansion might lie in her future; at other times, she thought that maybe a periodic flirtation with bulimia had something to do with the fact that she could still sit on a bicycle seat without requiring the services of a proctologist to dismount.

Jilly, too, was a believer, but she'd never made a novena in the hope of petitioning for a merciful exemption from gluteus muchomega. Her reticence in this matter arose not because she doubted that such a petition would be effective, but only because she was incapable of raising the issue of her butt in a spiritual conversation with the Holy Mother.

She had practiced bulimia for two miserable days, when she was thirteen, before deciding that daily volitional vomiting was worse than living two thirds of your life in stretchable ski pants, with a quiet fear of narrow doorways. Now she pinned all her hopes on dry toast for breakfast and wizardly advances in plastic surgery.

The ice and vending machines were in an alcove off the covered walkway that served her room, no more than fifty feet from her door. A faint breeze, coming off the desert, was too hot to cool the night and so dry that she half expected her lips to parch and split with an audible crackle; hissing faintly, this current of air seemed to serpentine along the covered passage as if it, too, were searching for something with which to wet its scaly lips.

En route, Jilly encountered a rumpled kindly-looking man who, apparently returning from the automated oasis, had just purchased a can of Coke and three bags of peanuts. His eyes were the faded blue of a Sonoran or a Mojave sky in August, when even Heaven can't hold its color against the intense bleaching light, but he wasn't native to the region, for his round face was pink, not cancerously tan, seamed by excess weight and by time rather than by the merciless Southwest sun.

Although his eyes didn't focus on Jilly, and though he wore the distracted half-smile of someone lost in a jungle of complex but pleasant thoughts, the man spoke as he approached her: 'If I'm dead an hour from now, I'd sure regret not having eaten a lot of peanuts before the lights went out. I love peanuts.'

This statement was peculiar at best, and Jilly was a young woman of sufficient experience to know that in contemporary America you should not reply to strangers who, unbidden, revealed their fears of mortality and their preferred deathbed snacks. Maybe you were dealing with a blighted soul who had been made eccentric by the stresses of modern life. More likely, however, you were being confronted by a drug-blasted psychopath who wanted to carve a crack pipe from your femur and use your skin as the cloth for a decorative cozy to cover his favorite beheading ax. Nevertheless, perhaps because the guy appeared so harmless, or maybe because Jilly herself was a tad wiggy after too long a period during which all her conversation had been conducted with a jade plant, she replied: 'For me, it's root beer. When my time is up, I want to cross a River Styx of pure root beer.'

Failing to acknowledge her response, he drifted serenely past, surprisingly light on his feet for a man his size, gliding almost as smoothly as an ice skater, his locomotion in sync with his half-loco smile.

She watched him walk away until she was convinced that he

was nothing worse than another weary soul who'd been wandering too long through the lonely immensity of the Southwest deserts – perhaps a tired salesman assigned to a territory so vast that it tested his stamina – dazed by the daunting distances between destinations, by sun-silvered highways that seemed to go on forever.

She knew how he might feel. Part of her unique stage shtick, her comedic ID, was to present herself as a true Southwest chick, a sand-sucking cactuskicker who ate a bowl of jalapeno peppers every morning for breakfast, who hung out in country-music bars with guys named Tex and Dusty, who was a full sun-ripened woman but also tough enough to grab a rattlesnake if it dared to hiss at her, crack it like a whip, and snap its brains out through its eye sockets. She booked dates in clubs all across the country, but she spent a significant part of her time in Texas, New Mexico, Arizona, and Nevada, staying in touch with the culture that had shaped her, keeping her shtick sharp, refining her material in front of boot-stompin' audiences that would relate to every righteous observation with whoops of approval but would likewise hoot her off the stage if she tried to pass off ketchup as salsa or if she went show-biz phony on them. Driving between these gigs was part of remaining a real and true sandsucker, and although she loved the barren badlands and the sweeping vistas of silver sage, she understood how the daunting emptiness of the desert could leave you smiling as vacuously as a sock puppet, and set you to talking of death and peanuts to an imaginary friend.

In the refreshments alcove, the vending machines offered three brands of diet cola, two brands of diet lemon-lime soda, and diet Orange Crush, but in the matter of root beer, her choice was between abstinence or the sugar-packed, big-ass-makin' real stuff. She pumped quarters with the abandon of a gambling grandma feeding a hot slot machine, and as three cans clattered one at a time into the delivery tray, she murmured a Hail Mary prayer, not with a physiology-related request attached, but just to store up a little goodwill in Heaven.

Carrying three cans of soda and a plastic bucket brimming with ice cubes, she made the short trip back to her room. She'd left the door ajar in anticipation of having full hands upon her return.

As soon as she opened a root beer, she'd have to call her mom in Los Angeles, have a good long mother-daughter gab about the curse of the family ass, new material for the act, who'd been shot recently in the neighborhood, whether the cutting from Fred was continuing to thrive under Mom's good care, whether Clone Fred was as cute as Fred the First. . . .

Shouldering inside, the first thing that she noticed was Fred, of course, who was a breath of Zen serenity in the colorful chaos of the clown-closet decor. And then on the desk, in the shade of Fred, she spotted the can of Coke, beaded with icy condensation, and the three bags of peanuts.

A fraction of an instant later, she saw the open black satchel on the bed. The smiling salesman had been carrying it. Probably his sample case.

Snake-cracking, sand-striding, Southwest Amazons need to be both mentally and physically quick to cope with romance-minded honky-tonk cowboys, both those who are loaded with Lone Star and those who are inexplicably sober. Jilly could fend off the most persistent cowpoke Casanova as fast and forcefully as she could dance Western swing, and her collection of swing-dance trophies filled a display case.

Nevertheless, although she understood the danger when she'd been in the motel room shy of two seconds, she couldn't react fast enough to save herself from the salesman. He came from behind her, locking one arm around her neck, pressing a rag over her face. The soft cloth stank of chloroform or ether, or perhaps of nitrous oxide. Not being a connoisseur of anesthetics, Jilly failed to identify the variety and the vintage.

She told herself *Don't breathe*, and knew that she should stamp hard on one of his feet, should drive an elbow into his gut, but her initial gasp of surprise, in the instant when the rag covered mouth and nose, undid her. When she tried to move her right foot, it was wobbly and seemed to be coming loose at the ankle, and she couldn't remember where her elbows were located or how they worked. Instead of *not* breathing, she breathed in again to clear her head, and this time she filled her lungs with the essence of darkness, as though she were a drowning swimmer, sinking, sinking. . . .

5

'Doodle-deedle-doodle.'
Was a name I gave my poodle.
'Doodle-deedle-doodle.'
On a flute my dog could tootle.

Dylan O'Conner's game had long been an effective defense against being driven into a screaming fit by his brother's occasional spells of monotonous chanting. In the current crisis, however, if he was not able to shut out Shep's voice, he would not be able to stay focused on the challenge posed by his bonds. He would still be taped to this chair, chewing on a cotton cud, when the nameless assassins arrived with the intention of testing his blood for the presence of *stuff* and then chopping him into bite-size carrion for the delectation of desert vultures.

As his fluttering hands rapidly constructed the two-dimensional temple, Shep said, 'Doodle-deedle-doodle.'

Dylan concentrated on his predicament.

The size of the rag in his mouth – a soggy wad large enough to make his entire face ache from the strain of containing it – prevented him from working his jaws as aggressively as he would have liked. Nevertheless, by persistently flexing his facial muscles, he loosened the strips of tape, which slowly began to peel up at the ends and to unravel like a mummy's wrappings.

He drew his tongue out from under the gag, contracted it behind that ball of cloth, and strove to press the foreign material out of his mouth. The extruding rag put pressure on the half-undone tape, which caused twinges of mild pain when, at a few points, the adhesive strips separated from his lips with a tiny prize of skin.

Like a giant human-moth hybrid regurgitating a disagreeable dinner in a low-budget horror movie, he steadily expelled the vile cloth, which slid wetly over his chin, onto his chest. Looking down, he recognized the saliva-soaked ejecta: one of his nearly knee-length white athletic socks, which Doc apparently had found in a suitcase. At least it had been a *clean* sock.

Half the tape had fallen away, but two strips remained, one dangling from each corner of his mouth, like catfish whiskers. He twitched his lips, shook his head, but the drooping lengths of tape clung fast.

At last he could shout for help, but he kept silent. Whoever came to free him would want to know what had happened, and some concerned citizen would call the police, who would arrive before Dylan could throw his gear – and Shep – into the SUV and hit the road. If killers were coming, any delay could be deadly.

Point in pine, gleaming brightly, the pocketknife awaited use.

He leaned forward, lowered his head, and clamped the rubber-coated handle of the knife in his teeth. Got a firm grip. Carefully worked the little instrument back and forth, widening the wound in the arm of the chair until he freed the blade.

'Doodle-deedle-doodle.'

Dylan once more sat up straight in the chair, biting on the handle of the pocketknife, staring cross-eyed at the point, on which a star of light twinkled. He was armed now, but he didn't feel particularly dangerous.

He dared not drop the knife. If it fell on the floor, Shepherd wouldn't pick it up for him. To retrieve it, Dylan would have to rock the chair, topple it sideways, and risk injury. Risking injury remained always near the top of his list of Things That Smart People Don't Do. Even if he toppled the chair without catastrophe, from that new and more awkward position, he might have a hard time getting his mouth around the handle again, especially if the knife bounced under the bed.

He closed his eyes and brooded on his options for a moment before making another move.

'Doodle-deedle-doodle.'

Because he was an artist, brooding was supposed to come easily to Dylan; however, he had never been *that* kind of artist, never one to wallow in bleak thoughts about the human condition or to despair over man's inhumanity to man. On an individual level, the human condition changed day by day, even hour by hour, and while you were soaking in self-pity over a misfortune, you might miss an opportunity for a redeeming triumph. And for every act of inhumanity, the species managed to commit a hundred acts of kindness; so if you were the type to brood, you would be more sensible if you dwelt on the remarkable goodwill with which most people treated others even in a society where the cultural elites routinely mocked virtue and celebrated brutality.

In this case, his options were so severely limited that although he might be an unskilled brooder, he was able quickly to arrive at a plan of action. Leaning forward again, he brought the cutting edge of the blade to one of the loops of glossy black tape that fixed his left wrist to an arm of the chair. Much like a goose bobbing its head, much as Shep sometimes spent hours *imitating* a goose bobbing its head, Dylan sawed with the pocketknife. The bonds began to part, and once his left hand was freed, he transferred the knife from teeth to fingers.

As Dylan quickly cut away the remaining restraints, the jigsaw junkie – now locking pieces in the picture at a frenetic pace that even methamphetamine could not have precipitated – altered his nonsense chant: 'Deedle-doodle-diddle.'

'I feel a pressure in my middle.'

'Deedle-doodle-diddle.'

'I think I have to piddle.'

6

Jilly opened her eyes and saw, blearily, the salesman and his identical twin bending over the bed on which she reclined.

Although she knew that she ought to be afraid, she had no fear. She felt relaxed. She yawned.

If the first brother was evil – and no doubt he was – then the second must be good, so she was not without a protector. In movies and often in books, moral character was distributed in exactly that ratio between identical siblings: one evil, one good.

She'd never known twins in real life. If she ever met any, she would not be able to trust both. Your trust ensured that you would be bludgeoned to death, or worse, in Act 2 or in Chapter 12, or certainly by the end of the story.

These two guys looked equally benign, but one of them slipped loose a rubber-tube tourniquet that had been knotted around Jilly's arm, while the second appeared to be administering an injection. Neither of these interesting actions could fairly be called evil, but they were certainly unsettling.

'Which of you is going to bludgeon me?' she asked, surprised to hear a slur in her voice, as though she had been drinking.

As one, with matching expressions of surprise, the twin salesmen looked at her.

'I should warn you,' she said, 'I know karaoke.'

Each of the twins kept his right hand on the plunger of the hypodermic syringe, but simultaneously each snatched up a white cotton handkerchief with his left hand. They were exquisitely choreographed.

'Not karaoke,' she corrected herself. 'Karate.' This was a lie, but she thought that she sounded convincing, even though her voice remained thick and strange. 'I know karate.'

The blurry brothers spoke in perfect harmony, their syllables precisely matched. 'I want you to sleep a little more, young lady. Sleep, sleep.'

As one, the wonderfully synchronized twins swept the white handkerchiefs through the air and dropped them on Jilly's face with such panache that she expected the cloths to transform magically into doves before they quite touched her skin. Instead, the damp fabric, reeking with the pungent chemistry of forgetfulness, seemed to turn black, like crows, like ravens, and she was borne away on midnight wings, into darkness deep.

Although she thought that she'd opened her eyes an instant after closing them, a couple minutes must have passed in that blink. The needle had been withdrawn from her arm. The twins no longer hovered over her.

In fact, only one of the men was present, and she realized that the other had not actually existed, had been a trick of vision. He stood at the foot of the bed, returning the hypodermic syringe to the leather satchel, which she'd mistaken for a kit of salesman's samples. She realized that it must be a medical bag.

He droned on about his life's work, but nothing he said made any sense to Jilly, perhaps because he was an incoherent psychopath or perhaps because the fumes of nepenthe, still burning in her nose and sinuses, rendered her incapable of understanding him.

When she tried to rise from the bed, she experienced a wave of vertigo that washed her back down onto the pillows. She clutched the mattress with both hands, as a shipwrecked sailor might cling to a raft of flotsam in a turbulent sea.

This sensation of tilting and spinning at last stirred up the fear that she knew she ought to feel but that until now had been an inactive sediment at the bottom of her mind. As her breathing grew shallow, quick, and frantic, her racing heart churned currents of anxiety through her blood, and fear threatened to darken into terror, panic.

She had never been interested in controlling others, but she'd always insisted on being the master of her own fate. She might make mistakes, *did* make mistakes – lots, lots – but if her life was destined to be screwed up, then she'd damn well do the job herself. Control had been taken from her, seized by force, maintained with chemicals, with drugs, for reasons that she could not understand even though she strained to remain focused on her tormentor's line of self-justifying patter.

With the surge of fear came anger. In spite of her karaoke-karate threat and her Southwest Amazon image, Jilly wasn't by nature a butt-kicking warrioress. Humor and charm were her weapons of choice. But here she saw an ample backside in which she emphatically wanted to bury a boot. As the salesman-maniac-doctor-whatever walked to the desk, to pick up his cola and three bags of peanuts, Jilly tried once more to rise in righteous rage.

Again, her box-spring raft tossed in the flamboyant sea of bad motel decor. A second attack of vertigo, worse than the first, spun a whirlpool of nausea through her, and instead of executing the butt-booting assault that she'd envisioned, she groaned. 'I'm gonna puke.'

Retrieving his Coke and peanuts, picking up his medical bag, the stranger said, 'You'd better resist the urge. The effects of the anesthesia linger. You could lose consciousness again, and if you pass out *while* regurgitating, you'll wind up like Janis Joplin and Jimi Hendrix, choking to death on your own vomit.'

Oh, lovely. She'd simply gone out to buy some root beer. Such an innocent undertaking. Not ordinarily a high-risk task. She had fully understood the need to compensate for the root-beer indulgence with a dry-toast breakfast, but she hadn't gone to the vending machines with any expectation whatsoever that by doing so she would put herself at risk of choking to death on her own upchuck. Had she known, she would have stayed in her room and drunk tap water; after all, what was good enough for Fred was good enough for her.

'Lie still,' the crackpot urged not with any element of command in his voice, but with what sounded like concern for her. 'Lie still, and the nausea and the vertigo will fade in two or three minutes. I don't want you to choke to death, that would be stupid, but I can't risk hanging around here, playing nursemaid. And remember, if they get their hands on me and discover what I've done, they'll come looking for anyone I've injected, and they'll kill you.'

Remember? Kill? *They?*

She had no memory whatsoever of any such previous warning, so she assumed that it must have been part of what he'd been talking about when her brain haze, now gradually clearing, had been as thick as London fog.

From the door, he looked back at her. 'The police won't be able to keep you safe from these people who're coming. There's no one to turn to.'

On the rolling bed, in this tilting room, she could not help but think about the chicken sandwich, slathered with chipotle mayonnaise, and the greasy French fries she'd eaten. She tried to concentrate on her assailant, desperate to devastate him with words in place of the boot that she hadn't been able to bury in his bottom, but her gorge kept trying to rise.

'Your only hope,' he said, 'is to get out of the search area before you're detained and forced to have a blood test.'

The chicken sandwich struggled within her as though it retained some of its chicken consciousness, as though the fowl were attempting to take a first messy step toward reconstitution.

Nevertheless, Jilly managed to speak, and she was at once embarrassed by the insult that escaped her, which would have been lame even if she had pronounced it without confusion: 'Siss my kass.'

In comedy clubs, she frequently dealt with hecklers, cracked their thick skulls, wrung their geek necks, stomped their malicious hearts till they cried for mama – metaphorically speaking, of course – using a dazzle of words as effective as the fists of Muhammad Ali in his prime. In postanesthesia disorientation, however, she was about as witheringly funny as chipotle mayonnaise, which right now was the least amusing substance in the known universe.

'As attractive as you are,' he said, 'I'm sure someone'll look after you.'

'Pupid srick,' she said, further mortified by the utter collapse of her once formidable verbal war machine.

'In the days ahead, you'd be best advised to keep your mouth shut about what happened here—'

'Cupid strick,' she corrected herself, only to realize that she had found a new way to mangle the same insult.

'—keep your head down—'

'Stupid prick,' she said with clarity this time, although the epithet had actually sounded more withering when mispronounced.

'—and never speak to anyone about what's happened to you, because as soon as it's known, you'll be a target.'

She almost spat the word at him, '*Hickdead*,' though such crude language, whether or not properly pronounced and clearly enunciated, was not her usual style.

'Good luck,' he said, and then he left with his Coke and his peanuts and his evil dreamy smile.

7

Having cut himself loose from the chair, having taken a quick piddle – *deedle-doodle-diddle* – Dylan returned from the bathroom and discovered that Shep had risen from the desk and had turned his back on the unfinished Shinto temple. Once he began to obsess on a puzzle, Shep could be lured from it neither with promises nor with rewards, nor by force, until he plugged in the final piece. Yet now, standing near the foot of the bed, staring intently at the empty air as though he perceived something of substance in it, he whispered not to Dylan, apparently not to himself, either, but as if to a phantom visible only to him: *'By the light of the moon.'*

During most of his waking hours, Shepherd radiated strangeness as reliably as a candle gave forth light. Dylan had grown accustomed to living in that aura of brotherly weirdness. He had been Shep's legal guardian for more than a decade, since their mother's untimely death when Shep was ten, two days before Dylan turned nineteen. After all this time, he could not easily be surprised by Shep's words or actions, as once he had been. Likewise, in his youth he had sometimes found Shep's behavior creepy rather than merely peculiar, but for many years, his afflicted brother had done nothing to chill the nape of Dylan's neck – until now.

'By the light of the moon.'

Shepherd's posture remained as stiff and awkward as always, but his current edginess wasn't characteristic. Though usually as smooth as the serene brow of Buddha, his forehead furrowed. His face gave itself to a ferocity he'd never exhibited before. He squinted at the apparition that only he could see, chewing on his lower lip, looking angry and worried. His hands cramped into fists at his sides, and he seemed to want to punch someone, though never before had Shepherd O'Conner raised a hand in anger.

'Shep, what's wrong?'

If the lunatic physician with a hypodermic syringe could be believed, they had to get out of here, and quickly. A speedy exit, however, would require Shep's cooperation. He seemed to be teetering on the edge of emotional turmoil, and if he was not calmed, he might prove difficult to manage in an excited state. He wasn't as big as Dylan, but he stood five ten and weighed 160 pounds, so you couldn't just grab him by the back of his belt and carry him out of the motel room as though he were a suitcase. If he decided he didn't want to go, he would wrap his arms around a bedpost or make a human grappling hook of himself in a doorway, hooking hands and feet to the jamb.

'Shep? Hey, Shep, you hear me?'

The boy appeared to be no more aware of Dylan now than when he'd been working the puzzle. Interaction with other human beings didn't come to Shepherd as easily as it came to the average person, or even as easily as it came to the average cave-dwelling hermit. At times he could connect with you, and as often as not, that connection would be uncomfortably intense; however, he spent most of his life in a world so completely his own and so unknowable to Dylan that it might as well have revolved around an unnamed star in a different arm of the Milky Way galaxy, far from this familiar Earth.

Shep lowered his gaze from an eye-level confrontation with the invisible presence, and although his stare fixed upon nothing more than a patch of bare carpet, his eyes widened from a squint, and his mouth went soft, as though he might cry. A progression of expressions fell across his face in swift succession, like a series of rippling veils, quickly transforming his grimace of anger to a wretched look of helplessness and tremulous despair. His tightly gripped ferocity swiftly sifted between his fingers, until his clenched fists, still at his sides, fell open, leaving him empty-handed.

When Dylan saw his brother's tears, he went to him, gently placed a hand on one shoulder, and said, 'Look at me, little bro. Tell me what's wrong. Look at me, see me, be here with me, Shep. Be here with me.'

At times, without coaching, Shep could relate almost normally, if awkwardly, to Dylan and to others. More often than not, however, he needed to be guided toward communication, constantly and patiently encouraged to make a connection and to maintain it once it had been established.

Conversation with Shep frequently depended on first making eye contact with him, but the boy seldom granted that degree of intimacy. He seemed to avoid such directness not solely because of his severe psychological disorder, and not merely because he was pathologically shy. Sometimes, in a fanciful moment, Dylan could almost believe that Shep's withdrawal from the world, beginning in early childhood, had occurred when he had discovered that he could read the secrets of anyone's soul by what was written in the eyes . . . and had been unable to bear what he saw.

'By the light of the moon,' Shep repeated, but this time with his gaze fixed on the floor. His whisper had fallen to a murmur, and with what sounded like grief, his voice broke more than once on those six words.

Shep seldom spoke, and when he did, he never spouted gibberish, even if sometimes it seemed to be gibberish as surely as Cheddar was a cheese. Within his every utterance lay motive and meaning to be discerned, although when he was at his most enigmatic, his message could not always be understood, in part because Dylan lacked the patience and the wisdom to solve the puzzle of the boy's words. In this case, his urgent and fiercely felt emotion suggested that what he meant to communicate was unusually important, at least to him.

'Look at me, Shep. We need to talk. Can we talk, Shepherd?'

Shep shook his head, perhaps in denial of what he seemed to see on the motel-room floor, in denial of whatever vision had brought tears to his eyes, or perhaps in answer to his brother's question.

Dylan put one hand under Shepherd's chin, gently lifted the boy's head. 'What's wrong?'

Maybe Shep read the fine print on his brother's soul, but even eye to eye, Dylan glimpsed nothing in Shepherd but mysteries more difficult to decipher than ancient Egyptian hieroglyphics.

As his eyes clarified behind waning tears, the boy said, 'Moon, orb of night, lunar lamp, green cheese, heavenly lantern, ghostly galleon, bright wanderer—'

This familiar behavior, which might be a genuine obsession

with synonyms or which might be just another technique to avoid meaningful communication, still occasionally annoyed Dylan, even after all these years. Now, with the unidentified golden serum circulating through his body and with the promise of ruthless assassins riding this way on the warm desert breeze, annoyance quickly swelled into irritation, exasperation.

'—silvery globe, harvest lamp, sovereign mistress of the true melancholy.'

Keeping one hand under his brother's chin, tenderly insisting upon attention, Dylan said, 'What's that last one – Shakespeare? Don't give me Shakespeare, Shep. Give me some real feedback. What's wrong? Hurry now, help me here. What's this about the moon? Why're you upset? What can I do to make you feel better?'

Having exhausted his supply of synonyms and metaphors for the moon, Shep turned next to the subject of *light*, speaking with an insistence that implied a greater meaning in these words than they otherwise seemed to possess: 'Light, illumination, radiance, ray, brightness, brilliance, beam, gleam, God's eldest daughter—'

'Stop it, Shep,' Dylan said firmly but not harshly. 'Don't talk *at* me. Talk to me.'

Shep made no effort to turn away from his brother. Instead, he simply closed his eyes, putting an end to any hope that eye contact would lead to useful communication. '—effulgence, refulgence, blaze, glint, glimmer—'

'Help me,' Dylan pleaded. 'Pack up your puzzle.'

'—shine, luster, sheen—'

Dylan looked down at Shep's stocking feet. 'Put on your shoes for me, kiddo.'

'—incandescence, candescence, afterglow—'

'Pack your puzzle, put on your shoes.' With Shepherd, patient repetition sometimes encouraged him to act. 'Puzzle, shoes. Puzzle, shoes.'

'—luminousness, luminosity, fulgor, flash,' Shep continued, his eyes jiggling behind his lids as though he were fast asleep and dreaming.

One suitcase stood near the foot of the bed, and the other lay open on top of the dresser. Dylan closed the open bag, picked up both pieces of luggage, and went to the door. 'Hey, Shep. Puzzle, shoes. Puzzle, shoes.'

Standing where his brother had left him, Shep chanted, 'Sparkle, twinkle, scintillation—'

Before frustration could build to head-exploding pressure, Dylan opened the door, carried the suitcases outside. The night continued to be as warm as a toaster oven, as parched as a burnt crust.

A dry drizzle of yellow lamplight fell on the largely empty parking lot, soaked into the pavement, was absorbed as efficiently by the blacktop as light might be captured by the heavy gravity of a black hole in space. Broad blades of sharp-edged shadows lent the night a quality of guillotine expectancy, but Dylan could see that the motel grounds did not yet seethe with the squads of promised pistol-packing killers.

His white Ford Expedition was parked nearby. Bolted to the roof, a watertight container held artist's supplies as well as finished paintings that he had offered for sale at a recent art festival in Tucson (where five pieces had sold) and would offer also in Santa Fe and at similar events thereafter.

As he opened the tailgate and quickly loaded the suitcases into the SUV, he looked left and right, and behind himself, leery of being assaulted again, as though crazed physicians armed with enormous syringes full of *stuff* could be expected to travel in packs as surely as did coyotes in desert canyons, wolves in forests primeval, and personal-injury attorneys at any prospect of product liability.

When he returned to the motel room, he found Shep where he had left him: standing in his stocking feet, eyes closed, exhibiting his annoyingly impressive vocabulary. '—fluorescence, phosphorescence, bioluminescence—'

Dylan hurried to the desk, broke apart the finished portion of the jigsaw, and scooped double handfuls of Shinto temple and cherry trees into the waiting box. He preferred to save time by leaving the puzzle, but he felt certain that Shep would refuse to go without it.

Shepherd surely heard and recognized the distinctive sound of pasteboard pieces being tumbled together in a pile of soft rubble. Ordinarily, he would have moved at once to protect his unfinished project, but not this time. Eyes closed, he continued urgently to recite the many names and forms of light: '—lightning, fulmination, flying flame, firebolt, oak-cleaving thunderbolts—'

Fitting the lid on the box, Dylan turned away from the desk and briefly considered his brother's shoes. Rockport walkers, just like Dylan's, but a few sizes smaller. Too much time would be required to get the kid to sit on the edge of the bed, to work his feet into the shoes, and to tie the laces. Dylan snatched them off the floor and placed them atop the puzzle box.

'—candlelight, rushlight, lamplight, torchlight—'

The point of injection in Dylan's left arm began to feel hot, and it itched. He resisted tearing off the cartoon-dog Band-Aid and scratching the puncture wound, because he feared that the colorful bandage concealed awful proof that the substance in the syringe had been worse than dope, worse than a mere toxic chemical, worse than any known disease. Under the little rectangle of gauze might wait a tiny but growing patch of squirming orange fungus or a black rash, or the first evidence that his skin had begun metamorphosing into green scales as he underwent a conversion from man to reptile. In full *X-Files* paranoia, he didn't have the courage to discover the reason for the itch.

'—firelight, gaslight, foxfire, fata morgana—'

Burdened with puzzle box and sibling footgear, Dylan hurried past Shep to the bathroom. He hadn't yet unpacked their toothbrushes and shaving gear, but he'd left a plastic pharmacy bottle, containing a prescription antihistamine, on the counter beside the sink. Right now, allergies were the least of his problems; however, even if he were being eaten alive by a vile orange fungus and simultaneously morphing into a reptile, while also being hunted by vicious killers, a runny nose and a sinus headache were complications best avoided.

'—chemiluminescence, crystalloluminescence, counterglow, Gegenschein—'

Returning from the bathroom, Dylan said hopefully, 'Let's go, Shep. Go, now, come on, *move.*'

'—violet ray, ultraviolet ray—'

'This is serious, Shep.'

'—infrared ray—'

'We're in trouble here, Shep.'

'—actinic ray—'

'Don't make me be mean,' Dylan pleaded.
'—daylight, dayshine—'
'Please don't make me be mean.'
'—sunshine, sunbeam—'

8

'Hickdead,' Jilly said again to the closed door, and then maybe she called a brief time-out, because the next thing she knew, she was no longer in the tilting-turning bed, but lay facedown on the floor. For an instant she couldn't remember the nature of this place, but then she gagged on a dirty-carpet stench that made it impossible to hope that she had checked into the presidential suite at the Ritz-Carlton.

After heroically rising to her hands and knees, she crawled away from the treacherous bed. When she realized that the telephone stood on the nightstand, she executed a 180-degree turn and crawled back the way she had come.

She reached up, fumbled at the travel clock, and then pulled the phone off the nightstand. It came easily, trailing a severed cord. Evidently, the peanut lover had cut it to prevent her from making a quick call to the cops.

Jilly considered crying out for help, but she worried that her assailant, if still in the vicinity, might be the first to respond. She didn't want another injection, didn't want to be quieted by a kick in the head, and didn't want to have to listen to any more of his droning monologue.

By focusing her attention and by bringing all her Amazonian strength to bear, she managed to lever herself off the floor and sit on the edge of the bed. This was a fine thing. She smiled, suddenly suffused with pride. Baby could sit up by herself.

Emboldened by this success, Jilly attempted to rise to her feet. She swayed on the way up, pressing her left hand against the nightstand to steady herself, but although she sagged slightly at the knees, she didn't collapse. Another fine thing. Baby could stand upright, as erect as any primate and more fully erect than some.

Best of all, she hadn't puked, as earlier she'd been sure she would. She no longer felt nauseated, just . . . peculiar.

Confident that she could stand without supportive furniture and that she would remember how to walk as soon as she tried, Jilly made her way from the bed to the door in a parabolic arc that compensated for the movement of the floor, which rolled lazily like the deck of a ship in mild seas.

The doorknob presented a mechanical challenge, but after she fumbled the door open and navigated the threshold, she found the warm night to be surprisingly more invigorating than the cool motel room. The thirsting desert air sucked moisture from her, and along with the moisture went some of her wooziness.

She turned right, toward the motel office, which lay at the end of a distressingly long and complicated series of covered walkways that seemed to have been patterned after any laboratory's rat maze.

Within a few steps, she realized that her Coupe DeVille had vanished. She had parked the car twenty feet from her room; but it no longer stood where she recalled leaving it. Empty blacktop.

She weaved toward the vacant parking slot, squinting at the pavement as though she expected to discover an explanation for the vehicle's disappearance: perhaps a concise but considerate memo –
IOU one beloved, midnight-blue Cadillac Coupe DeVille, fully loaded.

Instead she found an unopened bag of peanuts, evidently dropped by the smiling salesman-who-wasn't-a-salesman, and a dead but still formidable beetle the size and shape of half an avocado. The insect lay on its glossy shell, six stiff legs sticking straight in the air, eliciting a far less emotional response from Jilly than would have a kitten or puppy in the same condition.

Harboring little interest in entomology, she left the bristling beetle untouched, but she stooped to pluck the bag of peanuts from the pavement. Having read her share of Agatha Christie mysteries, she had been convinced instantly upon spotting the peanuts that here lay a valuable clue for which the police would be grateful.

When she rose to her full height once more, she realized that the warm dry air had not purged her of the lingering effects of the anesthetic as completely as she'd thought. As a whirl of dizziness came and passed, she wondered if she had been mistaken about where she'd parked the Coupe DeVille. Perhaps it had been twenty feet to the *left* of her motel room instead of to the right.

She peered in that direction and saw a white Ford Expedition, just twelve or fifteen feet away. The Cadillac might be parked on the far side of the SUV.

Stepping over the beetle, she returned to the covered walkway. She approached the Expedition, realizing that she was headed in the direction of the vending-machine alcove where she would find more of the root beer that had gotten her in all this trouble in the first place.

When she passed the SUV and didn't find her Coupe DeVille, she became aware of two people hurrying toward her. She said, 'The smiley bastard stole my car,' before she realized what an odd couple she had encountered.

The first guy – tall, as solid as an NFL linebacker – carried a box approximately the size of a pizza container with a pair of shoes balanced on top. In spite of his intimidating size, he didn't seem the least threatening, perhaps because he had a bearish quality. Not a rip-your-guts-out grizzly bear, but a burly Disney bear of the gosh-how-did-I-get-my-butt-stuck-in-this-tire-swing variety. He wore rumpled khaki pants, a yellow-and-blue Hawaiian shirt, and a wide-eyed worried expression that suggested he'd recently robbed a hive of honey and expected to be hunted down by a swarm of angry bees.

With him came a smaller and younger man – maybe five feet nine or ten, about 160 pounds – in blue jeans and a white T-shirt featuring a portrait of Wile E. Coyote, the hapless predator of the Road Runner cartoons. Shoeless, he accompanied the larger man with reluctance; his right sock appeared to be snugly fitted, but his loose left sock flapped with each step.

Although the Wile E. fan shuffled along with his arms dangling limply at his sides, offering no resistance, Jilly assumed he would have preferred not to go with the bearish man, because he was being pulled by his left ear. At first she thought she heard him protesting this indignity. When the pair drew closer and she could hear the younger guy more clearly, however, she couldn't construe his words as a protest.

'—electroluminescence, cathode luminescence—'

The bearish one halted in front of Jilly, bringing the smaller man to a stop as well. In a voice much deeper – but no less gentle – than that of Pooh, of Pooh Corners, he said, 'Excuse me, ma'am, I didn't hear what you said.'

Head tilted under the influence of the hand that gripped his left ear, the younger man kept talking, though perhaps not either to his burly keeper or to Jilly: '—nimbus, aureola, halo, corona, parhelion—'

She couldn't be certain whether this encounter was in reality as peculiar as it seemed to be or whether the lingering anesthetic might be distorting her perceptions. The prudent side of her argued for silence and for a sprint toward the motel office, away from these strangers, but the prudent side of her had hardly more substance than a shadow, so she repeated herself: 'The smiley bastard stole my car.'

'—aurora borealis, aurora polaris, starlight—'

Seeing the focus of Jilly's attention, the giant said, 'This is my brother, Shep.'

'—candlepower, foot-candle, luminous flux—'

'Pleased to meet you, Shep,' she said, not because she was in fact pleased to meet him, but because she didn't know what else to say, never having been in precisely this situation before.

'—light quantum, photon, *bougie decimale*,' said Shep without meeting her eyes, and continued rattling out a meaningless series of words as Jilly and the older brother conversed.

'I'm Dylan.'

He didn't look like a Dylan. He looked like a Bruno or a Samson, or a Gentle Ben.

'Shep has a condition,' Dylan explained. 'Harmless. Don't worry. He's just . . . not normal.'

'Well, who is these days?' Jilly said. 'Normality hasn't been attainable since maybe 1953.' Woozy, she leaned against one of the posts that supported the walkway cover. 'Gotta call the cops.'

'You said "smiley bastard."'

'Said it twice.'

'What smiley bastard?' he asked with such urgency that you would have thought the missing Cadillac had been his, not hers.

'The smiley, peanut-eating, needle-poking, car-stealing bastard, *that's* what bastard.'

'Something's on your arm.'

Curiously, she expected to see the beetle resurrected. 'Oh. A Band-Aid.'

'A bunny,' he said, his broad face cinching with worry.

'No, a Band-Aid.'

'Bunny,' he insisted. 'The son of a bitch gave you a bunny, and I got a dancing dog.'

The walkway was well enough lighted for her to see that both she and Dylan sported children's Band-Aids: a colorful capering rabbit on hers, a jubilant puppy on his.

She heard Shep say, 'Lumen, candle-hour, lumen-hour,' before she tuned him out again.

'I have to call the cops,' she remembered.

Dylan's voice, thus far earnest, grew more earnest still, and quite grave, as well: 'No, no. We don't want cops. Didn't he tell you how it is?'

'He who?'

'The lunatic doctor.'

'What doctor?'

'Your needle-poking bastard.'

'He was a doctor? I thought he was a salesman.'

'Why would you think he was a salesman?'

Jilly frowned. 'I'm not sure now.'

'Obviously, he's some sort of lunatic doctor.'

'Why's he knocking around a motel, attacking people and stealing Coupe DeVilles? Why isn't he just killing patients in HMOs like he's supposed to?'

'Are you all right?' Dylan asked, peering more closely at her. 'You don't look well.'

'I almost puked, then I didn't, then I almost did again, but then I didn't. It's the anesthetic.'

'What anesthetic?'

'Maybe chloroform. The lunatic salesman.' She shook her head. 'No, you're right, he must be a doctor. Salesmen don't administer anesthetics.'

'He just clubbed me on the head.'

'Now that sounds more like a salesman. I gotta call the cops.'

'That's not an option. Didn't he tell you professional killers are coming?'

'I'm glad they're not amateurs. If you have to be killed, you might as well be killed efficiently. Anyway, you believe *him*? He's a thug and a car thief.'

'I think he was telling the truth about this.'

'He's a lying sack of excrement,' she insisted.

Shep said, 'Lucence, refulgency, facula,' or at least that's what it sounded like, although Jilly wasn't entirely sure that any of those collections of syllables were actually words.

Dylan shifted his attention from Jilly to something beyond her, and when she heard the roar of engines, she turned in search of the source.

Past the parking lot lay a street. An embankment flanked the far side of the street, and atop that long slope, the interstate highway followed the east-to-west trail of the moon. Traveling at a reckless speed, three SUVs descended the arc of an exit ramp.

'—light, illumination, radiance, ray—'

'Shep, I think you've started repeating yourself,' Dylan noted, though he remained riveted on the SUVs.

The three vehicles were identical black Chevrolet Suburbans. As darkly tinted as Darth Vader's face shield, the windows concealed the occupants.

'—brightness, brilliance, beam, gleam—'

Without even a token application of brakes, the first Suburban exploded past the stop sign at the bottom of the exit ramp and angled across the heretofore quiet street. This was the north side of the motel, and the entrance to the parking lot lay toward the front of the enterprise, to the east. At the stop sign, the driver had shown no respect for the uniform highway-safety code; now, with gusto, he demonstrated a lack of patience with traditional roadway design. The Suburban jumped the curb, churned through a ten-foot-wide landscaping zone, spitting behind it a spray of dirt and masticated masses of flowering lantana, briefly took flight off another curb, made a hard four-tire landing in the parking lot, about sixty feet from Jilly, executed a sliding turn at the cost of considerable rubber, and raced west toward the back of the motel.

'—effulgence, refulgence, blaze—'

The second Suburban followed the first, and the third pursued the second, chopping up additional servings of lantana salad. But once in the parking lot, the second turned east instead of continuing to pursue the first, and sped toward the front of the motel. The third streaked straight toward Jilly, Dylan, and Shep.

'—glint, glimmer—'

Just when Jilly thought the oncoming SUV might run them down, as she was deciding whether to dive to the left or to the right, as she considered again the possibility that she might puke, the third driver proved to be as flamboyant a showman as the first two. The Suburban braked so hard that it nearly stood on its nose. Upon its roof, a rack of four motorized spotlights, previously dark, suddenly blazed, swiveled, tilted, took perfect aim, and shed enough wattage on its quarry to bake the marrow in their bones.

'—luminosity, fulgor, flash—'

Jilly felt as though she were standing not before a mere earthly vehicle, but in the awesome presence of an extraterrestrial vessel, being body-scanned, mind-sucked, and soul-searched by data-gathering rays that, in six seconds flat, would count the exact number of atoms in her body, review her entire lifetime of memories beginning with her reluctant exit from her mother's birth canal, and issue a printed chastisement for the deplorably frayed condition of her underwear.

After a moment, the spots switched off, and ghost lights like luminous jellyfish swam before her eyes. Even if she hadn't been dazzled, she wouldn't have been able to get a glimpse of the driver or of anyone else in the Suburban. The windshield appeared not merely to be tinted, but to be composed of an exotic material that while perfectly transparent to those within the SUV, appeared from the outside to be as impenetrable to light as absolute-black granite.

Because Jilly, Dylan, and Shep were not the quarry of this search – not yet – the Suburban turned away from them. The driver stomped on the accelerator, and the vehicle shot eastward, toward the front of the motel, once more following the second SUV, which had already rounded the corner of the building with a shriek of tires and had vanished from sight.

Shep fell silent.

Referring to the lunatic doctor who had warned that violent men would follow in his wake, Dylan said, 'Maybe he wasn't a lying sack of excrement, after all.'

9

These were extraordinary times, peopled by ranting maniacs in love with violence and with a violent god, infested with apologists for wickedness, who blamed victims for their suffering and excused murderers in the name of justice. These were times still hammered by the utopian schemes that had nearly destroyed civilization in the previous century, ideological wrecking balls that swung through the early years of this new millennium with diminishing force but with sufficient residual power to demolish the hopes of multitudes if sane men and women weren't vigilant. Dylan O'Conner understood this turbulent age too well, yet he remained profoundly optimistic, for in every moment of every day, in the best works of humanity as in every baroque detail of nature, he saw beauty that lifted his spirit, and everywhere he perceived vast architectures and subtle details that convinced him the world was a place of deep design as surely as were his own paintings. This combination of realistic assessment, faith, common sense, and enduring hope ensured that the events of his time seldom surprised him, rarely struck terror in him, and never reduced him to despair.

Consequently, when he discovered that Jillian Jackson's friend and traveling companion, Fred, was a member of the stonecrop family of succulents, native to southern Africa, Dylan was only mildly surprised, not in the least terrified, and encouraged rather than despondent. Dealing with any other Fred, not a plant, would almost certainly have entailed more inconvenience and greater complications than would coping with the little green guy in the glazed terra-cotta pot.

Mindful of the three black Suburbans circling the motel, a trio of hungry sharks cruising a sea of asphalt, Jilly hurriedly packed her toiletries. Dylan loaded her train case and her single suitcase in his Expedition, through the tailgate.

Commotion of any kind always distressed poor Shepherd, and when anxious, he could be at his most unpredictable. Now, cooperative when cooperation might have been least expected from him, the boy climbed docilely into the SUV. He sat beside the canvas tote bag that contained a variety of items to occupy him during long road trips, on those occasions when he grew bored after hours of staring into empty space or studying his thumbs. Because Jilly insisted that she would hold Fred on her lap, Shep had the backseat to himself, a solitude that would moderate his anxiety.

Arriving at the Expedition with the pot in both hands, for the first time appearing free of the lingering effects of anesthesia, the woman had second thoughts about getting into a vehicle with two men whom she'd met only minutes ago. 'For all I know, you could be a serial killer,' she told Dylan as he held open the front passenger's door for her and Fred.

'I'm not a serial killer,' he assured her.

'That's exactly what a serial killer would say.'

'It's exactly what an innocent man would say, too.'

'Yes, but it's exactly what a serial killer would say.'

'Come on, get in the truck,' he said impatiently.

Reacting sharply to his tone, she said, 'You're not the boss of me.'

'I didn't say I was the boss of you.'

'Nobody in my family's been bossed in any recent century.'

'Then I guess your real last name must be Rockefeller. Now will you *please* get in the truck?'

'I'm not sure I should.'

'You remember those three Suburbans that looked like something the Terminator might drive?'

'They weren't interested in us, after all.'

'They will be soon,' he predicted. 'Get in the truck.'

'"Get in the truck, get in the truck." The way you say it is so totally serial killer.'

Frustrated, Dylan demanded, 'Do serial killers generally travel with their disabled brothers? Don't you think that would get in the way of doing a lot of grisly work with chain saws and power tools?'

'Maybe he's a serial killer, too.'

From the backseat, Shep peered at them: head cocked, wide-eyed, blinking in bewilderment, looking less like a psychopath than like a big puppy waiting to be driven to the park for a session of Frisbee.

'Serial killers don't always look crazy-violent,' Jilly said. 'They're cunning. Anyway, even if you're not a killer, you might be a rapist.'

'You're a wonderfully cordial woman, aren't you?' Dylan said sourly.

'Well, you might be a rapist. How would I know?'

'I'm not a rapist.'

'That's just what a rapist would say.'

'For God's sake, I'm not a rapist, I'm an artist.'

'They aren't mutually exclusive.'

'Listen, lady, you approached *me* for help. Not the other way around. How do I know what you are?'

'One thing for sure, you know I'm not a rapist. That's not anything men have to worry about, is it?'

Nervously surveying the night, expecting the black Suburbans to reappear with a roar at any moment, Dylan said, 'I'm not a serial killer, a rapist, a kidnapper, bank robber, mugger, pickpocket, cat burglar, embezzler, counterfeiter, shoplifter, or jaywalker! I've had two speeding tickets, paid a fine on an overdue library book last year, kept a quarter and two dimes I found in a pay phone instead of returning them to the telephone company, wore wide neckties for a while after skinny ones were in fashion, and once in a park I was accused of not picking up my dog's crap when it wasn't even my dog, *when in point of fact I didn't even have a dog!* Now you can get in this truck and we can scram, or you can stand here dithering about whether I do or whether I don't look like Charles Manson on a bad-hair day, but with or without you, I am getting out of Dodge City before those stunt drivers come back and the bullets start to fly.'

'You're amazingly articulate for an artist.'

He gaped at her. 'What's *that* supposed to mean?'

'I've just always found artists far more visually than verbally oriented.'

'Yeah, well, I'm plenty verbal.'

'Suspiciously so for an artist.'

'What, you still think I'm Jack the Ripper?'

'Where's the proof you aren't?'

'And a rapist?'

'Unlike me, you *could* be,' she observed.

'So I'm a raping, killing itinerant artist.'

'Is that a confession?'

'What do you do – drum up business for psychiatrists? You go around all the time making people crazy so the shrinks will always have business?'

'I'm a comedian,' she declared.

'You're amazingly unfunny for a comedian.'

She bristled as obviously as a porcupine. 'You've never seen me perform.'

'I'd rather eat nails.'

'Judging by your teeth, you've eaten enough to build a house.'

He flinched from the insult. 'That's unfair. I've got nice teeth.'

'You're a heckler. Anything's fair with hecklers. Hecklers are lower than worms.'

'Get out of my truck,' he demanded.

'I'm not in your truck.'

'Then get into it so I can drag you out.'

Scorn as dry as old bones and as thick as blood lent a dangerous new texture to her voice: 'Do you have issues with people like me?'

'People like you? What is that – crazy people? Unfunny comedians? Women who have unnatural relationships with plants?'

Her scowl was storm-cloud dark. 'I want my bags back.'

'Delighted,' he assured her, at once heading for the back of the Expedition. 'And how fitting – bags for the bag.'

Following him, carrying Fred, she said, 'I've been hanging out with grown men too long. I've forgotten how delectable the wit of twelve-year-old boys can be.'

That stung. Raising the tailgate, he glared at her. 'You can't begin to imagine how much I wish right now I *was* a serial killer.'

'Were,' she said.

'What?'

'You wish you *were* a serial killer. In English grammar, when a statement is in obvious contradiction to reality, the subjunctive mood requires a plural verb after a singular noun or pronoun in conditional clauses beginning with *if*, but also in subordinate clauses following verbs like *wish*.'

Working up a mouthful of sarcasm, Dylan spat out his reply: 'No shit?'

'None whatsoever,' she assured him.

'Yeah, well, I'm a semiarticulate, visually oriented artist,' he reminded her as he removed her suitcase from the Expedition and put it down hard on the pavement. 'I'm no more than half a step above a barbarian, one step above a monkey.'

'Another thing—'

'I knew there would be.'

'If you put your mind to it, I'm sure you'll be able to think of plenty of acceptable synonyms for *feces*. I'd be grateful if you wouldn't use crude language around me.'

Plucking her train case out of the cargo space, Dylan said, 'I don't intend to use much more language of any kind around you, lady. Thirty seconds from now, you'll be a dwindling speck in my rearview mirror, and the instant you're out of sight, I'll forget you ever existed.'

'Fat chance. Men don't forget me easily.'

He dropped her train case, not actually aiming for her foot, but characteristically hopeful. 'Hey, you know, I stand corrected. You're absolutely right. You are every bit as unforgettable as a bullet in the chest.'

An explosion shook the night. Motel windows rattled, and the aluminum awning over the walkway thrummed softly as pressure waves traveled through it.

Dylan felt the shock of the blast in the blacktop under his feet, as if a fossilized Tyrannosaurus rex in deep rock strata were stirring in its eternal sleep, and he saw the dragon's breath of fire in the east-southeast, toward the front of the motel.

'Show time,' said Jillian Jackson.

10

Even as the dragon turned over deep in the earth and as the echo of its roar continued to wake motel guests, Dylan returned Jillian Jackson's two pieces of luggage to the cargo space in the Expedition. Before he quite realized what he was doing, he'd closed the tailgate.

By the time he climbed in behind the steering wheel, his feisty passenger was in the seat beside him, holding Fred on her lap. They slammed their doors in unison.

He started the engine and glanced over his shoulder to be sure that his brother was wearing a seat belt. Shep sat with his right hand flat on top of his head and his left hand atop his right, as though this ten-finger helmet would protect him from the next explosion and from falling debris. His stare matched Dylan's for an instant, but the connection proved too intense for the boy. When Shep closed his eyes and found insufficient privacy in self-imposed blindness, he turned his head toward the window beside him and faced the night, with his eyes still squeezed shut.

'Go, *go*,' Jilly urged, suddenly eager to commit herself to a road trip with a man who might be a cannibalistic sociopath.

Too law-abiding to jump curbs and destroy landscaping, Dylan drove to the front of the sprawling motel to reach the exit lane. Not far from the portico that overhung the entrance to the registration office, he discovered the source of the fire. A car had exploded.

This was not your typical aesthetically pleasing motion-picture kind of exploded car: not dressed by a set designer, not carefully positioned according to the artistic sensibilities of a director, the pattern and size and color of the flames not calculated for maximum prettiness by a pyrotechnics specialist collaborating with a stunt coordinator. These less than cinematic flames were a sour muddy orange as dark as bloodied tongues, and out of the many mouths of the blaze spewed a vomitus of greasy black smoke. The trunk lid had blown off, crumpling into a snarled mass as ugly as any example of modern sculpture, and had landed on the roof of one of the three black Suburbans that surrounded the burning wreckage at a distance of twenty feet. Having been pitched partway through the windshield by the force of the blast, the dead driver lay half in and half out of the vehicle. His clothes must have been reduced to ashes by a storm of fire during the few seconds following the explosion. Now his very substance fueled the pyre, and the seething flames that he produced by sacrifice of fat and flesh, of marrow, were unnervingly different from those that consumed the automobile: rancid yellow veined with red as dark as vinegary Cabernet, with somber green reminiscent of things putrescent.

Unable to look away from this horror, Dylan was ashamed of his inability to break free of the grip of grisly curiosity. Truth resided in ugliness as well as in beauty, and he blamed his macabre fascination on the curse of the artist's eye, although he recognized that this excuse was self-serving. Setting aside self-deception, the ugly truth might be that an enduring fault in the human heart made death perversely attractive.

'That's my Coupe DeVille,' Jilly said, sounding more shocked than angry, visibly stunned by the realization that her life had so abruptly gone wrong in a sleepy Arizona town that was little more than an interstate-highway rest stop.

Ten or twelve men had gotten out of the matched Suburbans, which stood with all the doors flung open. Instead of being dressed in dark suits or in paramilitary gear, these guys wore desert-resort clothes: white or tan shoes, white or cream-yellow pants, regular shirts and polo shirts in a variety of pastels. They appeared to have spent a relaxing day on a golf course and the early evening in a clubhouse bar, cooked by a day of sun and stewed in gin, but not one of them exhibited the alarm or even the surprise that you would expect of average duffers who had just witnessed a catastrophe.

Although Dylan didn't have to drive past the burning Cadillac to reach the exit lane from the motel, a few of these sporty types turned from the fire to stare at the Expedition. They didn't look like accountants or business executives, or like doctors or real-estate developers: They looked rougher and even more dangerous than attorneys. Their faces were expressionless, hard masks as lacking in animation as carved stone except for the reflections of firelight that flickered from ear to ear and chin to brow. Their eyes glittered darkly, and though they tracked the Expedition as it departed, none demanded that it halt; none gave pursuit.

Their hard-chased prey had been brought down. The lunatic doctor had perished in the Cadillac, evidently before they could capture and question him. With him must have been consumed what he referred to as his life's work, as well as all evidence that vials of his mysterious *stuff* were missing. For now this posse or pack – or whatever these men were – believed that the hunt had reached a successful conclusion. If fortune favored Dylan, they would never learn otherwise, and he would be spared a bullet in the head.

He slowed the SUV, then brought it to a full stop, gawking with obvious morbid curiosity at the blazing car. Proceeding without pause might have seemed suspicious.

Beside him, Jilly understood the strategy of his hesitant departure. 'It's hard to play the ghoul when you know the victim.'

'We didn't *know* him, and just a couple minutes ago, you called him a sack of excrement.'

'He's not the victim I'm talking about. I'm glad that smiley bastard's dead. I'm talking about the love of my life, my beautiful midnight-blue Coupe DeVille.'

For a moment, some of the make-believe golfers watched Dylan and Jilly goggling at the burning wreckage. God knew what they might make of Shepherd, who sat in the backseat with his hands still flattened atop his head, as disinterested in the fire as in everything else beyond his own skin. When the men turned away from the Expedition, dismissing its driver and passengers as the usual crash-scene oafs, Dylan took his foot off the brake and moved on.

At the end of the exit lane lay the street across which he had ventured not an hour ago to purchase cheeseburgers and French fries, heart disease on the installment plan. Though he'd never had a chance to eat that dinner.

He turned right on the street and headed toward the freeway as the caterwaul of sirens rose in the distance. He didn't speed.

'What're we going to do?' Jillian Jackson asked.

'Get away from here.'

'And then?'

'Get farther away from here.'

'We can't just run forever. Especially when we don't know who or what we're running from – or why.'

Her observation contained too much truth and common sense to allow argument, and as Dylan searched for a reply, he found that he'd become as verbally challenged as she believed all artists were.

Behind Dylan, as they reached the ramp to the interstate, his brother whispered, *By the light of the moon.*

Shepherd breathed those words only once, which was a relief, considering his penchant for repetition, but then he began to cry. Shep was not a weepy kid. He had wept seldom in the past seventeen years, since he'd been a child of three, when his retreat from the pains and disappointments of this world had become all but complete, since he had begun to live most of each day in a safer world of his own creation. Yet now: tears twice in one night.

He didn't shriek or wail, but cried quietly: thick sobs twined with thin mewling, sounds of misery swallowed before they were fully expressed. Although he labored to stifle his emotion, Shep could not entirely conceal the terrible power of it. Some unknowable grief or anguish racked him. As revealed by the rearview mirror, his usually placid countenance – under his hat of stacked hands, framed by his elbows – was wrenched by a torment as disturbing as that on the face in Edvard Munch's famous painting, *The Scream.*

'What's wrong with him?' Jilly asked as they arrived at the top of the ramp.

'I don't know.' Dylan worriedly shifted his attention between the road ahead and the mirror. 'I don't know.'

As though melting, Shepherd's hands slid slowly from the top of his head, down his temples, but firmed up again, hardening into fists just below his ears. He ground his knuckles against his cheekbones, as though he were resisting a fearsome inner pressure that threatened to fracture his facial structure, stretch his flesh, and forever balloon his features into a freakshow face.

'Dear God, I don't know,' Dylan repeated, aware of the tremor of distress in his voice as he transitioned from the entrance ramp onto the first eastbound lane of the interstate.

Traffic, all of it faster than the Expedition, raced through the Arizona night toward New Mexico. Distracted by his brother's whimpers and groans of despair, Dylan couldn't match the pace set by the other motorists.

Then good Shep – docile Shep, peaceful Shep – did something that he had never done before: With his clenched fists, he began to strike himself hard in the face.

Awkwardly balancing the potted jade plant on her lap, turned halfway around in her seat, Jilly cried out in dismay. 'No, Shep, don't. Honey, don't!'

Although putting distance between themselves and the men in the black Suburbans was imperative, Dylan signaled a right turn, drove onto the wide shoulder of the highway, and braked to a stop.

Pausing in his self-administered punishment, Shep whispered, *'You do your work,'* and then he hit himself again, again.

11

Having gotten out of the Expedition to allow Dylan O'Conner a degree of privacy with his brother, Jilly parked her not-yet-big butt on the guardrail. She sat with her unprotected back to a vastness of desert, where venomous snakes slithered in the heat of the night, where tarantulas as hairy as the maniacal mullahs of the Taliban scurried in search of prey, and where the creepiest species native to this cruel realm of rock and sand and scraggly scrub were even more fearsome than serpents or spiders.

The creatures that might be stalking Jilly from behind were of less interest to her than those that might approach on the eastbound lanes in synchronized black Suburbans. If they would blow up a mint-condition '56 Coupe DeVille, they were capable of any atrocity.

Although no longer nauseated or lightheaded, she didn't feel entirely normal. Her heart wasn't jumping like a toad in her chest, as it had been during their flight from the motel, but it wasn't beating as calm as a choirgirl's, either.

As calm as a choirgirl. That was a saying Jilly had picked up from her mother. By *calm*, Mom hadn't meant merely *quiet and composed*; she had also meant *chaste* and *God-loving*, and much more. When as a child Jilly had fallen into a pout or had flung herself high into a fit of pique, her mother reliably recommended to her the shining standard of a choirgirl, and when Jilly had been a teenager excited by the smooth moves of any acne-stippled Casanova, her mother had suggested somberly that she live up to the moral model of the oft-cited and essentially mythical choirgirl.

Eventually Jilly in fact became a member of their church choir, partly to convince her mother that her heart remained pure, partly because she fantasized that she was destined to be a world-famous pop singer. A surprising number of pop-music goddesses had sung in church choirs in their youth. A dedicated choirmaster – who was also a voice coach – soon convinced her that she was born to sing backup, not solo, but he changed her life when he asked, 'What do you want to sing for anyway, Jillian, when you've got such a big talent for making people laugh? When they just *can't* laugh, people turn to music to lift their spirits, but laughter is always the preferred medicine.'

Here, now, along the interstate, far from church and mother, but longing for both, sitting as straight-backed on a steel guardrail as ever she had sat on a choir bench, Jilly put one hand to her throat and felt the systolic throb in her right carotid artery. Although the beat was faster than the pulse of a devout choirgirl calmed by hymns of divine love and by a beautifully raised *Kyrie eleison*, it didn't race with outright panic. Instead it counted a quick cadence familiar to Jilly from several early turns on comedy-club stages, when her material had not connected with the audience. This was the hurried heartbeat of a rejected performer when humiliating minutes remained in the spotlight before a hostile crowd. Indeed, she felt that telltale clamminess on her brow, that damp chill on the nape of her neck, in the small of her back, and on her palms – an icy moistness that had but one name dreaded from the high proscenium arches of Broadway to the lowest stages of boondocks honkytonks: *flop sweat*.

The difference this time was that the troubled heartbeat and the cold sweat weren't merely the consequences of her standup-comedy act collapsing under her, but arose from a dreadful suspicion that her *life* might be falling apart. Which would make this the *ultimate* flop sweat.

Of course, maybe she was being melodramatic. More than once she had been accused of that tendency. Yet undeniably here she sat in a desolate desert, far from anyone who loved her, in the company of a decidedly odd pair of strangers, half convinced that any authorities to whom she turned would prove to be in league with the men who had blown up her cherished Cadillac. Worse, with every heartbeat, her blood carried an unknown corruption deeper into her tissues.

On consideration, she realized that in this instance, reality involved more frantic action, inspired more exaggerated emotions, and encouraged less respect for cause and effect than any melo-drama ever staged. 'Melodramatic, my ass,' she muttered.

Through the open back door of the Expedition, Jilly had a clear view of Dylan O'Conner sitting beside Shep and talking – ceaselessly, earnestly talking. The roar and whistle of passing traffic prevented her from hearing anything he said, and judging by Shepherd's faraway gaze, Dylan might as well have been alone, bending no ear but his own.

At first he held his younger brother's hands to put a stop to the self-administered blows that had brought a thin flow of blood from the kid's left nostril. In time, he released Shep and simply sat beside him, bent forward, head lowered, forearms on his thighs, hands clasped, but still talking, talking.

Jilly's inability to hear Dylan over the traffic noise created the impression that he spoke in a discreet murmur to his brother. The dim light in the SUV and the posture of the men – side by side, close and yet apart – brought to mind a confessional. The longer that she watched the brothers, the more completely the illusion developed, until she could smell the wood polish with which the confessional booths of her youth had been maintained and also the steeped-in scent of decades of smoldering incense.

A strangeness overcame her, a sense that the scene before her possessed meaning beyond what the five senses could perceive, that within it wound layers of mysteries and that at the core of all the mysteries lay . . . something transcendent. Jilly was too firmly rooted to this world to be a medium or a mystic; never before had she been seized by such a peculiar mood as this.

Although the night could not possibly be redolent of anything more exotic than the astringent alkaline breath of the Sonoran desert and the exhaust fumes of passing vehicles, the atmosphere between Jilly and the two O'Conners nevertheless appeared to thicken with a thin haze of incense. This enwrapping spicy perfume – cloves, myrrh, olibanum – was no longer a mere *memory* of fragrance; it had become as real and as true to this moment as were the star-shot sky above her and the loose gravel of the highway shoulder under her feet. In the cloistered interior of the Expedition, the fine particles of aromatic smoke in the gauzy air refracted and reflected the ceiling light, painting blue and gold aureoles around the O'Conners, until she might have sworn that the two brothers, rather than the small lamp above them, were radiant.

In this tableau, she would have expected Dylan to fulfill the role of priest, for of the two, Shepherd seemed to be the lost soul. But Dylan's expression and posture were those of a penitent, while Shep's blank stare appeared to be not empty but contemplative. As the younger brother began to nod slowly, rhythmically, he acquired the gracious aspect of a cassocked padre spiritually empowered to grant absolution. Jilly sensed that this unexpected reversal of roles revealed a truth of deep significance, but she could not grasp what it might be, and she could not understand why the subtleties of the relationship between these two men should be of such intense interest to her or should, in fact, impress her as being key to her salvation from her current circumstances.

Strangeness upon strangeness: She heard the sweet silvery laughter of children, although no children were present, and immediately as these musical peals of merriment arose, a flutter of wings soared after them. Surveying the vault of stars, she glimpsed no birds silhouetted against the constellations, yet the turbulence of wings increased and with it the laughter, until she rose to her feet and turned slowly around, around, in bafflement, wonderment.

Jilly knew no word to describe the extraordinary experience unfolding for her, but *hallucination* didn't seem to be applicable. These sounds and scents had neither the dreamlike insubstantiality nor the hyperrealistic intensity that she might have expected of hallucinations, but were of a vividness precisely matched to the elements of the night that she knew to be real: neither more nor less resonant than the grumble and swish of passing traffic, neither more nor less sweet-smelling than the traffic fumes were odorous.

Still turning to the encircling sound of wings, she saw tiers of candles in the desert south of her position, perhaps twenty feet beyond the guardrail. At least a double score of votive candles, racked in small ruby glasses, jeweled the darkness.

If this was dreamlight, it played on reality with a remarkable respect for the laws of physics. The metal rack stood at the foot of a smooth dune, among scattered clumps of struggling sage, casting a precise and accurate shadow made possible by the bright votives that it supported. Prowling chimeras of reflected fire shook their lions' manes and wriggled their serpents' tails across the sand, while the silvery-green leaves of the vegetation lapped at the wine-red light, glistening as though they were tongues savoring a crimson zinfandel. The illumination didn't imprint irrationally on the landscape, as the supernatural radiance of a vision might have been splashed in gaudy disregard for reason, but integrated logically with every element of the scene.

Also to the south but a few yards east of the candles and even closer to the guardrail, a single pew stood in want of a church, and if it faced a sanctuary and a high altar, both remained invisible. One end of this long wooden bench was buried in the slope of a dune; a woman in a dark dress anchored the other end.

This very vista, without pew and candles, had in distant times known the thunder of wild horses; and now Jilly's heart galloped with a sound that seemed to be as loud as hooves pounding across a desert plain. Her flop sweat had become an even icier perspiration than any she had known in failure on a stage, and instead of a mere dread of humiliation, she had been seized by the fear that she might be losing her mind.

The woman in the blue or black dress, perched upon the pew, wore her raven hair to the small of her back. In respect of God, a white lace mantilla draped her head, and incidentally hung forward along the side of her face, concealing her features. Lost in her prayers, she seemed to be oblivious of Jilly and to be unaware that her house of worship had disappeared around her.

Always the air was battered by wings, even louder than before, and ever closer, so that Jilly could clearly identify the particular feathery flutter of pinions and thus be certain that she heard birds rather than the leathery flight of bats. So close they swooped, with an air-cutting *thrum* and the eerie whisklike sound of wing vanes spreading, folding, spreading like the ribs of a Japanese fan, and yet she couldn't see them.

She turned, turned, she turned in search of birds, until before her once more stood the open door of the SUV, beyond which Dylan and Shep were still elevated on the seat of the false confessional, as radiant as apparitions. Dylan remained unaware of Jilly's encounter with the uncanny, as disconnected from her as his younger brother was perhaps forever lost to him, and she could not call his attention to the candles or to the worshiping woman because fear had stolen her voice, had nearly robbed her of breath, as well. The squall of wings became a storm, more tempestuous by the second, a spiraling rataplan that rapped all the way through her and drummed upon her bones. These sounds, hard as ratcheting gears, turned her, turned her, as did the whirlwind stirred by the ghostly wings, a turbulence that tossed her hair and buffeted her face, until she rotated again to the sight of the votive candles and to the penitent on the pew.

Flash, a pale something flared before her face, followed at once by a brighter flash, by a feathery flicker as luminous as a lambent flame. In but a blink, a frenzied scintillation of doves or pigeons became visible, beating all around her. This fury of wings implied a wickedness of beaks, and Jilly feared for her eyes. Before she could raise her hands to protect herself, a hard *crack* lashed the night, as loud as a god's whip, terrifying the flock into a greater tempest. A wave of wings splashed her face, and she cried out, but soundlessly because no cork had ever stoppered a bottle as effectively as terror plugged her throat. Dashed by this spray of wings, she blinked, expecting to be blinded, but all the birds were instead banished by the blink, gone as abruptly as they had appeared, not merely invisible as before, but gone with all their sound, with all their fury.

Gone, too, the rack of candles in the dunes. And the mantilla-mantled woman, cast back to an unknown church with the pew on which she had arrived.

A short sharp bark of pent-up air popped from Jilly's uncorked throat. With the first shuddery inhalation that followed, she detected what might have been the dead-last smell that she would have wanted if she'd been asked to make a list of a thousand odors. Blood. Subtle but distinctive, unmistakable, here was the scent of slaughter and of sacrifice, of tragedy and glory: faintly metallic, a whiff of copper, a trace of iron. More than a white wave of wings had splashed her face. With trembling and tentative hands, she touched her throat, chin, cheeks, and as she gazed with revulsion at the evidence on her fingers, she recognized a matching wetness on her lips and tasted the same substance that her fingertips revealed. She screamed, this time not silently.

12

Blacker than the barren land in this moonlit gloom, the highway sometimes seemed to unravel ahead of the Expedition, leading Jilly and the brothers O'Conner into chaos and oblivion. At other times, however, it appeared instead to be raveling itself up from chaos and into an orderly ball, steadily winding them toward a rigorously plotted and inescapable destiny.

She didn't know which possibility scared her more: running into an ever thornier and more tangled thicket of troubles, into a briar patch where every prickling turn brought her to another sanity-shaking encounter with the unknown – or discovering the identity of the smiling man with the needle and laying open the mystery of the golden liquid in the syringe.

In twenty-five years of life, she had learned that understanding didn't always – or even often – bring peace. Currently, since returning to her motel room with root beer, she existed in a purgatory of ignorance and confusion, where life resembled a waking nightmare or at least a bad and edgy dream. But if she found answers and a final resolution, she might discover that she was trapped in a living hell that would make her yearn for the comparative serenity and comfort of even this nerve-fraying purgatory.

As before, Dylan drove without his full attention on the road, repeatedly checking the rearview mirror and periodically glancing over his right shoulder to assure himself that Shep was not in any way harming himself, but now *two* worries distracted him from his driving. Following Jilly's dramatic roadside performance – her babble of birds and blood – the attention that Dylan paid to her had the same brother's-keeper quality that colored his attitude toward Shepherd.

'You actually tasted it – the blood, I mean?' he asked. 'Actually smelled it.'

'Yeah. I know it wasn't real. You didn't see it. But it seemed real enough.'

'Heard the birds, felt their wings.'

'Yeah.'

'Do hallucinations usually involve all five senses – or involve them so completely?'

'It wasn't any hallucination,' she said stubbornly.

'Well, it for sure wasn't real.'

She glared at him and saw that he wisely recognized the mortal danger of continuing to insist that she – Southwest Amazon, fearless cactuskicker – was susceptible to hallucinations. In her estimation, hallucinations were only one step removed from such quaint female complaints as the vapors, fainting spells, and persistent melancholy.

'I'm not an hysteric,' she said, 'or an alcoholic in withdrawal, or a consumer of psychedelic mushrooms, thank you very much, so the word *hallucination* doesn't apply.'

'Call it a vision, then.'

'I'm not Joan of Arc, either. God isn't sending me messages. Enough already. I don't want to talk about this anymore, not right now, not for a while.'

'We've got to—'

'I said not now.'

'But—'

'I'm scared, all right? I'm scared, and talking it to death isn't going to make me less scared, so time-out. Time-out.'

She understood why he would regard her with new concern and even with a measure of wariness, but she didn't like being the object of his solicitude. Even the compassion of friends was difficult for her to bear; and the sympathy of strangers could easily curdle into pity. She would not tolerate pity from anyone. She bristled at the thought of being perceived as weak or unfortunate, and she had no capacity whatsoever for being patronized.

Indeed, Dylan's glances, each of which glistened with dewy commiseration, so deeply annoyed Jilly that she soon grew desperate to distract herself from them. She unhooked her safety harness, drew her legs under herself, leaving potted Fred in full possession of the passenger's foot space, and turned half sideways in her seat to watch over Shep, making it possible for his brother to pay more attention to the road.

Dylan had left a first-aid kit with Shep. Much to Jilly's surprise, the young man opened it on the seat beside him and made proper use of its contents, although in a state of such intense concentration and with an expression of such blank detachment that he seemed to be machinelike. With swabs soaked in hydrogen peroxide, he patiently removed the obstructing clots of blood from his left nostril, which had played like a whistle with each breath he took, proceeding so delicately that the crimson flow did not resume. His brother had said this was a mere bloody nose, not a broken one, and Shep seemed to confirm the diagnosis, tending to his injury without one wince or hiss of pain. Employing cotton balls moistened with rubbing alcohol, he scrubbed the dried blood from his upper lip, out of the corner of his mouth, and off his chin. He had skinned a couple knuckles on his teeth; he treated these minor abrasions with alcohol followed by dabs of Neosporin. With the thumb and forefinger of his right hand, he tested his teeth, one by one, molar to molar, top and then bottom; each time he confirmed that a tooth was firmly in place, he paused to say, 'Quite as it should be, m'lord.' Judging by every indication – by his refusal to make eye contact; by his otherworldly air; by the absence of any nobleman in the SUV, either lord or duke, or prince-in-waiting – Shep wasn't speaking to anyone present. 'Quite as it should be, m'lord.' His ministrations were methodical to the point of robotism, and often his movements had an awkwardness that suggested a robot from which the mechanical kinks and the programming errors had not yet been entirely eliminated.

More than once, Jilly tried to chat with Shepherd, but every effort at communication failed. He spoke only to the Lord of Teeth, dutifully making his report.

'He's capable of conversation,' Dylan told her. 'Although even at his best, what he lays on you isn't the kind of sparkling repartee that'll make him a hit at cocktail parties. It's his own brand of conversation, what I call Shepspeak, but it's not without interest.'

In the backseat, Shep tested a tooth and announced, 'Quite as it should be, m'lord.'

'But you won't be able to get a dialogue going with him anytime soon,' Dylan continued, 'not when he's rattled like this. He doesn't handle commotion well, or deviation from routine. He's best when the day goes exactly as he expects it to, right on schedule, quiet and boring. If breakfast, lunch, and dinner are always exactly on time, if every dish at every meal is on the narrow menu of foods acceptable to him, if he doesn't encounter too many new people who try to talk to him . . . then you might make a connection with him and have yourself a real gabfest.'

'Quite as it should be, m'lord,' Shep declared, ostensibly not in confirmation of what his brother had said.

'What's wrong with him?' Jilly asked.

'He's been diagnosed autistic, also high-functioning autistic. He's never violent, and sometimes he's highly communicative, so he was once even diagnosed with Asperger syndrome.'

'Ass burger?'

'A-S-P-E-R-G-E-R, emphasis on *per*. Sometimes Shep seems totally high-functioning and sometimes not so high as you would hope. Mostly, I don't think easy labels apply. He's just Shep, unique.'

'Quite as it should be, m'lord.'

'He's said that fourteen times,' Dylan noted. 'How many teeth in the human mouth?'

'I think . . . thirty-two, counting four wisdom teeth.'

Dylan sighed. 'Thank God his wisdom teeth were pulled.'

'You said he needs stability. Is it good for him to be bouncing around the country like a Gypsy?'

'Quite as it should be, m'lord.'

'We don't bounce,' Dylan replied with an edge that suggested he had taken offense at her question, though she intended none. 'We have a schedule, a routine, goals to be attained. Focus. We have focus. We drive in style. This isn't a horse-drawn wagon with hex signs painted on the sides.'

'I just meant he might be better off in an institution.'

'That'll never happen.'

'Quite as it should be, m'lord.'

Jilly said, 'Not all those places are snake pits.'

'The only thing he's got is me. Drop him in an institution, and he won't have anything.'

'It might be good for him.'

'No. It would kill him.'

'For one thing, maybe they could keep him from hurting himself.'

'He won't hurt himself.'

'He just did,' she noted.

'Quite as it should be, m'lord.'

'That was a first and a fluke,' Dylan said with what sounded more like hope than like conviction. 'It won't happen again.'

'You never imagined it would happen the first time.'

Although they were already exceeding the legal limit and though traffic conditions were not conducive to even greater speed, Dylan accelerated steadily.

Jilly sensed that he was trying to outrun more than just the men in the black Suburbans. 'No matter how fast you drive, Shep's still in the backseat.'

'Quite as it should be, m'lord.'

Dylan said, 'The lunatic doctor gives you an injection, and an hour later, or whatever, you experience an altered state of—'

'I *said* I want a time-out from that.'

'And I don't want to talk about *this*,' he declared emphatically, 'about institutions, sanitariums, care homes, places where people might as well be canned meat, where they're put on a shelf and dusted from time to time.'

'Quite as it should be, m'lord.'

'All right,' Jilly relented. 'Sorry. I understand. It's really none of my business anyway.'

'That's right,' Dylan concurred. 'Shep isn't *our* business. He's *my* business.'

'All right.'

'Okay.'

'Quite as it should be, m'lord.'

'Twenty,' Jilly counted.

Dylan said, 'But your altered state of consciousness *is* our business, not just yours, but yours and mine, because it's related to the injection—'

'We don't know that for sure.'

Certain expressions took exaggerated form on his broad rubbery face, as if he were in fact a cartoon bear who had stepped out of an animated realm into the real world, had shaved his furry mug, and had set himself the tricky task of passing for human. In this instance, his disbelief pulled his features into a configuration worthy of Sylvester the cat on those occasions when the scheming feline had been tricked by Tweety bird into walking off the edge of a cliff. 'Oh, but we *do* know that for sure.'

'We do not,' she insisted.

'Quite as it should be, m'lord.'

Jilly continued: 'And I don't like the term *altered state* any more than I like *hallucination*. It makes me sound like a doper.'

'I can't believe we're arguing over vocabulary.'

'I'm not arguing. I'm just saying what I don't like.'

'If we're going to talk about it, we have to call it *something*.'

'Then let's not talk about it,' she suggested.

'We *have* to talk about it. What the hell are we supposed to do – drive at random the rest of our lives, here and there and everywhere, keeping on the move, and *not* talking about it?'

'Quite as it should be, m'lord.'

'Speaking of driving,' Jilly said, 'you're going way too fast.'

'I am not.'

'You're doing over ninety.'

'It only looks that way from your angle.'

'Oh, yeah? What's it look like from *your* angle?'

'Eighty-eight,' he admitted, and eased up on the accelerator. 'Let's call it a . . . *mirage*. That doesn't imply mental instability, drug use, or religious hysteria.'

'Quite as it should be, m'lord.'

'I was thinking maybe *phantasm*,' Jilly said.

'I can live with phantasm.'

'But I think I like mirage better.'

'Great! Fantastic! And we're in the desert, so it fits.'

'But it wasn't actually a mirage.'

'I know that,' he hastened to assure her. 'It was its own thing, special, unique, impossible to properly name. But if you were hit by this mirage because of the stuff in the damn needle—' He interrupted himself, sensing her rising objection: 'Oh, get real! Common sense tells us the two things *must* be related.'

'Common sense is overrated.'

'Not in the O'Conner family.'

'I'm not a member of the O'Conner family.'

'Which relieves us of the need to change our name.'

'Quite as it should be, m'lord.'

She didn't want to argue with him, for she knew that they were in this together, but she couldn't restrain herself: 'So there's not room in the O'Conner family for people like me, huh?'

'There's that "people like me" business again!'

'Well, it seems to be an issue with you.'

'It's not an issue with me. It's an issue with *you*. You're way too sensitive or something, like a boil just waiting to burst.'

'Lovely. Now I'm a bursting boil. You've sure got a talent for getting under people's skin.'

'Me? I'm the easiest guy in the world to get along with. I've never gotten under anyone's skin in my life – until you.'

'Quite as it should be, m'lord.'

'You're doing over ninety again,' she warned him.

'Eighty-nine,' he disagreed, and this time he didn't ease up on the accelerator. 'If you were hit by that mirage because of the stuff in the injection, then I'll probably be hit with one, too.'

'Which is another reason you shouldn't be doing over ninety.'

'Eighty-nine,' he corrected, and reluctantly allowed the speed of the SUV to fall.

'The crazy son-of-a-bitch salesman jacked the stuff into your arm first,' Jilly said. 'So if it always causes mirages, you should have had one before I did.'

'For maybe the hundredth time – he wasn't a salesman. He was some lunatic doctor, some psycho scientist or something. And come to think of it, he said the stuff in the needle does lots of different things to different people.'

'Quite as it should be, m'lord.'

'Different things? Like what?'

'He didn't say. Just different. He also said something like . . . the effect is always interesting, often astonishing, and *sometimes* positive.'

She shuddered with the memory of whirling birds and flickering votive candles. 'That mirage wasn't a positive effect. So what else did Dr. Frankenstein say?'

'Frankenstein?'

'We can't keep calling him a lunatic doctor, psycho scientist, crazy son-of-a-bitch salesman. We need a name for him until we can find out his real name.'

'But Frankenstein . . .'

'What about it?'

Dylan grimaced. He took one hand off the steering wheel to make a gesture of equivocation. 'It feels so . . .'

'Quite as it should be, m'lord.'

'Feels so what?'

'Melodramatic,' he decided.

'Everyone's a critic,' she said impatiently. 'And why's this word *melodramatic* being flung at me all the time?'

'I never flung it before,' he objected, 'and I wasn't referring to you personally.'

'Not you. I didn't say it was you. But it might as well have been you. You're a man.'

'I don't follow that at all.'

'Of course you don't. You're a man. With all your common sense, you can't follow anything that isn't as perfectly linear as a line of dominoes.'

'Do you have *issues* with men?' he asked, and the self-satisfied, back-at-you look on his face made her want to smack him.

'Quite as it should be, m'lord.'

Simultaneously and with equal relief, Jilly and Dylan said, *'Twenty-eight!'*

In the backseat, all teeth tested and found secure, Shep put on his shoes, tied them, and then settled into silence.

The speedometer needle dropped, and gradually so did Jilly's tension, although she figured she wouldn't again achieve a state of serenity for another decade.

Cruising at seventy miles an hour, though he probably would have claimed that he was only doing sixty-eight, Dylan said, 'I'm sorry.'

The apology surprised Jilly. 'Sorry for what?'

'For my tone. My attitude. Things I said. I mean, normally you couldn't *drag* me into an argument.'

'I didn't drag you into anything.'

'No, no,' he quickly amended. 'That's not what I meant. You didn't drag. You didn't. I'm just saying normally I don't get angry. I hold it in. I manage it. I convert it into creative energy. That's part of my philosophy as an artist.'

She couldn't repress her cynicism as skillfully as he claimed to manage his anger; she heard it in her voice, felt it twist her features and harden them as effectively as if thick plaster had been applied to her face to cast a life mask titled *Scorn*. 'Artists don't get angry, huh?'

'We just don't have much negative energy left after all the raping and killing.'

She had to like him for that comeback. 'Sorry. My excrement detector always goes off when people start talking about their philosophy.'

'You're right, actually. It's nothing so grand as a philosophy. I should have said it's my modus operandi. I'm not one of those angry young artists who turns out paintings full of rage, angst, and bitter nihilism.'

'What *do* you paint?'

'The world as it is.'

'Yeah? And how's the world look to you these days?'

'Exquisite. Beautiful. Deeply, strangely layered. Mysterious.' Word by word, as though this were an oft-repeated prayer from which he drew the comfort that only profound faith can provide, his voice softened both in tone and volume, and into his face came a radiant quality, after which Jilly was no longer able to see the cartoon bear that heretofore he had resembled. 'Full of meaning that eludes complete understanding. Full of a truth that, if both felt and also logically deduced, calms the roughest sea with hope. More beauty than I have the talent or the time to capture on canvas.'

His simple eloquence stood so at odds with the man whom he had seemed to be that Jilly didn't know what to say, though she realized she must not give voice to any of the many acerbic put-downs, laced with venomous sarcasm, that made her tongue tremble as that of any serpent might flutter in anticipation of a bared-fang strike. Those were easy replies, facile humor, both inadequate and inappropriate in the face of what seemed to be his sincerity. In fact, her usual self-confidence and her wise-ass attitude drained from her, because the depth of thought and the modesty revealed by his answer unsettled her. To her surprise, a needle of inadequacy punctured her as she'd rarely been punctured before, leaving her feeling . . . empty. Her quick wit, always a juggernaut with sails full of wind, had morphed into a small skiff and had come aground in shallow water.

She didn't like this feeling. He hadn't meant to humble her, but here she was, reduced. Having been a choirgirl, having been churched more of her life than not, Jilly understood the theory that humility was a virtue and also a blessing that ensured a happier life than the lives of those who lived without it. On those occasions when the priest had raised this issue in his homily, however, she had tuned him out. To young Jilly, living with full humility, rather than with the absolute minimum of it that might win God's approval, had seemed to be giving up on life before you started. Grown-up Jilly felt pretty much the same way. The world was full of people who were eager to diminish you, to shame you, to put you in your place and to keep you down. If you embraced humility too fully, you were doing the bastards' work for them.

Gazing forward at the raveling or unraveling highway, which-ever it might be, Dylan O'Conner appeared serene, as Jilly had not before seen him, as she had never expected to see him in these dire circumstances. Apparently the very thought of his art, contemplating the challenge of adequately celebrating the world's beauty on a two-dimensional canvas, had the power to keep his dread at bay, at least for a short time.

She admired the apparent confidence with which he had embraced his calling, and she knew without asking that he'd never enter-tained a backup plan if he failed as an artist, not as she had fantasized about a fallback career as a best-selling novelist. She envied his evident certainty, but instead of being able to use that envy to stoke a little fire of healthy anger that might chase off the chill of inadequacy, she settled deeper into a cold bath of humility.

In her self-imposed silence, Jilly heard once more the faint silvery laughter of children, or heard only the memory of it; she could not be sure which. As ephemeral as a cool draft against her arms and throat and face, whether felt or imagined, feathery wings flicked, flicked, and trembled.

Closing her eyes, determined not to succumb to another mirage if one might be pending, she succeeded in deafening herself to the children's laughter.

The wings withdrew, as well, but an even more disturbing and astonishing sensation overcame her: She grew intimately, acutely aware of every nerve pathway in her body, could feel – as heat, as a tingle of current – the exact location and the complex course of all twelve pairs of cranial nerves, all thirty-one pairs of spinal nerves. If she'd been an artist, she could have drawn an exquisitely accurate map of the thousands upon thousands of axons in her body, and could have rendered each axon to the precise number of neurons that comprised its filamentous length. She was aware of millions of electrical impulses carrying information along sensory fibers from far points of her body to her spinal cord and brain, and of an equally high traffic of impulses conveying instructions from the brain to muscles and organs and glands. Into her mind came the three-dimensional cartography of the central nervous system: the billions of interconnected nerve cells in the brain and spinal cord, seen as points of light in numerous colors, alive in shimmering and vibrant function.

She became conscious of a universe within herself, galaxy after galaxy of scintillant neurons, and suddenly she felt as though she were spiraling into a cold vastness of stars, as though she were an astronaut who, on an extravehicular walk, had snapped the tether that linked her safely to her spacecraft. Eternity yawned before her, a great swallowing maw, and she drifted fast, faster, faster still, into this internal immensity, toward oblivion.

Her eyes snapped open. The unnatural self-awareness of neurons, axons, and nerve pathways faded as abruptly as it had seized her.

Now the only thing that felt peculiar was the point at which she had received the injection. An itch. A throbbing. Under the bunny Band-Aid.

Paralyzed by dread, she could not peel off the bandage. Shaken by shudders, she could only stare at the tiny spot of blood that had darkened the gauze from the underside.

When this paralytic fear began to subside, she looked up from the crook of her arm and saw a river of white doves flowing directly toward the Expedition. Silently they came out of the night, flying westward in these eastbound lanes, came by the hundreds, by the thousands, great winged multitudes, dividing into parallel currents that flowed around the flanks of the vehicle, forming a third current that swept across the hood, up and over the windshield, following the slipstream away into the night, as hushed as birds in a dream without sound.

Although these uncountable legions rushed toward the truck with all the blinding density of any blizzard, allowing not one glimpse of the highway ahead, Dylan neither spoke of them nor reduced his speed in respect of them. He gazed forward into these white onrushing shoals and seemed to see not one wing or gimlet eye.

Jilly knew this must be an apparition only she could perceive, a flood of doves where none existed. She fisted her hands in her lap and chewed on her lower lip, and while her pounding heart provided the drumming not furnished by the soundless wings of the birds, she prayed for these feathered phantoms to pass, even though she feared what might come after them.

13

Phantasm soon gave way to reality, and the highway clarified out of the last seething shoals of doves gone now to boughs and belfries.

Gradually Jilly's heart rate subsided from its frantic pace, but each slower beat seemed as hard struck as when her fear had been more tightly wound.

Moon behind them, wheel of stars turning overhead, they traveled in the hum of tires, in the whoosh-and-swish of passing cars, in the grind-and-grumble of behemoth trucks for a mile or two before Dylan's voice added melody to the rhythm: 'What's *your* modus operandi? As a comedian.'

Her mouth was dry, her tongue thick, but she sounded normal when she spoke. 'My material, I guess you mean. Human stupidity. I make fun of it as best I can. Stupidity, envy, betrayal, faithlessness, greed, self-importance, lust, vanity, hatred, senseless violence . . . There's never a shortage of targets for a comedian.' Listening to herself, she cringed at the difference between the inspirations he claimed for his art and those she acknowledged for her stage work. 'But that's how all comedians operate,' she elaborated, dismayed by this impulse to justify herself, yet unable to repress it. 'Comedy is dirty work, but someone has to do it.'

'People need to laugh,' he said inanely, reaching for this trite bit of reassurance as though he sensed what she'd been thinking.

'I want to make them laugh till they cry,' Jilly said, and at once wondered where *that* had come from. 'I want to make them feel . . .'

'Feel what?'

The word that she had almost spoken was so inappropriate, so out of phase with what everyone expected a comedian's motivations to be, that she was confused and disturbed to hear it in the echo chamber of her mind. *Pain.* She'd almost said, *I want to make them feel pain.* She swallowed the word unspoken and grimaced as if it had a bitter taste.

'Jilly?'

The dark charm of self-examination abruptly had less appeal than the threat-filled night from which they'd both taken a brief holiday and to which she preferred to return. Frowning at the highway, she said, 'We're headed east.'

'Yeah.'

'Why?'

'Black Suburbans, explosions, gorillas in golf clothes,' he reminded her.

'But I was headed west before all this . . . all this excrement happened. I've got a three-night gig in Phoenix next week.'

In the backseat, Shepherd broke his silence: 'Feces. Feculence. Defecation.'

'You can't go to Phoenix now,' Dylan objected. 'Not after all this, after your mirage—'

'Hey, end of the world or not, I need the money. Besides, you don't book a date, then back out at the last minute. Not if you want to work again.'

'Movement. Stool. Droppings,' said Shep.

'Did you forget about your Cadillac?' Dylan asked.

'How could I forget? The bastards blew it up. My beautiful Coupe DeVille.' She sighed. 'Wasn't it beautiful?'

'A jewel,' he agreed.

'I loved those tastefully subdued tail fins.'

'Elegant.'

'Its howitzer-shell front bumper.'

'Very howitzery.'

'They put the name, *Coupe DeVille*, in gold script on the sides. That was such a sweet detail. Now it's all blown up, burned, and stinking of one toasted Frankenstein. Who forgets such a thing?'

Shep said, 'Manure. Ordure.'

Jilly asked, 'What's he doing now?'

'A while ago,' Dylan reminded her, 'you told me I was crude. You suggested I find polite synonyms for a certain word that offended you. Shep accepted your challenge.'

'Crap. Coprolite.'

'But that was back before we left the motel,' she said.

'Shep's sense of time isn't like yours and mine. Past, present, and future aren't easily differentiated for him, and sometimes he acts as if they're all the same thing and happening simultaneously.'

'Poopoo,' said Shep. 'Kaka.'

'My point about the Caddy,' Dylan continued, 'is that when those thugs in polo shirts discover it doesn't belong to Frankenstein, that it's registered to one Jillian Jackson, then they're going to come looking for you. They'll want to know *how* he got your car, whether you gave it to him willingly.'

'I knew I should've gone to the cops. Should've filed a stolen-vehicle report like a good citizen would. Now I look suspicious.'

'Doodoo. Diaper dump.'

'If Frankenstein was right,' Dylan warned, 'maybe the cops can't protect you. Maybe these people can pull rank on the cops.'

'Then I guess we'd have to go to – who? The FBI?'

'Maybe you can't escape these guys. Maybe they can pull rank on the FBI, too.'

'Who in God's name are they – the Secret Service, the CIA, Santa Claus's elf gestapo out making their who's-been-naughty list?'

'Cow pie. Waste.'

'Frankenstein didn't say who they were,' Dylan reported. 'He just said if they find the stuff in our blood, we'll be as dead as dinosaurs and buried where our bones won't ever be found.'

'Yeah, maybe that's what he said, but why should we believe him anyway? He was a mad scientist.'

'Evacuation. Voidance. Toilet treasure.'

'He wasn't mad,' Dylan averred.

'You called him a lunatic.'

'And you called him a salesman. We've called him a lot of things in the heat of the moment—'

'Potty packing. Outhouse input. Excreta.'

'—but given his options,' Dylan continued, 'considering that he *knew* those guys were on his tail and were going to kill him, he took the most logical, rational action available to him.'

Her mouth opened as wide as if she were assuming the cooperative position for a root canal. *'Logical? Rational?'* She reminded herself that she didn't really know Mr. Dylan O'Conner. In the end, he might prove to be more peculiar than his brother. 'Okay, let me get this straight. The smiley creep chloroforms me, shoots Dr. Jekyll juice or something into my veins, steals my fabulous car, gets himself blown up – and in your enlightened view, that behavior qualifies him to coach the university debating team?'

'Obviously, they'd pushed him into a corner, time was running out, and he did the only thing he *could* do to save his life's work. I'm sure he didn't intend to get himself blown up.'

'You're as insane as he was,' Jilly decided.

'Dejecta. Bulldoody.'

'I'm not saying that what he did was *right*,' Dylan clarified. 'Only that it was logical. If we operate under the assumption that he was just nuttier than a one-pound jar of Jif, we're making a mistake that could get us killed. Think about it: If we die, he loses. So he wants us to stay alive, if only because we're his . . . I don't know . . . because we're his living experiments or something. Consequently, I have to assume that everything he told me was meant to *help* us stay alive.'

'Filth. Dung. A withdrawal from the bowel bank.'

Immediately to the north and south of the interstate lay plains as black as ancient hearthstones stained by the char of ten thousand fires, with isolated mottlings as gray as ashes where moonlight and starlight glimmered off the reflective surfaces of desert vegetation and mica-flecked rock formations. Directly east, but also curving toward the highway with viselike relentlessness from the northeast and the southeast, the Peloncillo Mountains presented a barren and forbidding silhouette: hard, black, jagged slabs darker than the night sky into which they thrust.

This wasteland offered no comfort to the mind, no consolation to the heart, and except for the interstate, it provided no evidence that it existed on a populated planet. Even along these paved lanes, the lights of the oncoming and receding traffic made no conclusive argument for a living population. The scene possessed an eerie quality that suggested the science-fiction scenario of a world on which all species had perished centuries before, leaving their domain as morbidly still as a glass-encased diorama through which the only movement was the periodic bustle of perpetual-motion machines engaged in ancient programmed tasks that no longer held any meaning.

To Jilly, this bleak vastness began to look like the landscape of Hell with all the fires put out. 'We're not going to get out of this alive, are we?' she asked in a tone entirely rhetorical.

'What? Of course we will.'

'*Of course?*' she said with a rich measure of disbelief. 'No doubt at all?'

'Of course,' he insisted. 'The worst is already behind us.'

'It's not behind us.'

'Yes, it is.'

'Don't be ridiculous.'

'The worst is behind us,' he repeated stubbornly.

'How can you say the worst is behind us when we have no idea what's coming next?'

'Creation is an act of will,' he said.

'What's that supposed to mean?'

'Before I create a painting, I conceive it in my mind. It exists from the instant it's conceived, and all that's needed to transform the conception into a tangible work of art are time and effort, paint and canvas.'

'Are we in the same conversation?' she wondered.

In the backseat, Shepherd sat in silence again, but now his brother spewed a prattle more disturbing than Shep's. 'Positive thinking. Mind over matter. If God created the heavens and the earth merely by *thinking* them into existence. The ultimate power in the universe is willpower.'

'Evidently not, or otherwise I'd have my own hit sitcom and be partying in my Malibu mansion right now.'

'Our creativity reflects divine creativity because we think new things into existence every day – new inventions, new architectures, new chemical compounds, new manufacturing processes, new works of art, new recipes for bread and pie and pot roast.'

'I'm not going to risk eternal damnation by claiming I make a pot roast as good as God's. I'm sure His would be tastier.'

Ignoring her interruption, Dylan said, 'We don't have godlike power, so we aren't able to transform our thought energy directly into matter—'

'God would whip up better side dishes than me, too, and I'm sure He's a whiz at beautiful table settings.'

'—but *guided* by thought and reason,' Dylan continued patiently, 'we can use other kinds of energy to transform existing matter into virtually anything we conceive. I mean, we spin thread to make cloth to sew into clothes. And we cut down trees to make lumber to build shelter. Our process of creation is a lot slower, clumsier, but it's fundamentally just one step removed from God's. Do you understand what I'm saying?'

'If I ever do, I absolutely insist you have me committed.'

Gradually accelerating once more, he said, 'Work with me here, okay? Can you make an effort?'

Jilly was irritated by his childlike earnestness and by his Pollyanna optimism in the shadow of the mortal danger that confronted them. Nevertheless, recalling how his eloquence had earlier humbled her, she felt a flush of warmth rise in her face, and for the moment she managed to put a lid on the sarcasm that a fire of frustration had set boiling. 'Okay, all right, whatever. Go ahead.'

'Assume we were made in God's image.'

'All right. Yeah? So?'

'Then it's also reasonable to assume that although we aren't able to create matter out of nothing and although we can't change existing matter solely by the application of thought, nevertheless even our less than godlike willpower might be able to influence the shape of things to come.'

'The shape of things to come,' she repeated.

'That's right.'

'The shape of things to come.'

'Exactly,' he confirmed, nodding happily, glancing away from the interstate to smile at her.

'The shape of things to come,' she repeated yet again, and then she realized that in her frustration and bewilderment, she sounded disturbingly like Shepherd. 'What *things*?'

'Future events,' he explained. 'If we're in God's image, then maybe we possess a small measure – a tiny but still useful fraction – of the divine power to shape things. Not matter, in our case, but *the future*. Maybe with the exercise of willpower, maybe we can shape our destiny, in part if not entirely.'

'What – I just imagine a future in which I'm a millionaire, then I'll become one?'

'You still have to make the right decisions and work hard . . . but, yeah, I believe all of us can shape our futures if we apply enough willpower.'

Still suppressing her frustration, keeping her tone light, she said, 'Then why aren't you a famous billionaire artist?'

'I don't want to be famous or rich.'

'Everyone wants to be famous and rich.'

'Not me. Life is complicated enough.'

'Money simplifies.'

'Money complicates,' he disagreed, 'and fame. I just want to paint well, and to paint better every day.'

'So,' she said, as the lid flew off her boiling pot of sarcasm, 'you're gonna imagine yourself a future where you're the next Vincent van Gogh, and just by wishing on a star, you'll one day see your work hanging in museums.'

'I'm sure going to try, anyway. Vincent van Gogh – except I'm imagining a future in which I keep both ears.'

Dylan's persistent good humor in the face of dire adversity had an effect on Jilly no less distressing than the damage that would be wrought with sandpaper vigorously applied to the tongue. 'And to make you get real about our situation, *I'm* imagining a future where I have to kick your *cojones* into your esophagus.'

'You're a very angry person, aren't you?'

'I'm a *scared* person.'

'Scared right now, sure, but *always* angry.'

'Not always. Fred and I were having a lovely relaxed evening before all *this* started.'

'You must have some pretty heavy unresolved conflicts from your childhood.'

'Oh, wow, you get more impressive by the minute, don't you? Now you're licensed to provide psychoanalysis when you're not painting circles around van Gogh.'

'Pump up your blood pressure any further,' Dylan warned, 'and you'll pop a carotid artery.'

Jilly strained a shriek of vexation through clenched teeth, because by swallowing it unexpressed, she might have imploded.

'All I'm saying,' Dylan pressed in an infuriatingly reasonable tone of voice, 'is that maybe if we think positive, the worst *will* be behind us. And for sure, there's nothing to be gained by negative thinking.'

She almost swung her legs off the seat, almost stomped her feet against the floorboard in a fit of frustration before she remembered that poor defenseless Fred would be trampled. Instead, she drew a deep breath and confronted Dylan: 'If it's so easy, why have you let Shepherd live such a miserable existence all these years? Why haven't you imagined that he just magically comes out of his autism and leads a normal life?'

'I have imagined it,' he replied softly and with a poignancy that revealed a plumbless sorrow over the condition of his brother. 'I've imagined it intensely, vividly, with all my heart, every day of my life, since as far back as I can remember.'

Infinite sky. Trackless desert. A vastness had been created inside the SUV to equal the daunting immensities of darkness and vacuum beyond these doors and windows, a vastness of her making. Succumbing to fear and frustration, she had unthinkingly crossed a line between legitimate argument and unwarranted meanness, needling Dylan O'Conner where she knew that he was already sorest. The distance between them, although but an arm's length, seemed now unbridgeable.

Both in the glare of the oncoming headlights and in the softer pearlescent glow of the instrument panel, Dylan's eyes glimmered as though he had repressed so many tears for so long that within his gaze were pent-up oceans. As Jilly studied him with more sympathy than she'd felt previously, even dim light proved bright enough to clarify that what had resembled sorrow might be a more acute pain: grief, long-sustained and unrelenting grief, as if his brother were not autistic, but dead and lost forever.

She didn't know what to say to make amends for her mean-ness. Whether she spoke in a whisper or in a shout, the usual words of an apology seemed insufficiently powerful to carry across the gulf that she had created between herself and Dylan O'Conner.

She felt like a pile of toilet treasure.

Infinite sky. Trackless desert. The bee hum of tires and the drone of engine wove a white noise that she quickly tuned out, until she might as well have been sitting in the dead silence that abides on the surface of an airless moon. She couldn't hear even the faint tide of her breathing or the slogging of her heart, or the singing of her old church choir that occasionally came to her in memory when she felt alone and adrift. She had not possessed a voice fine enough to perform a solo, but she'd shown a talent for harmony, and among her choral sisters and her brothers all robed alike, holding a hymnal identical to each of theirs, she had been warmed by a profound sense of community that she had not known before or since. Sometimes Jilly felt that the excruciatingly difficult task of establishing rapport with an audience of strangers and inducing them to laugh against their will at the stupidity and meanness of humanity was far easier than closing the distance between any two human beings and keeping them even tenuously bonded for any length of time whatsoever. The infinite sky, the trackless desert, and the isolation of each armored heart were characterized by the same nearly impenetrable remoteness.

Along the shoulder of the highway, tongues of light licked up here and there from the dark gravel, and for an instant Jilly feared a return of votive candles and of displaced church pews, feared the reappearance of bloodless birds and sprays of ectoplasmic blood, but she quickly realized that these quick cold flames were nothing but reflections of their headlights flaring off the curved shards of broken bottles.

The silence fell not to her or to Dylan, but to the gentle ax of Shepherd's voice monotonously chopping through the same three-word mantra familiar from television commercials: 'Fries not flies, fries not flies, fries not flies. . . .'

Jilly was baffled as to why Shep would choose to chant the advertising slogan of the very restaurant at which she had bought dinner less than two hours ago, but then she realized that he must have seen the promotional button that the counter clerk had pinned to her blouse.

'Fries not flies, fries not flies. . . .'

Dylan said, 'I was clubbed down as I was returning to the room with the bags of takeout. We never had dinner. I guess he's hungry.'

'Fries not flies, fries not flies,' said Shep, rocking from side to side in his seat.

As Dylan took one hand off the steering wheel and reached to the breast pocket of his Hawaiian shirt, Jilly realized he wore a toad pin that matched hers. Against the tropical-flower pattern of the colorful fabric, the grinning cartoon amphibian had not been easy to see.

'Fries not flies, fries not flies. . . .'

When Dylan removed the promotional gimcrack from his shirt, a strange thing happened, and the night took another unexpected turn. Holding the button between thumb and forefinger, reaching toward the console that separated the front seats, as though he was intending to deposit the unwanted pin in the trash receptacle, he appeared to vibrate, not violently, yet with too much force for the episode to be deemed a mere shudder, vibrated as though an electrical current were quivering through his body. His tongue fluttered rapidly against the roof of his mouth, producing a peculiar noise not unlike that of a stalled car straining to start: *'Hunnn-na-na-na-na-na-na-na-na-na-na!'*

He managed to hold on to the steering wheel with his left hand, but his foot either eased up on the accelerator or slipped off the pedal altogether. The Expedition's reckless speed began to plummet from a perilous 95 miles per hour to a merely dangerous 85, to a still hazardous 75.

'Hunnn-na-na-na-na-na-na-na-na-na,' he stuttered, and with the final syllable, he snapped the toad button out of his fingers as though he were shooting a game of marbles. He stopped vibrating as abruptly as he had begun.

The little metal disc pinged off the window in the passenger's door, inches from Jilly's face, ricocheted off the dashboard, dropped out of sight among Fred's maze of branches and succulent leaves.

Although they were decelerating, Jilly sensed that because she had slipped out of her safety harness, she was at grave risk, sensed also that she didn't have enough time to shrug into the straps and engage the buckle. Instead she pivoted to face front, clutched the seat with her left hand almost desperately enough to puncture the leather upholstery, and with her right hand grabbed the padded assist bar immediately above the passenger's door. Just as Dylan confirmed the value of her intuition by all but standing on the brakes, she braced her feet against the dashboard. Knees bent to absorb whatever shock might come, she launched into a mental recitation of the Hail Mary prayer, not with a petition to be spared from the curse of a fat ass but with a plea to save her ass regardless of what grotesque dimensions it might acquire in years to come.

Maybe the Expedition's speed fell as far as 60, maybe even as low as 50, in two seconds flat, but it was still traveling so fast that no sane person would have tried to execute a hard turn at this velocity. Evidently, Dylan O'Conner fully embraced madness: He let up on the brakes, pulled the steering wheel hand-over-hand to the left, pumped the brakes again, swung the truck off the pavement, and cranked it through a rubber-burning spin.

Whirling up a cloud of dust, the Expedition rotated on the wide shoulder of the highway. Gravel tattooed the undercarriage: a fierce *ponk-plink-crack* as unnerving as machine-gun fire. Spinning into the glare of approaching headlights, Jilly inhaled a lung-stretching breath with the desperate greediness for life of a condemned woman hearing the thin whistle of a descending guillotine blade. She shrieked as they came around to their starting position, and she failed to use a polite synonym for *feces* as they spun yet another 120 degrees and jolted to a stop facing northwest.

Here the eastbound and westbound lanes of the interstate were separated by a sixty-foot-wide median without a guardrail, relying solely on a center swale to prevent out-of-control vehicles from crossing easily into oncoming traffic. The instant that the SUV rocked to a stop, as Jilly sucked in another here-comes-the-death-blow breath deep enough to sustain her during an underwater swim across the English Channel, Dylan abandoned the brake pedal for the accelerator and drove down the slope, diagonally crossing the median.

'What're you doing?' she demanded.

He was extraordinarily focused, as she'd never seen him before, concentrating more intensely on the descent into the shallow swale than he had on the sight of her blazing Coupe Deville, than he had concentrated on self-battered Shep in the backseat confessional. Bruin big, he filled his half of the front seat to overflowing. Even in normal circumstances – or in as normal as any circumstances under which Jilly had known him – he *hulked* over the steering wheel, but now he hulked more aggressively than before, head thrust toward the windshield, face screwed into a bearish scowl, stare fixed on the bright swaths that the headlights cut through the dark depression into which he piloted the SUV.

He failed to answer her question. His mouth hung open as if in astonishment, as though he couldn't quite believe that he had put the Expedition through a controlled spin or that he was barreling across the median toward the westbound lanes.

All right, he wasn't barreling yet, but the truck continued to accelerate as it reached the low point of the swale. If they crossed the declivity and hit the rising slope at the wrong angle and at too high a speed, the SUV would roll because rolling was something that SUVs did well when they were badly driven and when the terrain was, like this, composed of shifting sand and loose shale.

She shouted – 'Don't!' – but he did. As the Expedition churned across the crumbling face of the upgrade, Jilly jammed her feet harder against the dashboard, wondering where the impact air bag might be stowed, dreading what would happen if the bag was in the dashboard and if it exploded around her feet, wondering whether it would jam her knees into her face, whether it would rupture around her shoes and spew skin-peeling hot gas at high pressure across her entire body. Those grotesque images and worse flashed through her mind, instead of the standard replay of her life to date (with the *Looney Tunes* soundtrack that would have been most appropriate), but she couldn't block them, so she held fast to the seat and to the assist bar and shouted – 'Don't!' – again to no avail.

Riddling the night behind them with twin barrages of tire-cast shale and sand, Dylan forced the Expedition up the northern incline of the median at an oblique angle, putting the vehicle to the ultimate roll test. Judging by the relentlessness with which gravity pulled Jilly toward the driver, just one more degree of tilt would tumble the SUV back into the swale.

Repeatedly as they ascended, four-wheel drive seemed to be at least two wheels shy of an adequate number to maintain traction. The truck lurched, rocked, but finally topped the rise onto the shoulder of the westbound lanes.

Dylan checked the rearview mirror, glanced at the side mirror, and rocketed into a gap in traffic, heading back the way they had come. Toward town. Toward the motel where the Coupe DeVille no doubt still smoldered. Into the trouble they had been trying to outrun.

Jilly had the crazy notion that the dangerous crossing of the median had been motivated by Shep's reminder – 'Fries not flies' – that he had not eaten dinner. The older brother's impressively deep commitment to the younger was admirable to a point, but a return to that burger bistro under these circumstances represented a colossal leap from the high ground of responsible stewardship into a swamp of reckless devotion.

'What're you doing?' she demanded again.

He answered this time, but his reply was neither reassuring nor informative: 'I don't know.'

She sensed a quality in his demeanor that was reminiscent of her desperate state of mind each time she found herself in the thrall of a mirage. Alarmed by the prospect of being driven at high speed by a man distracted by hallucinations or worse, she said, 'Slow down, for God's sake. Where are you going?'

Accelerating, he said, 'West. Somewhere west. A place. Some place.'

'Why?'

'I feel the pull.'

'The pull of what?'

'The west. I don't know. I don't know what or where.'

'Then why are you going anywhere at all?'

As if he were the simplest of men for whom this conversation had taken a philosophical turn no less beyond his comprehension than the arcane discoveries of molecular biology, Dylan rolled his gaze toward her, revealing as much white of the eyes as does a dog cringing in bewilderment from harsh words that it can't understand. 'It just . . . feels right.'

'*What* feels right?'

'Going this direction, going west again.'

'Aren't we driving straight back into trouble?'

'Yeah, probably, I think so.'

'Then pull over, stop.'

'Can't.' An instant sweat slicked his face. 'Can't.'

'Why?'

'Frankenstein. The needle. The *stuff*. It's started. Something's happening to me.'

'What something?'

'Some weird shit.'

In the backseat, Shepherd said, 'Manure.'

14

Weird manure indeed.

As though he were fleeing from a fast-moving fire or outrunning an avalanche of tumbling rock and ice and snow, Dylan O'Conner was flogged by a sense of urgency so intense that his heart jumped like that of a rabbit running in the shadow of a wolf. He had never suffered feelings of persecution and had never taken methamphetamine, but he supposed this must be how a man with paranoid delusions would feel if he mainlined a near-lethal dose of liquid speed.

'I'm jacked up,' he told Jilly, pressing the accelerator, 'and I don't know why, and I can't get down.'

God alone knew what she made of that. Dylan himself wasn't sure what he'd been trying to convey.

In fact, he didn't feel that he was running from danger, but that he was being drawn inexorably *toward* something by the world's largest electromagnet, which pulled him by the iron in his blood. His sense of urgency was matched by an irresistible compulsion to *move*.

The urgency had no apparent cause, and the compulsion related to no specific object. He simply *needed* to go west, and he felt constrained to race after the setting moon with all possible haste.

Instinct, he told Jilly. Something in his blood that said *go*, something in his bones that said *hurry*, a race-memory voice speaking through his genes, a voice that he knew he dared not ignore, because if he resisted its message, something terrible would happen.

'Terrible?' she asked. 'What?'

He didn't know, he only *felt*, as a stalked antelope feels the cheetah lurking a hundred yards away behind a screen of tall grass, and as a parched cheetah senses the presence of a water hole miles away across the veldt.

Trying to explain himself, he'd let up on the accelerator. The speedometer needle quivered at 85. He pumped it toward 90.

In this traffic, on this highway, in this vehicle, driving at ninety miles per hour wasn't only illegal and imprudent, but foolish, and worse than foolish – moronic.

He wasn't able either to shame or argue himself into reacting responsibly to the risk. Shep's life and Jilly's, as well as his own, were jeopardized by this monomaniacal determination to move and to move fast, faster, always west, *west*. On another night or even at an earlier hour this night, the mere recognition of his accountability for their safety would have caused Dylan to slow down, but now all moral considerations and even his survival instinct were overruled by this feverish compulsion.

Macks and Peterbilts, sedans, coupes, SUVs, pickups, vans, auto carriers, motor homes, tanker trucks raced westward, weaving back and forth from lane to lane, and without once slowing, Dylan plunged the Expedition through the gaps in traffic as expertly as an eagle-eyed tailor speed-threading a long series of needles.

As the speedometer indicated 92, his fear of crashing into another vehicle influenced him less than did the pure animal need to *move*. When it eased past 93, he grew concerned about the waves of vibrations that rattled the chassis, but not concerned enough to be able to cut their speed.

This urgent necessity, this sense that he must drive hard or die, exceeded mere compulsion, possessed him so fully as to be no less than an obsession, until with every rushing breath he heard within his mind the dire admonition *You're running out of time*, and heard with every racing heartbeat the exhortation *Faster!*

Encountering chuckholes, cracks, and patches in the pavement, the tires stuttered as hard as rapping hammers, and Dylan worried about the consequences of a blowout at this lightning pace, but he pressed the Expedition to 96, taxing the shock absorbers, torturing the springs, onward to 97, with engine screaming and wind of their own manufacture shrieking at the windows, to 98, between bracketing big rigs, around a sleek Jaguar with a cruise-missile *whoosh* that elicited a disapproving blast of the sports car's horn, to 99.

He remained aware of Jilly beside him, still braced for disaster with her sneakered feet against the dashboard, frantically struggling to shrug into her safety harness and to buckle herself to the seat. Peripheral vision suggested and a glance confirmed that she'd fallen into a state of unadulterated terror. He supposed she was saying something to him, shouting objections to his heedless, headlong westward rush. In fact he could hear her voice, which had grown hollow and low and distorted, as though hers was a taped recitation being replayed at the wrong speed; he couldn't understand a word.

Before the speedometer registered 100, to an even greater degree when it read 101, each irregularity in the pavement translated with magnified effect to the steering wheel, which tried to spin out of his grip. Fortunately, the sudden sweat that earlier slathered his face and moistened his palms had already dried in the steady blast of air conditioning. He maintained control at 102, at 103, but though he held the wheel, he couldn't lift his foot from the accelerator.

Greater velocity didn't at all diminish his overwhelming need for speed, and indeed, the faster the Expedition went, the greater Dylan's sense of urgency grew, and the more compelled he became to push the vehicle still harder, more relentlessly. He felt drawn by black-hole gravity, across the event horizon, beyond which neither matter nor radiation could escape the power of a crushing vortex. *Move, move, MOVE* became his mantra, movement with no deducible purpose, movement for movement's sake, westward, westward, on the trail of the long-lost sun and the still visible but receding moon.

Perhaps this frenzied plunge toward an unknown yet desperately needed object was how Frankenstein's unluckiest injected subjects felt in the frantic moments before their plummeting IQs dropped them through a trapdoor to the land of imbecility, idiocy.

If it doesn't obliterate your personality or totally disrupt your capacity for linear thinking, or reduce your IQ by sixty points . . .

Ahead loomed the town that they had departed with such haste a short while ago, when they'd feared nothing more than the appearance of a train of black Suburbans in the rearview mirror, gleaming like Death's gondolas given wheels.

Dylan expected to experience an irresistible pull toward the freeway exit near the motel where Jilly's Coupe DeVille had served as their tormentor's flaming casket. A glance at the instrument panel – 104 miles per hour – caused his briskly trotting heart to break into a gallop. He couldn't navigate that curving ramp at half their current velocity. He prayed that if compelled to leave the interstate, he would overcome this rage for speed in time to avoid crashing through the guardrail and tumbling to the bottom of an embankment in a test-to-destruction of Ford Motor Company's safety engineering.

As they approached the dreaded exit, he tensed, but he felt no strange attraction for it. They shot past the off-ramp as though they were a stunt team gearing up toward a jump over sixteen parked buses.

South of the interstate, among the bright clutter of road-service enterprises, the motel sign glowed with an ominous quality. The red neon inspired thoughts of blood, fire; it brought to mind myriad scenes of Hell as conceived with morbid passion by everyone from pre-Renaissance artists to contemporary comic-book illustrators.

The rhythmic spurt of roof-rack beacons atop emergency vehicles splashed the walls of the distant motel. Thin ribbons of gray smoke still rose from the charred hulk of the Coupe DeVille.

In little more than half a minute, the smoldering carnage lay a mile behind them. They were closing rapidly on the second of two exits that served the town, more than three miles west of the first.

As their speed at last began to fall rapidly and as Dylan flicked the right-turn signal, Jilly might have thought that he'd regained control of himself. He was, however, no more the master of his fate than he'd been when he'd spun the SUV out of the eastbound lanes and crossed the median. Something called him, like a siren to a sailor, and he continued to be powerless to resist this unknown summoning force.

He took the western exit too fast, but not fast enough to slide or roll the Expedition. At the bottom of the ramp, when he saw no traffic on the quiet surface street, he ran the stop sign without hesitation and turned left into a residential area, with utter disregard for the laws of man and physics.

'Euca, euca, euca, eucalyptus,' Dylan heard himself chanting, speaking without volition, spooked by this new turn of events not solely because it was *weird*, but because he sounded dismayingly like Shep. 'Eucalyptus, eucalyptus five, no, not five, eucalyptus six, no, eucalyptus sixty.'

Although visually oriented, he was a bookish man as well; and over the years he'd read a few novels about people seized by mind-controlling aliens, one about a girl possessed by a demon, one about a guy ridden by the ghost of a dead twin, and he supposed that this was how he might feel if, in reality, an evil extraterrestrial or a malevolent spirit took up residence in his body with the power to override his will. He wasn't aware, however, of any invading entity squirming within his flesh or crawling the surface of his brain; he remained rational enough to reason that what had gotten into him was nothing more than the mysterious contents of that 18-cc syringe.

This analysis did not reassure him.

For no reason, just because it felt right, he turned left at the first cross street, drove three blocks, his voice growing more urgent by the moment, insistent and loud enough to drown out whatever Jilly was saying: 'Eucalyptus six, eucalyptus zero, eucalyptus five, sixty-five, no, five sixty, maybe, or fifty-six. . . .'

Although he had slowed to forty miles an hour, he almost sped past the street sign bearing the name of the very tree about which he had been babbling: EUCALYPTUS AVENUE.

He tapped the brakes, wheeled left, climbed and descended the curb at the corner of the intersection, drove into Eucalyptus Avenue.

Too narrow to be correctly called an avenue, hardly wider than a lane, the street featured not a single eucalyptus, as far as he could discern, but was flanked by Indian laurels and by old olive trees with exquisitely gnarled trunks and limbs that cast a wild wickerwork of shadows in the amber glow of streetlamps. Either the eucalyptuses had perished and had been replaced ages ago, or the street had been named by an arboricultural ignoramus.

Beyond the trees stood modest houses, old but for the most part well maintained: stucco *casetas* with barrel-tile roofs, suburban ranch-style houses with clean lines but little character, here and there a two-story structure that seemed to have been displaced from Indiana or Ohio.

He began to accelerate, but then impetuously braked and swung the Expedition to the curb in front of 506 Eucalyptus Avenue. At the end of a brick walkway stood a two-story clapboard house with a deep front porch.

Switching off the engine, popping the release on his safety harness, he said, 'Stay here with Shep.'

Jilly responded, but Dylan didn't understand her. Although from this point he would be on foot, the urgency and sense of mission that had swiveled him out of an eastward flight into this westward odyssey had not diminished. His heart still knocked so forcibly and so fast that the inner percussion half deafened him, and he had neither the patience nor the presence of mind to ask her to repeat herself.

When he threw open the driver's door, she snared a handful of his Hawaiian shirt and held fast. She had the grip of a griffin; her fingers hooked like talons in the fabric.

Dark anxiety clouded her beauty, and her sable-brown eyes, once as limpid and sharp with purpose as those of a sentinel eagle, were muddy with worry. 'Where did you go?' she demanded.

'Here,' he said, pointing to the clapboard house.

'I mean on the road. You were a world away. You forgot I was even with you.'

'Didn't forget,' he disagreed. 'No time. Stay with Shep.'

Griffin-tough, she tried to hold him back. 'What's going on here?'

'Hell if I know.'

Maybe he *didn't* pry Jilly's fingers out of his shirt with a cruel force uncharacteristic of him, and maybe he *didn't* shove her violently away from him. He wasn't sure how he tore loose of the woman, but he got out of the Expedition. Leaving the driver's door hanging open behind him, he rounded the front of the SUV, heading toward the house.

Darkness ruled the first floor, but light shone behind the curtains of half the upstairs windows. Someone was home. He wondered if they were aware of his approach, if they were waiting for him – or if his appearance at their doorstep would come as a surprise to them. Perhaps they instinctively sensed something rushing toward them as Dylan himself had been aware of being drawn to an unknown place, by a power inexplicable.

He heard a noise that seemed to come from the right, at the side of the house.

Halfway along the front walk toward the porch, he veered off the herringbone bricks. He crossed the lawn to the driveway.

Attached to the house: a carport. Under the carport, an aging Buick stood beyond the reach of the waning moonlight as during the day it would shelter from the fierce desert sun.

Hot metal pinged and ticked as it cooled. The vehicle had arrived here only recently.

Past the open end of the carport, toward the back of the house, a noise arose: a jangling, as of keys on a ring.

Though a sense of urgency continued to plague him undiminished, Dylan stood motionless beside the car. Listening. Waiting. Uncertain what to do next.

He didn't belong here. He felt as if he were a lurking thief, although as far as he knew, he hadn't come to this place to steal anything.

On the other hand, the operative phrase was *as far as he knew*. Under the influence of the injected *stuff*, he might discover himself driven to commit heinous acts of which he would previously have been incapable. Theft might be the least of the crimes from which he would be powerless to turn away.

He thought of *Dr. Jekyll and Mr. Hyde*, the inner beast released and sent roaming.

From the moment he had succumbed to the urgent need to drive west, his fear had been sharp, but also it had been sheathed in a blunting thickness of compulsion and confusion. Now he wondered if the substance circulating in him might be the chemical equivalent of a demon saddling his soul and digging spurs into his heart. He shuddered, and an icy blade of fear flayed his nerves and caused the skin to prickle with dread on his arms and on the nape of his neck.

Again, not far away, he heard the soft brass ring of keys on keys. Hinges creaked, perhaps those of a door.

At the back of the house, light bloomed behind daisy-patterned curtains at the ground-floor windows.

He didn't know what to do, and then he did: He touched the handle on the driver's door of the Buick. Cascades of sparks whirled across his vision, phantom fireflies in flight *behind* his eyes.

Inside his head, he heard a fizzing-crackling electrical sound, the same as he had heard earlier in the Expedition, when he'd touched the button that bore the cartoon toad's grinning face. Some kind of seizure afflicted him, frightening but fortunately less severe than full convulsions, and as his tongue vibrated against the roof of his mouth, he heard himself make that queer, half-mechanical sound again. *'Hunnn-na-na-na-na-na-na-na!'*

This episode proved to be briefer than the first, and when he attempted to quell the stutter, he at once fell silent, instead of having to let it run its course, as had been the case previously.

With the final *na*, he was on the move again. Quietly, quietly through the carport, around the corner of the house.

Shallower than the veranda at the front of the house, the back porch also featured plainer posts. The steps were concrete instead of brick.

When his hand enfolded the knob on the back door, fireflies flew inside his head, but this bright swarm numbered fewer than the two that had flown in advance of it. The accompanying electric crackle sounded less cataclysmic than before. Clenching his teeth, pressing his tongue firmly against the roof of his mouth, he avoided making any sound this time.

The lock was not engaged. The knob turned when he tried it, and the door opened when he pushed inward.

Dylan O'Conner crossed a threshold that was not his to cross, entered uninvited, appalled by this bold trespass, yet compelled to proceed.

The plump, white-haired woman in the kitchen wore a candy-striped uniform. She looked weary and troubled, different from the fresh and cheerful Mrs. Santa Claus that she'd been when, a couple hours ago, she had taken his order for burgers and had fixed the toad pin to his shirt.

A large white bag of takeout, discount dinner from her job, stood on the counter near the cooktop. This potpourri of grease and onion and cheese and charbroiled meat had already flooded the room with a delicious melange of aromas.

She stood beside the kitchen table, her once-pink face fading toward gray, captured by an expression between worry and despair. She stared down at an arrangement of objects on the Formica tabletop, a still life unlike any that the old masters had ever painted: two empty cans of Budweiser, one upright, one on its side, both partly crushed; a scattered collection of pills and capsules, many white, some pink, a few green giants; an ashtray containing two roaches – not the kind that had ever crawled or nested under the warm motor of a refrigerator, but the butt ends of two marijuana joints.

The woman didn't hear Dylan enter, didn't glimpse the movement of the door from the corner of her eye, and for a moment she remained unaware of him. When she realized that she had a visitor, she shifted her gaze from the table to his face, but she seemed to have been too numbed by the tableau on the Formica to be immediately surprised or alarmed by his unexpected arrival.

He saw her alive, dead, alive, dead, and the faint cold fear that thrilled through his veins thickened into terror.

15

Dylan crossing in front of the Expedition, through the headlight beams, his yellow-and-blue shirt as bright as any afternoon on Maui, might have vanished before Jilly's eyes, stepping out of this world into an alternate reality, and she would have been surprised but not astonished. The hazardous return drive to town had been a high-speed journey squarely into the Twilight Zone, and after her vision in the desert and the river of spirit doves, she might not be capable of astonishment again this side of the grave.

When Dylan *didn't* vanish in front of the truck, when he reached the brick walkway and started toward the house, Jilly turned her head to look at Shepherd in the backseat.

She caught him watching her. They locked stares. His green eyes widened at the shock of contact, and then he closed them.

'You stay here, Shep.'

He didn't answer.

'Don't move out of that seat. We'll be right back.'

Under his pale lids, his eyes twitched, twitched.

When Jilly glanced toward the house, she saw Dylan angling from the brick walk toward the driveway.

Leaning across the console, she doused the headlights. Switched off the engine. Plucked the keys from the ignition.

'Did you hear me, Shep?'

His shuttered eyes appeared to be full of dreams, marked by more REM than those of a sleeping man thrashed by nightmares.

'Don't move, stay here, don't move, we'll be right back,' she counseled as she opened the passenger's door and swiveled on her seat, keeping her legs up to spare Fred from injury.

Olives littered the sidewalk and squished underfoot, as though recently the neighbors had gathered here for an outdoor martini party but had discarded their cocktail garnishes instead of eating them.

Dylan followed the driveway into the layered tarps of shadow that draped the sedan in the carport, though he remained in sight.

A breath of breeze as dry as stirred gin with a single drop of vermouth inspired a subtle silken rustle from the olive trees. Over this seductive swish, Jilly heard *Hunnn-na-na-na-na-na-na-na!*

His eerie stutter spiraled down her cochleae to the bottom of her ears and seemed to leap from there into her spine, vibrating from vertebra to vertebra, shaking shivers from her.

With the utterance of the final syllable, Dylan disappeared toward the back of the carport.

Making olive paste underfoot as she crossed the public sidewalk, shuffling through the grass to clean her shoes, Jilly hurried toward the place where he'd been just before darkness swallowed him.

≈ ≈ ≈

Her face plump and sweet, ideal for Christmas cards, was in the next instant drawn, bleak, fit for Halloween. In a quiver of shadow cast by something invisible, her white and glossy hair became tangled and matted with blood, but in a shimmer of light that had no apparent source, red tangles smoothed and clarified again into white glossy locks. A face pale pink under snowy hair withered into grainy gray when framed by clotted curls and snarls. Her eyes met Dylan's with bewilderment, but then shocked wide and filled with cold mortality – and yet an instant later were alert, aware, startled once more.

Dylan saw her alive, dead, alive, dead, one image rising out of the other, briefly asserting its reality, then submerging in its antithesis. He didn't know beyond doubt what this hideous apparition meant, if in fact it meant anything at all, but he glanced at his hands, expecting them to appear alternately clean and filthy with the woman's blood. When the vision of violence did not involve his hands, his innards nevertheless remained a clenched mass of dread, and he raised his eyes to her face once more, half convinced that whatever power had driven him to this place would eventually use him as the instrument of her death.

'Cheeseburgers, French fries, apple pies, and vanilla shakes,' she said, proving either that he had been memorable during his brief visit to the takeout counter or that her powers of recollection were formidable.

Instead of answering her, Dylan found himself stepping to the kitchen table and picking up one of the empty cans of Budweiser. The fireflies flew again within the bone cave of his skull, but he heard far less of the fizz-and-crackle of arcing electrical current than he had heard before, and behind his clenched teeth, not one convulsive spasm plagued his tongue.

'Get out of the house,' he advised the woman. 'You're not safe here. Hurry, go, *now*.'

Whether she went or stayed, he didn't know, because even as he spoke, he dropped the beer can on the table and at once turned from her. He didn't look back. Could not.

He hadn't yet come to the end of this bizarre journey begun in the Expedition and continued here on foot. Beyond the kitchen, past an open door, lay a plank-floored hallway softened by a threadbare, rose-patterned runner. His sense of urgency renewed, Dylan was drawn forward toward some dark destination.

Reaching the carport, Jilly peered back toward the Expedition, where the streetlamps, filtered through olive branches, revealed Shepherd in silhouette, in the backseat where he had been told to stay.

Past the Buick, out of the carport, she hurried to the rear of the house, stirring up a cloud of pale moths when she brushed against a camellia bush with blooms as full and red as maidens' hearts.

The back door stood open. A rectangle of outfalling kitchen light revealed a porch floor painted pearl-gray and remarkably free of dust for the porch of a house in a desert town.

Even under these extraordinary circumstances, she might have halted at the threshold, might have politely rapped knuckles against the jamb of the open door. The sight of the familiar white-haired woman in the kitchen, lifting the receiver of a wall-mounted phone, alarmed and emboldened Jilly, however, and she stepped off the porch, onto the freshly polished yellow-and-green basket-weave linoleum.

By the time Jilly surprised her, the woman had pressed 9, pressed 1, on the telephone keypad. Jilly took the receiver from her grasp, and hung up before the second 1 could be entered.

If the police had been summoned, eventually the men in the black Suburbans would have followed.

No longer the cheerful purveyor of fast food and have-a-nice-day sentiments, wearied by a long day's work, haggard by worry, confused by the events of the past minute, this Disneyesque grandmother wrung her hands as though to squeeze the nervous tremors from them. With a note of amazed recognition, she said, 'You. Chicken sandwich, French fries, root beer.'

'Big man, Hawaiian shirt?' Jilly inquired.

The woman nodded. 'He said I wasn't safe here.'

'Not safe why?'

'He said get out of the house *now*.'

'Where did he go?'

Although well wrung, her hand remained sodden with tremors as she pointed shakily toward the open door to the downstairs hallway, where soft rose-colored light glowed at the far end, past a gauntlet of shadows.

≈ ≈ ≈

Walking on roses, green leaves, and thorns, he passed openings arched like the entrances to arbors, with dark rooms beyond, where anything might be growing in the gloom. One room to the right and two on his left worried him, even though he was drawn to none of them and could most likely assume that his compulsion to keep moving meant the danger still lay ahead rather than to either side.

He had no doubt that something dangerous waited to be met. The mysterious attractant that had pulled him through the Arizona night would not prove to be a pot of gold, nor would this house likely ever lie at the end of any rainbow.

Toad pin to car door to beer can, he had followed a trail of strange energy left behind by the white-haired woman's touch.

Marjorie. Just now he knew she was Marjorie, though her uniform had not featured a name tag.

Toad pin to kitchen, he had been seeking Marjorie, for in the invisible residue that her touch left on inanimate objects, he had read the pattern of her destiny. He had felt the broken threads in the tapestry of her fate and had somehow known that they would be broken here, this night.

From the half-crushed beer can onward, he stalked a new quarry. Unknowingly, Marjorie had been prey when she'd entered her home; and Dylan sought her would-be killer.

Having arrived at even this half-formed understanding of the nature of the looming confrontation, he realized that pressing onward was an act of reckless valor, if not evidence of insanity, but yet he was not able to retreat a single step. He was constrained to proceed by the same unknown and overmastering power that had forced him to turn back from the promise of New Mexico and to drive westward at speeds in excess of a hundred miles per hour.

The hallway led to a modest front foyer, where a blown-glass lamp under a rose silk shade stood on a small table with a delicate carved fretwork skirt. This was the sole source of light beyond the kitchen, and it barely illuminated the rising staircase as far as the landing.

When Dylan put one hand on the newel post at the bottom of the stairs, he experienced again the predator's psychic spoor, the same that he had found upon the beer can, as clear to him as a fugitive's unique scent is unmistakable to a bloodhound. The character of these traces was different from the quality of those Marjorie had left on the toad pin and the car door, for in these he sensed a malignancy, as though they had been laid down by a spirit that passed this way on cloven hooves.

He took his hand off the newel cap and stared for a moment at the polished curve of darkly stained poplar, searching for evidence of any residue of either a physical or a supernatural nature, but finding none. His fingerprints and palm print overlaid those of the beer drinker, and though not one loop or arch or whorl could be seen by the unassisted eye, police-lab technicians would later be able to make visible – with fixative chemicals, powder, and oblique light – irrefutable proof that he'd once been here.

The certainty that fingerprints exist – all but invisible and yet sufficiently recoverable to convict a man of any crime from theft to murder – provided an analogy that allowed Dylan more easily to believe that with their very touch, people might leave behind something more peculiar but every bit as real as natural oils impressed with the patterns of skin ridges.

The rose-decorated runner up the center of the stairs appeared to be as worn as the similar carpet in the lower hall. The pattern here looked bolder, featuring fewer flowers and more brambles, as though to signify that station by station in this journey, Dylan's task was growing thornier.

Ascending although reason could present no argument to ascend, he slid his right hand along the banister. Lingering traces of the malevolent entity flared against his palm and sparked against his fingertips, but fireflies no longer swarmed through his head. The internal electrical sizzle had been silenced as completely as his convulsing tongue had been stilled by the time that he'd touched the beer can in the kitchen. He had adjusted to this uncanny experience, and neither his mind nor his body any longer offered resistance to these currents of supernatural sensation.

Even unknown intruders and a perception of impending violence could not long stifle the white-haired woman's natural amiableness, which had no doubt been enhanced with motivational steroids during training provided by the fast-food franchise for which she worked. Worry twitched into a fragile smile, and she offered one hand to be shaken even though it was doing a fine job of shaking itself. 'I'm Marjorie, dear. What's your name?'

Jilly would have gone into the downstairs hall in search of Dylan if her only responsibility had been Shepherd, but Dylan had left her with a second, this woman. She didn't want to leave Shep alone in the SUV much longer, and if she left Marjorie alone within reach of a telephone, more small-town cops would be milling around this place than you'd find at a *Mayberry RFD* convention.

Besides, Dylan had told Marjorie to get out of the house because she wasn't safe here, but the old girl seemed to have lived nearly seventy years while remaining a naif incapable of recognizing peril even when the wickedly gleaming edge of it was descending toward her neck. If Jilly didn't get her out of here, Marjorie might remain in the kitchen, vaguely concerned but not alarmed, even if a plague of ravenous locusts swarmed out of the pantry and gouts of molten lava erupted from the sink drain.

'I'm Marjorie,' she repeated, her fragile smile trembling like a crescent of froth that might dissolve back into the pool of worry that had flooded her features. Still extending her hand, she clearly expected a name in return – a name that she would give to the cops later when, inevitably, she eventually summoned them.

Putting an arm around Marjorie's shoulders, encouraging her toward the back door, Jilly said, 'Sweetie, you can just call me Chicken-sandwich-French-fries-root-beer. "Chicky" for short.'

≈   ≈   ≈

Each further contact with the spoor on the banister suggested that the person whose trail Dylan followed was more malevolent than the previous trace had revealed. By the time that he turned at the landing and climbed the second flight into the gloom at the top of the stairs, he understood that in the upper rooms waited an adversary who could be vanquished not by a mere artist lacking any firsthand experience of violence, but by no less than a dragon slayer.

Hardly more than a minute ago, downstairs, when he had seen the woman alive but also as she might eventually appear in the aftermath of murder, he had felt undiluted terror for the first time slither into him. Now it tightened its serpent coils around his spine.

'*Please*,' Dylan whispered, as though he still believed that he stood here in the iron control of – and at the mercy of – an unknown external force. '*Please*,' he repeated, as though it were not becoming manifestly clear that this sixth sense had been conferred upon him – or cursed upon him – by whatever elixir the syringe contained, and as though it were not equally clear that he continued on this dangerous course utterly without coercion. His whispered *please* could rightly be directed toward no one but himself. He was driven by motives that he could not understand, but they were nonetheless his motives and his alone.

He could turn and leave. He *knew* the choice was his to make.

Also he understood that the way down and out of this house would be easier than the path ahead.

When he realized that he was indeed in full control of himself, a remarkable calm settled through him with the rare grace of windless snow layering smooth contours over a racked landscape. He stopped shaking. When his clenched teeth relaxed, his jaw muscles stopped twitching. His sense of urgency subsided, and his heartbeat grew slower and less forceful until he thought that his cardiac muscle might not explode, after all. Unwinding from his spine, the serpent of cold terror bit its tail and swallowed itself entirely.

He stood at the head of the stairs, at the brink of the dark hall, knowing that he could turn back, knowing that he would instead go forward, but *not* knowing why, and for the moment not needing to know. By his own assessment, he was not a courageous man, not born to travel battlefields or to police mean streets. He admired heroism, but he didn't expect it of himself. Although his motivation here remained a mystery, he understood himself well enough to be sure that selflessness wasn't a factor; he would go forward because intuitively he sensed that to retreat would not be in his best interests. Because he couldn't yet consciously process all the strange information gathered by his uncannily heightened perceptions, logic led him to rely on his instincts more than might ordinarily have been prudent.

Rose light climbed the trellis of the stairs only as far as the lower landing. The dark bowers before Dylan were brightened only – and barely – by the glow of a lamp behind a door that had been left half an inch ajar on the right side of the hall.

As best he could discern, three rooms lay upstairs: the lamplit chamber at the end, a nearer door also on the right, and a single room on the left.

When Dylan took three steps to the first door on the right, fear crept upon him once more: a manageable anxiety, the judicious apprehension of a fireman or a cop, not the burden of terror under which he'd labored from the kitchen, along the lower hall, to the top of the stairs.

The psychic spoor of his quarry contaminated the doorknob. He nearly withdrew his hand, but intuition – his new best friend – urged him to proceed.

A faint rasp of the latch, a whisper of dry hinges. A frosted-glass window lustrous with the cadmium-yellow glow of a streetlamp, veined by the shadow of an olive branch, allowed enough light to reveal a deserted bathroom.

He proceeded to the second room on the right, where a blade of brighter light cut through the half-inch crack between the door and jamb. Both instinct and reason prevented him from putting his eye to that narrow space, lest the metaphorical blade be joined by a real knife that would blind him for his spying.

When he cupped his hand around this doorknob, Dylan knew that he had found the lair of the sick soul he sought, for the spoor was a hundredfold more potent than what he'd encountered thus far. The psychic trace left by his quarry wriggled like a centipede against his palm, squirmed, writhed, and he knew that beyond this door lay a colony of Hell established on the wrong side of death.

16

Crossing the threshold at the back door, Marjorie remembered her take-out dinner, which she'd left behind, and she wanted to return to the kitchen to fetch the bag 'while the cheeseburger is still warm.'

With the patience of a giant bird or other costumed teacher from Sesame Street defining a new word for a child whose ability to focus had been atomized by an overdose of Ritalin, Jilly kept the woman on the move by explaining that a warm cheeseburger would be no comfort if she was dead.

Apparently, Dylan had given Marjorie only a vague warning, had not specified that the four-burner gas oven was about to explode, had not predicted that an earthquake would at any moment shake her house into one of those piles of smoking rubble that the gleeful vultures of the media found so picturesque. Nevertheless, in light of recent events, Jilly took his premonition seriously, regardless of its lack of specificity.

Using happy talk and cunning psychology that Big Bird would have heartily endorsed, Jilly coddled Marjorie through the door, onto the back porch, to the head of the steps that led down to the back lawn.

At that point the older woman applied her impressive weight to a squinching maneuver with her feet, creating suction between the tread on her rubber-soled shoes and the glossy paint on the porch floor. This clever trick made her as immovable as Hercules had ever been when, sentenced to be drawn and quartered, he had proved himself the equal of two teams of torturing horses.

'Chicky,' the woman said to Jilly, choosing not to address her by her full fast-food name, 'does he know about the knives?'

'He who?'

'Your fella.'

'He's not my fella, Marj. Don't make assumptions like that. He's not my type. What knives?'

'Kenny likes knives.'

'Who's Kenny?'

'Kenny junior, not his father.'

'Kids,' Jilly commiserated, still urging the woman to move.

'Kenny senior's in a prison in Peru.'

'Bummer,' Jilly said, referring both to Kenny senior's Peruvian incarceration and to her own inability to tumble Marjorie down the porch stairs.

'Kenny junior, he's my oldest grandson. Nineteen.'

'And he likes knives, huh?'

'He collects them. Very pretty knives, some of them.'

'That sounds swell, Marj.'

'I'm afraid he's back on the drugs again.'

'Knives and drugs, huh?' Jilly said, trying to rock the woman to break the shoe suction and get her moving.

'I don't know what to do. I don't. He gets crazy on the drugs sometimes.'

'Crazy, drugs, knives,' Jilly said, talking the pieces of the Kenny puzzle into place, glancing nervously toward the kitchen door that stood open behind them.

'He's going to have a breakdown sooner or later,' Marj worried. 'He's going to go over the edge someday.'

'Sweetie,' Jilly said, 'I think today's the day.'

≈ ≈ ≈

Not just a single centipede but a nest of them, writhing knots of centipedes, seemed to squirm against the palm of Dylan's hand.

He didn't release the knob in revulsion because simultaneously he sensed the appealing traces of another and better personality layered with the spoor of the sick soul. He received impressions of a shining but anxious heart whose refuge, curiously, was in the same place as the dragon's lair.

Cautiously he pushed open the door.

A large bedroom had been partitioned exactly at the midpoint as clearly as though a line had been painted across the floor, up the left-hand wall, across the ceiling, and down the right-hand wall. The division had been effected not with any boundary markers, however, but by the dramatic contrast between the interests and the characters of the two residents who shared these lodgings.

In addition to a bed and nightstand, the nearer half of the room featured bookshelves stocked with paperbacks. Wall space remained for an eclectic collection of three posters. In the first, a 1966 A.C. Shelby Cobra convertible rocketed along a highway toward a dazzling red sunset; with its low profile, sensuously rounded lines, and a silver finish that reflected the Technicolor sky, this sports car was the embodiment of speed, joy, freedom. Beside the Cobra hung a solemn portrait of a grumpy-looking C. S. Lewis. The third was a poster of the famous photograph of U.S. Marines raising Old Glory at the summit of a battle-scarred hill on Iwo Jima.

Furnished with another bed and nightstand, the farther half of the room had no books, no posters. There, the walls served as display racks for a bristling collection of edge weapons. Thin poniards and wider daggers, dirks, stilettos, one saber, one scimitar, kukris and katars from India, a skean dhu from Scotland, a short-handled halberd, bayonets, falchions, bowies, yataghans . . . Many blades were etched with elaborate designs, handles ornately carved and painted, pommels and quillons sometimes plain but often elaborately decorated.

In the nearer half of the room stood a small desk. On it, neatly arranged, were a blotter, a pen set, a canister of pencils, a thick dictionary, and a scale model of the 1966 A. C. Shelby Cobra.

In the far zone, a work table held a plastic replica of a human skull and a collapsed stack of pornographic videos.

The nearer realm was dusted, swept, more elaborately appointed than a monk's cell but every bit as neat as any friar's habitat.

Disorder ruled in the far kingdom. The bedclothes were tangled. Dirty socks, discarded shoes, empty soda and beer cans, and crumpled candy wrappers littered the floor, the nightstand, and the shelf atop the headboard of the bed. Only the knives and other edge weapons had been arranged with care – if not with loving calculation – and judging by the mirror-bright gleam of every blade, much time had been devoted to their maintenance.

A pair of suitcases stood side by side in the center of the room, on the border between these rival encampments. A black cowboy hat with a green feather in the band was perched atop the luggage.

All this Dylan noted in one quick survey of the scene lasting but three or four seconds, much as he had long been accustomed to absorbing entire landscapes in vivid detail with an initial sweeping gaze, in order to assess at first glance, before his head overruled his heart, whether the subject merited the time and the energy that he would have to expend to paint it and to paint it well. The talent with which he'd been born included instant photographic perception, but he dramatically enhanced it with training, as he imagined that a gifted young cop consciously honed his natural skills of observation until he earned detective status.

As any good cop would have done, Dylan began and ended this initial sweep with the detail that most immediately and strikingly defined the scene: a boy of about thirteen sat in the nearest bed, wearing jeans and a New York City Fire Department T-shirt, shackled at the ankles, cruelly gagged, and handcuffed to the brass headboard.

$\sim$ $\sim$ $\sim$

Marj did her immovable-object shtick far better than Jilly could pull off her irresistible-force act. Still anchored to the porch at the top of the steps, she said worriedly, 'We've got to get him.'

Although Dylan wasn't her fella, Jilly didn't know how otherwise to refer to him, since she didn't want to use his real name in front of this woman and because she didn't know what food *he* had ordered earlier. 'Don't worry. My fella will get him, Marj.'

'I don't mean get Kenny,' Marj said with more distress than she had shown previously.

'Who do you mean?'

'Travis. I mean Travis. All he's got is books. Kenny has knives, but Travis has just his books.'

'Who's Travis?'

'Kenny's little brother. He's thirteen. Kenny has a breakdown, it'll be Travis who gets broke.'

'And Travis – he's in there with Kenny?'

'Must be. We've got to get him out.'

At the far end of the back porch from them, the kitchen door still stood open. Jilly didn't want to return to the house.

She didn't know why Dylan had come here at high speed, risking life and limb and increased insurance premiums, but she doubted that he'd been compelled by a belated need to thank Marj for her courteous service or by a desire to return the toad button so that it might be given to another customer who would better appreciate it. Based on what little information Jilly possessed and considering what an *X-Files* night this had become, the smart-money bet was that Mr. Dylan Something's-happening-to-me O'Conner had raced to this house to stop Kenny from doing a bad thing with his knife collection.

If a burst of psychic perception had led Dylan to Kenny of the Many Knives, whom he had apparently never met previously, then logic suggested that he would be aware of Travis, too. When he encountered a thirteen-year-old boy armed with a book, he wasn't going to mistake the kid for a doped-up nineteen-year-old knife maniac.

That train of thought, however, was derailed by the word *logic*. The events of the past couple hours had thrown baby Logic out the window with the bathwater of reason. Nothing happening to them this night would have been possible in the rational world where Jilly had grown up from choirgirl to comedian. This was a new world, either with an entirely new logic that she hadn't puzzled out yet or with no logic at all, and in such a world, *anything* could happen to Dylan in a strange house, in the dark.

Jilly didn't like knives. She had become a comedian, not part of a knife-throwing act. She desperately didn't want to go into a house with a knife collection and a Kenny.

Two minutes ago, when Jilly had entered the kitchen and had hung up the telephone one digit short of disaster, poor Marj seemed dazed, numb. Now the candy-striped semizombie was rapidly transforming into an emotionally distraught grandmother capable of reckless action. 'We gotta get Travis!'

The last thing Jilly needed was a knife in her chest, but the *next-to-last* thing she needed was a hysterical grandmother barging back into the house, complicating Dylan's situation, most likely going for the phone again the moment she caught sight of it and was reminded that the police were always waiting to serve.

'You stay here, Marj. You stay right here. This is my job. I'll find Travis. I'll get him out of there.'

As Jilly turned away, having committed to being braver than she preferred to be, Marj grabbed her by the arm. 'Who *are* you people?'

You people. Jilly almost reacted to those two innocent words, *you people*, rather than to the question. She almost said, *What do you mean – YOU PEOPLE? You have a problem with people like me?*

During the past couple years, however, as she had gained some acceptance with her act and had achieved at least a small measure of success, her hot-tempered knee-jerk reactions to perceived insults had seemed increasingly stupid. Even in response to Dylan – who for some reason had the power to push her go-nuts button as no one before him – even in response to *him*, the knee-jerk reactions were stupid. And under current circumstances, they were dangerously distracting, as well.

'Police,' she lied with surprising ease for a former choirgirl. 'We're police.'

'No uniforms?' Marj wondered.

'We're undercover.' She didn't offer to produce a badge. 'Stay here, sweetie. Stay here where it's safe. Let the pros handle this.'

∽ ∽ ∽

The boy in the FDNY T-shirt had been overpowered, beaten, and most likely knocked unconscious, although he had revived by the time Dylan entered his room. One blackened and swollen eye. Abraded chin. Blood caked in his left ear from a blow to the side of the head.

Pulling strips of adhesive tape off the kid's face, prying a red rubber ball from the pale-lipped mouth, Dylan vividly recalled being helpless in the motel-room chair, remembered gagging on the athletic sock, and he discovered in himself a settled anger like long-banked coals ready to flare white-hot when fanned by one breath of righteous outrage. This potentially volcanic anger seemed out of character for an easygoing man who believed that even the most savage heart could be brought out of darkness by the recognition of the deeply beautiful design of the natural world, of life. For years he'd turned the other cheek so often that at times he must have looked like a spectator at a perpetual tennis match.

His anger wasn't fueled by what he had suffered, however, nor even by what he might yet have to endure as his *stuff*-driven fate played out in days to come, but by sympathy for the boy and by pity for all victims in this age of violence. After Judgment, perhaps the meek *would* inherit the earth for their playing field, as promised; but meanwhile, the vicious had their sport, day after bloody day.

Dylan had always been aware of injustice in the world, but he'd never cared as intensely as this, had never before felt the twisting auger of injustice boring through his heart. The poignancy and purity of his anger surprised him, for it seemed greatly out of proportion to the apparent cause. One battered boy was not Auschwitz, not the mass graves of Khmer Rouge Cambodia, not the World Trade Center.

Something profound was happening to him, all right, but the transfiguration wasn't limited to the acquisition of a sixth sense. Deeper and more fearsome changes were occurring, tectonic shifts in the deepest bedrock of his mind.

Gag removed, free to speak, the boy proved self-controlled and capable of getting at once to the quick of the situation. Whispering, his gaze fixed on the open door as if it were a portal through which the most hideous troops in Hell's army might march at any moment, he said, 'Kenny's wired at least six ways. Full-on psycho. Got a girl in Grandma's room, I think he'll kill her. Then Grandma. Then me. He'll kill me last 'cause he hates me most.'

'What girl?' Dylan asked.

'Becky. Lives down the street.'

'Little girl?'

'No, seventeen.'

The chain that wrapped the boy's ankles and bound them together had been secured with a padlock. The links between the two bracelets of his handcuffs had been passed behind one of the vertical rails on the brass headboard, tethering him to the bed.

'Keys?' Dylan asked.

'Kenny's got 'em.' At last the boy's gaze shifted from the open door, and he met Dylan's eyes. 'I'm stuck here.'

Lives were in the balance now. Although bringing in the cops would almost certainly draw the black-Suburban crowd, as well, with mortal consequences for Dylan and Shep and Jilly, he was morally compelled to call 911.

'Phone?' he whispered.

'Kitchen,' breathed the boy. 'And one in Grandma's room.'

Intuition told Dylan that he didn't have time to go to the kitchen to make the call. Besides, he didn't want to leave the boy up here alone. As far as he knew, premonition was not a part of his psychic gift, but the air cloyed about him, thickening with the expectation of violence; he would have wagered his soul that if the killing had not already begun, it would start before he reached the bottom of the rose-festooned stairs.

Grandma's room had a phone, but evidently it also had Kenny. When Dylan went in there, he would need more than a steady finger for the touch-tone keypad.

Once more the blades on the walls drew his attention, but he was repulsed by the prospect of slashing anyone with sword or machete. He didn't have the stomach for such wet work.

Aware of Dylan's renewed interest in the knives, and evidently sensing his disinclination to use one, the boy said, 'There. By the bookcase.'

A baseball bat. One of the old-fashioned hardwood kind. Dylan had swung a lot of them in his childhood, although never at a human being.

Any soldier or cop, or any man of action, might have disagreed with him, but Dylan preferred the baseball bat to a bayonet. It felt good in his hands.

'Full-on psycho,' the boy reminded him, as if to say that the bat should be swung first, with no resort to reason or persuasion.

To the threshold. The hall. Across the hall to the only second-floor room that he'd not yet investigated.

This final door, closed tight, wasn't outlined by even a thin filament of light.

A hush fell over the house. Ear to the jamb, Dylan listened for a telltale sound from six-way-wired Kenny.

≈   ≈   ≈

Some performers eventually confused make-believe with truth, and to a degree grew into their invented personas, swaggering

117

through the real world as though they were always on a stage. Over the past few years, Jilly had half convinced herself that she was the ass-kicking Southwest Amazon whom she claimed to be when she appeared before an audience.

Returning to the kitchen, she discovered much to her dismay that in a crunch, image and reality were not, in her case, the same thing. As she searched quickly for a weapon, drawer to drawer, cupboard to cupboard, the bones in her legs jellified, while her heart hardened into a sledge that hammered against her ribs.

By any standard of law or combat, a butcher knife qualified as a weapon. But the nearly arthritic stiffness with which her right hand closed on the handle convinced her that she'd never be comfortable wielding it on anything more responsive than a chuck roast.

Besides, to use a knife, you had to get in close to your enemy. Assuming that she might have to thump Kenny enough to stop him, if not actually waste him, Jilly preferred to thump him from as great a distance as possible, preferably with a high-powered rifle from a neighboring rooftop.

The pantry was just a pantry, not also an armory. The heaviest weaponry on its shelves were cans of cling peaches in heavy syrup.

Then Jilly noticed that Marj apparently had been plagued by an ant problem, and with a flash of inspiration, she said, '*Ah.*'

~ ~ ~

Neither the baseball bat nor his righteous anger made Dylan sufficiently brave or sufficiently foolish to crash into a dark room in search of a dope-crazed, hormone-crazed, just-plain-crazed teenager with more types of edge weapons than Death himself could name. After easing the door open – and feeling the tingle of psychic spoor – he waited in the hallway, his back to the wall, listening.

He heard enough nothing to suggest that he might be adrift in the vacuum of deep space, and as he began to wonder if he had gone deaf, he decided that Kenny must be no less patient than he was full-on psychotic.

Although Dylan wanted to do this about as much as he wanted to wrestle a crocodile, he edged into the open doorway, reached around the casing into the room, and felt the wall for the light switch. He assumed that Kenny stood poised to respond to such a maneuver, and his expectations of having his hand pinned to the wall with a knife were so high that he was not far short of astonished when he still had all his fingers after flipping the switch.

Grandma's room didn't have a ceiling fixture, but one of two nightstand lamps came on: a ginger jar painted with tulips, crowned by a pleated yellow shade in the shape of a coolie hat. Soft light and soft shadows shared the space.

Two other doors served the room. Both were closed. One most likely led to a closet. A bathroom might lie behind the other.

The drapes at the three windows were neither long enough nor full enough to conceal anyone.

A freestanding, full-length, oval-shaped mirror occupied one corner. No one lurked behind it, but Dylan's reflection occupied its face, looking less frightened than he felt, bigger than he thought of himself.

The queen-size bed was positioned so that Kenny might be hiding on the far side, lying on the floor, but no other furniture offered concealment.

Of more immediate concern was the figure on the bed. A thin chenille spread, a blanket, and a top sheet were tossed in disarray, but someone appeared to be lying under them, concealed head to foot.

As in countless prison-escape movies, this might actually have been pillows arranged to mimic the human form, except that the bedclothes trembled slightly.

By opening the door and switching on the light, Dylan already had announced his presence. Cautiously approaching the bed, he said, 'Kenny?'

Under the tumbled bedding, the ill-defined figure stopped shaking. For a moment it froze and lay as still as any cadaver beneath a morgue sheet.

Dylan gripped the baseball bat with both hands, ready to swing for the fences. 'Kenny?'

The hidden form began to twitch, as though with uncontainable excitement, with nervous energy.

The door that might lead to a closet: still closed. The door that might lead to a bathroom: still closed.

Dylan glanced over his shoulder, toward the hall door.

Nothing.

He grappled for the name that the shackled boy mentioned, the name of the threatened girl from down the street, and then he had it: 'Becky?'

The mysterious figure twitched, twitched, so *alive* beneath the covers, but it did not reply.

Although he dared not club what he could not see, Dylan was loath to put his hand to the bedclothes to toss them aside, for the same reason that he would have been reluctant to pull back the tarp on a woodpile if he suspected that a rattlesnake coiled among the cords.

He also wasn't eager to use the fat end of the baseball bat to lift the bedclothes out of the way. While entangled with the covers, the bat would be an ineffective weapon, and although this maneuver would leave Dylan vulnerable for only the briefest moment, a moment would be all that Kenny needed if he shot off the bed and out from under the rising covers, armed with a specialty knife well designed for evisceration.

Soft light, soft shadows.

House hushed.

The shape, twitching.

17

Jilly in the downstairs hall, archway to archway, past three lightless rooms, listened at each threshold, detected nothing, and moved onward to the foyer, past the lamp table, to the foot of the stairs.

Starting to climb, she heard a metallic *plink* behind her, and halted on the second step. *Plink* was followed by *tat-a-tat* and by a quick strumming – *zzziiinnnggg* – and then by utter stillness.

The noises had seemed to come from the first room inside the front door, directly opposite the foyer. Probably the living room.

When you were trying to avoid a run-in with a young man whose own grandmother's best assessment of him boiled down to *crazy-drugs-knives*, you didn't want to hear peculiar metallic sounds coming out of a dark room at your back. The subsequent silence did not have – could never possibly have – the innocent quality of the silence that had preceded *plink*.

With the unknown ahead, but now also behind her, Jilly did not suddenly discover the elusive inner Amazon, but she didn't freeze or cringe in fear, either. Her stoic mother and a few bad breaks long ago had taught her that adversity must be faced forthrightly, without equivocation; Mom counseled that you must tell yourself that every misfortune was custard, that it was cake and pie, and you must eat it up and be done with it. If grinning Kenny lurked in the pitch-black living room, stropping knives against each other loud enough to be confident that she would hear him, Jilly had an entire picnic of trouble laid out for her.

She retreated from the stairs into the foyer once more.

Plink, plink. Tick-tick-tick. Zing . . . zzziiinnnggg!

≈ ≈ ≈

Short of inhaling a gale like the big bad wolf in the fairy tale and blowing the covers off the bed, Dylan either had to stand here waiting for the shrouded figure to make the first move, which invited disaster more certainly than did taking action, or he must unveil the twitching form to learn its name and intentions.

Holding the baseball bat upraised in his right hand, he seized the bedclothes with his free hand and whipped them aside, revealing a black-haired, blue-eyed, barefoot teenage girl in cut-off jeans and a sleeveless blue-checkered blouse.

'Becky?'

Fright possessed her face, her electroshock-wide eyes. Tremors of fear flowed through her in plentiful rillets that repeatedly backed up into an overspilling twitch, jerking her head, her entire body, with the force he'd seen translated through the covers.

Her stricken gaze remained fixed on the ceiling as if she were unaware that help had arrived. Her obliviousness had the quality of a trance.

As he repeated her name, Dylan wondered if she might have been drugged. She seemed to be in a semiparalytic state and unaware of her surroundings.

Then, without glancing at him, she spoke urgently between teeth more than half clenched: *'Run.'*

With the bat raised in his right hand, he remained acutely aware of the open hallway door and of the two closed doors, alert for any sound, movement, swell of shadow. No threat arose on any side, no brutish figure that clashed with the daisy wallpaper, the yellow drapes, and the luminously reflective collection of satin-glass perfume bottles on the dresser.

'I'll get you out of here,' he promised.

He reached for her with his free hand, but she didn't take it. She lay stiff and shaking, attention still focused fearfully on the ceiling as if it were lowering toward her, a great crushing weight, as in one of those old movie serials featuring a villain who built elaborate machines of death when a revolver would have done the job better.

'Run,' Becky whispered with a note of greater desperation, *'for God's sake, run.'*

Her shaking, her paralysis, her frantic admonitions rattled his nerves, which were already rattling like hailstones on a tin roof.

In those old serials, a calculated dose of curare might reduce a victim to the helpless condition of this woman, but not in the real world. Her paralysis was probably psychological, though nonetheless hampering. To lift her off the bed and carry her from the room, he would have to put down the baseball bat.

'Where's Kenny?' he whispered.

At last her gaze lowered from the ceiling, toward the corner of the room in which one of the closed doors waited.

'There?' he pressed.

Becky's eyes met his for the first time . . . and then at once shifted again toward the door.

Warily Dylan moved around the foot of the bed, crossing the remainder of the room. Kenny might come at him from any-where.

Bedsprings sang, and the girl grunted as she exerted herself.

Turning, Dylan saw Becky no longer lying face-up, saw her risen to her knees, and rising still, all the way to her feet upon the bed, with a knife in her right hand.

$\approx$ $\approx$ $\approx$

Tonk. Twang. Plink.

Eating up trouble as though it were custard, but not pleased by the taste, Jilly reached the archway on the *tonk*, found the light switch on the *twang*. On the *plink*, she bathed the threat in light.

The furious beating of wings almost caused her to reel backward. She expected the tumult of doves or pigeons that had spiraled around her by the side of the highway, or the blinding blizzard of birds that she alone had seen while in the Expedition. But the flock made no appearance, and after the briefest spate of flapping, the wings fell silent.

Kenny wasn't sharpening knives. Unless he proved to be crouched behind an armchair or a sofa, Kenny wasn't even present.

Another series of metallic sounds drew her attention to a cage. It hung five or six feet off the floor, supported by a base similar to that of a floor lamp.

With tiny taloned feet, a parakeet clung to the heavy-gauge wire that formed the bars of its habitat; using its beak, the feathered prisoner plucked at those same restraints. With a sweep of its fluid neck, the parakeet strummed its beak back and forth across a swath of bars as if it were a handless harpist playing a glissando passage: *zzziiinnnggg, zzziiinnnggg.*

Her tattered reputation as a warrioress having been further diminished by mistaking a parakeet for a mortal threat, Jilly retreated from this moment of humiliation. Returning to the stairs, she heard once more the bird's vigorously feathered drumming of the air, as though it were demanding the freedom to fly.

The rap and rustle of wings so vividly recalled her paranormal experiences that she resisted an urge to flee the house, and instead fled up toward Dylan. The bird grew quiet by the time she reached the midpoint landing, but remaining in flight from the *memory* of wings, she hurried to the upper floor with too little caution.

Fake fear had washed out of Becky's blue eyes, and a mad glee had flooded into them.

She launched herself off the bed in a frenzy, slashing wildly with the knife. Dylan twisted out of her way, and Becky proved to have more enthusiasm for murder than practice at it. She stumbled, nearly fell, barely escaped skewering herself, and shouted, 'Kenny!'

Here came Kenny through the door that Becky had not indicated. He had certain qualities of an eel: lithe and quick to the point of sinuousness, lean but muscular, with the mad pressure-pinched eyes of a creature condemned to live in cold, deep, rancid waters. Dylan half expected Kenny's teeth to be pointed and backward-hooked like the teeth of any serpent, whether on land or in water.

He was a young man with flair, dressed in black cowboy boots, black jeans, a black T-shirt, and a black denim jacket brightened by embroidered green Indian designs. The embroidery matched the shade of the feather in the cowboy hat that had been perched atop the suitcases in the bedroom across the hall.

'Who're *you*?' Kenny asked Dylan, and without waiting for an answer, he demanded of Becky, 'Where the hell's the old bitch?'

The white-haired woman in the candy-striped uniform, home from a hard day's work, was no doubt the old bitch for whom these two had lain in wait.

'Who cares who he is,' Becky said. 'Just kill him, then we'll find the old pus bag and gut her.'

The shackled boy had misunderstood the relationship between his brother and the girl. Cold-blooded conspirators, they intended to slaughter Grandma and little brother, perhaps steal whatever pathetic trove of cash the woman had hidden in her mattress, toss Kenny's two suitcases in the car, and hit the road.

They might make a stop farther along the street at Becky's house to pick up her luggage. Maybe they intended to kill her family, too.

Whether or not their plan subsequent to this snafu would prove successful, right now they had Dylan in a pincer play. They were well positioned to dispatch him quickly.

Kenny held a knife with a twelve-inch blade and two wickedly sharp cutting edges. The rubber-coated, looped handle featured a finger-formed grip that appeared to be user-friendly and difficult to dislodge from a determined hand.

Less designed for war than for the kitchen, Becky's weapon would nevertheless chop a man as effectively as it might have been used to dismember a chicken for a stew pot.

Considerably longer than either blade, the baseball bat provided Dylan with the advantage of reach. And he knew from experience that his size warned off punks and drunks who might otherwise have taken a whack at him; most aggressive types assumed that only a brute could reside within the physique of a brute, when in fact he had the heart of a lamb.

Perhaps Kenny hesitated also because he didn't understand the situation any longer, and worried about murdering a stranger without knowing how many others might also be in the house. The homicidal meanness in those eely eyes was tempered by a cunning akin to that of the serpent in Eden.

Dylan considered trying to pass himself off as a police officer and claiming that backup was on the way, but even if the lack of a uniform could be explained, the use of a baseball bat instead of a handgun made the cop story a hard sell.

Whether or not a drop of prudence seasoned the drug-polluted pool of Kenny's mind, Becky was all intense animal need and demon glee, certain not to be dissuaded for long by the reach of the bat or by her adversary's size.

With one foot, Dylan feinted toward Kenny, but then spun more directly toward the girl and swung the bat at the hand in which she held the knife.

Becky was perhaps a high-school gymnast or one of the legions of ballerina wannabes on whom multitudes of loving American parents had squandered countless millions with the certainty that they were nurturing the next Margot Fonteyn. Although not talented enough for Olympic competition or for the professional dance theater, she proved to be quick, limber, and more coordinated than she had appeared to be when she'd flung herself off the bed. She fell back, avoiding the bat with a cry of premature triumph – 'Ha!' – and at once sprang to her right to get out of the way of the backswing, half crouching to contract her leg muscles, the better to move with power when she decided *how* to move.

Under no illusions that Kenny's better judgment would ensure his continued hesitancy if an ideal opening appeared, Dylan borrowed some moves from Becky, though he probably looked less like a failed ballerina than like a dancing bear. He rounded on the embroidered cowboy just as Kenny came in for the kill.

The kid's moray eyes revealed not the feral ferocity of Becky, but the calculation of a sneak and the incomplete commitment of a coward who was bravest with a weak adversary. He was a monster, but not the savage equal of his blue-eyed squeeze, and he made the mistake of slipping in for the kill instead of lunging full-out. By the time Dylan turned toward him, the bat arcing high, Kenny should have been rushing forward with enough momentum to duck under the bat and drive the blade home. Instead, he flinched, juked back, and fell victim to his lack of nerve.

With a Babe Ruth *crack*, the bat broke Kenny's right forearm. In spite of the looped handle and formed grip, the knife flew out of his hand. Kenny seemed almost to lift off his feet, as though he were a two-base hit if not an out-of-the-park home run.

As the screaming kid failed to take flight and instead dropped like a bunt, Dylan could sense Becky coming at his back and knew that a dancing bear could never outmaneuver a psychotic ballerina.

~ ~ ~

As she reached the next-to-the-last step, Jilly heard someone shout 'Kenny!' She halted short of the upstairs hall, unsettled that the cry had come neither from Dylan nor from a thirteen-year-old boy. Urgent and shrill, the voice had been female.

She heard other noises, then a man's voice, likewise not Dylan's and not that of a boy, though she couldn't discern what he said.

Having come to warn Dylan that young Travis was up here with Kenny, but also having followed to help him if he needed help, she couldn't freeze on these steps and yet retain her self-respect. For Jillian Jackson, self-respect had been won with considerable effort through a childhood that, except for the example set by her mother, had provided fertile ground for seeds of self-doubt and excessive self-effacement. She would not here relinquish what she had struggled so long and hard to capture.

Hurrying out of the stairwell, Jilly saw a spill of soft light coming from an open door on the left, brighter light issuing from a door farther along on the right – and doves erupting through a closed window at the end of the hallway, a vision of doves that left the panes intact in their wake.

The birds made no sounds – no coos or cries, nor the faintest thrum of wings. When they exploded around and over her, cataracts of white feathers, a thousand piercing gazes, a thousand yawning beaks, she didn't expect to feel them, but she did. The breeze stirred by their passage was spicy with incense. Their wing tips brushed her body, arms, and face.

Staying close to the left wall, she moved quickly forward into a storm of white wings as dense as the feathery blizzard that earlier had swept across the Expedition. She feared for her sanity, but she didn't fear the birds, which meant her no harm. Even if they had been real, they would not have pecked or blinded her. She sensed that they were in fact proof of *augmented* vision, although even as this thought occurred to her, she had no idea what augmented vision might be; for the moment it was a thing she understood instinctively, emotionally, rather than intellectually.

Although she could not be harmed by these phenomena, the timing of the birds' appearance couldn't have been worse. She needed to find Dylan, and real or not, the birds were a hindrance to the search.

'*Ha!*' exclaimed someone close at hand, and an instant later, Jilly felt on her left the open doorway that the seething flock had hidden from her view.

She stepped across the threshold, and the birds vanished. Before her lay a bedroom revealed by a single lamp. And here was Dylan, too, armed with a baseball bat, bracketed by a young man – Kenny? – and a teenage girl, both brandishing knives.

The bat cut the air with a *whoosh*, the young man screamed, and the wickedly sharp knife, tumbling free, clattered against a walnut highboy.

When Dylan swung the bat, the teenage girl behind him tensed, for an instant tightening down in her crouch. As Kenny shrieked in pain, the girl drew her knife back in striking position, certain to spring forward and bury it in Dylan before he could turn to deal with her.

On the move even as the girl uncoiled out of her crouch, Jilly shouted, '*Police!*'

Monkey-agile, the girl whipped around but also sidestepped to avoid turning her back on Dylan, to keep him in sight.

Her eyes were as blue as any sky adorned with cherubim on any chapel ceiling, but also radiant with dementia surely spawned by psychosis-inducing drugs.

A Southwest Amazon at last, but too squeamish to risk destroying the girl's eyes, Jilly aimed lower with the instant ant death. The nozzle on the can that she'd found in the pantry had two settings: SPRAY and STREAM. She had set it on STREAM, which would reach ten feet, according to the label.

Perhaps because of her excitement, her homicidal exhilaration, the girl was breathing through her mouth. The stream of insecticide went straight in, like an arc of water from a drinking fountain, moistening lips, bathing tongue.

Although instant ant death had a notably less severe effect on a teenage girl than it would have on an ant, it wasn't received with lip-smacking delight. Less refreshing than cool water, this drink at once took all the fight out of the girl. She flung the knife aside. Gagging, wheezing, spitting, she staggered to a door, yanked it open, slapped at the wall switch until the lights came on, revealing a bathroom. At the sink, the girl cranked on the cold water, cupped her hands, and repeatedly flushed out her mouth, sputtering and choking.

On the floor, groaning, crying with a particularly annoying note of self-pity, Kenny had curled up like a shrimp.

Jilly looked at Dylan and shook the can of insecticide. 'From now on, I'm going to use this on hecklers.'

'What did you do with Shep?'

'The grandmother told me about Kenny, the knives. Aren't you going to say *"Thanks for saving my butt, Jilly"*?'

'I told you not to leave Shep alone.'

'He's all right.'

'He's *not* all right, out there by himself,' he said, raising his voice as though he had some legitimate authority over her.

'Don't you shout at me. Good lord, you drove here like a maniac, wouldn't tell me why, bailed out of the truck, wouldn't tell me why. And I'm supposed to – what? – to sit out there, just shift my brain into neutral like your good little woman, and wait like a stupid turkey standing in the rain with its mouth open, gawking at the sky, until it drowns?'

He glowered at her. 'What are you talking about turkeys?'

'You know *exactly* what I'm talking about.'

'And it's not raining.'

'Don't be obtuse.'

'You have no sense of responsibility,' he declared.

'I have a *huge* sense of responsibility.'

'You left Shep alone.'

'He won't go anywhere. I gave him a task to keep him busy. I said, "Shepherd, because of your rude and overbearing brother, I'm going to need at least one hundred polite synonyms for *asshole*." '

'I don't have time for this bickering.'

'Who started it?' she accused, and turned away from him, and might have left the room if she'd not been halted by the sight of the doves.

The flock still streamed through the hallway, past the open bedroom door, toward the stairs. By this time, if these apparitions had been real, the house would have been so fully packed that extreme bird pressure would have blown out all the windows as surely as a gas leak and a spark.

She willed them to vanish, but they flew, they flew, and she turned her back on them, fearing for her sanity once more. 'We've got to get out of here. Marj will call the cops sooner or later.'

'Marj?'

'The woman who gave you the toad pin and somehow started all this. She's Kenny's grandma, Travis's. What do you want me to do?'

≈ ≈ ≈

In the bathroom, on her knees at the toilet, Becky had begun to reconsider her dinner, if not the entire direction of her life.

Dylan pointed to a straight-backed chair. He saw that Jilly got the message.

The bathroom door opened outward. With the chair tipped back and wedged under the knob, Becky would be imprisoned until the police arrived to let her out.

Dylan didn't think that the girl would recover sufficiently to cut him to ribbons, but he didn't want to be vomited on, either.

On the floor, six-way-wired Kenny had come unstrung. He was all tears and snot and spit bubbles, but still dangerous, speaking more curses and obscenities than sense, demanding immediate medical attention, promising revenge, and given half a chance he might prove whether or not his teeth were snake-sharp.

A threat to cave in Kenny's skull sounded phony to Dylan when he made it, but the kid took it seriously, perhaps because he would not have hesitated to crush Dylan's skull if their roles had been reversed. On demand, he produced handcuff and padlock keys from one of his embroidered shirt pockets with mother-of-pearl button snaps.

Jilly seemed reluctant to follow Dylan out of the bedroom, as if she feared other miscreants against whom insecticide might prove to be an inadequate defense. He assured her that Becky and Kenny were the sum of all evil under this roof. Nevertheless, wincing, hesitant, she crossed the hallway to the shackled boy's room as though fear half blinded her, and repeatedly she glanced toward the window at the end of the hall, as if she saw a ghostly face pressed to the glass.

As he freed Travis, Dylan explained that Becky was not morally fit to compete in the Miss All-American Teen Pageant, and then they went downstairs to the kitchen.

When Marj rushed in from the back porch to embrace her grandson and to wail about his blackened eye, Travis all but disappeared in cuddling candy-stripe.

Dylan waited for the boy to half extract himself and then said, 'Both Becky and Kenny need medical attention—'

'And a prison cell until their social security kicks in,' Jilly added.

'—but give us two or three minutes before you call nine-one-one,' Dylan finished.

This instruction baffled Marj. 'But you *are* nine-one-one.'

Jilly fielded that peculiar question: 'We're one of the ones, Marj, but we're not the other one or the nine.'

Although this further baffled Marj, it amused Travis. The boy said, 'We'll give you time to split. But this is fully weird, it's practically mojo. Who the heck are you two?'

Dylan couldn't summon a reply, but Jilly said, 'Damned if we know. This afternoon we could have told you who we are, but right now we don't have a clue.'

In one sense her answer was true and grimly serious, but it only puckered Marj's face in deeper bafflement and widened the boy's grin.

Upstairs, Kenny pleaded loudly for help.

'Better get movin',' Travis advised.

'You don't know what we were driving, never saw our wheels.'

'That's true,' Travis agreed.

'And you'll do us the favor of not watching us leave.'

'As far as we know,' said Travis, 'you took a running leap and flew away.'

Dylan had asked for three minutes because Marj and Travis would have difficulty explaining a greater delay to the cops; but if Shep had wandered off, they were ruined. Three minutes wouldn't be long enough to find him.

Except for the breeze in the olive trees, the street was quiet. In the house, Kenny's muffled shouts wouldn't carry to a neighbor.

At the curb, driver's door open, the Expedition waited. Jilly had doused the headlights and switched off the engine.

Even as they crossed the front lawn, Dylan saw Shepherd in

the backseat, face illuminated by the reflected glow of a battery-powered book light bouncing up at him from the page he was reading.

'Told you,' Jilly said.

Relieved, Dylan didn't snap at her.

Through the dusty window at Shepherd's side, the title of the book could be seen: *Great Expectations*, by Charles Dickens. Shep was a fiend for Dickens.

Dylan settled behind the wheel, slammed the door, figuring more than half a minute had passed since they'd left Travis to watch the wall clock in the kitchen.

Legs folded on the passenger's seat to spare her jade plant on the floor, Jilly held out the keys, then snatched them back. 'What if you go nuts again?'

'I didn't go nuts.'

'Whatever it was you did, what if you do it again?'

'I probably will,' he realized.

'I better drive.'

He shook his head. 'What did you see upstairs, on the way to Travis's room? What did you see when you looked toward the window at the end of the hall?'

She hesitated. Then she surrendered the keys. 'You drive.'

As Travis counted off the first minute in the kitchen, Dylan executed a U-turn. They followed the route they had taken earlier on Eucalyptus Avenue, with its dearth of eucalyptuses. By the time Travis would have called 911, they had traveled surface streets to the interstate.

Dylan took I-10 east, toward the end of town where by now the Cadillac might have stopped smoldering, but he said, 'I don't want to stay on this. I have a hunch it won't be safe a whole lot longer.'

'Tonight's not a night for ignoring hunches,' she noted.

Eventually he departed the interstate in favor of U.S. Highway 191, an undivided two-lane blacktop that struck north through dark desolation and carried little traffic at this hour. He didn't know where 191 led, and right now he didn't care. For a while, where they went didn't matter, as long as they kept moving, as long as they put some distance between themselves and the corpse in the Coupe DeVille, between themselves and the house on Eucalyptus Avenue.

For the first two miles on 191, neither he nor Jilly spoke, and as the third mile began to clock up on the odometer, Dylan started to shake. Now that his adrenaline levels were declining toward normal and now that the primitive survivalist within him had returned to his genetic subcellar, the enormity of what had happened belatedly hit him. Dylan strove to conceal the shaking from Jilly, knew that he was unsuccessful when he heard his teeth chatter, and then realized that she was trembling, too, and hugging herself, and rocking in her seat.

'D-d-d-damn,' she said.

'Yeah.'

'I'm not W-w-wonder Woman,' she said.

'No.'

'For one thing, I don't have big enough hooters for the job.'

He said, 'Me neither.'

'Oh, man, those *knives*.'

'They were honking big knives,' he agreed.

'You with your baseball bat. What – were you out of your mind, O'Conner?'

'Must've been out of my mind. You with your ant spray – that didn't strike me as the epitome of rationality, Jackson.'

'Worked, didn't it?'

'Nice shot.'

'Thanks. Where we lived when I was a kid, I got lots of practice with roaches. They move faster than Miss Becky. You must've been good at baseball.'

'Not bad for an effete artist. Listen, Jackson, it took guts to come upstairs after you knew about the knives.'

'It took stupidity, is what it took. We could've been killed.'

'We could've been,' he acknowledged, 'but we weren't.'

'But we could've been. No more of that run-jump-chase-fight crap. No more, O'Conner.'

'I hope not,' he said.

'I mean it. I'm serious. I'm tellin' you, no more.'

'I don't think that's our choice to make.'

'It's sure my choice.'

'I mean, I don't think we control the situation.'

'I *always* control my situation,' she insisted.

'Not this situation.'

'You're scaring me.'

'I'm scaring me, too,' he said.

These admissions led to a contemplative silence.

The high moon, lustrous silver at its pinnacle, grew tarnished as it became a low moon in the west, and the romantic desert table it once brightened became a somber setting suitable for a last supper.

Brown bristling balls of tumbleweed trembled at the verge of the road, dead yet eager to roam, but the night breeze didn't have enough power to send them traveling.

Moths traveled, however, small white ghost moths and larger gray specimens like scraps of soiled shroud cloth, eerily illumined by the headlights, swooping over and around the SUV but seldom striking the windshield.

In classic painting, butterflies were symbols of life, joy, and hope. Moths – of the same order as butterflies, Lepidoptera – were in all cases symbols of despair, deterioration, destruction, and death. Entomologists estimate the world is home to thirty thousand species of butterflies, and four times that many moths.

In part, a mothy mood gripped Dylan. He remained edgy, twitchy, as if the insulation on every nerve in his body were as eaten away as the fibers of a wool sweater infested with larvae. As he relived what had happened on Eucalyptus Avenue and as he wondered what might be coming next, spectral moths fluttered the length of his spine.

Yet anxiety didn't own him entirely. Contemplation of their uncertain future flooded Dylan with a choking disquiet, but each time the disquiet ebbed, exhilaration flowed in to take its place, and a wild joy that nearly made him laugh out loud. He was simultaneously sobered by anxiety that threatened to become apprehension – and also intoxicated with the possibilities of this glorious new power that he understood only imperfectly.

This singular state of mind was so fresh to his experience that he wasn't capable of crafting the words – or the images, for that matter – to explain it adequately to Jilly. Then he glanced away from the empty highway, from trembling tumbleweeds and kiting moths, and knew at once, by her expression, that her state of mind precisely matched his.

Not only weren't they in Kansas anymore, Toto, they weren't in predictable Oz, either, but adrift in a land where there were sure to be greater wonders than yellow-brick roads and emerald cities, more to fear than wicked witches and flying monkeys.

A moth snapped hard against the windshield, leaving a gray dusty substance on the glass, a little kiss of Death.

18

Earth's magnetic pole might shift in a twink, as some scientists theorized it had done in the past, resulting in an entirely new angle of rotation, causing catastrophic changes in the surface of the planet. Current tropical zones could in an instant be plunged into an arctic freeze, leaving startled soft-body Miami retirees clawing for survival in 100-degree-below-zero cold, in blizzards so bitter that the snow came not in the form of flakes, but as spicules, needlelike crystals as hard as glass. Colossal tectonic pressures would cause continents to buckle, fracture, fold. Rising up in massive tides, oceans would slop over coastlines, crash across the Rockies and the Andes and the Alps alike. New inland oceans would form, new mountain ranges. Volcanoes would vomit forth great burning seas of Earth's essence. With civilization gone and billions dead, small scattered bands of survivors would face the daunting task of forming tribes of hunters and gatherers.

In the final hour of his program, Parish Lantern and call-ins from his nationwide radio audience discussed the likelihood of a pole-shift striking within the next fifty years. Because Dylan and Jilly were for the moment still too busy digesting their recent experiences to talk anymore about them, they listened to Lantern as they drove north on this lonely desert highway, where it was possible to believe simultaneously that civilization had already vanished in a planetary cataclysm and that the earth was timeless, unchanging.

'You listen to this guy all the time?' he asked Jilly.

'Not every night, but a lot.'

'It's a miracle you're not suicidal.'

'His show isn't usually about doom. Mostly it's time travel, alternate realities, whether we have souls, life after death. . . .'

In the backseat, Shep continued reading Dickens, granting the novelist a form of life after death. On the radio, the planet crushed and burned and drowned and blew away human civilization and most of the animal kingdom, as though all life were pestilence.

When they reached the town of Safford, about forty minutes after they exited the interstate, Shepherd said, 'Fries not flies, fries not flies, fries not flies. . . .'

Maybe it was time to stop and devise a plan of action, or maybe they had not yet analyzed their situation to a degree that allowed for planning, but in either case, Dylan and Shep were in want of the dinner they had missed. And Jilly expressed the need for a drink.

'First we need new license plates,' Dylan said. 'When they trace that Cadillac to you, they'll go unit to unit in the motel, looking for you. When they find you've lit out and that Shep and I didn't stay the night we'd paid for, they might link us.'

'No *might* about it. They will,' she said.

'The motel records have the make, model, license-plate number. At least we can change the plate number and not be so easily made.'

On a quiet residential street, Dylan parked, took screwdrivers and pliers from the Expedition tool kit, and went looking for Arizona plates. He found an easily detached pair on a pickup in the driveway of a weather-silvered cedar ranch house with a dead front lawn.

Throughout the theft, his heart pounded. The guilt he felt was out of proportion to such a minor crime, but his face burned with shame at the prospect of being caught in the act.

After he had purloined the plates, he drove around town until he found a school. The parking lot was deserted at this hour. In those shadows, he replaced his California plates with the Arizona pair.

'With luck,' he said as he got behind the wheel once more, 'the owner of that pickup won't notice the plates missing until tomorrow.'

'I hate trusting in luck,' Jilly said. 'I've never had much.'

'Fries not flies,' Shepherd reminded them.

A few minutes later, when Dylan parked in front of a restaurant adjacent to a motel, he said, 'Let me see the pin. Your toad button.'

She unpinned the smiling amphibian from her blouse but withheld it. 'What do you want it for?'

'Don't worry. It's not going to set me off like the other one did. That's over. That business is finished.'

'Yeah, but what if?' she worried.

He handed the car keys to her.

Reluctantly, she exchanged the pin for the keys.

Thumb on the toad face, forefinger against the back of the pin, Dylan felt a quiver of psychic spoor, the impression of more than one individual, perhaps Grandma Marjorie overlaid by Jillian Jackson, but neither invoked in him the compulsion to hurry-move-find-do that had harried him to the house on Eucalyptus Avenue.

Dropping the button in the little trash basket in the console, he said, 'Nothing. Or next to nothing. It wasn't the pin itself that set me off. It was . . . Marjorie's impending death that somehow I sensed on the first pin. Does that make sense?'

'Only here in Nutburg, USA, where we seem to live now.'

'Let's get you that drink,' he said.

'Two.'

Crossing the parking lot to the front door of the restaurant, Shep walked between them. He carried *Great Expectations* with the little battery-powered light attached, reading intently as he walked.

Dylan had considered taking the book away from him, but Shepherd had been through a lot this evening. His routines had been disrupted, which usually filled him with anxiety. Worse, he had endured more excitement in a couple hours than he had experienced in the previous ten years, and Shepherd O'Conner usually had no ability to cope with excitement.

Being directly addressed by too many strangers at an art show could tax his tolerance for conversational stimulation even though he never replied to any of them. Too much lightning in a thunderstorm or too much thunder, or too much roaring rain, for that matter, could fill his capacity for commotion to overflowing, whereupon he would succumb to a panic attack.

Indeed, that Shep had not panicked at the motel, that he had not curled up like a defensive pill bug and had not shaken with spasms of apprehension when he'd seen the burning Coupe DeVille, that he hadn't squealed and pulled his hair at some point during Dylan's reckless drive to Marjorie's house – these were great wonders if not miracles of self-control compared to his customary behavior when confronted by the more mundane agitations of daily life.

Right now, *Great Expectations* was his life raft in an evening swamped by turmoil. Clinging to the book, he was able to convince himself that he was safe, and he could push from his awareness all the violations of comforting routine, also blind and deafen himself to the otherwise drowning tides of stimulation.

Awkward movements and poor physical coordination were symptoms of Shep's condition, but walking while reading didn't lead to either a stiffer gait or a more pronounced shuffle. Dylan had the feeling that if confronted by a flight of steps, his brother might negotiate every riser without putting Mr. Dickens on hold for a moment.

No steps awaited them at the restaurant entrance, but when Dylan touched the door, a fizz of latent psychic energy effervesced against his palm, the pads of his fingers, and he almost released the handle.

'What?' Jilly asked, always alert.

'Something I'm going to have to get used to.' Vaguely he sensed numerous personalities expressed by the preternatural residue on the door handle, like layers of dried sweat from many hands.

The restaurant presented a split personality, as though against the laws of physics, a diner and a steakhouse had occupied the same place at the same time without triggering a catastrophic explosion. Plastic-looking red leatherette booths and red-leatherette chairs with chrome legs were mismatched with real mahogany tables. Expensive cut-glass ceiling fixtures cast rich prismatic light not on carpet, but on an easy-to-clean, wood-pattern vinyl floor. Waiters and waitresses wore black suits, crisp white shirts, and natty black string ties; but the busboys shambled among the tables in their street clothes, coordinated only by the same stupid-looking pointy paper hats and by similar surly expressions.

With the dinner rush far behind, only a third of the restaurant tables were occupied. Customers lingering over dessert, liqueurs, and coffee were engaged in low, pleasantly boozy conversations. Only a few took notice of Shep as – preceded by Jilly, followed by Dylan – he allowed the hostess to lead him to a booth, remaining absorbed in his book every step of the way.

Shep would rarely sit next to a window in a restaurant because he didn't want 'to be looked at by people inside *and* people out.' Dylan requested a booth distant from the windows, and he sat on one side of the table with his brother, across from Jilly.

She looked uncommonly fresh, considering what she'd been through – and remarkably calm for a woman whose life had been upended and whose future was as difficult to read as a wad of tea leaves in a dark room. Hers was not a cheap beauty, but one that would wear well with time, that would take many hard washings and keep its color in more than one sense.

When he picked up the menu that the hostess had placed on the table before him, Dylan shuddered as if he'd touched ice, and he put it down at once. Deposited by previous patrons, a lively patina of emotions, wants, needs, hungers squirmed on the plastic menu cover and seemed to crackle against his skin, like a charge of static electricity, much stronger than what he'd felt on the door handle.

During their drive north from the interstate, he'd told Jilly about the psychic spoor. Now she understood at once why he had put down the menu. 'I'll read mine to you,' she said.

He found that he liked looking at her while she read, liked it so much that repeatedly he had to remind himself to listen to her recitation of salads, soups, sandwiches, and entrees. Her face soothed him perhaps as much as *Great Expectations* soothed Shep.

While he watched Jilly read aloud, Dylan placed his hands flat on his menu again. As he expected based on his experience at the restaurant door, the initial boiling rush of strange impressions quickly subsided to a quiet simmer. And now he learned that with a conscious effort, he could entirely quell these uncanny sensations.

As she informed him of the last of the dinner selections, Jilly looked up, saw Dylan's hands on his menu, and clearly realized that he had allowed her to read to him only to have an excuse to gaze at her openly, without the challenge of a direct return stare. Judging by her complex expression, she had mixed feelings about the various implications of his scrutiny, but at least part of her response was a lovely, even though uncertain, smile.

Before either of them could speak, the waitress returned. Jilly asked for a bottle of Sierra Nevada. Dylan ordered dinner for Shep and for himself, and requested that Shep's plate be served five minutes before his own.

Shepherd continued to read: *Great Expectations* flat on the table in front of him, the book light switched off. Hunching forward, he lowered his face within eight or ten inches of the page, although he had no vision problems. While the waitress was present, Shep moved his lips as he scanned the lines of type, which was his way of subtly establishing that he was occupied and that she would be rude if she was to address him.

Because no other diners were near them, Dylan felt comfortable discussing their situation. 'Jilly, words are your business, right?'

'I guess maybe you could say that.'

'What's this one mean – *psychotropic*?'

'Why's it important?' she asked.

'Frankenstein used it. He said the *stuff*, the stuff in the syringe, was psychotropic.'

Without looking up from his book, Shep said, 'Psychotropic. Affecting mental activity, behavior, or perception. Psychotropic.'

'Thank you, Shep.'

'Psychotropic drugs. Tranquilizers, sedatives, antidepressants. Psychotropic drugs.'

Jilly shook her head. 'I don't think that weird juice was any of those things.'

'Psychotropic drugs,' Shep elucidated. 'Opium, morphine, heroin, methadone. Barbiturates, meprobamate. Amphetamines, cocaine. Peyote, marijuana, LSD, Sierra Nevada beer. Pscyhotropic drugs.'

'Beer isn't a drug,' Jilly corrected. 'Is it?'

Eyes still tracking Dickens's words back and forth across the page, Shep seemed to be reading aloud: 'Psychotropic intoxicants and stimulants. Beer, wine, whiskey. Caffeine. Nicotine. Psychotropic intoxicants and stimulants.'

She stared at Shep, not sure what to make of his contributions.

'Forgot,' Shepherd said in a chagrined tone. 'Psychotropic inhalable-fume intoxicants. Glue, solvents, transmission fluid. Psychotropic inhalable-fume intoxicants. Forgot. Sorry.'

'If it had been a drug in any traditional sense,' Dylan said, 'I think Frankenstein would have used that word. He wouldn't have called it *stuff* so consistently, as if there wasn't an existing word for it. Besides, drugs have a limited effect. They wear off. He sure gave me the impression that whatever this crap does to you is permanent.'

The waitress arrived with bottles of Sierra Nevada for Jilly and Dylan, and with a glass of Coca-Cola, no ice. Dylan unwrapped the straw and put it in the soda for his brother.

Shepherd would drink only through a straw, though he didn't care if it was paper or plastic. He liked cola cold, but wouldn't tolerate ice with it. Cola, a straw, *and* ice in a glass at the same time offended him for reasons unknown to everyone except Shepherd himself.

Raising a frosty glass of Sierra Nevada, Dylan said, 'Here's to psychotropic intoxicants.'

'But not to the inhalable-fume variety,' Jilly qualified.

He detected faint quivering energy signatures on the cold glass: perhaps the psychic trace of a member of the kitchen staff, certainly the trace of their waitress. When he willed himself not to feel these imprints, the sensation passed. He was gaining control.

Jilly clinked her bottle against his glass, and drank thirstily. Then: 'There's nowhere to go from here, is there?'

'Of course there is.'

'Yeah? Where?'

'Well, not to Phoenix. That wouldn't be smart. You have that gig in Phoenix, so they're sure to go looking for you there, wanting to know why Frankenstein had your Cadillac, wanting to test your blood.'

'The guys in the Suburbans.'

'They might be different guys in different vehicles, but they'll be related.'

'Who were those phony duffers, anyway? Cloak-and-dagger types, you think? Or some secret police agency? Aggressive door-to-door magazine salesmen?'

'Any of that, I guess. But not necessarily bad guys.'

'They blew up my car.'

'As if I could forget. But they blew it up only because Frankenstein was in it. We can be pretty sure *he* was a bad guy.'

'Just because they blew up a bad guy doesn't mean they're good guys,' she noted. 'Bad guys blow up bad guys sometimes.'

'Lots of times,' he agreed. 'But to avoid all the blowing up, we'll go around Phoenix.'

'Around Phoenix to what?'

'Maybe stay on secondary highways, go north somewhere big

and empty where they wouldn't think to look first, maybe up near the Petrified Forest National Park. We could be there in a few hours.'

'You make this sound like a vacation. I'm talking about – where do I go with my *life*.'

'You're focusing on the big picture. Don't do that,' he advised. 'Until we know more about this situation, it's pointless to focus on the big picture – and it's depressing.'

'Then what should I focus on? The *little* picture?'

'Exactly.'

She drank some beer. 'And what is the little picture?'

'Getting through the night alive.'

'The little picture sounds as depressing as the big picture.'

'Not at all. We just have to find a place to hole up and *think*.'

The waitress brought Shepherd's dinner.

Dylan had ordered for his brother based on the kid's taste and on the ease with which this particular meal could be customized to conform to Shep's culinary requirements.

'From Shep's viewpoint,' Dylan said, 'shape is more important than flavor. He likes squares and rectangles, dislikes roundness.'

Two oval slices of meat loaf in gravy formed the centerpiece of this platter. Using Shep's knife and fork, Dylan trimmed the edges off each slice, forming rectangles. After setting the trimmings aside on Shep's bread plate, he cut each slice into bite-size squares.

When he first picked up the utensils, he'd felt a psychic buzz but again he'd been able to dial it below his threshold of awareness.

The steak fries featured beveled rather than blunt ends. Dylan quickly cut the points from each crisp piece of potato, forming them into simple rectangles.

'Shep'll eat the points,' he explained, stacking those small golden nibs beside the altered fries, 'but only if they're separate.'

Already cubed, the carrots posed no problem. He had to separate the peas, however, mash them, and form them into square forkfuls.

Dylan had ordered bread in place of a roll. Three sides of each slice were straight; the fourth was curved. He cut off the arcs of crust and put them with the meat-loaf trimmings.

'Fortunately, the butter isn't whipped or formed into a ball.' He stripped three foil-wrapped pats of butter and stood them on end beside the bread. 'Ready.'

Shepherd put aside the book as Dylan slid the plate in front of him. He accepted the utensils and ate his geometric meal with the blinkered attention he exhibited when reading Dickens.

'This happens every time he eats?' Jilly asked.

'This or something like it. Some foods have different rules.'

'What if you don't go through this rigmarole?'

'This isn't rigmarole to him. It's . . . bringing order to chaos. Shep likes things orderly.'

'But what if you just shove it in front of him the way it comes and say "Eat"?'

'He won't touch it,' Dylan assured her.

'He will when he gets hungry enough.'

'Nope. Meal after meal, day after day, he'll turn away from it until he passes out from low blood sugar.'

Regarding him with what he chose to read as sympathy rather than pity, she said, 'You don't date much, do you?'

He answered with a shrug.

'I need another beer,' Jilly said as the waitress arrived with Dylan's dinner.

'I'm driving,' he said, declining a second round.

'Yeah, but the way you've been driving tonight, another beer could only help.'

Maybe she had a point, maybe she didn't, but he decided to live with uncharacteristic abandon. 'Two,' he told the waitress.

As Dylan began to eat chicken and waffles in anarchic disregard for the shape and size of each bite, Jilly said, 'So let's say we go north a couple hundred miles, find a place to hole up and think. What exactly do we think about – other than how totally screwed we are?'

'Don't be so negative all the time.'

She bristled better than a wire brush. 'I'm not negative.'

'You aren't exactly as cheerful as the Dalai Lama.'

'For your information, I was a nothing once, a wadded-up-thrown-away-Kleenex of a kid. Shy, shaky shy, rubbed so thin by life I half believed sunlight passed through me. Could've given timid lessons to a mouse.'

'Must've been a long time ago.'

'You wouldn't have bet a dollar against a million bucks I'd ever get up on a stage, or join a choir before that. But I had hope, great hope, had this dream of me as a something, a somebody, this *positive* dream of me as a performer, for God's sake, and I dragged myself up out of shaky-shy nothing until I started to live that dream.'

As she drained the last of the beer, she glared at Dylan over the upturned bottle.

He said, 'No argument – you've got good self-esteem. I never said different. It's not you that you're negative about. It's the rest of the world.'

She looked as if she might hit him with the empty bottle, but then she put it down, slid it aside, and surprised him: 'That's fair enough. It's a hard world. And most people are hard, too. If you call that negative thinking, I call it realism.'

'Lots of people are hard, but not most. Most are just scared or lonely, or lost. They don't know why they're here or what's the purpose, the reason, so they wind up half dead inside.'

'I suppose you know the purpose, the reason,' she said.

'You make me sound smug.'

'Don't mean to. Just curious what you think it is.'

'Everyone has to figure it out for himself,' he said, which was in truth how he felt. 'And you're one who will because you want to.'

'*Now* you sound smug.' She looked as if she might whack him with the bottle, after all.

Shepherd picked up one of the three pats of unwrapped butter and popped it in his mouth.

When Jilly grimaced, Dylan said, 'Shep likes bread and butter, but not in the same bite. You don't want to see him eat a mayonnaise-and-bologna sandwich.'

'We're doomed,' she said.

Dylan sighed, shook his head, said nothing.

'Get real, okay? They start shooting at us, what rules will Shep have about how we're allowed to dodge the bullets? Always dodge left, never right. You can weave but you can't duck – unless it's a day of the week that has the letter *u* in it, in which case you can duck, but you can't weave. How fast can he run while reading, and what happens when you try to take the book away from him?'

'It won't be that way,' Dylan said, but he knew she was right.

Jilly leaned toward him, her voice lowering, but gaining in

intensity what it lost in volume: 'Why won't it? Listen, you've got to admit, even if it were just you and me in this mess together, we'd be on a greased slope in glass shoes. So then hang a hundred-sixty-pound, butter-munching millstone around our necks, and what chance do we have?'

'He's not a millstone,' Dylan said stubbornly.

To Shep, she said, 'Sweetie, no offense, but if we have any hope of getting through this, the three of us, we've got to face facts, speak the truth. We lie to ourselves, we're dead. Maybe you can't help being a millstone, but maybe you can, and if you can, then you've got to work with us.'

Dylan said, 'We've always been a great team, me and Shep.'

'Team? Some team. You two couldn't run a three-legged sack race without the sack ending up on somebody's *head.*'

'He ain't heavy—'

'Oh, don't say it,' she interrupted. 'Don't you dare say it, O'Conner, don't you dare, you hope-drunk lunatic, you power-of-positive-thinking nutball.'

'He ain't heavy, he's my—'

'—idiot-savant brother,' she finished for him.

Patiently, quietly, Dylan explained: 'No. An idiot savant is mentally defective with a low IQ, but with an exceptional talent in one special field, such as the ability to solve complex mathematical problems at lightning speed or to play any musical instrument upon first picking it up. Shep's got a high IQ, and he's exceptional in more ways than one. He's just . . . some kind of autistic.'

'We're doomed,' she repeated.

Shepherd chewed another pat of butter with enthusiasm, all the while staring at his plate from a distance of just ten inches, as though he, like Dylan, had discovered the purpose of life, and as though that purpose were meat loaf.

19

Each time the door opened and a customer entered, Dylan tensed. The SUV crowd couldn't have tracked them this fast. And yet . . .

The waitress brought the second round of beers, and after Jilly drew cold comfort from a swallow of Sierra Nevada, she said, 'So we hole up somewhere around the Petrified Forest and . . . You said what? You said *think*?'

'Think,' Dylan confirmed.

'Think about what, besides how to stay alive?'

'Maybe we can figure out how to track down Frankenstein.'

'You forget he's dead?' she asked.

'I mean, track down who he was before they killed him.'

'We don't even have a name, except the one we made up.'

'But he was evidently a scientist. Medical research. Developing psychotropic drugs, psychotropic *stuff*, psychotropic something, which gives us a key word. Scientists write papers, produce articles for journals, give lectures. They leave a trail.'

'Intellectual breadcrumbs.'

'Yeah. And if I think about it, I might remember more of what the bastard said back there in my motel room, other key words. With enough key words, we can go on the Internet and winnow through the researchers working to enhance brain function, related areas.'

'I'm no tech whiz,' she said. 'Are you?'

'No. But this search doesn't take technical expertise, just patience. Even some of those stuffy science journals run photos of their contributors, and if he was near the top of his field, which it seems he must've been, then he'll have gotten newspaper coverage. As soon as we find a photo, we have a name. Then we can read about him and find out what he's been working on.'

'Unless his research was all top secret, like the Manhattan Project, like the formula for fudge-covered Oreos.'

'There you go again.'

'Even if we get the full skinny on him,' she said, 'how does that help us?'

'Maybe there's a way to undo what he did to us. An antidote or something.'

'Antidote. What – we toss frog tongues, bat wings, and lizard eyes in a big cauldron, stew them up with some broccoli?'

'Here comes Negative Jackson, vortex of pessimism. The folks at DC Comics ought to develop a new superhero around you. They go in for brooding, depressive superheroes these days.'

'And you're a Disney book. All sugar and talking chipmunks.'

In a Wile E. Coyote T-shirt, hunched over his dinner plate, Shep snickered, either because the Disney crack rang his bell or because he found the remaining meat loaf amusing.

Shepherd wasn't always as disconnected as he appeared to be.

'What I'm saying,' Dylan continued, 'is that maybe his work was controversial. And if so, then it's possible some of his colleagues opposed his research. One of them will understand what was done to us – and might be willing to help.'

'Yeah,' she said, 'and if a lot of money is needed to finance the research to find this antidote, we can always get a few billion from your uncle Scrooge McDuck.'

'You have a better idea?'

She stared at him as she drank her beer. One swallow. Two.

'I didn't think so,' he said.

Later, when the waitress brought the check, Jilly insisted on paying for the two beers that she'd ordered.

From her attitude, Dylan deduced that paying her own way was an issue of honor with her. Further, he suspected that she would no more graciously accept a nickel for a parking meter than she would take ten bucks for two beers and a tip.

After putting the tenner on the table, she counted the contents of her wallet. The calculation didn't require much time or higher mathematics. 'I'll need to find an ATM, make a withdrawal.'

'No can do,' he said. 'Those guys who blew up your car – if they have any kind of law-enforcement connections, which they probably do, then they'll be able to follow a plastic trail. And quick.'

'You mean I can't use credit cards, either?'

'Not for a while, anyway.'

'Big trouble,' she muttered, staring glumly into her wallet.

'It's not big trouble. Not considering our other problems.'

'Money trouble,' she said solemnly, 'is never *little* trouble.'

In that one statement, Dylan could read whole chapters from the autobiography of her childhood.

Although he didn't know for sure that the men in pursuit of her could have connected Jilly to him and Shep, Dylan decided not to use any of his plastic, either. When the restaurant ran his card through their point-of-sale verification machine, the transaction would register in a credit-clearing center. Any legitimate law-enforcement agency or any gifted hacker with dirty money behind him, monitoring that center either with a court order or secretly, might be running software that could track selected individuals immediately upon the execution of a credit-card purchase.

Paying with cash, Dylan was surprised to feel no charge of uncanny energy on the currency, which had passed through uncountable hands before coming into his possession in a bank withdrawal a couple days ago. This suggested that unlike finger-prints, psychic spoor faded completely away with time.

He told the waitress to keep the change, and he took Shep to the men's room, while Jilly visited the ladies'.

'Pee,' Shep said as soon as they walked into the lavatory and he knew where they were. He put his book on a shelf above the sinks. 'Pee.'

'Pick a stall,' Dylan said. 'I think they're all unused.'

'Pee,' Shep said, keeping his head down, peering up from under his brow as he shuffled to the first of the four stalls. From behind the door, as he latched it, he said, 'Pee.'

A robust seventy-something man with a white mustache and white muttonchops stood at one of the sinks, washing his hands. The air smelled of orange-scented soap.

Dylan approached a urinal. Shep couldn't produce at a urinal because he feared being spoken to while indisposed.

'Pee,' Shep called out from behind his stall door. 'Pee.'

In any public restroom, Shepherd became so uncomfortable that he needed to be in continuous voice contact with his brother, to assure himself that he hadn't been abandoned.

149

'Pee,' Shep said, growing anxious in his stall. 'Dylan, pee. Dylan, Dylan. *Pee!*'

'Pee,' Dylan replied.

Shep's spoken *pee* served a purpose similar to that of a signal broadcast by submarine sonar apparatus, and Dylan's response was equivalent to the return *ping* that signified the echolocation of another vessel, in this case a known and friendly presence in the scary depths of the men's room.

'Pee,' said Shep.

'Pee,' Dylan replied.

In the mirrored wall above the urinals, Dylan observed the retiree's reaction to this verbal sonar.

'Pee, Dylan.'

'Pee, Shepherd.'

Puzzled and uneasy, Mr. Muttonchops looked back and forth from the closed stall to Dylan, to the stall, as if something not only strange but also perverse might be unfolding here.

'Pee.'

'Pee.'

When Mr. Muttonchops realized that Dylan was watching him, when their eyes met in the mirror above the urinals, the retiree quickly looked away. He turned off the water at the sink, without rinsing the orange-scented lather off his hands.

'Pee, Dylan.'

'Pee, Shepherd.'

Dripping frothy suds from his fingers, shedding iridescent bubbles that floated in his wake and settled slowly to the floor, the retiree went to a wall dispenser and cranked out a few paper towels.

At last came the sound of Shepherd's healthy stream.

'Good pee,' said Shep.

'Good pee.'

Reluctant to pause long enough to dry his soapy hands, the man fled the lavatory with the wad of paper towels.

Dylan went to a different sink from the one that the retiree had used – and then had an idea that led him to the towel dispenser.

'Pee, pee, pee,' Shep said happily, with great relief.

'Pee, pee, pee,' Dylan echoed, returning with a towel to the retiree's sink.

Shielding his right hand with the paper towel, he touched the faucet that the retiree had so recently shut off. Nothing. No fizz. No crackle.

He touched the fixture barehanded. Lots of fizz and crackle.

Again with the paper towel. Nothing.

Skin contact was required. Maybe not just hands. Maybe an elbow would work. Maybe feet. All sorts of ludicrous comic possibilities occurred to him.

'Pee.'

'Pee.'

Dylan rubbed the faucet vigorously with the towel, scrubbing away the soap and water that the retiree had left on the handle.

Then he touched it with his bare hand once more. The senior citizen's psychic spoor remained as strong as it had been previously.

'Pee.'

'Pee.'

Evidently, this latent energy couldn't simply be wiped away as fingerprints could be, but it dissipated gradually on its own, like an evaporating solvent.

At another sink, Dylan washed his hands. He was drying them near the towel dispenser when Shepherd came out of the fourth stall and went to the sink that his brother had just used.

'Pee,' Shepherd said.

'You can see me now.'

'Pee,' Shep insisted as he turned on the water.

'I'm right here.'

'Pee.'

Refusing to be drawn into the sonar game when they were within sight of each other, Dylan tossed his crumpled towels in the waste can, and waited.

A riot of bizarre thoughts tumbled through his head, like an immense load of colorful laundry in a laundromat-size clothes dryer. One of those thoughts was that Shep had gone into the first stall but had come out of the fourth.

'Pee.'

Dylan went to the fourth stall. The door stood ajar, and he shouldered it open.

Partitions separated the stalls, with twelve or fourteen inches of air space at the bottom. Shepherd could have dropped flat on the floor and wriggled from stall one to number four, under intervening partitions. Possible but highly unlikely.

'Pee,' Shep repeated, but with less enthusiasm, reluctantly coming to the conclusion that his brother would not participate any longer.

As fastidious about personal cleanliness as he was about the geometrical presentation of his meals, Shep had a post-toilet routine from which he never deviated: vigorously scrub the hands once, rinse them thoroughly, then scrub and rinse again. Indeed, as Dylan watched, Shep began the second scrub.

The kid had a special concern about the sanitary conditions in public lavatories. He regarded even the most well-maintained restroom with paranoid suspicion, certain that all known diseases and some not yet discovered were busily festering on every surface. Having read the *American Medical Association Encyclopedia of Medicine*, Shep could recite a list of virtually all known diseases and infections if you were foolish enough to ask him to do so, and if he happened to be relating to the outer world well enough to hear your request – and if you had a sufficient number of hours to listen, since he would be all but impossible to stop once he got started.

Now, with the second rinse completed, Shep's hands were red from excessive scrubbing and from water turned up so hot that he'd hissed in discomfort as he had endured it. Mindful of the deadly and cunning microorganisms hiding in plain sight on the chrome faucet handle, he turned the water off with his elbow.

Dylan could not imagine any circumstances under which Shepherd would lie facedown on a lavatory floor and slither under a series of partitions between toilet stalls. In fact, if it ever were to happen, you could be certain that simultaneously, in a sporting-goods store somewhere, Satan would be buying ice skates.

Besides, his white T-shirt remained immaculate. He hadn't been mopping the floor with it.

Holding his hands high, like a surgeon expecting an assisting nurse to sheath them in latex gloves, Shep crossed the room to the towel dispenser. He waited for his brother to turn the crank, which he would not touch with clean hands.

'Didn't you go into the first stall?' Dylan asked.

Head lowered in his customary shy posture, but also cocked so he could look up sideways at the towel machine, Shepherd frowned at the handle and said, 'Germs.'

'Shep, when we came in here, didn't you go straight into the first stall?'

'Germs.'

'Shep?'

'Germs.'

'Hey, come on, listen to me, buddy.'

'Germs.'

'Give me a break, Shep. Will you listen to me, please?'

'Germs.'

Dylan cranked out a few towels, tore them off the perforated roll, and handed them to his brother. 'But then didn't you come out of the fourth stall?'

Scowling at his hands, drying them energetically, obsessively, instead of merely blotting them on the paper, Shep said, 'Here.'

'What'd you say?'

'Here.'

'What do you hear?'

'Here.'

'I don't hear anything, little bro.'

'H-e-r-e,' Shep spelled with some effort, as if pronouncing each letter at an emotional cost.

'What do you want, bro?'

Shep trembled. 'Here.'

'Here what?' Dylan asked, seeking clarification even though he knew that clarification wasn't likely to be granted.

'There,' said Shep.

'There?' Dylan asked.

'There,' Shep agreed, nodding, though continuing to focus intently on his hands, still trembling.

'There where?'

'Here.' The note in Shep's voice might have been impatience.

'What're we talking about, buddy?'

'Here.'

'Here,' Dylan repeated.

'There,' said Shep, and what had seemed to be impatience matured instead into a strained note of anxiety.

Trying to understand, Dylan said, 'Here, there.'

'Here, th-th-there,' Shep repeated with a shudder.

'Shep, what's wrong? Shep, are you scared?'

'Scared,' Shep confirmed. 'Yeah. Scared. Yeah.'

'What're you scared of, buddy?'

'Shep is scared.'

'Of what?'

'Shep is scared,' he said, beginning to shake more violently. 'Shep is scared.'

Dylan put his hands on his brother's shoulders. 'Easy, easy now. It's okay, Shep. There's nothing to be scared about. I'm right here with you, little bro.'

'Shep is scared.' The kid's averted face had faded as pale as whatever haunting spirits he might have glimpsed.

'Your hands are clean, no germs, just you and me, nothing to be afraid of. Okay?'

Shepherd didn't reply but continued to shake.

Resorting to the singsong cadences with which his brother most often could be calmed in moments of emotional turmoil, Dylan said, 'Good clean hands, no dirty germs, good clean hands. Gonna go now, go now, hit the road now. Okay? Gonna roll. Okay? You like the road, on the road again, on the road, goin' places where we never been. Okay? On the road again, like old Willie Nelson, you and me, rollin' along. Like always, rollin'. The old rhythm, the rhythm of the road. You can read your book, read and ride, read and ride. Okay?'

'Okay,' said Shep.

'Read and ride.'

'Read and ride,' Shep echoed. The urgency and tension drained out of his voice even though he still shivered. 'Read and ride.'

As Dylan had calmed his brother, Shep had continued to dry his hands with such energy that the towels had shredded. Crumpled rags and frayed curls of damp paper littered the floor at his feet.

Dylan held Shep's hands until they stopped trembling. Gently, he pried open the clenched fingers and removed the remaining tatters of the paper towels. He wadded this debris and threw it in the nearby trash can.

Placing a hand under Shep's chin, he tipped the kid's head up. The moment their eyes met, Shep closed his.

'You okay?' Dylan asked.

'Read and ride.'

'I love you, Shep.'

'Read and ride.'

A pinch of color had returned to the kid's wintry cheeks. The lines of anxiety in his face slowly smoothed away as crow tracks might be erased from a mantle of snow by a persistent breeze.

Although Shep's outer tranquility became complete, his inner weather remained troubled. Shuttered, his eyes twitched behind his pale lids, jumping from sight to sight in a world that only he could see.

'Read and ride,' Shep repeated, as if those three words were a calming mantra.

Dylan regarded the bank of toilet stalls. The door of the fourth stood open, as he had left it after he'd checked on the nature of the partitions. The doors of the two middle stalls were ajar, and that of the first remained tightly closed.

'Read and ride,' said Shep.

'Read and ride,' Dylan assured him. 'I'll get your book.'

Leaving his brother beside the towel dispenser, Dylan retrieved *Great Expectations* from the shelf above the sinks.

Shep stood where he'd been left, head still raised even though Dylan's supporting hand had been removed. Eyes closed, but busy.

Carrying the book, Dylan went to the first stall. He tried the door. It wouldn't open.

'Here, there,' Shep whispered. Standing with his eyes closed, arms slack at his sides, and hands open with both palms facing front, Shepherd had an otherworldly quality, as though he were a medium in a trance, bisected by the membrane between this world and the next. If he had risen off the floor, his levitation would have conformed to his appearance so completely that you would not have been much surprised to see him floating in the air. Although Shep's voice remained recognizably his own, he almost seemed to speak for a seance-summoned entity from Beyond: *'Here, there.'*

Dylan knew that no one could be in the first stall. Nevertheless he dropped to one knee and peered under the door to confirm what he understood to be a certainty.

'Here, there.'

He got up and tried the door again. Not just stuck. Locked. From the inside, of course.

A faulty latch, perhaps. Loose, the drop bar might have fallen into the latch channel when no one had been in the stall.

Maybe Shepherd had *approached* this first compartment, as Dylan had seen him do, but had found it inaccessible, and had at once moved to the fourth without Dylan noticing.

'*Here, there.*'

The chill found bone first, not skin, and radiated through Dylan from the core of every limb. Fear iced his marrow, although not fear alone; this was also a chill of not entirely unpleasant expectation and of awe inspired by some mysterious looming event that he sensed much in the manner that a storm petrel, winging under curdled black clouds, senses the glorious tempest before being alerted by either lightning or thunder.

Strangely, he glanced at the mirror above the sink, prepared to see a room other than the lavatory in which he stood. His expectation of wonders outstripped the capacity of the moment to deliver them, however, and the reflection proved to be the mundane facts of toilet stalls and urinals. He and Shep were the only figures occupying the reversed image, though he didn't know who or what else he might have expected.

With one last puzzled glance at the locked stall door, Dylan returned to his brother and put one hand on his shoulder.

At Dylan's touch, Shepherd opened his eyes, lowered his head, let his shoulders slump forward, and in general reassumed the humble posture in which he shuffled through life.

'Read and ride,' Shep said, and Dylan said, 'Let's roll.'

20

Jilly waited pensively near the cashier's station, by the front door, gazing out at the night, as radiant as a princess, perhaps the heir of a handsome Roman emperor who had ventured in conquest south of Sidra's shores.

Dylan nearly stopped midrestaurant to study her and to lock in his memory every detail of the way she looked at this moment in the dialed-down, bevel-sheared light from the cut-glass ceiling fixtures, for he wanted to paint her eventually just as she stood now.

Always preferring to remain in motion in any public place, lest a hesitation should encourage a stranger to speak to him, Shepherd allowed no slightest pause, and Dylan was drawn after his brother by their invisible chain.

Bringing hand to hat brim, a departing customer graciously tipped his Stetson to Jilly as she stepped aside to give him easier access to the door.

When she looked up and saw Dylan and Shep approaching, palpable relief chased the pensive expression from her face. Something had happened to her in their absence.

'What's wrong?' he asked when he reached her.

'I'll tell you in the truck. Let's get out of here. Let's go.'

Opening the door, Dylan put his hand on fresh spoor. Bleakness, an oppressive sense of solitude, a dark-night-of-the-soul loneliness pierced him and filled him with an emotional desolation as blasted, burnt, and ash-shrouded as a landscape in the aftermath of an all-consuming fire.

He tried immediately to insulate himself from the power of the latent psychic print on the door handle, as he had learned to do with the restaurant menu. This time, however, he wasn't able to resist the influx of energy.

With no memory of crossing the threshold, Dylan found himself outside and on the move. Even hours past sundown, the mild desert night withdrew the banked heat of the day from the blacktop, and he detected the faint scent of tar under the kitchen odors that rose from the restaurant roof vents.

Glancing back, he saw Jilly and Shep standing in the open door, already ten feet behind him. He had dropped Shep's book, which lay on the pavement between him and them. He wanted to retrieve the book and return to Shep and Jilly. He could not. 'Wait here for me.'

Car to pickup to SUV, he was impelled to venture farther into the parking lot, not with the urgency that had earlier caused him to turn the Expedition on a dime and leave nine cents change, but with a nonetheless motivating perception that an important opportunity would shortly be foreclosed if he didn't act. He knew that he wasn't out of control, that on a subconscious level he understood exactly what he was doing, and why, as he had subconsciously understood his purpose when he had driven pell-mell and hell-bent to the house on Eucalyptus Avenue, but he *felt* out of control just the same.

This time the magnet proved to be not a grandmotherly woman in a candy-striped uniform, but an aging cowboy wearing tan Levi's and a chambray shirt. Arriving just as the guy settled behind the wheel of a Mercury Mountaineer, Dylan prevented him from shutting the door.

From the psychic trace on this door handle, he again encountered the heart-deadening loneliness familiar from the imprint back at the restaurant, a despondency bordering on despair.

A lifetime of outdoor work had given the man in the Mountaineer a cured-leather face, but the decades of sun that crimped and cockled his skin had not left any light in him, and the years of wind had not piped much life into his bones. Burnt out, worn thin, he seemed to be a scraggy gnarl of tumbleweed tenuously rooted to the earth, waiting only for the gust that would break him loose from life.

The old man didn't tip his Stetson as he'd tipped it at Jilly upon leaving the restaurant, but he didn't react with irritation or alarm, either, when Dylan blocked the door. He had the look of a guy who had always been able to take care of himself, regardless of the nature of the threat or tribulation – but there was also about him the aura of a man who didn't much care what happened next.

'You've been searching for something,' Dylan said, although he had no idea what words were coming from him until he'd spoken them and could afterward review their meaning.

'Don't need Jesus, son,' the cowboy replied. 'Already found him twice.' His azurite-blue eyes took in more light than they gave out. 'Don't need trouble, either, nor do you.'

'Not something,' Dylan corrected. 'You're looking for someone.'

'Isn't just about everybody, one way or another?'

'You've been looking a long time,' Dylan said, though he still had no idea where this might be leading.

Through a squint that seemed wise enough to filter truth from illusion, the old man studied him. 'What's your name, son?'

'Dylan O'Conner.'

'Never heard of you. So how'd you hear of me?'

'Didn't hear of you, sir. I don't know who you are. I just . . .' Words that had come without volition now failed him on command. After a hesitation, he realized that he would have to tell a piece of the truth, reveal part of his secret, if they were to proceed. 'You see, sir, I have these moments of . . . intuition.'

'Don't count on it at the poker table.'

'Not just intuition. I mean . . . I know things when there's no way to know. I feel, I know, and . . . I make connections.'

'Some sort of spiritist, you're sayin'?'

'Sir?'

'You're a diviner, soothsayer, psychic – that sort of thing?'

'Maybe,' Dylan said. 'It's just this weirdness that's happened to me lately. I don't make money at it.'

Those worn features that seemed incapable of a smile might have formed one, although it was drawn lightly, as with a feather on the weathered sandstone of his face, and was so short-lived that it might have been only the tic of a wince. 'If what I'm hearin' is your usual pitch, I'm amazed you don't have to pay folks to listen.'

'You think you've come to the end of whatever road you've been following.' Once more Dylan was unaware of what he would say before he said it. 'You think you've failed. But maybe you haven't.'

'Go on.'

'Maybe she's near right now.'

'She?'

'I don't know, sir. That just came to me. But whoever she is, you know who I mean.'

That analytic squint fixed Dylan once more, this time with a certain merciless quality like the piercing scrutiny of a police detective. 'Step back a piece. Give me room to get out.'

As the old man exited the big Mercury SUV, Dylan surveyed the night for Jilly and Shep. They had ventured a few feet farther from the restaurant since he'd last seen them, but only far enough for Jilly to retrieve the copy of *Great Expectations* that Dylan had dropped. She stood at Shepherd's side, watchful, in the wound-tight posture of one who wondered if this time, too, there would be knives.

He looked out toward the street, as well. No black Suburbans. Nonetheless, he sensed they had stayed too long in Safford.

'Name's Ben Tanner.'

When Dylan looked away from Shep and Jilly, he discovered the old man offering one worn and callused hand.

He hesitated, concerned that a handshake would expose him to a supercharged version of the bleak loneliness and the despondency that he had sensed in Tanner's psychic imprint, emotion a thousand times more intense by direct contact than what he'd experienced by exposure to the spoor, so powerful that it would knock him to his knees.

He couldn't remember if he had touched Marjorie when he'd found her standing beside the pill-littered kitchen table, but he didn't believe he had. And Kenny? After administering baseball-bat justice, Dylan demanded handcuff and padlock keys from the pants-wetting knife maniac; however, after producing the keys from a shirt pocket, Kenny had given them to Jilly. To the best of Dylan's recollection, he had not touched the vicious little coward.

No strategy to avoid Tanner's hand would leave their fragile rapport undamaged, so Dylan shook it – and discovered that what he had felt so poignantly in the man's latent psychic imprint could not be felt in equal measure, or at all, in the man himself. The mechanism of his sixth sense was no less mysterious than the source of it.

'Come down from Wyoming near a month ago,' Tanner said,

'with some leads, but they had no more substance than gnat piss.'

Dylan reached past Tanner to touch the handle on the driver's door.

'Been rattlin' from one end of Arizona to the other, and now I'm on my way home, where maybe I should've stayed.'

In the psychic trace, Dylan felt again the geography of a burnt-out soul, that continent of ashes, that despondent world of soundless solitude he had encountered when, hand to door, he had left the restaurant.

Although he had not consciously framed the question, Dylan heard himself asking, 'How long has your wife been dead?'

The reappearance of the intimidating squint suggested that the old man still suspected a con, but the pertinence of the question lent Dylan some credibility. 'Emily's been gone eight years,' Tanner said in the matter-of-fact tone with which men of his generation felt obliged to conceal their tenderest emotions, but in spite of the squint, those azurite eyes betrayed the drowning depth of his grief.

To have known by some form of clairvoyance that this stranger's wife was dead, to have *known* it rather than merely to have suspected it, to *know intimately* the devastation that this death had wrought in Tanner, made Dylan feel like a brazen intruder exploring the most private spaces of a victim's house, like a sneak who picked the locks on diaries and read the secrets of others. This repugnant aspect of his uncanny talent far outweighed the exhilaration he had felt after the successful confrontation at Marjorie's house, but he couldn't suppress these revelations, which rose into his awareness like water bubbling at a wellhead.

'You and Emily started looking for the girl twelve years ago,' Dylan said, though he didn't know to what girl he referred or yet grasp the nature of their search.

Grief made way for surprise. 'How do you know these things?'

'I said "girl," but she'd have been thirty-eight even then.'

'Fifty now,' Tanner confirmed. For a moment he seemed to be more amazed by the number of lost decades than by the knowledge that Dylan had acquired by divination: 'Fifty. My God, where does a life go?'

Releasing the door handle, Dylan was drawn away from the

Mercury by an unknown but more powerful attractant, and once again he was on the move. Almost as an afterthought, he called back to Tanner, 'This way,' as though he had a clue as to where he might be going.

Prudence no doubt counseled the old man to climb in his truck and lock the doors, but his heart was involved now, and prudence had little influence with him. Hurrying at Dylan's side, he said, 'We figured we'd find her sooner than later. Then we learned the system was dead-set against us.'

A swooping shadow, a *thrum* overhead. Dylan looked up in time to see a desert bat snare a moth in midflight, the killing silhouetted against a tall parking-lot lamp. This sight would not have chilled him on another night, but chilled him now.

An SUV in the street. Not a Suburban. But cruising past slowly. Dylan watched until it passed out of sight.

The bloodhound of intuition led him across the parking lot to a ten-year-old Pontiac. He touched the driver's door, and every nerve end in his hand received the psychic spoor.

'You were twenty,' Dylan said, 'Emily just seventeen, when the girl came along.'

'We had no money, no prospects.'

'Emily's parents had died young, and yours were . . . useless.'

'You know what you *can't* know,' Tanner marveled. 'That's exactly how it was. No family to back us up.'

When the faintly fizzing trace on the driver's door did not electrify Dylan, he moved around the Pontiac to the passenger's side.

At his heels, the old man said, 'Still, we'd have kept her no matter how hard things got. But then in Emily's eighth month—'

'A snowy night,' Dylan said. 'You were in a pickup truck.'

'No match for a semi.'

'Both your legs were broken.'

'Broke my back, too, and internal injuries.'

'No health insurance.'

'Not a dime. And I was a year gettin' back on my feet.'

At the front door on the passenger's side, Dylan found an imprint different from the one on the driver's door.

'Broke our hearts to give that baby up, but we prayed it was the best thing for her.'

Dylan detected a sympathetic resonance between the psychic trace of this unknown person and that of Ben Tanner.

'By God, you're the true thing,' the old man said, abandoning his skepticism more quickly than Dylan would have thought possible. Songless for so long, hope – that feathered thing perched in his soul – was singing again to Ben Tanner. 'You're real.'

No matter what might come, Dylan remained compelled to follow this incident to its inevitable conclusion. He could no more easily turn away than a rainstorm could reverse course and pour upward from the puddled earth into the wrung-out thunderheads from which it had fallen. Nevertheless, he was loath to raise the old man's hopes, for he couldn't foresee the end point. He couldn't guarantee that the father-and-child reunion that seemed miraculously in process was, in fact, destined to occur this night – or ever.

'You're real,' Tanner repeated, this time with a disquieting reverence.

Dylan's hand tightened around the Pontiac door handle, and in his mind a connection occurred with the solid *ca-chunk* of railroad cars coupling. 'Dead man's trail,' he murmured, not sure what he meant, but not thrilled by the sound of it. He turned from the car toward the restaurant. 'There's an answer here, if you want it.'

Seizing Dylan by the arm, halting him, Tanner said, 'You mean the girl? In there? Where I just was?'

'I don't know, Ben. It doesn't work that way with me. No clear visions. No final answers till I reach the end. It's like a chain, and I go link by link, not knowing what the last link is until I've got it.'

Choosing to ignore the warning implicit in Dylan's words, the old man said wonderingly, 'I wasn't actually looking for her here. Not in this town, this place. Pulled off the road, came for dinner, that's all.'

'Ben, listen, I said there's an answer here, but I don't know if the answer is the girl herself. Be prepared for that.'

The old man had taken his first taste of hope not a minute ago, and already he was drunk with it. 'Well, like you said, if this isn't the last link, you'll find the next one, and the one after that.'

'All the way to the last link,' Dylan agreed, recalling the relentlessness of the compulsion that had driven him to Eucalyptus Avenue. 'But—'

'You'll find my girl, I know you will, I know.' Tanner didn't seem to be the type who could flip from despair to joy in a manic moment, but perhaps the prospect of resolving fifty years of regret and remorse was sufficiently exhilarating to effect an immediate emotional transformation even in a stoic heart. 'You're an answer to prayers.'

In truth, Dylan might have been at least mildly enthusiastic about playing hero twice in one night, but his enthusiasm curdled when he realized how devastated Ben Tanner would be if this chase didn't have a storybook ending.

Gently, he broke the old man's grip on his arm and continued toward the restaurant. Since there was no turning back, he wanted to finish this as quickly as possible and put an end to the suspense.

Jinking bats, now three in number, frolicked in their aerial feast, and the paper-fragile exoskeleton of each doomed moth made a faint but audible crunch when snapped in those rodent teeth: entire death announcements in crisp strokes of exclamatory punctuation.

If Dylan had believed in omens, these lamplit bats would have warranted a pause for consideration. And if they were an omen, they certainly didn't portend success in the search for Ben Tanner's girl.

Dead man's trail.

The words returned to him, but he still didn't know what he ought to infer from them.

If a chance existed that the old man's long-lost daughter would be found inside the restaurant, then perhaps it was equally likely that she was dead and that who waited to be discovered instead at the end of this particular chain was the physician who had attended her during her final hours or the priest who'd given her last rites. No less possible: She might not merely have died; she might have been murdered, and at dinner this evening might be the policeman who had found her body. Or the man who had murdered her.

With the buoyant Ben at his side, Dylan paused when he reached Jilly and Shep, but made no introductions, offered no explanations. He handed his keys to Jilly, leaned close, and said, 'Get Shep belted in. Get out of the parking lot. Wait for me half a block that way.' He pointed. 'Keep the engine running.'

Events in the restaurant, whether they proved to be good or bad, might cause sufficient commotion to ensure that the employees and the customers would be interested enough in Dylan to watch him through the big front windows when he left. The SUV must not be near enough for anyone to read the license plates or to discern clearly the make and model of the vehicle.

To her credit, Jilly asked no questions. She understood that in his *stuff*-driven condition, Dylan couldn't do other than what he was impelled to do. She accepted the keys, and she said to Shep, 'Come on, sweetie, let's go.'

'Listen to her,' Dylan told his brother. 'Do what she says,' and he led Ben Tanner into the restaurant.

The hostess said, 'I'm sorry, but we're no longer seating for dinner.' Then she recognized them. 'Oh. Forget something?'

'Saw an old friend,' Dylan lied, and headed into the dining area with the confidence that although he didn't know where he was going, he would arrive at where he needed to be.

The couple sat at a corner table. They appeared to be in their middle to late twenties.

Too young to be Ben Tanner's daughter, the woman looked up as Dylan approached her without hesitation. A pretty, fresh-faced, sun-browned brunette, she had eyes that were a singular shade of blue.

'Excuse me for interrupting,' Dylan said, 'but do the words *dead man's trail* mean anything to you?'

Smiling uncertainly but as though prepared to be delighted, the woman glanced at her companion. 'What's this, Tom?'

Tom shrugged. 'A setup for some joke, I guess, but it's not my joke, I swear.'

Turning her attention to Dylan once more, the woman said, 'Dead Man's Trail is a desert back road 'tween here and San Simon. Just dirt and tire-snapped rattlesnakes. It's where me and Tom first met.'

'Lynette was changing a flat tire when I saw her,' Tom said. 'Helped her tighten the lugs, and the next thing I knew, she used some hoodoo or other to make me propose marriage.'

Smiling affectionately at Tom, Lynette said, 'I cast a spell on you, all right, but the purpose was to turn you into a warty toad and make you hop away forever. And here you are instead. That'll teach me not to slack off on my spellcastin' practice.'

On the table, two small gifts, as yet unwrapped, and a bottle of wine indicated a special evening. Although Lynette's simple dress appeared inexpensive, the care with which she had done her makeup and brushed her hair suggested she'd worn her best. The aging Pontiac in the parking lot further supported the conclusion that an evening as fancy as this must be a rare treat for them.

'Anniversary?' Dylan asked, relying on deduction rather than on clairvoyance.

'As if you didn't already know,' said Lynette. 'Our third. Now who put you up to this, and what's next?'

Surprise froze her smile when Dylan briefly touched the stem of her wineglass to reacquaint himself with her psychic imprint.

He felt again the unique trace that had been on the passenger's door of the Pontiac, and in his mind another connection occurred with the *ca-chunk* of coupling railroad cars. 'I believe your mother told you that she was adopted, told you as much as she knew.'

The mention of her mother thawed Lynette's smile. 'Yes.'

'Which was nothing more than her adopted parents knew – that she'd been given up by a couple somewhere in Wyoming.'

'Wyoming. That's right.'

Dylan said, 'She tried to find her real parents, but she didn't have enough money or time to keep at it.'

'You knew my mother?'

Fully dissolve a heavy concentration of sugar in an ordinary bowl of water, suspend a string in this mixture, and in the morning you will find that rock-sugar crystals have formed upon the string. Dylan seemed to have lowered a long mental string into some pool of psychic energy, and the facts of Lynette's life crystallized on it much faster than sugar would separate from water.

'She died two years ago this August,' he continued.

'The cancer took her,' Tom confirmed.

Lynette said, 'Forty-eight is too young to go.'

Repulsed by the continued invasion of this young woman's heart, but unable to restrain himself, Dylan felt her still-sharp anguish at the loss of her beloved mother, and he read her secrets as they crystallized on his mental string: 'The night your mom died, the next-to-last thing she said to you was, "Lynnie, someday you should go lookin' for your roots. Finish what I started. We can better figure where we're goin' if we know where we come from."'

Astonished that he could be privy to the exact words her mother had spoken, Lynette began to rise, but at once sat down, reached for her wine, perhaps remembered that he had put his fingers to the stem of the glass, and left the drink untouched. 'Who . . . who are you?'

'There in the hospital, the night she died, the *last* thing she ever said to you was . . . "Lynnie, I hope this won't count against me wherever I'm goin' from here, but as much as I love God, I love you more."'

By reciting those words, he wielded an emotional sledgehammer. When he saw Lynette's tears, he was appalled that he had broken her pretty anniversary mood and had knocked her into memories unsuitable for celebration.

Yet he knew why he'd swung so hard. He had needed to establish his bona fides before introducing Ben Tanner, ensuring that Lynette and the old man would more immediately connect, thereby allowing Dylan to finish his work and to slip away as quickly as possible.

Although Tanner had hung back until now, he'd been near enough to hear that his dream of a father-daughter reunion would not become a reality in this life, but also that another unexpected miracle was here occurring. Having taken off his Stetson, he turned it nervously in his hands as he came forward.

When Dylan saw that the old man's legs were shaking and that his joints seemed about to fail him, he pulled out one of the two unused chairs at the table. As Tanner put his hat aside and sat down, Dylan said, 'Lynette, while your mom hoped one day to find her blood kin, they were looking for her, too. I'd like you to meet your grandfather – your mother's father, Ben Tanner.'

The old man and the young woman stared wonderingly at each other with matching azurite-blue eyes.

While Lynette was silenced by her astonishment, Ben Tanner produced a snapshot that he had evidently fished out of his wallet while standing behind Dylan. He slid the photo across the table to his granddaughter. 'This is my Emily, your grandma, when she was almost as young as you. It breaks my heart she couldn't live to see you're the image of her.'

'Tom,' Dylan said to Lynette's husband, 'I see there's but an inch of wine left in that bottle. We're going to need something more to celebrate, and I'd be pleased if you'd let me buy this one.'

Bewildered by what had happened, Tom nodded, smiled uncertainly. 'Uh, sure. That's nice of you.'

'I'll be right back,' Dylan said, with no intention of keeping that promise.

He went to the cashier's station by the front door, where the hostess had just paid out change to a departing customer, a florid-faced man with the listing walk of one who had drunk more of his dinner than he had chewed.

'I know you're not serving dinner any longer,' Dylan said to the hostess. 'But can I still send a bottle of wine to Tom and Lynette over there?'

'Certainly. The kitchen's closed, but the bar's open for another two hours.'

She knew what they had ordered, a moderately priced Merlot. Dylan mentally added a tip for the waitress, put cash on the counter.

He glanced back at the corner table, where Tom, Lynette, and Ben were intensely engaged in conversation. Good. None of them would see him leave.

Shouldering through the door, stepping outside, he discovered that Jilly had moved the Expedition from the parking lot, as he had requested. The SUV stood in the street, at the curb, half a block north.

Angling in that direction, he encountered the florid-faced man who had left the restaurant ahead of him. The guy apparently had some difficulty remembering where he'd parked his car or perhaps even what car he'd been driving. Then he focused on a silver Corvette and made for it with the hunched shoulders and the head-down determination of a bull spotting a matador with unfurled cape. He didn't charge as fast as a bull, however, nor as directly, but tacked left and right, left and right, like a sailor changing the course of his vessel by a series of maneuvers, singing a slurred and semicoherent version of the Beatles' 'Yesterday.'

Fumbling in the pockets of his sport coat, the drunk found his car keys but dropped a wad of currency. Oblivious of the money on the blacktop behind him, he blundered on.

'Mister, you lost something,' Dylan said. 'Hey, fella, you're gonna want this.'

In the melancholy mood of 'Yesterday,' singing mushily of his many troubles, the drunk did not respond to Dylan, but weaved toward the Corvette with the newfound key held at arm's length ahead of him, as though it were a dowsing rod without which he would be unable to find his way across the last ten feet of pavement to his vehicle.

Picking up the wad of cash – Dylan felt a cold slippery twisting serpent in his hand, smelled something goatish and rank, heard an internal buzzing as of angry wasps. At once he knew that the drunken fool lurching toward the Corvette – Lucas something, Lucas Croaker or Crocker – was more despicable than a drunk, more sinister than a mere fool.

21

Even drunk and stumbling, this Lucas Crocker should be feared. After casting aside the wad of cash saturated in repulsive spoor, Dylan rushed him from behind, with no further warning.

Crocker looked flabby in his loose-fitting slacks and jacket, but he was as solid as a whiskey keg, which in fact he smelled like. Body-checked forcefully, he slammed against the Corvette hard enough to rock it, and slobbered a final word of Beatles' lyrics against the glass even as he broke the driver's-side window with his face.

Most men would have gone down, stayed down, but Crocker roared in rage and reared back with such Brahman power that he appeared to have been invigorated by the rib-cracking impact with the sports car. He pistoned his arms, jabbed with his elbows, thrashed, bucked, and rolled his meaty shoulders like a rodeo beast casting off a flyweight rider.

Far from flyweight, Dylan was nonetheless cast off. He staggered backward, almost fell, but stayed on his feet, and wished that he had kept the baseball bat.

Nose broken, face cracked in a crimson grin, Crocker rounded on his adversary with diabolic delight, as though stimulated by the prospect of having his teeth knocked out, excited by the certainty of greater pain, as if this were *just* the kind of entertainment that he preferred. He charged.

The advantage of size would not have been enough to spare Dylan ruinous injury, and perhaps the advantage of sobriety wouldn't have been enough either; but size and sobriety *and* raw anger gave him a precious edge. When Crocker charged with drunken enthusiasm, Dylan lured the man by making a come-on gesture, stepped aside almost too late, and kicked him in the knee.

Crocker sprawled, rapped the pavement with his forehead, and found it less accommodating than a car window. Nevertheless, his fighting spirit proved less breakable than his face, and he pushed at once onto his hands and knees.

Dylan drew courage from the volcanic anger that he'd first felt upon seeing the beaten boy shackled to the bed in that room divided between books and knives. The world was full of victims, too many victims and too few defenders of them. The hideous images that had passed into him from the wad of cash, sharp images of Lucas Crocker's singular depravity and cruelty, still ricocheted through his mind, like destructive radioactive particles. The righteous anger that flooded Dylan washed before it all fear regarding his own safety.

For a painter of idyllic nature scenes, for an artist with a peaceful heart, he could deliver a remarkably vicious kick, place it with the accuracy of any mob enforcer, and follow it with another. Sickened by this violence, he nonetheless remained committed to it without compunction.

As Crocker's broken ribs tested how resistant his lungs were to puncture, as his smashed fingers fattened into unclenchable sausages, as his rapidly swelling lips transformed his fierce grin into the goofy smile of a stocking doll, the drunk evidently decided that he'd had enough fun for one evening. He stopped trying to get to his feet, collapsed onto his side, rolled onto his back, lay gasping, groaning.

Breathing hard but unhurt, Dylan surveyed the parking lot. He and Crocker were alone. He was pretty sure that no traffic had passed in the street during the altercation. No one had seen.

His luck wouldn't hold much longer.

The keys to the Corvette gleamed on the pavement near the car. Dylan confiscated them.

He returned to the bloodied, gasping man and noticed a phone clipped to his belt.

In Crocker's boiled-ham face, cunning little pig eyes watched for an easy opportunity.

'Give me your phone,' Dylan said.

When Crocker made no move to obey, Dylan stepped on his broken hand, pinning the swollen fingers to the blacktop.

Cursing, Crocker used his good hand to detach the phone from his belt. He held it out, eyes wet with pain but as cunning as before.

'Slide it across the pavement,' Dylan directed. 'Over there.'

When Crocker did as instructed, Dylan stepped off his injured hand without doing further damage.

Spinning, the telephone came to rest about a foot from the wad of currency. Dylan went to the phone, plucked it off the blacktop, but left the money untouched.

Spitting out broken teeth or window glass along with words as mushy as his smashed lips, Crocker asked, 'You aren't robbing me?'

'I only steal long-distance minutes. You can keep your money, but you're going to get one hell of a phone bill.'

Having been sobered by pain, Crocker was now bleary-eyed only with bewilderment. 'Who *are* you?'

'Everybody's been asking me that same question tonight. I guess I'll have to come up with a name that resonates.'

Half a block north, Jilly stood beside the Expedition, watching. Perhaps, if she'd seen Dylan getting his ass kicked, she would have come to his aid with a can of insecticide or aerosol cheese.

Hurrying toward the SUV, Dylan glanced back, but Lucas Crocker made no attempt to get up. Maybe the guy had passed out. Maybe he had noticed the bats feeding greedily on the moths in the lamplight: That spectacle would appeal to him. It might even be the kind of thing he found inspiring.

By the time Dylan reached the Expedition, Jilly had returned to the front passenger's seat. He got in and shut his door.

Her psychic trace upon the steering wheel felt pleasant, rather like immersing work-sore hands in warm water enhanced with curative salts. Then he became aware of her anxiety. As if a live electrical wire had been dropped into the hand bath. With an act of will, he tuned out all those vibrations, good and bad.

'What the hell happened back there?' Jilly asked.

Handing the phone to her, he said, 'Get me the police.'

'I thought we didn't want them.'

'Now we do.'

Headlights appeared in the street behind them. Another slow-moving SUV. Maybe the same one that had earlier drifted by well below the speed limit. Maybe not. Dylan watched it pass. The driver didn't appear to be interested in them. A true professional, of course, would conceal his interest well.

In the backseat, Shepherd had returned to *Great Expectations*. He seemed remarkably calm.

The restaurant fronted on Federal Highway 70, the route that Dylan wanted. He headed northwest.

After using the telephone keypad, Jilly listened, then said, 'Guess the town's too small for nine-one-one service.' She keyed in the number for directory assistance, asked for the police, and passed the phone back to Dylan.

Succinctly, he told the police operator about Lucas Crocker, half drunk and fully thrashed, waiting for an ambulance in the restaurant parking lot.

'May I have your name?' she asked.

'That's not important.'

'I'm required to ask your name—'

'And so you have.'

'Sir, if you were a witness to this assault—'

'I committed the assault,' Dylan said.

Law-enforcement routine seldom took a strange turn here in the sleepy heart of the desert. The unsettled operator was reduced to repeating his statement as a question. 'You committed the assault?'

'Yes, ma'am. Now, when you send that ambulance for Crocker, send an officer, too.'

'You're going to wait for our unit?'

'No, ma'am. But before the night's out, you'll arrest Crocker.'

'Isn't Mr. Crocker the victim?'

'He's my victim, yes. But he's a perpetrator in his own right. I know you're thinking it's me you'll want to be arresting, but trust me, it's Crocker. You also need to send another patrol car—'

'Sir, filing a false police report is—'

'I'm not a hoaxer, ma'am. I'm guilty of assault, phone theft, breaking a car window with a man's face – but I'm not into pranks.'

'With a man's face?'

'I didn't have a hammer. Listen, you also need to send a second patrol car and an ambulance to the Crocker residence out on . . .

Fallon Hill Road. I don't see a house number, but as small as this town is, you probably know the place.'

'You're going to be there?'

'No, ma'am. Who's out there is Crocker's elderly mother. Noreen, I think her name is. She's chained in the basement.'

'Chained in the basement?'

'She's been left in her own filth for a couple weeks now, and it's not a pretty situation.'

'You chained her in the basement?'

'No, ma'am. Crocker wrangled a power of attorney, and he's starving her to death while he gradually loots her bank accounts and sells off her belongings.'

'And where can we find you, sir?'

'Don't you worry about me, ma'am. You're going to have your hands full enough tonight.'

He pushed END, then switched the phone off and handed it to Jilly. 'Wipe it clean and throw it out the window.'

She used a Kleenex and disposed of it with the phone.

A mile later, he handed the keys to the Corvette to her, and she tossed those out the window, as well.

'It'd be ironic if we were stopped for littering,' she said.

'Where's Fred?'

'While I was waiting for you, I moved him into the cargo space, so I could have legroom.'

'You think he's okay back there?'

'I braced him between suitcases. He's solid.'

'I meant psychologically okay.'

'Fred's highly resilient.'

'You're pretty resilient yourself,' he said.

'It's an act. Who was the old cowboy?'

As he was about to answer her question, Dylan suffered a delayed reaction to the confrontation with Lucas Crocker and to the purity of evil that he'd experienced so intimately from contact with the wad of money. He felt as though clouds of frenzied moths swarmed within him, seeking a light they couldn't find.

Already he had driven through the dusty outskirts of Safford and into relatively flat land that in the night, at least, seemed almost as devoid of the human stain as it had been in the Mesozoic Era, tens of millions of years ago.

He pulled onto the shoulder of the highway and stopped. 'Give me a minute. I need to get . . . to get Crocker out of my head.'

When he closed his eyes, he found himself in a cellar, where an old woman lay in chains, caked with filth. With an artist's attention to minutiae and to the meaning of it, Dylan furnished the scene with baroque details as significant as they were disgusting.

He had never actually seen Lucas Crocker's mother when he had touched her son's dropped money in the parking lot. This cellar and this wretchedly abused woman were constructs of his imagination, and they most likely in no way resembled either the real cellar or the real Noreen Crocker.

Dylan didn't *see* things with his sixth sense, not any more than he heard or smelled or tasted them. He simply, instantly *knew* things. He touched an object rich with psychic spoor, and knowledge arose in his mind as though summoned from memory, as though he were recalling events that he had once read in a book. Thus far this knowledge had usually been the equivalent of a sentence or two of linked facts; at other times, it equaled paragraphs of information, pages.

Dylan opened his eyes, leaving the imagined Noreen Crocker in that squalid cellar even as the real woman might at this very moment be listening to the approaching sirens of her rescuers.

'You okay?' Jilly asked.

'I'm maybe not quite as resilient as Fred.'

She smiled. 'He's got the advantage of not having a brain.'

'Better get moving.' He popped the handbrake. 'Put some distance between ourselves and Safford.' He drove onto the two-lane highway. 'For all we know, the guys in the black Suburbans have a statewide alert out to law-enforcement agencies, asking to be informed of any unusual incidents.'

At Dylan's request, Jilly got an Arizona map out of the glove box and studied it with a penlight while he drove northwest.

North and south of them, the black teeth of different mountain ranges gnawed at the night sky, and as they traveled the intervening Gila River Valley here between those distant peaks, they seemed to be traversing the jaw span of a yawning leviathan.

'Seventy-eight miles to the town of Globe,' Jilly said. 'Then if you really think it's necessary to avoid the Phoenix area—'

'I really think it's necessary,' he said. 'I prefer not to be found charred beyond recognition in a burnt-out SUV.'

'At Globe, we'll have to turn north on Highway 60, take it all the way up to Holbrook, near the Petrified Forest. From there, we can pick up Interstate 40, west toward Flagstaff or east toward Gallup, New Mexico – if it matters which way we go.'

'Negative Jackson, vortex of pessimism. It'll matter.'

'Why?'

'Because by the time we get there, something will have happened to make it matter.'

'Maybe by the time we get up to Holbrook, we'll have gotten so good at positive thinking that we'll have thought ourselves into being billionaires. Then we'll go west and buy a mansion overlooking the Pacific.'

'Maybe,' he said. 'One thing I'm buying for sure, soon as the stores open in the morning, wherever we are.'

'What's that?'

'Gloves.'

22

Outside Globe, Arizona, past midnight, they stopped at a service station where the night man had almost finished closing. Nature had given him an unfortunately thin fox face, which he failed to enhance with a hedgehog haircut. In his twenties, he had the surly manner of a fourteen-year-old with a severe hormonal imbalance. According to the tag on his shirt, his name was SKIPPER.

Perhaps Skipper would have switched on the pumps again and would have filled the Expedition's tank if Dylan had offered a credit card, but no bookmaker in Vegas would have been naive enough to quote odds in favor of that outcome. At the mention of cash, however, his crafty eyes sharpened on the promise of an easy skim, and his poor attitude improved from surly to sullen.

Skipper turned on the pumps but not the exterior lights. In the dark, he filled the tank while Dylan and Jilly cleaned bug splatters and dust off the windshield and the tailgate glass, no more likely to offer assistance than he was likely to start reciting Shakespeare's sonnets with a perfect seventeenth-century English accent.

When Dylan caught Skipper watching Jilly with obvious lascivious interest, a low-grade fever of anger warmed his face. Then, with some surprise, he wondered when he'd become possessive of her – and why he thought he had any reason or right to be possessive.

They had known each other less than five hours. True, they had been subjected to great danger, enormous pressures, and consequently they had discovered more about each other's character than they might have learned during a long acquaintance under ordinary circumstances. Nevertheless, the only fundamental thing he knew about Jilly was that she could be depended upon in a pinch, that she did not back down. This wasn't a bad thing to know about anyone, but it wasn't a full portrait, either.

Or was it?

As he finished cleaning the windshield, angered by Skipper's leer, Dylan wondered if this one thing he knew about Jilly might be all he needed to know: She deserved his trust. Perhaps everything else that mattered in a relationship grew from trust – from a tranquil faith in the courage, integrity, and kindness of the other person.

He decided that he was losing his mind. The psychotropic *stuff* had affected his brain in more ways than he yet knew. Here he was thinking about committing his life to a woman who *already* thought he was a Disney comic book, all sugar and talking chipmunks.

They were not an item. They weren't even friends. You didn't make a true friend in mere hours. They were at most fellow survivors, victims of the same shipwreck, with a mutual interest in staying afloat and remaining alert for sharks.

Regarding Jilly Jackson, he wasn't feeling possessive. He was only *protective*, just as he felt toward Shep, just as he would feel toward a sister if he had one. Sister. Yeah, right.

By the time he accepted cash for the gasoline, Skipper brightened from surliness to sullenness to peevishness. Making no pretense of adding the currency to the station receipts, he tucked the money in his wallet with a pinched look of spiteful satisfaction.

The total had been thirty-four dollars; but Dylan paid with two twenties and suggested that the attendant keep the difference. He did not want the change, because those bills would carry Skipper's spoor.

He had been careful not to touch the fuel pumps or anything else on which the attendant might have left a psychic imprint. He didn't want to know the nature of Skipper's soul, didn't want to feel the texture of his mean life of petty thefts and petty hatreds.

Regarding the human race, Dylan was as much of an optimist as ever. He still liked people, but he'd had enough of them for one day.

~ ~ ~

Traveling north from Globe, through the Apache Mountains, with the San Carlos Indian Reservation to the east, Jilly gradually became aware that something had changed between her and Dylan

O'Conner. He wasn't relating to her quite as he had previously. He glanced away from the road more frequently than before, studying her in what he believed to be a surreptitious manner, and so she pretended not to notice. A new energy flowed between them, but she couldn't define it.

Finally she decided she was just tired, too exhausted and too stressed to trust her perceptions. After this eventful night, lesser mortals than Jillian Jackson, Southwest Amazon, might have lost their sanity altogether, so a little paranoia was nothing to worry about.

From Safford to Globe, Dylan had told her about the encounter with Lucas Crocker. He'd also recounted the story of Ben Tanner and his granddaughter, which revealed an application of his sixth sense that was more appealing than being drawn into the depraved psychotic worlds of people like Crocker and like Kenny of the Many Knives.

Now, as the lights of Globe receded, as Shep remained quietly engaged with *Great Expectations*, Jilly brought Dylan up to speed on the unsettling incident in the women's restroom at the restaurant.

At one of the sinks, as she'd washed her hands, she had looked up at the mirror and had seen a reflection of the bathroom that was accurate in every detail except one. Where the toilet stalls should have been, three dark wood confessionals stood instead; the carved crosses on the doors were brightened by gold leafing.

'I turned around to look directly, and there were only toilet stalls, as there should have been. But when I looked at the mirror again . . . the confessionals were still reflected in it.'

Rinsing her hands, unable to take her eyes off the mirror, she had been watching when the door of one of the confessionals slowly opened. A priest came out of the booth, not with a smile, not with a prayer book, but in a sliding heap, dead and drenched in blood.

'I got the hell out of the bathroom,' she said, shivering at the memory. 'But I can't turn this off, Dylan. These visions keep coming at me, and they *mean* something.'

'Visions,' he said. 'Not *mirages*?'

'I was in denial,' she admitted. She slipped one fingertip under the gauze pad of the Band-Aid that covered the point of injection in her arm, and she gently fingered the sore, slightly swollen puncture wound. 'But I'm not playing that game anymore. These are visions, all right. Premonitions.'

The first town ahead was Seneca, thirty miles away. Twenty-eight miles beyond Seneca lay Carrizo. Both were just wide spots in the road. Dylan was driving deeper into one of those many areas in the Southwest known separately and collectively as the Big Lonely.

'In my case,' he said, 'I seem to be making connections between people and places, regarding events that happened in the past or that are already underway in current time. But you think you're seeing some event in the future.'

'Yeah. An incident in a church somewhere. It's going to happen. And soon, I think. Murder. Mass murder. And somehow . . . we're going to be there when it goes down.'

'You see us there? In your visions?'

'No. But why else would these same images keep coming to me – the birds, the church, all of it? I'm not having premonitions about train wrecks in Japan, airplane crashes in South America, tidal waves in Tahiti. I'm seeing something in my own future, our future.'

'Then we don't go anywhere near a church,' Dylan said.

'Somehow . . . I think the church comes to us. I don't think there's any way we can avoid it.'

A rapid moonset left the night with none but starlight, and the Big Lonely seemed to get bigger, lonelier.

Dylan didn't pilot the Expedition as if it were a wingless jet, but he pushed it hard. He completed what should have been more than a three-hour drive in two and a half hours.

For a town of five thousand, Holbrook boasted an unusual number of motels. It provided the only convenient lodging for tourists who wanted to visit the Petrified Forest National Park or various Native American attractions at nearby Hopi and Navajo Indian reservations.

No five-star resorts were among the accommodations, but Dylan wasn't looking for amenities. All he wanted was a quiet place where the cockroaches were discreet.

He chose the motel farthest from service stations and other businesses likely to get noisy in the morning. At the registration counter, he presented a sleepy-eyed desk clerk with cash in advance, no credit card.

The clerk required a driver's license. Dylan was loath to give it, but refusal would arouse suspicion. He had already given an Arizona license-plate number, and not the one on the plates that he had stolen. Fortunately, the sleepy clerk seemed not to be intrigued by the apparent conflict between a California license and Arizona plates.

Jilly didn't want adjoining rooms. After all that had happened, even if they left the door open between rooms, she'd feel isolated.

They booked a single unit with two queen-size beds. Dylan and Shep would share one, and Jilly would take the other.

The usual decor of bold clashing patterns, calculated to conceal stains and wear, gave Dylan a faint case of motion sickness. He was bone tired, too, and grainy-eyed, suffering from a killer headache.

By 3:10 A.M., they had transferred the essential luggage to the room. Shep wanted to bring the Dickens novel, and Dylan noticed that although the boy had appeared to be absorbed in the book throughout the ride north, he was on the same page that he'd been reading in the restaurant, all the way back in Safford.

Jilly used the bathroom first, and when she came out, teeth brushed and ready for bed, she still wore street clothes. 'No pajamas tonight. I want to be ready to move fast.'

'Good idea,' Dylan decided.

Shep had responded to an evening of chaos and shattered routines with remarkable equanimity, so Dylan didn't want to push him further by making him forgo his customary sleepwear. One straw too many, and Shep might break out of his stoic silence into a hyperverbal mode, which could last for hours, ensuring that none of them got any sleep.

Besides, Shep wore pretty much the same thing in bed and out of it. His daytime wardrobe consisted of a collection of identical white T-shirts featuring Wile E. Coyote, and a collection of identical blue jeans. At night he put on a fresh Wile E. Coyote T-shirt and a pair of black pajama pants.

Seven years ago, in a state of hysterical despair over the decisions required to dress each morning, Shep had rebelled against a varied wardrobe. Thereafter, he would wear only jeans and Wile E.

The nature of his fascination with the infamous coyote was not clear. When in the mood for cartoon mayhem, he watched Road Runner videos for hours. Sometimes he laughed with delight; at other times, he followed the action as solemnly as though it were the moodiest of Swedish cinema; and on still other occasions, he watched quietly, with bottomless sorrow, tears sliding ceaselessly down his cheeks.

Shepherd O'Conner was an enigma wrapped in a mystery, but Dylan wasn't always sure that the mystery had a solution or that the enigma possessed any meaning. The great stone heads of Easter Island, as enigmatic as anything on earth, stared with mysterious purpose toward the sea, but they were stone inside as well as out.

After brushing his teeth twice and flossing twice, after washing his hands twice before toilet and twice after, Shep returned to the bedroom. He sat on the edge of the bed and took off his slippers.

'You're still wearing socks,' Dylan noted.

Shepherd always slept barefoot. But when Dylan knelt to remove the socks, the kid swung his legs into bed and pulled the covers up to his chin.

Deviations from routine were forced on Shep, always to his deep dismay; he never *chose* to make them.

Dylan worried, 'Are you all right, kiddo?'

Shepherd closed his eyes. There would be no communication on the issue of socks.

Maybe his feet were cold. The in-window air conditioner didn't cool the room evenly, but sent icy drafts chasing along the floor.

Maybe he was worried about germs. Germs on the carpet, germs on the bedclothes, but only germs that infected feet.

Maybe if you excavated around one of those Easter Island stone heads, you'd find the rest of a giant statue buried in the earth, and maybe when you revealed its feet, the statue would be wearing stone socks, for which an explanation would be as hard to come by as an explanation for Shep's new preference for bedtime footwear.

Dylan was too headachy and too wrung-out weary to care about what the psychotropic *stuff* might be doing in his brain, let alone to worry about Shepherd's socks. He took his turn in the bathroom, wincing at the haggard face that confronted him in the mirror.

∾ ∾ ∾

Jilly lay in her bed, staring at the ceiling.

Shep lay in his bed, staring at the backside of his eyelids.

The hum and rumble of the airconditioner, at first annoying, settled into a lulling white noise that would mask the bang of car doors and the voices of other guests who might rise with the dawn.

The air conditioner would also ensure that they could not hear the specific engine-noise pattern of a souped-up Suburban or the stealthy sounds of assassins preparing to storm their room.

For a while, Jilly tried to work up a little fear about their vulnerability, but in fact she felt safe in this place, for a while. Physically safe, anyway.

Without an urgent concern for her immediate safety, without active fear to distract her, she couldn't stave off a discouragement that came close to despair. Dylan believed they had a chance to track down Frankenstein's identity and learn the nature of the injections, but she didn't share his confidence.

For the first time in years, she wasn't in control of her life. She *needed* control. Otherwise, she felt as she had felt for too much of her childhood: weak, helpless, at the mercy of pitiless forces. She loathed being vulnerable. Accepting victimhood, taking refuge in it, was to her a mortal sin, yet it seemed now that she had no choice but acceptance.

Some psychotropic hoodoo elixir was at work in her brain, at work *on* her brain, which filled her with horror when she dared to think about it. She'd never done drugs, had never been drunk, because she valued her mind and didn't want to lose any significant number of brain cells. During all the years when she'd had nothing else, she'd had her intelligence, her wit, her rich imagination. Jilly's mind had been a formidable weapon against the world and a refuge from cruelty, from adversity. If eventually she developed the gluteus muchomega that plagued the women in her family, if her ass grew so fat that she had to be driven everywhere on a flatbed truck, she had always figured that she'd still have her mind and all the satisfactions of that inner life. But now a worm crawled through her brain, not a worm in the literal sense, perhaps, but a worm of change, and she could not know what would be left of her or even *who* she might be when the worm of change had finished remaking her.

Although earlier she had been exhilarated when she and Dylan had dealt with the murderous Kenny and Becky, she could not get in touch again with the fine sense of empowerment that for a while had lifted her. Concerned about the oncoming violence foreseen in visions, she could not convince herself that the gift of clairvoyance might again help her to save others – or that it might, in time, leave her more in control of her destiny than she had ever been before.

Negative Jackson. She'd never had much faith in other people, but she'd long had an abiding faith in herself. Dylan had been right about that. But her faith in herself began to desert her.

From his bed, Shepherd whispered, 'Here, there.'

'What is it, sweetie?'

'Here, there.'

Jilly raised herself on one elbow.

Shep lay on his back, eyes closed. Anxiety pleated his forehead.

'Are you okay, Shepherd?'

'Shep is scared,' he whispered.

'Don't be scared.'

'Shep is scared.'

'We're safe here, now, for a while,' she assured him. 'Nobody can hurt you.'

His lips moved, as though he were speaking, but no sound issued from him.

Shepherd was not as big as his brother, but he was bigger than Jilly, a full-grown man, yet he seemed small beneath the sheets. Hair tousled, mouth pinched in a grimace of fear, he looked childlike.

A pang of sympathy pierced her when she realized that Shepherd had lived twenty years without any meaningful control over his life. Worse, his need for routine, the limits he put on what he would wear, his elaborate rules about food: All these things and more revealed a desperate need to establish a sense of dominion wherever possible.

His silence held. His lips stopped moving. The fear did not fade from his face, but it settled into softer lines, as if mellowing from acute fright to chronic dismay.

Jilly settled back upon her pillow, grateful that she had not been born in a trap as inescapable as Shep's, but she also worried that by the time the worm of change finished with her, she might be more like Shep than not.

A moment later, Dylan came out of the bathroom. He'd taken off his shoes, which he put beside the bed that he would share with his brother.

'You okay?' he asked Jilly.

'Yeah. Just . . . burnt out.'

'God, I'm sludge.'

Fully clothed, ready for an emergency, he got into bed, lay staring at the ceiling, but did not turn out the nightstand lamp.

After a silence, he said, 'I'm sorry.'

Jilly turned her head to look at him. 'Sorry about what?'

'Maybe from the motel on, I've done all the wrong things.'

'Such as?'

'Maybe we should've gone to the police, taken a chance. You were right when you said we can't run forever. I've got an obligation to think for Shep, but I've no right to drag you down with us.'

'Accountable O'Conner,' she said, 'vortex of responsibility. As broody as Batman. Call DC Comics, quick.'

'I'm serious.'

'I know. It's endearing.'

Still staring at the ceiling, he smiled. 'I said a lot of things to you tonight that I wish I hadn't said.'

'You had provocation. I made you nuts. And I said worse things. Listen . . . it just makes me crazy to have to depend on anyone. And . . . especially on men. So this situation, it pushes all my buttons.'

'Why especially men?'

She turned away from him to gaze at the ceiling. 'Let's say your dad walks out on you when you're three years old.'

After a silence, he encouraged her: 'Let's say.'

'Yeah. Let's say your mother, she's this beauty, this angel, this hero who's always there for you, and nothing bad should ever happen to her. But he beats her up so bad before he goes that she loses one eye and walks with two canes the rest of her life.'

Though weary and in need of sleep, he had the grace to wait for her to tell it at her own pace.

Eventually, she said, 'He leaves you to the miseries of welfare and the contempt of government social workers. Bad enough. But then a couple times each year, he'd visit for a day, two days.'

'Police?'

'Mom was afraid to call them when he showed up. The bastard said if she turned him in, when he got bail, then he'd come back and take her other eye. And one of mine. He would have done it, too.'

'Once he'd walked out, why come back at all?'

'To keep us scared. Keep us down. And he expected a share of her welfare money. And we always had it for him because we ate a lot of dinners free at the church kitchen. Most of our clothes came without charge from the church thrift shop. So Daddy always got his share.'

Her father rose in her memory, standing at the apartment door, smiling that dangerous smile. And his voice: *Come to collect the eye insurance, baby girl. You got the eye-insurance premium?*

'Enough about that,' she told Dylan. 'This isn't meant to be a pity party. I just wanted you to understand it isn't you I've got a problem with. It's just . . . being dependent on anyone.'

'You didn't owe me an explanation.'

'But there it is.' Her father's face persisted in memory, and she knew that even as tired as she was, she wouldn't sleep until she had exorcised it. '*Your* dad must have been great.'

He sounded surprised. 'Why do you say that?'

'The way you are with Shep.'

'My dad raised venture capital to help high-tech entrepreneurs start up new companies. He worked eighty-hour weeks. He might've been a great guy, but I never spent enough time with him to know. He got in some deep financial problems. So two days before Christmas, near sunset, he drove to this beach parking lot with a great view of the Pacific. Cold day. No swimmers, no surfers. He connected a hose to the tailpipe, put the other end into the car through a window. Then he got in behind the wheel and also took an overdose of Nembutal. He was thorough, my dad. Always a backup plan. He went out with one of the most spectacular sunsets of the year. Shep and I watched it from the hill behind our house, miles away from that beach, and of course we didn't know he was watching it, too, and dying.'

'When was this?'

'I was fifteen. Shep was five. Almost fifteen years ago.'

'That's hard,' she said.

'Yeah. But I wouldn't trade you situations.'

'So where did you learn?'

'Learn what?'

'To take such good care of Shep.'

He switched off the lamp. In the darkness, he said, 'From my mom. She died young, too. She was great, so tender with Shep. But sometimes you can learn the right lesson from a bad example, too.'

'I guess so.'

'No need to guess. Look at yourself.'

'Me? I'm all screwed up,' she said.

'Name me someone who isn't.'

Trying to think of a name to give him, she eventually drifted into sleep.

The first time that she woke, rising out of a dreamless bliss, she heard Dylan snoring softly.

The room was cold. The air conditioner had shut off.

She had not been awakened by Dylan's snoring, but perhaps by Shepherd's voice. Three whispered words: 'Shep is scared.'

Judging by the direction from which his voice arose, she thought he was still in bed.

'Shep is scared.'

'Shep is brave,' she whispered in reply.

'Shep is scared.'

'Shep is brave.'

Shepherd fell silent, and when the silence held, Jilly found sleep again.

When next she woke, she heard Dylan still snoring softly, but fingers of sunshine pried at every edge of the blackout drapes, not the thinner light of dawn, but the harsher glare of midmorning sun.

She became aware of another light, arising from beyond the half-open bathroom door. A bloody radiance.

Her first thought was *fire*, but even as she bolted out of bed, with that word stuck in her throat, she realized that this was not the flickering light of flames, but something quite different.

23

Shaken out of dreams, Dylan sat up, stood up, into his shoes, before he was fully conscious, like a firefighter so trained in the routine of an alarm response that he could answer the firehouse bell and shrug into his turnout coat while still asleep, and then wake up sliding down the pole.

According to the travel clock on the nightstand, the morning had crept around to 9:12, and according to Jilly, they had trouble, a message she conveyed to him not in words but in a look, her eyes wide and shining with worry.

Dylan saw first that Shep wasn't in bed, wasn't anywhere in the motel room.

Then he noticed the fiery glow beyond the half-closed bathroom door. Fiery but not fire. The hellfire-red of a nightmare, scarlet ocher overlaid on aniline black. An orange-red, muddy-red radiance with the bristle-at-your-eyes texture of the light in a nocturnal scene shot with infrared film. The dire-red, hungry-red glow in the eyes of a night-hunting snake. This had all of those qualities, but none of them adequately described it, because it defied description and would defy his talent if ever he tried to render it on canvas.

The bathroom had no windows. This couldn't simply be morning sun filtered through a colorful curtain. The standard fluorescent fixture above the sink couldn't produce such an eerie shine.

How odd that mere light could instantly make his gut clench, his chest tighten, and his heart gallop. Here was a peculiar luminosity that appeared nowhere in nature, that was not quite like anything he had seen before in the works of man, either, and therefore it snagged at every fiber of superstition in the fabric of his soul.

As he drew near the bathroom, he discovered that when this glow touched him, he was able to *feel* it, and not merely as he would have felt the heat of the summer sun when stepping out of the shade of a tree. This light seemed to *crawl* on his skin, to bustle like hundreds of ants, initially on his face as he first stepped into the wedge of outfalling brightness, but then more busily on his right hand as he put it against the door.

Although Jilly, at his side, remained less directly illuminated than Dylan, her face had a faint red sheen. With one glance, he saw that she, too, experienced the extraordinary tactility of this light. With a start and with a little grimace of revulsion, she wiped at her face with one hand, as though she had walked into the clingy spokes and spirals of a spider's web.

Dylan wasn't a science buff, except as knowledge in the fields of biology and botany served to improve the accuracy of his depiction of the natural world in his paintings, and he didn't qualify as even an armchair physicist. But he knew that deadly types of radiation, including that from a nuclear bomb, never stimulated the sense of touch, just as the less mortal X-rays administered in a dentist's office never caused the slightest tingle when passing through your jaw; the survivors of the historic blast in Hiroshima, who later died of radiation poisoning, had never felt the many billions of subatomic particles piercing their bodies.

Although he doubted that the flesh-prickling effect of the light represented a danger, he hesitated anyway. He might have pulled the door shut, might have turned away, leaving his curiosity unsatisfied, if Shep had not been on the other side and perhaps in need of help.

When he spoke his brother's name, he didn't receive a reply. This came as no surprise. While Shep was more talkative than your average stone, he often proved no more *responsive* than granite. Dylan called out again, and pushed open the door after the second silence.

He was prepared for the sight of the shower stall. The toilet, too. The sink, the mirror, the towel rack.

What Dylan had not been prepared for, what caused his adrenal gland to squirt another dose of epinephrine into his bloodstream, what caused his guts to tweak in a less than pleasant fashion was the doorway in the wall beside the sink, where earlier no door had been. The source of the strange red light lay beyond this postern.

Hesitantly, he crossed the threshold into the bathroom.

Doorway didn't accurately convey the nature of this mysterious opening. It wasn't rectangular, but round, like a hatch in a bulkhead between two compartments in a submarine. *Hatch* didn't qualify as the *mot juste*, either, because no architrave surrounded the hole in the wall.

Indeed, the six-foot-diameter opening itself appeared to lack depth, as though it had been painted on the wall. No header, no jamb, no threshold. And yet the scene beyond appeared convincingly three-dimensional: a radiant red tunnel dwindling to a disc of blue light.

Dylan had seen masterpieces of trompe l'oeil in which artists, relying on nothing more than paint and their talent, had created illusions of space and depth that completely deceived the eye. This, however, was not merely a clever painting.

For one thing, the murky red glow from the luminous walls of the tunnel penetrated to the motel bathroom. This queer light glimmered in the vinyl floor, reflected off the mirror – and *crawled* on his exposed skin.

Furthermore, those tunnel walls ceaselessly turned, as if this were a passage in a carnival funhouse, a sideshow monkey barrel in which to test your balance. Trompe l'oeil painting could produce the illusion of depth, texture, and reality – but it could not provide an illusion of motion.

Jilly stepped into the bathroom beside Dylan.

He placed a restraining hand on her shoulder.

Together they marveled at the tunnel, which appeared to be at least thirty feet long.

Impossible, of course. Another motel unit backed up to this one; plumbing-to-plumbing design saved construction costs. A hole cut in the wall would reveal only another bathroom identical to theirs. Not a tunnel, never a tunnel. There was nothing to bore a tunnel *through*; the bathroom had not been built into the side of a mountain.

Nonetheless, a tunnel. He closed his eyes. Opened them. Tunnel. Six feet in diameter. Glowing, revolving.

Welcome to the monkey barrel. Buy a ticket, test your balance.

In fact, someone had already entered the barrel. Silhouetted against a disc of azure light, a man stood at the far end of the passageway.

Dylan had no doubt that the distant figure was Shep. Out there past the terminus of the tunnel, his back to them, Shepherd gazed into the blue beyond.

So if under Dylan the floor seemed to shift, if he felt that he might drop through a hole into a shaft as deep as eternity, this was not an associated effect of the tunnel. This was just a psychological response to the sudden perception that reality, as he'd always known it, was less stable than he had assumed.

Breathing hard, exhaling words in a hot rush, Jilly sought an explanation for the impossible: 'The hell with this, the hell with it, I'm not awake, I can't be awake.'

'You're awake.'

'You're probably part of the dream.'

'This isn't a dream,' he said, sounding shakier than she did.

'Yeah, right, not a dream – that's exactly what you'd say if you were part of the dream.'

He had put a restraining hand on her shoulder not because he feared that she would rush forward into the tunnel, but because he half expected that she would be swept into it against her will. The revolving walls suggested a whirlpool that might inexorably swallow anyone who ventured too close to the mouth of it. Second by second, however, his fear of a cyclone suction receded.

'What's happening,' she asked, 'what is this, what the *hell* is this?'

Not a whisper of sound issued from the realm beyond the wall. The turning surface of the tunnel looked as though it ought to be emitting a noisy scrape and rumble, or at least the liquid sound of churning magma, but it revolved in absolute silence.

No air escaped the opening, neither a breath of heat nor the faintest cool draft. No scent, either. Only the light.

Dylan moved closer to the portal.

'Don't,' Jilly worried.

At the brink, he tried first to examine the transition point between the bathroom wall and the entrance to the tunnel, but the junction of the two proved to be . . . fuzzy . . . a blur that would not resolve into concrete detail no matter how hard he squinted at it. In fact, his hackles rose and his gaze repeatedly slid away from the joint line as though some deep primitive part of him knew that by looking too directly at such a thing, he would risk glimpsing a secret kingdom of fearsome entities behind the veil of this world, beings that operated the machinery of the universe itself, and that such a sight invited instant madness.

When he'd been thirteen, fourteen, he'd read H. P. Lovecraft and thrilled to those macabre tales. Now he couldn't shake the unnerving feeling that Lovecraft had written more truth than fiction.

Abandoning an attempt to examine the point of transition between bathroom and tunnel, he stood at the brink and squinted at a spot on the revolving walls, trying to determine the nature of the material, its solidity. On closer study, the passage seemed to be formed from shining mist, or maybe he was peering along a tunnel of pure energy; this was not unlike a god's-eye view down the funnel of a tornado.

Tentatively, he placed his right hand on the wall beside the mysterious gateway. The painted sheetrock felt slightly warm and gratifyingly normal.

Sliding his hand to the left, across the bathroom wall, toward the opening, he hoped to be able to *feel* the point of transition from motel to tunnel and to understand how the connection was made. But as his hand slid off the sheetrock and into the apparently open doorway, he detected no details of structure, nothing but a coldness – and also the red light crawling more vigorously than ever across his upraised palm.

'No, don't, *no!*' Jilly warned.

'No, what?'

'No, don't go in there.'

'I'm not going in there.'

'You look like you're going in there.'

'Why would I go in there?'

'After Shep.'

'No way am I going in there.'

'You'd jump off a cliff after Shep.'

'I wouldn't jump off a cliff,' he impatiently assured her.

'You'd jump off a cliff,' she insisted. 'Hope to catch him on the way down, hope to carry him down into a haystack. You'd jump, all right.'

He just wanted to test the reality of the scene before him, to confirm that indeed it had true dimension, that it was a gateway and not just a window, an actual entry point to some otherworldly place rather than merely a view of it. Then he would retreat and think over the situation, try to arrive at a logical course of action with which to approach this monumentally illogical development.

Firmly pressing his right hand against the plane where the wall should have been, he discovered no sheetrock underlying the image of the tunnel, encountered no resistance whatsoever. He reached out of the bathroom, into that forbidding other realm, where the air proved to be icy, and where the baleful light squirmed over and around his fingers not like hundreds of ants any longer, but like thousands of hard-shell beetles that might strip the flesh from his bones.

If he'd allowed himself to be guided by instinct, he would have withdrawn his hand at once; but he believed that he needed to explore this incredible situation more fully. He reached farther through the gateway, extending his hand in there to the wrist, and although he winced at the bitter cold, was nearly overwhelmed by revulsion at the hideous crawly sensation, he reached in still farther, all the way to his elbow, and then, of course, as instinct might have warned him if he had been listening, the tunnel *took* him.

24

Dylan didn't walk the length of the tunnel, didn't run, didn't tumble, didn't fly through it, had no sense of being in transit, but went from the motel bathroom to Shep's side in an instant. He felt his shoes slip off the vinyl tiles and simultaneously bite into soft earth, and when he looked down, he discovered that he was standing in knee-high grass.

His abrupt arrival stirred scores of tiny midges into spiraling flight from the golden-brown grass, which appeared crisp from months of summer heat. A few startled grasshoppers leaped for safety.

Upon touchdown, Dylan explosively spoke his brother's name – '*Shep!*' – but Shepherd didn't acknowledge his arrival.

Even as Dylan registered that he stood upon a hilltop, under a blue sky, on a warm day, in a mild breeze, he turned from the vista that fascinated Shepherd and looked back where he expected the tunnel to be. Instead, he found a six-foot-diameter view of Jillian Jackson standing in the motel bathroom, not at the end of the red passageway, but immediately in front of him, as though she were a foot from him, as though he were looking at her through a round window that had no frame.

From the bathroom, Shepherd had appeared to be standing far away, a fragile silhouette against blue light. Viewed from this end, however, Jilly loomed life-size. Yet Dylan knew at once that from where she stood, the woman perceived him as a tiny figure at Shep's side, for she leaned toward the tunnel entrance where he himself had so recently stood, and she squinted worriedly at him, straining to see his distant face.

Her mouth opened, her lips moved. Perhaps she called his name, but though she appeared to be only inches from him, Dylan couldn't hear her, not even faintly.

The view of the bathroom, floating like a huge bubble here on the hilltop, disoriented him. He grew lightheaded. The land seemed to slide under him as though it were a sea, and he felt that he had been shanghaied by a dream.

He wanted to step at once out of the dry grass and back into the motel, for in spite of the fact that he had arrived on this hilltop physically intact, he feared that he must nevertheless have left some vital part of himself back there, some essential thread of mind or spirit, without which he'd soon unravel.

Instead, propelled by curiosity, he moved around the gateway, wondering what side view it presented. He discovered that the portal wasn't in the least similar either to a window or a bubble, but more resembled a giant coin balanced on edge. From the side, it had the narrow profile of a dime, though it lacked the serrations to be found on the milled edges of most coins. The thin silvery line, arcing out of the sun-browned grass and all but vanishing against the backdrop of bright blue sky, might in fact have been narrower than the edge of a dime, hardly more than a filament, as though this gate were but a disc as translucent and thin as the membrane of a fly's wing.

Dylan waded through grass all the way around to the back of the portal, out of sight of his brother.

Viewed from a point 180 degrees opposite his first position, the gateway offered the identical sight as from the front. The shabby motel bathroom. Jilly anxiously leaning forward – squinting, worried.

Not being within sight of Shep made Dylan nervous. He quickly continued around the gate to the point at his brother's side from which he had begun this inspection.

Shep stood as Dylan had left him: arms hanging slackly at his sides, head cocked to the right, gazing west and down upon a familiar vista. His wistful smile expressed both melancholy and pleasure.

Rolling hills mantled in golden grass lay to the north and south, here and there graced by widely separated California live oaks that cast long morning shadows, and this particular hill rolled down to a long meadow. West of the meadow stood a Victorian house with an expansive back porch. Beyond the house: more lush meadows, a gravel driveway leading to a highway that followed the coastline.

A quarter of a mile to the west of those blacktop lanes, the Pacific Ocean, a vast mirror, took the color of the sky and condensed it into a deeper and more solemn blue.

Miles north of Santa Barbara, California, on a lightly populated stretch of coast, half a mile from the nearest neighbor, this was the house in which Dylan had grown up. In this place, their mother had died more than ten years ago, and to this place, Dylan and Shep still returned between their long road trips to arts festival after arts festival across the West and Southwest.

'This is nuts!' His frustration burst from him in those three words much the way *This sucks!* might have erupted from him if he'd learned that his lottery ticket had missed the hundred-million-dollar prize by one digit, and as *Ouch!* or something more rude might have passed his lips if he'd hit his thumb with a hammer. He was confused, he was scared, and because his head might have exploded if he'd stood here as silent as Shep, he said again, 'This is nuts!'

Miles farther north, in the deserted parking lot of a state beach, their father had committed suicide fifteen years ago. From this hill, unaware that their lives were soon to change, Dylan and Shep had watched the spectacular December sunset that their dad had viewed through a haze of Nembutal and carbon-monoxide poisoning as he had settled into an everlasting sleep.

They were hundreds of miles from Holbrook, Arizona, where they had gone to bed.

'Nuts, this is nuts,' he expanded, 'totally, fully nuts with a nut filling and more nuts on top.'

Warm sunshine, fresh air faintly scented by the sea, crickets singing in the dry grass: As much as it might feel like a dream, all of it was real.

Ordinarily, Dylan would not have turned to his brother for the answer to any mystery. Shepherd O'Conner wasn't a source of answers, not a wellhead of clarifying insights. Shep was instead a bubbling font of confusion, a gushing fountain of enigmas, a veritable geyser of mysteries.

In this instance, however, if he didn't turn to Shepherd, he might as well seek answers from the crickets in the grass, from the fairy midges that swooned through the day on lazy currents of sun-warmed air.

'Shep, are you listening to me?'

Shep smiled a half-sorrowful smile at the house below them.

'Shep, I need you to be with me now. Talk to me now. Shep, I need you to tell me how you got here.'

'Almond,' Shep said, 'filbert, peanut, walnut—'

'Don't do this, Shep.'

'—black walnut, beechnut, butternut—'

'This isn't acceptable, Shep.'

'—cashew, Brazil nut—'

Dylan stepped in front of his brother, seized him firmly by the shoulders, shook him to get his attention. 'Shep, look at me, see me, be with me. How did you get here?'

'—coconut, hickory nut—'

Shaking his brother harder, violently enough to make the litany of nuts stutter out of the boy, Dylan said, 'That's it, enough, no more of this shit, *no more!*'

'—chestnut, kola nut—'

Dylan let go of Shep's shoulders, clasped his hands around his brother's face, holding his head in a ten-finger vice. 'Don't you hide from me, don't you pull your usual crap, not with *this* going on, Shep, not now.'

'—pistachio, pine nut.'

Although Shepherd strove mightily to keep his chin down, Dylan relentlessly forced his brother's head up. 'Listen to me, talk to me, *look at me!*'

Muscled into a confrontation, Shepherd closed his eyes. 'Acorn, betel nut—'

Ten years of frustration, ten years of patience and sacrifice, ten years of vigilance to prevent Shep from unintentionally hurting himself, thousands of days of shaping food into neat rectangular and square morsels, uncounted hours of worrying about what would happen to Shepherd if fate conspired to have him outlive his brother: All of these things and so many more had pressed on Dylan, each a great psychological stone, had piled one atop another, atop another, dear God, until he felt crushed by the cumulative weight, until he could no longer say with any sincerity, *He ain't heavy, he's my brother*, because Shepherd was heavy, all right, a burden immeasurable, heavier than the boulder that Sisyphus had been condemned forever to roll up a long dark hill in Hades, heavier than the world on the back of Atlas.

'—pecan, litchi nut—'

Pressed between Dylan's big hands, Shepherd's features were scrunched together, puckered and pouted like those of a baby about to burst into tears, and his speech was distorted.

'—almond, cashew, walnut—'

'You're repeating yourself now,' Dylan said angrily. 'Always repeating yourself. Day after day, week after week, the maddening routine, year after year, always the same clothes, the narrow little list of crap you'll eat, always washing your hands twice, always nine minutes under the shower, never eight, never ten, always precisely nine, and all your life with your head bowed, staring at your shoes, always the same stupid fears, the same maddening tics and twitches, deedle-doodle-deedle, always the endless repetition, the endless *stupid* repetition!'

'—filbert, coconut, peanut—'

With the index finger of his right hand, Dylan attempted to lift the lid of his brother's left eye, tried to pry it open. 'Look at me, Shep, look at me, look, look.'

'—chestnut, hickory nut—'

Although standing with his arms slack at his sides and offering no other resistance, Shep squeezed his eyes shut, foiling Dylan's insistent finger.

'—butternut, Brazil nut—'

'Look at me, you little shit!'

'—kola nut, pistachio—'

'LOOK AT ME!'

Shep stopped resisting, and his left eye flew open, with the lid pressed almost to his eyebrow under the tip of Dylan's finger. Shep's one-eyed stare, as direct a moment of contact as ever he'd made with his brother, was an image suitable for any horror-movie poster: the essence of terror, the look of the victim just before the alien from another world rips his throat open, just before the zombie tears his heart out, just before the lunatic psychiatrist trepans his skull and devours his brain with a good Cabernet.

LOOK AT ME . . . LOOK AT ME . . . Look at me . . .

Dylan heard those three words echoing back from the surrounding hills, decreasing in volume with each repetition, and though he knew that he was listening to his own furious shout, the voice sounded like that of a stranger, hard and sharp with a steely anger of which Dylan would have thought himself incapable, but also cracking with a fear that he recognized too well.

One eye tight shut, the other popped to the max, Shepherd said, 'Shep is scared.'

They were looking at each other now, just like Dylan had wanted, eye to eye, a direct and uncompromising connection. He felt pierced by his brother's panicked stare, as breathless as if his lungs had been punctured, and his heart clenched in pain as though skewered by a needle.

'Shep is s-s-scared.'

The kid was scared, sure enough, flat-out terrified, no denying that, perhaps more frightened than he'd ever been in twenty years of frequent bouts of fright. And while but a moment ago he might have been afraid of the radiant tunnel by which he had traveled in a blink from the eastern Arizona desert to the California coast, his alarm now arose from another cause: his brother, who in an instant had become a stranger to him, a shouting and abusive stranger, as though the sun had played a moon trick, transforming Dylan from a man into a vicious wolf.

'Sh-shep is scared.'

Horrified by the expression of dread with which his brother regarded him, Dylan withdrew his pinning finger from Shep's arched eyelid, let go of the kid's head, and stepped back, shaking with self-disgust, remorse.

'Shep is scared,' the kid said, both eyes open wide.

'I'm sorry, Shep.'

'Shep is scared.'

'I'm so sorry. I didn't mean to scare you, buddy. I didn't mean what I said, not any of it, forget all that.'

Shepherd's shocked-wide eyelids lowered. He let his shoulders slump, too, and bowed his head and cocked it to one side, assuming the meek demeanor and the awkward posture with which he announced to the world that he was harmless, the humble pose that he hoped would allow him to shuffle through life without calling attention to himself, without inviting any notice from dangerous people.

The kid hadn't forgotten the confrontation this quickly. He was still plenty scared. He hadn't gotten over his hurt feelings, either, not in a wink; he might never get over them. Shepherd's sole defense in every situation, however, was to mimic a turtle: quickly pull all the vulnerable parts under the shell, hunker down, hide in the armor of indifference.

'I'm sorry, bro. I don't know what got into me. No. No, that isn't true. I know exactly what got into me. The old jimjams, the whimwhams, the old boogeyman bitin' on my bones. I got scared, Shep. Hell, I *am* scared, so scared I can't think straight. And I don't like being scared, don't like it one bit. It's not something I'm used to, and so I took my frustration out on you, and I never should've done that.'

Shepherd shifted his weight from left foot to right, right foot to left. The expression with which he stared at his Rockports wasn't difficult to read. He didn't appear to be terrified anymore – anxious, yes, but at least not electrified with fright. Instead he seemed to be startled, as though surprised that anything could scare his big brother.

Dylan peered past Shepherd to the magical round gateway, at the motel bathroom for which he would never have imagined that he could feel a nostalgic yearning as intense as what swelled in his heart at this moment.

One hand visored over her eyes, squinting the length of the red tunnel, clearer to Dylan than he must be to her, Jilly looked terrified. He hoped that she remained more frightened of reaching into the tunnel than of being left behind and alone, because her arrival here on the hilltop could only complicate matters.

He poured out further effusive apologies to Shepherd, until he realized that too many mea culpas could be worse than none at all. He was salving his own conscience at the cost of making his brother nervous, essentially poking at Shep in his shell. The kid shifted more agitatedly from one foot to the other.

'Anyway,' Dylan said, 'the stupid thing is, I shouted at you because I wanted you to tell me how you got here – but I already knew somehow you must have done it yourself, some new wild talent of your own. I don't understand the mechanics of what you've done. Even you probably don't grasp the mechanics of it any more than I understand how I feel a psychic trace on a door handle, how I read the spoor. But I knew the rest of what must've happened before I asked.'

With an effort, Dylan silenced himself. The surest way to calm Shepherd was to stop jabbering at him, stop overloading him with sensory input, grant him a little quiet.

In the barest breath of ocean-scented breeze, the grass stirred as languidly as seaweed in deep watery gardens. Gnats nearly as tiny as dust motes circled lazily through the air.

High in the summer sky, a hawk glided on thermal currents, in search of field mice three hundred feet below.

At a distance, traffic on the coast highway raised a susurration so faint that even the feeble breeze sometimes erased the sound. When the growl of a single engine rose out of the background murmur, Dylan shifted his attention from the hunting hawk to the graveled driveway and saw a motorcycle approaching his house.

The Harley belonged to Vonetta Beesley, the housekeeper who came once a week, whether Dylan and Shep were in residence or not. During inclement weather, she drove a supercharged Ford pickup perched high on fifty-four-inch-diameter tires and painted like a crimson dragon.

Vonetta was a fortyish woman with the winning personality and the recreational interests of many a Southern good old boy. A superb housekeeper and a first-rate cook, she had the strength and the guts – and would most likely be delighted – to serve as a bodyguard in a pinch.

The hilltop lay so far behind and above the house that Vonetta would not be able to identify Dylan and Shep at this distance. If she noticed them, however, and if she found them to be suspicious, she might take the Harley off-trail and come up here for a closer look. Concern for her own safety would not be an issue, and she would be motivated both by a sense of duty and a taste for adventure.

Maybe Dylan could concoct a half-assed story to explain what he and his brother were doing here when they were supposed to be on the road in New Mexico, but he didn't have the talent for deception or the time to craft a story to explain the gateway, the motel bathroom here on the hill, and Jilly peering cluelessly out at them as though she were Alice unsuccessfully attempting to scope the nature of the enchanted realm on the far side of the looking glass.

He turned to his little brother, prepared to risk agitating the kid anew by suggesting that the time had come to return to Holbrook, Arizona.

Before Dylan could speak, Shepherd said, 'Here, there.'

Dylan was reminded of the men's restroom at the restaurant in Safford, the previous evening. *Here* had referred to stall number one. *There* had referred to stall number four. Shep's first jaunt had been short, toilet to toilet.

Dylan recalled no eerie red radiance on that occasion. Perhaps because Shep had closed the gateway behind him as soon as he'd passed through it.

'Here, there,' Shep repeated.

Head lowered, Shep looked up from under his brow, not at Dylan but at the house below the hill, beyond the meadow, and at Vonetta on the Harley.

'What're you trying to say, Shep?'

'Here, there.'

'Where is there?'

'Here,' said Shep, scuffing the grass with his right foot.

'And where is here?'

'There,' said Shep, tucking his head down farther and turning it to the right, peering back past his shoulder toward Jilly.

'Can we go back where we started,' Dylan urged.

On her motorcycle, Vonetta Beesley followed the driveway around the house to the detached garage.

'Here, there,' Shep said.

'How do we get back to the motel safely?' Dylan asked. 'Just reach in from this end, just step into the gateway?'

He worried that if he went through the portal first and found himself back in the motel, Shep wouldn't follow him.

'Here, there. There, here,' said Shep.

On the other hand, if Shep made the return trip first, the gate might immediately close up after him, stranding Dylan in California until he could get back to Holbrook, Arizona, by conventional means, thus requiring Jilly to fend for herself and the kid in the meantime.

Common sense insisted that everything strange happening to them came out of Frankenstein's syringes. Therefore, Shepherd must have been injected and must have acquired the power to open the gate. He found it, activated it. Or more likely he created it. Consequently, in a sense, the gate operated according to Shep's rules, which were unknown and unknowable, which meant that traveling by means of the gate was like playing poker with the devil using an unconventional deck of cards with three additional suits and a whole new court of royals between jack and queen.

Vonetta brought the Harley to a stop near the garage. The engine swallowed its growl.

Dylan was reluctant to take Shepherd's hand and plunge together into the gateway. If they had come to California by teleportation – and what else but teleportation could explain this? – if each of them had been instantaneously deconstructed into megatrillions of fellow-traveling atomic particles upon falling out of the motel bathroom and had then been perfectly reconstructed upon emerging onto this hilltop, they might find it necessary or at least wise to make such a journey one at a time, to avoid . . . commingling their assets. Dylan had seen the old movie *The Fly*, in which a teleporting scientist had undertaken a short trip from one end of his laboratory to the other, hardly farther than Shepherd's toilet-to-toilet experiment, unaware that a lowly housefly accompanied him, resulting in disaster on a scale usually achieved only by politicians. Dylan didn't want to wind up back at the motel wearing Shepherd's nose on his forehead or with Shepherd's thumb bristling from one of his eye sockets.

'Here, there. There, here,' Shep repeated.

Behind the house, Vonetta put down the kickstand. She climbed off the Harley.

'No here. No there. Herethere,' Shep said, making a single noun from two. 'Herethere.'

They were actually conducting a conversation. Dylan had only the dimmest understanding of what Shepherd might be trying to tell him; however, for once he felt certain that his brother was listening to him and that what Shep said was in direct response to the questions that were asked.

With this in mind, Dylan sprang to the most important question pending: 'Shep, do you remember the movie *The Fly*?'

Head still lowered, Shep nodded. '*The Fly*. Released to theaters in 1958. Running time – ninety-four minutes.'

'That's not important, Shep. Trivia isn't what I'm after. What

I want to know is do you remember what happened to the scientist?'

Far below them, standing beside the motorcycle, Vonetta Beesley took off her crash helmet.

'The cast included Mr. David Hedison as the scientist. Miss Patricia Owens, Mr. Vincent Price—'

'Shep, don't do this.'

'—and Mr. Herbert Marshall. Directed by Mr. Kurt Neumann who also directed *Tarzan and the Leopard Woman*—'

Here was the kind of conversation that Dylan called *Shepspeak*. If you were willing to participate, involving yourself in patient give-and-take, you could spend an entertaining half-hour together before you reached data overload. Shep had memorized prodigious quantities of arcane information about subjects that were of particular interest to him, and sometimes he enjoyed sharing it.

'—*Son of Ali Baba, Return of the Vampire*—'

Vonetta hung her helmet from the handlebars of the bike, peered up at the hawk that circled to the east of her, and then spotted Shep and Dylan high on the hill.

'—*It Happened in New Orleans, Mohawk,* and *Rocketship X-M* among others.'

'Shep, listen, let's get back to the scientist. You remember the scientist got into a teleportation booth—'

'*The Fly* was remade as *The Fly* in 1986.'

'—and there was a fly in the booth too—'

'Running time of this remade version—'

'—but the scientist didn't know—'

'—is one hundred minutes.'

'—it was there with him.'

'Directed by Mr. David Cronenberg,' said Shepherd. 'Starring Mr. Jeff Goldblum—'

Standing down there beside her big motorcycle, Vonetta waved at them.

'—Miss Geena Davis, and Mr. John Getz.'

Dylan didn't know whether or not he should wave at Vonetta. From this distance, she couldn't possibly know who he and Shep were, but if he gave her too much to work with, she might recognize him by his body language.

'Other films directed by Mr. David Cronenberg include *The Dead*

Zone, which was good, a scary but good movie, Shep liked *The Dead Zone*—'

Vonetta might be able to see the suggestion of a third person on the hilltop – Jilly – but she wouldn't be able to discern enough of the gateway to understand the full strangeness of the situation up here.

'—*The Brood* and *They Came from Within*. Shep didn't like those 'cause they were too bloody, they were full of sloppy stuff. Shep doesn't ever want to see those again. None of that stuff anymore. Not again. None of that stuff.'

Deciding that to wave at the woman might be to encourage her to come up the hill for a visit, Dylan pretended not to see her. 'Nobody is going to make you watch another Cronenberg movie,' he assured his brother. 'I just want you to think about how the scientist and the fly got all mixed up.'

'Teleportation.'

Apparently suspicious, Vonetta put on her helmet.

'Teleportation!' Dylan agreed. 'Yes, that's exactly right. The fly and the scientist teleported together, and they got mixed up.'

Still addressing the ground at his feet, Shepherd said, 'The 1986 remake was too icky,'

'You're right, it was.'

'Gooey scenes. Bloody scenes. Shep doesn't like gooey-bloody scenes.'

The housekeeper mounted her Harley once more.

'The first version wasn't gooey-bloody,' Dylan reminded his brother. 'But the important question is—'

'Nine minutes in the shower is just right,' said Shepherd, unexpectedly harking back to Dylan's critical tirade.

'I suppose it is. Yes, I'm sure it is. Nine minutes. You're absolutely right. Now—'

'Nine minutes. One minute for each arm. One minute for each leg. One minute—'

Vonetta tried to fire up the Harley. The engine didn't catch.

'—for the head,' Shepherd continued. 'Two full minutes to wash everything else. And two minutes to rinse.'

'If we jump back to the motel together,' Dylan said, 'right now, the two of us hand-in-hand, are we going to wind up like the fly and the scientist?'

Shep's next words were saturated with an unmistakable note of wounded feelings: 'Shep doesn't eat crap.'

Baffled, Dylan said, 'What?'

When Vonetta keyed the ignition again, the Harley answered with proud power.

'Shep doesn't eat a narrow little list of crap like you said, a narrow little list of crap. Shep eats food just like you.'

'Of course you do, kiddo. I only meant—'

'Crap is shit,' Shepherd reminded him.

'I'm sorry. I didn't mean any of that.'

Straddling the Harley, both feet still on the ground, Vonetta gunned the throttle a few times, and the roar of the engine echoed across the meadow, through the hills.

'Poopoo, kaka, diaper dump—'

Dylan almost cried out in frustration, but he swallowed hard, and maintained his composure. 'Shep, listen, buddy, bro, listen—'

'—doodoo, cow pie, bulldoody, and all the rest as previously listed.'

'Exactly,' Dylan said with relief. 'As previously listed. You did a good job previously. I remember them all. So are we going to wind up like the fly and the scientist?'

With his head bowed so far that his chin touched his chest, Shep said, 'Do you hate me?'

The question rocked Dylan. And not solely the question, but the fact that Shepherd had spoken of himself in the first person instead of the third. Not do you hate *Shep*, but do you hate *me*. He must feel deeply wounded.

Behind the house, Vonetta turned the Harley out of the driveway and rode across the backyard toward the meadow.

Dylan knelt on one knee in front of Shep. 'I don't hate you, Shep. I couldn't if I tried. I love you, and I'm scared for you, and being scared just made me pissy.'

Shep wouldn't look at his brother, but at least he didn't close his eyes.

'I was mean,' Dylan continued, 'and you don't understand that, because you're never mean. You don't know how to be mean. But I'm not as good as you, kiddo, I'm not as gentle.'

Shepherd appeared to boggle at the grass around his bedroom

slippers, as though he had seen an otherworldly creature creeping through those bristling blades, but he must instead be reacting to the astonishing idea that, in spite of all his quirks and limitations, he might in some ways be superior to his brother.

At the end of the mown yard, Vonetta rode the Harley straight into the meadow. Tall golden grass parted before the motorcycle, like a lake cleaving under the prow of a boat.

Returning his full attention to Shepherd, Dylan said, 'We have to get out of here, Shep, and right away. We have to get back to the motel, to Jilly, but not if we're going to end up like the scientist and the fly.'

'Gooey-bloody,' said Shep.

'Exactly. We don't want to end up gooey-bloody.'

'Gooey-bloody is bad.'

'Gooey-bloody is very bad, yes.'

Brow furrowed, Shep said solemnly, 'This isn't a Mr. David Cronenberg film.'

'No, it isn't,' Dylan agreed, heartened that Shep seemed to be as tuned in to a conversation as he ever could be. 'But what does that mean, Shep? Does that mean it's safe to go back to the motel together?'

'Herethere,' Shep said, compressing the two words into one, as he had done before.

Vonetta Beesley had traveled half the meadow.

'Herethere,' Shep repeated. 'Here is there, there is here, and everywhere is the same place if you know how to fold.'

'Fold? Fold what?'

'Fold here to there, one place to another place, herethere.'

'We're not talking teleportation, are we?'

'This is not a Mr. David Cronenberg film,' Shep said, which Dylan took to be a confirmation that teleportation – and therefore the catastrophic commingling of atomic particles – was not an issue.

Rising off his knee to full height, Dylan put his hands on Shepherd's shoulders. He intended to plunge with his brother into the gateway.

Before they could move, the gateway came to them. Facing Shep, Dylan was also facing the magical portal behind Shep when the image of Jilly in the motel bathroom abruptly *folded* as though it were a work of origami in progress, like one of those tablet-paper cootie catchers that kids made in school for the purpose of teasing other kids: folded forward, folded around them, folded them up inside it, and folded away from California.

25

Half crazed with worry, Jilly almost snapped completely when the radiant tunnel in front of her appeared to fracture from the center and then *folded* upon the fracture lines. Although she thought the red passageway folded inward upon itself, simultaneously she had a sense of it blooming toward her, causing her to step backward in alarm.

In place of the tunnel, she was confronted by shifting geometric patterns in shades of red and black, similar to what might be seen in a kaleidoscope, except that these designs were breathtakingly three-dimensional, continually evolving. She feared falling into them, not down necessarily, but also up and around, feared tumbling like a weightless astronaut into blossoming patterns forever, to eternity.

In fact, the awesome structure that loomed in the wall defied her sense of vision, or perhaps defied her mental capacity to grasp and analyze what her eyes revealed. It seemed markedly more real than anything else in the bathroom, real but so infinitely strange that her terrified gaze ricocheted off one peculiar detail after another, as though her mind fled from the consideration of the true complexity of the construct. Repeatedly she perceived a depth greater than three dimensions, but didn't possess the ability to lock on that perception and hold it, even though a small and panicky inner voice of intuition counted *five*, and then *seven*, and kept counting after she refused to listen to it anymore.

Almost at once, new colors intruded upon the red and black: the blue of a summer sky, the golden shade of certain beaches and of ripe wheat. Among the countless thousands of tiles in this ceaselessly re-forming mosaic, the percentage of red and black rapidly declined as the blue and gold increased. She thought she saw, then *knew* she saw, then tried *not* to see fragments of human forms distributed widely through the kaleidoscopic patterns: here a staring eye, and there a finger, and there an ear, as if a stained-glass portrait had been shattered and tossed in the air by a cyclone wind. She thought that she also glimpsed a toothy portion of Wile E. Coyote's grinning visage, then saw the merest scrap of a familiar blue-and-yellow Hawaiian shirt, and another scrap *there*.

No more than five or six seconds passed from the instant that the tunnel folded upon itself until Dylan and Shepherd *unfolded* into the bathroom and appeared before Jilly as whole and normal as ever they had been. Behind them, where the tunnel had once churned with red light, there was now only an ordinary wall.

With obvious relief, Dylan exhaled a pent-up breath and said something like, 'No gooey-bloody.'

Shep declared, 'Shep is dirty.'

Jilly said, 'You son of a bitch,' and punched Dylan in the chest.

She hadn't pulled the punch. The blow made a satisfying *thwack*, but Dylan was too big to be rocked off his feet as Jilly had hoped he would be.

'Hey!' Dylan protested.

Head bowed, Shep said, 'Time to shower.'

And Jilly repeated herself, 'You son of a bitch,' as she hit Dylan again.

'What's wrong with you?'

'You said you weren't going in there,' she angrily reminded him, and punched still harder.

'Ow! Hey, I didn't *intend* to go.'

'You went,' she accused, and she swung at him again.

With one of his open hands as big as a catcher's mitt, he caught her fist and held it, effectively ending her assault. 'I went, yeah, okay, but I really didn't intend to go.'

Shepherd remained patient but persistent: 'Shep is dirty. Time to shower.'

'You told me you wouldn't go,' Jilly said, 'but you went, and left me here *alone*.'

She didn't quite know how Dylan had gotten hold of her by both wrists. Restraining her, he said, 'I came back, we both came back, everything's all right.'

'I couldn't *know* you'd come back. As far as I knew, you'd never come back or you'd come back dead.'

'I had to come back alive,' he assured her, 'so you'd have a fair chance to kill me.'

'Don't joke about this.' She tried to wrench loose of him but couldn't. 'Let go of me, you bastard.'

'Are you going to hit me again?'

'If you don't let go of me, I'll tear you to pieces, I swear.'

'Time to shower.'

Dylan released her, but he kept both hands raised as though he expected that he would have to catch further punches. 'You're such an angry person.'

'Oh, you're damn right I'm an angry person.' She trembled with anger, shook with fear. 'You said you wouldn't go in there, then you went in there anyway, and I was *alone*.' She realized that she was shaking more with relief than with either fury or fear. 'Where the *hell* did you go?'

'California,' Dylan said.

'What do you mean "California"?'

'California. Disneyland, Hollywood, Golden Gate Bridge. You know, California?'

'California,' said Shep. 'One hundred sixty-three thousand seven hundred and seven square miles.'

With a thick note of disbelief in her voice, Jilly said, 'You went through the wall to California?'

'Yeah. Why not? Where'd you think we went – Narnia? Oz? Middle Earth? California's weirder than any of those places, anyway.'

Shep evidently knew a lot about his native state: 'Population, approximately thirty-five million four hundred thousand.'

'But I don't think we actually went through the wall,' Dylan said, 'or through anything at all. Shep folded here to there.'

'Highest point, Mount Whitney—'

'Folded what to where?' Jilly asked.

'—fourteen thousand four hundred ninety-four feet above sea level.'

As her anger settled and as relief brought with it a measure of calm and clarity, Jilly realized that Dylan was exhilarated. A little nervous, yes, and maybe a little fearful, too, but largely exhilarated, almost boyishly exuberant.

Dylan said, 'He folded reality maybe, space and time, one or both, I don't know, but he folded here to there. What did you fold, Shep? What exactly was it you folded?'

'Lowest point,' said Shep, 'Death Valley—'

'He'll probably be on this California thing for a while.'

'—two hundred eighty-two feet below sea level.'

'What did you fold, bro?'

'State capital – Sacramento.'

'Last night he folded stall one to stall four,' Dylan said, 'but I didn't realize it at the time.'

'Stall one to stall four?' Jilly frowned, working the pain out of the hand with which she'd punched him. 'Right now Shep's making more sense than you are.'

'State bird – California valley quail.'

'In the men's room. He folded toilet to toilet. He went in number one and came out number four. I didn't tell you about it, because I didn't realize what had happened.'

'State flower – golden poppy.'

Jilly wanted to be clear on this: 'He teleported from one toilet to another?'

'No, teleportation isn't involved. See – I came back with my own head, he came back with his own nose. No teleportation.'

'State tree – California redwood.'

'Show her your nose, Shep.'

Shepherd kept his head bowed. 'State motto – "Eureka," which means, "I have found it."'

'Believe me,' Dylan told Jilly, 'it's his own nose. This isn't a David Cronenberg film.'

She thought about that last statement for a moment while Dylan grinned at her and nodded, and then she said, 'I know I haven't even had breakfast yet, but I need a beer.'

Shepherd disapproved. 'Psychotropic intoxicant.'

'He's talking to me,' Jilly said.

'Yeah,' Dylan said.

'I mean not *at* me. Talking *to* me. Sort of.'

'Yeah, he's going through some changes.' Dylan lowered the lid on the toilet. 'Here, Shep, sit down here.'

'Time to shower,' Shep reminded them.

'All right, soon, but sit down here first.' Dylan maneuvered his brother to the closed toilet and persuaded him to sit.

'Shep is dirty. Time to shower.'

After kneeling in front of his brother, Dylan quickly examined his arms. 'I don't see anything.'

'Time to shower. Nine minutes.'

Dylan removed Shepherd's bedroom slippers, and set them aside. 'Want to bet which cartoon?'

Bewildered, Jilly wanted that beer more than ever. 'Cartoon?'

Head lowered, Shep watched his brother set aside the slippers. 'Nine minutes. One minute for each arm.'

'Bunny or puppy,' Dylan said.

Examining the adhesive bandage on her arm, Jilly saw that it was loose but that it still concealed the needle mark.

Dylan peeled the sock off Shepherd's right foot.

'One minute,' Shep said, 'for each leg—'

Moving closer, Jilly watched as Dylan examined his brother's bare foot. 'If he was injected,' she said, 'why not in the arm?'

'—and one minute for the head—'

'He was working a jigsaw puzzle at the time,' Dylan said.

'So?'

'—and two full minutes to wash everything else—'

'You've never seen my brother work a puzzle. He's fast. His hands keep moving. And he's focused.'

'—two minutes to rinse,' Shep finished. Then he added, 'Cat.'

'He's so focused,' Dylan continued, 'you can't persuade him to stop until he's completed the puzzle. You can't *force* him to stop. He wouldn't care what you did with his feet because he doesn't work the puzzle with his feet. But you couldn't immobilize one of his arms.'

'Maybe he was chloroformed, like me.'

Having found no obvious puncture mark on Shepherd's right foot, Dylan said, 'No. When I went across the street to get takeout, he was doing jigsaw, and when I woke up taped to the chair, Shep was still flying through the puzzle.'

Inexplicably, Shep interjected, 'Cat.'

'If he'd been chloroformed, he wouldn't have gotten over the effects that quickly,' Jilly said, remembering the disorientation that had lingered after she'd awakened.

'Cat.'

'Besides, having a chloroform-soaked rag clamped to his face would have been even more traumatic for Shep than it was for you. A lot more. He's fragile. After regaining consciousness, he'd have been either highly emotional or he'd have curled up in the fetal position and refused to move. He wouldn't have gone back to the puzzle as if nothing had happened.'

Dylan stripped the sock from Shepherd's left foot.

Shepherd's Band-Aid featured a cartoon cat.

'Cat,' said Shep. 'Shep bet cat.'

Carefully Dylan peeled off the tape.

'Shep wins,' said Shep.

More than half a day after the injection had been administered, the puncture remained inflamed and slightly swollen.

The sight of Shep's stigmata sent a shiver through Jilly that she could not entirely explain.

She removed her bunny-decorated bandage. The site of her injection looked identical to Shepherd's.

Dylan's cartoon puppy proved to conceal a needle puncture that matched his brother's and Jilly's wounds. 'He told me the stuff does something different to everyone.'

Glancing at the wall where the tunnel had been, Jilly said, 'In Shepherd's case, something *way* different.'

'"The effect is without exception interesting,"' Dylan quoted Frankenstein, as he had quoted him before, '"frequently astonishing, and sometimes positive."'

Jilly saw the wonder in Dylan's face, the shining hope in his eyes. 'You think this is positive for Shep?'

'I don't know about the talent to . . . to fold things. Whether that might be a blessing or a curse. Only time will tell. But he's talking more, too. And talking more directly to me. Now that I look back on it, he's been changing ever since this happened.'

She knew what Dylan was thinking and what he dared not say, for fear of tempting fate: that by virtue of the injection, with the aid of the mysterious psychotropic *stuff*, Shep might find his way out of the prison of his autism.

Negative Jackson might be a name she'd earned. Perhaps at her worst she was, as well, a vortex of pessimism, never regarding her own life and prospects, but often regarding the likelihood that most people and society in general would always find a hellbound handbasket in which to be carried to destruction. But she didn't think she was being pessimistic – or even negative – when she looked upon this development with Shep and sensed more danger in it than hope, less potential for enlightenment than for horror.

Staring down at the tiny red point of inflammation on his foot, Shepherd whispered, *'By the light of the moon.'*

In his heretofore innocent face, Jilly saw neither the vacant stare nor the benign expression, nor the wrenching anxiety, that had thus far pretty much defined his apparent emotional range. A hint of acrimony colored his voice, and his features tightened in a bitter expression that might have represented something more caustic than mere bitterness. Anger perhaps, rock-hard and long-nurtured anger.

'He said this before,' Dylan revealed, 'as I was trying to get him out of our motel room last night, just before we met you.'

'You do your work,' Shep whispered.

'This too,' Dylan said.

Shepherd's shoulders remained slumped, and his hands lay in his lap, palms up almost as if he were meditating, but his clouded face betrayed an inner storm.

'What's he talking about?' Jilly asked.

'I don't know.'

'Shep? Who're you talking to, sweetie?'

'You do your work by the light of the moon.'

'Whose work, Shep?'

A minute ago, Shepherd had been as connected to them and to the moment as she had ever seen him. Now he had gone away somewhere as surely as he had stepped through the wall to California.

She crouched beside Dylan and gently took one of Shep's limp hands in both her hands. He didn't respond to her touch. His hand remained as slack as that of a dead man.

His green eyes were alive, however, as he stared down at his foot, at the floor, perhaps seeing neither, seeming to gaze instead at someone or something that, in memory, profoundly troubled him.

'*You do your work by the light of the moon,*' he whispered once more. This time the suggestion of anger in his face was matched by an unmistakable raw edge to his voice.

No clairvoyant vision settled upon Jilly, no vivid premonition of terror to come, but ordinary intuition told her to be alert and to expect deadly surprises.

26

Shepherd returned from his private moonlit place to the realization that he still needed to shower.

Although Jilly retreated to the bedroom, Dylan remained in the bathroom with his brother. He didn't intend to leave Shepherd alone anytime soon, not with this latest herethere complication to worry about.

As Shep pulled off his T-shirt, Dylan said, 'Kiddo, I want you to promise me something.'

Shucking off his jeans, Shep made no reply.

'I want you to promise me that you won't fold here to there, won't go anywhere again like that, unless you clear it with me.'

Shep skinned out of his briefs. 'Nine minutes.'

'Can you make me that promise, Shep?'

Sliding the shower curtain aside, Shep said, 'Nine minutes.'

'This is serious, buddy. None of this folding until we have a better understanding of what's happening to us, to all of us.'

Shep turned on the shower, gingerly slipped one hand in the spray, adjusted the controls, and tested the temperature again.

Often people made the mistake of assuming that Shepherd must be severely retarded and that he required far more assistance to take care of himself than was in fact the case. He could groom himself, dress himself, and deal successfully with many simple tasks of daily life other than food preparation. You should never ask Shep to make a flaming dessert or even to toast a Pop-Tart. You didn't want to hand him the keys to your Porsche. But he was intelligent, and perhaps even smarter than Dylan.

Unfortunately, in his case intelligence remained isolated from performance. He had come into this world with some bad wiring. He was like a Mercedes sports car with a powerful engine that had not been connected to the drive train; you could race that engine all day, and it would sound as pretty as any engine ever built, but you wouldn't go anywhere.

'Nine minutes,' Shep said.

Dylan handed the Minute Minder to him: a mechanical timer made for use in the kitchen. The round white face featured sixty black checks, a number at every fifth check.

Shep brought the device close to his face, scrutinizing it as though he had never seen it before, and carefully set the dial at nine minutes. He picked up a bar of Neutrogena, the only soap he would use in the shower, and he stepped into the tub, holding the Minute Minder by the dial to prevent the timer from engaging.

To avoid an attack of claustrophobia, Shep always showered with the curtain open.

Once he was under the spray, he stood the Minute Minder on the edge of the tub, releasing the dial. The ticking proved audible above the hiss and splash of water.

The timer always got wet. In a couple months, rust would have made it useless. Dylan bought the gadgets by the dozen.

Immediately Shep began to soap his left arm, directly applying the Neutrogena. Although he wouldn't look at the Minute Minder again, he would allot precisely the desired amount of time to each area of his body. Two or three seconds before the timer went off, he would anticipate it by loudly announcing *Ding!* with a note of satisfaction.

Perhaps he kept track of the elapsing time by counting the ticks of the Minute Minder – one per second. Or maybe after all these years of precisely timed baths, Shep had developed a reliable inner clock.

For the past decade, Dylan had been chronically aware of his own clock relentlessly counting off his life, but he had refused to think too much about time, about where he would be either in nine minutes or in six months, a year, two years. He would be painting the world, of course, traveling to art festivals, making a circuit of galleries across the West. And looking after Shep.

Now his inner watchworks ticked not faster but more insistently, and he couldn't stop contemplating the suddenly fluid nature of his future. He no longer knew where he might be tomorrow or in what situation he would find himself by sunset this very day, let alone where twelve months might take him. To one who'd lived a singularly predictable life for ten years, these new circumstances should have been frightening, and they *were*, scary as hell, but they were also undeniably exciting, almost exhilarating.

He was surprised that the prospect of novelty had so much appeal for him. He had long conceived himself to be a man of constancy, who respected tradition, who loved what was immemorial and did not share the interest in newness for the sake of newness that had made this society so rootless and so in love with flash.

Guilt brought a blush to his face as he remembered his tirade on the hilltop, when he had railed at Shepherd about 'maddening routine' and 'stupid repetition,' as though the poor kid had any choice to be other than what he was.

Being exhilarated by the possibility of revolutionary change in his life, while having no clue whether the coming changes would be for good or ill, at first struck him as reckless. Then in light of the recognition that those changes held more peril for Shepherd than for anyone, this excitement had to be judged worse than recklessness: It seemed selfish, shallow.

Face to face with himself in the mirror, he argued silently that his rush to embrace change, any change, was nothing more and nothing worse than a reflection of his eternal optimism. Even if it had been made aloud, that argument would not have resonated with the ring of truth. Dismayed by the man he saw, he turned away from the mirror, but even though he counseled himself to face this newly fluid future with more caution, even with alarm, his excitement had not been in the least diminished.

No one would ever accuse Holbrook, Arizona, of being a noisy hub of commerce. Except perhaps during the Old West Celebration in June, the Gathering of Eagles show of Native American art in July, and the Navajo County Fair in September, an armadillo could cross any local street or highway at a pace of its own choosing with little risk of death by motor vehicle.

Nevertheless, Jilly discovered that this two-star motel provided an in-room modem link separate from the phone line. In this regard, at least, they might as well have been holed up in the Peninsula hotel in Beverly Hills.

Ensconced at the small desk, she opened her laptop, jacked in, and cruised onto the Internet. She had begun to search for sites concerned with scientific research into enhanced brain function by the time that Shepherd, in the bathroom, cried out *'Ding!'* and the Minute Minder rang off the final second of his nine-minute shower.

She ruled out sites related to improving mental acuity through vitamin therapy and diet. Frankenstein had not seemed to be the kind of guy who'd been devoted to natural foods and homeopathic medicine.

In addition she had no interest in sites related to yoga and to other forms of meditation. Even the most brilliant scientist couldn't take the principles of a meditative discipline, liquify them, and inject them as though they were flu vaccine.

Showered, hair still damp, wearing a fresh pair of jeans and a clean Wile E. Coyote T-shirt, Shepherd returned from the bathroom.

Dylan followed him for a couple steps and said, 'Jilly, can you keep an eye on Shep? Be sure he doesn't . . . go anywhere.'

'Sure.'

Two additional straight-backed chairs faced each other across a small table near the window. She brought one of them to the desk, intending for Shep to sit beside her.

Instead, he ignored her invitation and went to a corner of the bedroom near the desk, where he stood with his back to the room.

'Shep, are you all right?'

He didn't reply. The wallpaper – beige, yellow, and pale-green stripes – had been sloppily joined where the walls met. Shepherd moved his head slowly up, slowly down, as though studying the error in the pattern match.

'Sweetie, is something wrong?'

Having twice surveyed the paperhanger's shoddy work from floor to ceiling, Shep stared straight ahead at the juncture of walls. His arms had hung slack at his sides. Now he raised his right arm as if he were swearing an oath: bent at the elbow, hand beside his face, palm flat and facing forward. After a moment, he began to wave as though he were not staring into a corner but through a window at someone he knew.

Dylan came out of the bathroom again, this time to get a change of clothes from his suitcase, and Jilly said, 'Who's he waving at?'

'He's not really waving,' Dylan explained. 'It's spasmodic, the equivalent of a facial tic. He can sometimes do it for hours.'

On further consideration, Jilly realized that Shepherd's wrist had gone limp and that his hand actually flopped loosely, not in the calculated wave of a good-bye or a greeting.

'Does he think he's done something wrong?' she asked.

'Wrong? Oh, because he's standing in the corner? No. He's just feeling overwhelmed at the moment. Too much input recently. He can't cope with all of it.'

'Who can?'

'By facing into a corner,' Dylan said, 'he's limiting sensory input. Reducing his world to that narrow space. It helps to calm him. He feels safer.'

'Maybe I need a corner of my own,' Jilly said.

'Just keep an eye on him. He knows I don't want him to . . . go anywhere. He's a good kid. Most of the time he does what he should. But I'm just afraid that this folding thing . . . maybe he won't be able to control it any more than he can control that hand right now.'

Shep waved at the wall, waved, waved.

Adjusting the position of her laptop, turning her chair at an angle to the desk in order to keep Shep in view while she worked, Jilly said to Dylan, 'You can count on me.'

'Yeah. I know I can.'

A tenderness in his voice compelled her attention.

His forthright stare had the same quality of assessment and speculation that had characterized the surreptitious glances with which he had studied her after they had refueled at that service station in Globe, the previous night.

When Dylan smiled, Jilly realized that she had been smiling first, that his smile was in answer to hers.

'You can count on me,' Shep said.

They looked at the kid. He still faced the corner, still waved.

'We know we can count on you, buddy,' Dylan told his brother.

'You never let me down. So you stay here, okay? Only here, no *there*. No folding.'

For the time being, Shep had said all that he had to say.

'I better get showered,' Dylan said.

'Nine minutes,' Jilly reminded him.

Smiling again, he returned to the bathroom with a change of clothes.

With Shepherd always in her peripheral vision, glancing up at him more directly from time to time, Jilly traveled the Net in search of sites related to the enhancement of brain function, mental acuity, memory . . . anything that might lead her to Frankenstein.

By the time that Dylan returned, shaved and showered, in a fresh pair of khaki pants, in a red-and-brown checkered shirt cut Hawaiian style and worn over his belt, Jilly had found some direction in their quest. She was primarily interested in several articles regarding the possibility of microchip augmentation of human memory.

As Dylan settled onto the chair beside her, Jilly said, 'They claim that eventually we'll be able to surgically install data ports in our brains and then, anytime we want, plug in memory cards to augment our knowledge.'

'Memory cards.'

'Like if you want to design your own house, you can plug in a memory card – which is really a chip densely packed with data – and instantly you'll know all the architecture and engineering required to produce a set of buildable plans. I'm talking everything from the aesthetic considerations to how you calculate the load-bearing requirements of foundation footings, even how you route plumbing and lay out an adequate heating-and-cooling system.'

Dylan looked dubious. 'That's what they say, huh?'

'Yeah. If you want to know everything there possibly is to know about French history and art when you take your first trip to Paris, you'll just plug in a memory card. They say it's inevitable.'

'They who?'

'A lot of big-brain techies, Silicon Valley research types out there on the cutting edge.'

'The same folks who brought us ten thousand bankrupt dot-com companies?'

'Those were mostly con men, power-mad nerds, and sixteen-year-old entrepreneurs, not research types.'

'I'm still not impressed. What do the brain surgeons say about all this?'

'Surprisingly, a lot of them also think eventually it'll be possible.'

'Supposing they haven't been smoking too much weed, what do they mean by "eventually"?'

'Some say thirty years, some say fifty.'

'But how does any of this relate to us?' he wondered. 'Nobody installed a data port in my skull yet. I just washed my hair, I would have noticed.'

'I don't know,' she admitted. 'But this feels like even if it isn't the right track, if I just follow it a little farther, it'll cross over the right one, and bring me to whatever area of research Frankenstein was actually involved in.'

He nodded. 'I don't know why, but I have the same feeling.'

'Intuition.'

'We're back to that.'

Getting up from the desk, she said, 'You want to take over the chase while I clean up my act?'

'Nine minutes,' he said.

'Not possible. *My* hair has some style to it.'

≈ ≈ ≈

Risking scalp burn from a too-relentless application of her hair dryer, Jilly returned to the motel bedroom, cleaned and fluffed, in forty-five minutes. She had dressed in a banana-yellow, short-sleeve, lightweight, stretchy-clingy knit sweater, white jeans tailored to prove that the big-ass curse plaguing her family had not yet resized her buttocks from cantaloupes to prize-winning pumpkins, and white athletic shoes with yellow laces to match the sweater.

She felt pretty. She hadn't cared about being pretty in weeks, even months, and she was surprised to care now, in the middle of an ongoing catastrophe, with her life in ruins and perhaps worse trials to come; yet she'd spent several minutes examining herself in the bathroom mirror, making carefully calculated adjustments to further prettify herself. She felt shameless, she felt shallow, she felt silly, but she also felt *fine*.

In his calming corner, Shepherd remained unaware that Jilly had returned prettier than she'd left. He no longer waved. His arms hung at his sides. He leaned forward, head bowed, the top of his skull actually pressed into the corner, in full contact with the striped wallpaper, as though to stand at any distance whatsoever from this sheltering juncture would make him vulnerable to an intolerably rich influx of sensory stimulation.

She hoped for considerably more reaction from Dylan than from Shepherd, but when he looked up from the laptop, he didn't compliment her on her appearance, didn't even smile. 'I found the bastard.'

Jilly was so invested in the expectation of a compliment that for a moment she couldn't compute the meaning of his words. 'What bastard?'

'The smiley, peanut-eating, needle-poking, car-stealing bastard, *that's* what bastard.'

Dylan pointed, and Jilly looked at the laptop screen, where a photograph showed their Dr. Frankenstein looking respectable and far less like a lunatic than he had appeared the previous night.

27

Lincoln Merriweather Proctor was, in this case, a name deceptive in every regard. *Lincoln* made you think of Abe, therefore suggesting the wisdom and the integrity of men who rose to greatness from humble origins. *Merriweather* added a light note, implying a calm untroubled soul, perhaps even one capable of entertaining moments of frivolity. A proctor was a person who supervised students, mentored them, who maintained order, stability.

This Lincoln Merriweather Proctor had been a child of privilege, educated first at Yale, then at Harvard. Judging by a quick sampling of his writings, to which Dylan guided her on the laptop, Jilly decided that Proctor's soul, far from being calm, was troubled by megalomaniacal visions of the total mastery of nature followed by the complete perversion of it. His life's work – the mysterious *stuff* in the syringe – didn't contribute to order and stability; it fostered uncertainty, terror, even chaos.

A certifiable prodigy, Proctor had earned two Ph.D.s – the first in molecular biology, the second in physics – by the age of twenty-six. Assiduously courted by academia and industry, he enjoyed prestigious positions with both, although before his thirtieth birthday, he had formed his own company and had proved that his greatest genius lay in his ability to attract enormous sums of investment capital to finance his research with the hope of discovering commercial applications of tremendous economic significance.

In his writing and his public speaking, however, Proctor had not merely pursued the creation of a business empire, but had dreamed of reforming society and in fact had hoped to change the very nature of humankind. In the scientific breakthroughs of the late twentieth century and in those certain to follow in the early twenty-first, he foresaw the opportunity to perfect humanity and to create utopia.

His expressed motives – compassion for those who suffered from poverty and disease, concern for the planet's ecosystem, a desire to promote universal equality and justice – sounded admirable. Yet when she read his words, Jilly heard in her mind vast ranks of marching boots and the rattle of chains in gulags.

'From Lenin to Hitler, utopians are all the same,' Dylan agreed. 'Determined to perfect society at any cost, they destroy it instead.'

'People can't be perfected. Not any I've ever known.'

'I love the natural world, it's what I paint. You see perfection everywhere in nature. The perfect efficiency of bees in the hive. The perfect organization of an anthill, a termite colony. But what makes humanity beautiful is our free will, our individuality, our endless striving in spite of our imperfection.'

'Beautiful . . . and terrifying,' she suggested.

'Oh, it's a tragic beauty, all right, but that's what makes it so different from the beauty of nature, and in its own way precious. There's no tragedy in nature, only process – and therefore no triumph, either.'

He kept surprising her, this bearish man with the rubbery face, dressed like a boy in khakis and an untucked shirt.

'Anyway,' he said, 'that stuff about plugging memory cards into data ports in the brain wasn't the track Proctor's research took, but you were right when you thought it might *cross* his track if we kept following it.'

He reached past her to use the laptop keyboard. New material flashed on the screen.

Pointing to a key word in a headline, he said, 'This is the train Proctor's been riding for a long time.'

Reading the word above his finger, Jilly said, 'Nanotechnology.' She glanced at Shep in the corner, half expecting him to provide the definition, but he remained engaged in an apparent attempt to press his head into the corner until his skull re-formed itself to fit the wedge where wall met wall.

'Nano as a unit of measure means "one billionth,"' Dylan revealed. 'A nanosecond is one billionth of a second. In this case, however, it means "very small, minute." Nanotechnology – very tiny machines, so tiny as to be invisible to the naked eye.'

Jilly mulled that over, but the concept wasn't easy to digest. 'Too tiny to be seen? Machines made of what?'

He looked expectantly at her. 'Are you sure none of this rings a bell?'

'Should it?'

'Maybe,' he said mysteriously. 'Anyway, these nanomachines are constructed of just a handful of atoms.'

'Constructed by who – elves, fairies?'

'Most people remember seeing this on the news maybe a decade ago – the corporate logo that some IBM researchers built out of maybe just fifty or sixty atoms. Lined up a handful of atoms and locked them in place to spell out those three letters.'

'Hey, yeah. I was in maybe tenth grade. Our science teacher showed us a picture of it.'

'They photographed it with a camera hooked up to a powerful electron microscope.'

'But that was pretty much just a tiny sign, not a machine,' she objected. 'It didn't *do* anything.'

'Yeah, but platoons of researchers have been burning up a lot of development funds designing nanomachines that *will* work. Machines that already do.'

'Teeny-tiny fairy machines.'

'If you want to think of it that way, yes.'

'Why?'

'Eventually, when the technology's perfected, the applications are going to be incredible, virtually infinite, especially in the medical field.'

Jilly tried to imagine at least one of the infinite applications of teeny-tiny machines performing teeny-tiny tasks. She sighed. 'I've spent too much of my life writing jokes, telling jokes, and stealing jokes. Now I *feel* like a joke. What applications?'

He pointed to the laptop screen. 'I've sourced up an interview that Proctor did a few years ago. It's in layman's terms, easy to grasp. Even I understood it.'

'Why don't you condense it for me?'

'All right. First, an application or two. Imagine a machine tinier than a blood cell, composed of a handful of atoms, but with the capacity to identify plaque on blood-vessel walls and the ability to remove it mechanically, safely. They're biologically interactive in function but fashioned from biologically inert atoms, so your body's immune system won't be triggered by their presence. And now imagine receiving an injection containing hundreds of thousands of these nanomachines, maybe millions.'

'Millions?'

He shrugged. 'Millions would fit in a few cc of a carrier fluid like glucose. It'd be a smaller syringe than Proctor used with us.'

'Creepy.'

'I suppose when the first vaccines were developed, people back then thought it was creepy to be injected with *dead germs* in order to build up an immunity against live ones.'

'Hey, I still don't like the sound of it.'

'So anyway, these millions of nanomachines would circulate end-lessly through your body, searching out plaque, gently scrubbing it away, keeping your circulatory system as clean as a whistle.'

Jilly was impressed. 'If that ever hits the market, welcome to the age of the guilt-free cheeseburger. And you know what? This *is* starting to sound a little familiar.'

'I'm not surprised.'

'But why should it?'

Instead of answering her question, he said, 'Nanomachines could detect and eliminate colonies of cancer cells before the tumor was half as large as the head of a pin.'

'Hard to see the downside to all this,' Jilly said. 'But we know for sure there is one. And why're you being enigmatic? Why do you think this should sound familiar to me?'

In the corner, Shep said, 'Herethere.'

'Oh, shit!' Dylan bolted from his chair so fast that he knocked it over.

'Herethere.'

Closer to Shepherd than Dylan was, Jilly reached the kid first. Approaching him, she didn't see anything out of the ordinary, no red tunnel to California or to anywhere else.

Shepherd no longer leaned with the top of his skull jammed into the juncture of walls. He had taken a step backward. He stood erect, head up, eyes focused intently on something that appeared to be a lot more interesting than anything Jilly could see.

He had raised his right hand again, as if taking an oath, but he hadn't started to wave. As Jilly arrived at his side, Shep reached in front of his face, to the point in midair at which he'd been staring, and between his thumb and forefinger, he took a pinch of . . . a pinch of nothing, as far as she could tell. When he tweaked that pinch of air, however, the corner of the room began to fold in upon itself.

'No,' Jilly said breathlessly, and though she knew that Shepherd often recoiled from contact, she reached in front of him and put her hand atop his. 'Don't do this, sweetie.'

Multiple segments of the tricolored stripes on the wallpaper, previously mismatched only at the corner, now bent everywhichway at radical angles to one another, and the corner became so distorted that Jilly could not follow the floor-to-ceiling line of it.

At Shep's other side, Dylan placed one hand on his brother's shoulder. 'Stay here, buddy. Right here with us, safe with us.'

The folding motion halted, but the corner remained tweaked into a surreal geometry.

Jilly seemed to be looking at this small portion of the world through an octagonal prism. Her mind rebelled at the spectacle, which defied reason to an extent that even the radiant tunnel in the wall had not done.

With the palm of her right hand still against the back of Shep's right hand, Jilly was afraid to struggle with him, for fear that any movement she made would further fold here to there, wherever *there* might be this time. 'Smooth it out, honey,' she urged, tremors creasing her voice as strangely as the walls were folded before her. 'Let it go, sweetie. Smooth it out like it ought to be.'

Between thumb and forefinger, Shepherd still pinched the fabric of reality.

Slowly he turned his head to look at Jilly. He met her eyes as directly as he had met them only once before: when he'd been in the backseat of the Expedition outside the house on Eucalyptus Avenue, just after Dylan had rushed away without explanation. Then, Shep had flinched from eye contact, had looked at once away.

This time he held her gaze. His green eyes appeared as deep as oceans and seemed to be lit from within.

'Do you feel it?' he asked.

'Feel what?'

'Feel how it works, the round and round of all that is.'

She supposed that by transmission through his hand, he expected her to feel what he felt between his thumb and forefinger, but she was aware only of his warm skin, of the sharpness of his metacarpals and his knuckles. She expected to detect tremendous tension, as well, to have an awareness of how hard Shep must be straining to achieve this incredible feat, but he seemed to be relaxed, as though folding this place to another required no more effort than folding a towel.

'Do you feel the beautiful of all that is?' he asked, addressing her with a directness that had no element of autistic detachment.

As beautiful as the secret structure of reality might be, this close an encounter with the mystery of it did not delight her as it seemed to enchant Shepherd, but instead crystallized an ice of terror in her bones. She wanted not to understand, but only to persuade him to close this gateway before he fully opened it.

'Please smooth it out, sweetie. Smooth it out again so I can feel how it unfolds.'

Although her father had been shot to death a year ago in a drug deal gone bad, Jilly had the fearful notion that if Shepherd didn't unfold this, if instead he folded it all the way and took them from *here* to *there*, she would abruptly come face to face with her hateful old man, as she had often opened the apartment door to the sight of his dangerous smile. She expected Shep to swing wide the gate to Hell as easily as he opened a gate to California, facilitating a father-and-daughter reunion. *Come to collect the eye insurance, baby girl. You got the eye-insurance premium?* As though Shep might unwittingly give her father a chance to reach out from Beyond to make good on his unfulfilled threat, blinding her in not one eye, but in both.

Shep's gaze drifted away from her. He refocused on his thumb and forefinger.

He had tweaked the pinch of nothing from left to right. Now he tweaked it right to left.

The wildly angled stripes in the wallpaper realigned themselves. The unbroken line of the corner, floor to ceiling, became clearly visible again, without a single zig or zag. What she had seemed to see through an octagonal prism, she here saw undistorted.

Squinting at the pinch point where Shep still squeezed something between thumb and forefinger, Jilly thought she saw the air *dimple* like a puckered film of thin plastic wrap.

Then his pale fingers parted, releasing whatever extraordinary fabric he had held.

Even viewed from the side, his green eyes appeared to cloud, and in place of the ocean's depth that had been revealed, there came now a shallowness, and in place of enchantment . . . a melancholy.

'Good,' Dylan said with relief. 'Thank you, Shep. That was just fine. That was good.'

Jilly let go of Shep's hand, and he lowered it to his side. He lowered his head, too, staring at the floor, slumping his shoulders, as though, for an instant liberated, he had once more accepted the weight of his autism.

28

Dylan moved the second chair from the table near the window, and the three of them sat in a semicircle at the desk, in front of the laptop, with Shepherd safely in the middle, where he could be more closely watched.

The kid sat with his chin against his chest. His hands lay in his lap, turned up. He appeared to be reading his palms: the heart line, head line, lifeline – and the many meaningful lines radiating out of the web between thumb and forefinger, that area known as the anatomical snuffbox.

Jilly's mother read palms – not for money, but for hope. Mom was never interested solely in the heart line, head line, and lifelines, but equally in the anatomical snuffbox, the interdigital pads, the heel of the hand, the thenar eminence, and the hypothenar.

Arms crossed on her chest, Jilly sat with her hands fisted in her armpits. She didn't like having her palms read.

Reading palms, reading tea leaves, interpreting Tarot cards, casting horoscopes – Jilly wanted nothing to do with any of that. She would never *concede* control of her future to fate, not for a minute. If fate wanted control of her, fate would have to club her senseless and *take* control.

'Nanomachine,' Jilly said, reminding Dylan where they had been interrupted. 'Scouring plaque off artery walls, searching out tiny groups of cancer cells.'

He stared worriedly at Shepherd, then nodded and finally met Jilly's eyes. 'You get the idea. In the interview there on the laptop, Proctor talks a lot about nanomachines that'll also be nanocomputers with enough memory to be programmed for some pretty sophisticated tasks.'

In spite of the fact that all three of them appeared to be living proof that Lincoln Proctor wasn't a fool, Jilly found this chatter of technological marvels almost as difficult to believe as Shepherd's power to fold. Or maybe she simply didn't *want* to believe it because the implications were so nightmarish.

She said, 'Isn't this ridiculous? I mean, how much memory can you squeeze into a computer smaller than a grain of sand?'

'In fact, smaller than a mote of dust. The way Proctor tells it, with a little background: The first silicon microchips were the size of a fingernail and had a million circuits. The smallest circuit on the chip was one hundredth as wide as a human hair.'

'All I really want to know is how to make audiences laugh until they puke,' she lamented.

'Then there were breakthroughs in . . . X-ray lithography, I think he called it.'

'Call it gobbledegook or fumfuddle if you want. It'll mean as much to me.'

'Anyway, some fumfuddle breakthrough made it possible to print one *billion* circuits on a chip, with features one thousandth the width of a human hair. Then two billion. And this was years ago.'

'Yeah, but while all these hotshot scientists were making their breakthroughs, I memorized one hundred and eighteen jokes about big butts. Let's see who gets more laughs at a party.'

The idea of nanomachines and nanocomputers swarming through her blood creeped her out no less than the idea of an extraterrestrial bug gestating in her chest a la *Aliens*.

'By shrinking dimensions,' Dylan explained, 'chip designers gain computer speed, function, and capacity. Proctor talked about multi-atom nanomachines driven by nanocomputers *made from a single atom*.'

'Computers no bigger than a single atom, huh? Listen, what the world really needs is a good portable washing machine the size of a radish.'

To Jilly, these minuscule, biologically interactive machines began to seem like fate in a syringe. Fate didn't need to sneak up on her with a club; it was already inside her and busily at work, courtesy of Lincoln Proctor.

Dylan continued: 'Proctor says the protons and electrons in one atom could be used as positive and negative switches, with millions of circuits actually etched onto the neutrons, so a single atom in a nanomachine could be the powerful computer that controls it.'

'Personally,' Jilly said, 'I'd rush out to Costco the moment I heard they were selling a reasonably priced teeny-tiny microwave oven that could double as a bellybutton ornament.'

Sitting here with her arms crossed and her hands in her armpits, she could barely make herself listen to Dylan because she knew where all this information was leading, and where it was leading scared the sweat out of her. She felt her armpits growing damp.

'You're scared,' he said.

'I'm all right.'

'You're not all right.'

'Yeah. What am I thinking? Who am I to know whether I'm all right or not all right? You're the expert on me, huh?'

'When you're scared, your wisecracks have a desperate quality.'

'If you'll search your memory,' she said, 'you'll discover that I didn't appreciate your amateur psychoanalysis in the past.'

'Because it was on target. Listen, you're scared, I'm scared, Shep is scared, we're all scared, and that's okay. We—'

'Shep is hungry,' said Shepherd.

They had missed breakfast. The lunch hour was drawing near.

'We'll get lunch soon,' Dylan promised his brother.

'Cheez-Its,' Shep said without looking up from his open palms.

'We'll get something better than Cheez-Its, buddy.'

'Shep likes Cheez-Its.'

'I know you do, buddy.' To Jilly, Dylan said, 'They're a nice square snack.'

'What would he do if you gave him those little cheese-cracker fish – what're they called, Goldfish?' she wondered.

'Shep *hates* Goldfish,' the kid said at once. 'They're shapey. They're all round and shapey. Goldfish suck. They're too shapey. They're *disgusting*. Goldfish stink. They suck, suck, suck.'

'You've hit on a sore point,' Dylan told Jilly.

'No Goldfish,' she promised Shep.

'Goldfish suck.'

'You're absolutely right, sweetie. They're totally too shapey,' Jilly said.

'*Disgusting.*'

'Yes, sweetie, totally disgusting.'

'Cheez-Its,' Shep insisted.

Jilly would have spent the rest of the day talking about the shapes of snack foods if that would have prevented Dylan from telling her more than she could bear to know about what those nanomachines might be doing inside her body right this very minute, but before she could mention Wheat Thins, he returned to the dreaded subject.

'In that interview,' Dylan said, 'Proctor even claims that one day millions of psychotropic nanomachines—'

Jilly winced. 'Psychotropic.'

'—might be injected into the human body—'

'Injected. Here we go.'

'—travel with the blood supply to the brain—'

She shuddered. 'Machines in the brain.'

'—and colonize the brain stem, cerebellum, and cerebrum.'

'Colonize the brain.'

'Disgusting,' Shep said, though he was most likely still talking about Goldfish.

Dylan said, 'Proctor envisions a forced evolution of the brain conducted by nanomachines and nanocomputers.'

'Why didn't somebody kill the son of a bitch years ago?'

'He says these nanomachines could be programmed to analyze the structure of the brain at a cellular level, firsthand, and find ways to improve the design.'

'I guess I failed to vote when Lincoln Proctor was elected to be the new god.'

Taking her hands out of her armpits, Jilly opened her fists and looked at her palms. She was glad that she didn't know how to read them.

Dylan said, 'These colonies of nanomachines might be able to create new connections between various lobes of the brain, new neural pathways—'

She resisted the impulse to put her hands to her head, for fear that she would feel some faint strange vibration through her skull, evidence of a horde of nanomachines busily changing her from within.

'—better synapses. Synapses are the points of contact between neurons in a neural pathway inside the brain, and apparently they become fatigued when we think or just when we stay awake too long. When they're fatigued they slow down our thought processes.'

Dead serious, not reaching for a wisecrack, she said, 'I could use a little synapse fatigue right now. My thoughts are spinning way too fast.'

'There's more in the interview,' Dylan said, pointing again at the laptop screen. 'I skimmed some of it, and there was a lot that I just didn't understand, a lot of fumfuddle about something called the precentral gyrus, and the postcentral gyrus, Purkinje cells . . . on and on with the arcane words. But I understood enough to realize what a hole we're in.'

No longer able to resist pressing her fingertips to her temples, Jilly felt no vibrations. Nevertheless, she said, 'God, it doesn't bear thinking about. Millions of tiny nanomachines and nanocomputers salted through your head, squirming around in there like so many bees, busy ants, making changes . . . It's not tolerable, is it?'

Dylan's face had gone gray enough to suggest that if his usual optimism had not burnt out, at least it had for the moment grown as dim as banked coals. 'It's got to be tolerable. We don't have any choice but to think about it. Unless we take the Shep option. But then who would cut *our* food into squares and rectangles?'

Indeed, Jilly couldn't decide whether talking about this machine infection or *not* talking about it would lead more surely and quickly to full-blown panic. She felt a dark winged terror perched within her, its feathers fluttering agitatedly, and she knew that if she didn't control it, didn't keep it firmly on its perch, if she allowed it to take flight, she might never bring it to roost again; and she knew that once it had flown long enough, frantically battering its pinions against the walls of every chamber in the mansion of her mind, her sanity would take flight with it.

She said, 'It's like being told you've got mad cow disease or brain parasites.'

'Except it's intended to be a boon to humanity.'

'Boon, huh? I'll bet somewhere in that interview, the nutcase used the term *master race* or *super race*, or something like it.'

'Wait'll you hear. From the day Proctor first conceived of using nanotechnology for the forced evolution of the brain, he knew exactly what the people who underwent it should be called. Proctorians.'

A thunderous bolt of anger was the ideal thing to distract Jilly from her terror and to keep it caged. 'What an egotistical, self-satisfied *freak!*'

'That's one apt description,' Dylan agreed.

Still apparently brooding about the superiority of square-cut snack crackers to the sucky-shapey Goldfish, Shep said, 'Cheez-Its.'

'Last night,' Dylan said, 'Proctor told me that if he weren't such a coward, he would have injected himself.'

'If he hadn't had the bad grace to get himself blown up,' Jilly declared, 'I'd inject the freak right now, get me an even bigger damn syringe than his, pump all those nanomachines straight into his brain through his ass.'

Dylan smiled a gray smile. 'You are an angry person.'

'Yeah. It feels good.'

'Cheez-Its.'

'Proctor told me he wasn't a fit role model for anyone,' Dylan said, 'that he had too much pride to be contrite. Kept rambling on about his character flaws.'

'What – that's supposed to make me go all gooey with compassion?'

'I'm just remembering what he said.'

Motivated partly by the twitchy feeling that she got from thinking about all those nanomachines roaming in her gray matter and partly by a sense of righteous outrage, Jilly became too agitated to sit still any longer. Supercharged with nervous energy, she wanted to go for a long run or perform vigorous calisthenics – or preferably, ideally, find someone whose ass needed kicking and then kick it until her foot ached, until she couldn't lift her leg anymore.

Jilly shot to her feet with such agitation that she startled Dylan into bolting off his chair, as well.

Between them, Shep stood, moving faster than Shep usually moved. He said, 'Cheez-Its,' raised his right hand, pinched a scrap of nothing between thumb and forefinger, tweaked, and folded all three of them out of the motel room.

29

Being an attractive, personable, and frequently amusing woman with no halitosis problem, Jillian Jackson had often been taken to lunch by young men who appreciated her fine qualities, but she had never before been *folded* to lunch.

She didn't actually witness herself folding, didn't see herself become the equivalent of a *Playboy* Playmate sans staples, nor did she feel any discomfort. The cheesy motel room and furnishings instantly rumpled into bizarrely juxtaposed fragments and then doubled-pleated-creased-crimped-ruckled-twilled-tucked *away* from her. Beveled shards of another place folded *toward* her, appearing somehow to pass *through* the receding motel room, the departure point shadowy and lamplit but the destination full of sunshine, so that for a moment she seemed to be inside a gigantic kaleidoscope, her world but a jumble of colorful mosaic fragments in the process of shifting from a dark pattern to a brighter one.

Objectively, transit time might have been nil; they might have gone from here to there instantaneously; but subjectively, she timed it at three or four seconds. Her feet slipped off motel-room carpet, the rubber soles of her athletic shoes stuttered a few inches across concrete, and she found herself standing with Dylan and Shepherd outside the front doors of a restaurant, a diner.

Shepherd had folded them back to the restaurant in Safford, where they had eaten dinner the previous night. This struck her as being a bad development because Safford was where Dylan had introduced the cowboy, Ben Tanner, to his lost granddaughter and, more important, where he had beaten the crap out of Lucas Crocker in the parking lot before calling the police to report that Crocker had been keeping his mother, Noreen, chained in the cellar. Even though the restaurant staff for the lunch shift probably didn't include any employees who'd been at work late the previous day, someone might recognize Dylan from a description, and in fact at least one cop might have returned today to examine the scene in daylight.

Then she realized that she was mistaken. They weren't all the way back in Safford. The establishment looked similar to the one in Safford because both shared the creatively bankrupt but traditional architecture of motel restaurants across the West, featuring a deep overhang on the roof to shield the big windows from the desert sun, low flagstone-faced walls supporting the windows, and flagstone-faced planters full of vegetation struggling to survive in the heat.

This was the coffee shop adjacent to the motel out of which they had just folded. Immediately south of them lay the motel registration office, and beyond the office, a covered walkway served a long wing of rooms, of which theirs was the next to last. Shepherd had folded them a grand distance of four or five hundred feet.

'Shep is hungry.'

Jilly turned, expecting to find an open gateway behind them, like the one Dylan had described on the hilltop in California, except that this one ought to provide a view not of the motel bathroom, but of the empty bedroom that they had a moment ago departed. Evidently, however, Shepherd had instantly closed the gate this time, for only the blacktop parking lot shimmered darkly in the noontime sun.

Twenty feet away, a young man in ranch clothes and a battered cowboy hat, getting out of a pickup truck that boasted a rifle rack, looked up at them, did a double take, but didn't cry out 'Teleporters' or 'Proctorians', or anything else accusatory. He just seemed mildly surprised that he had not noticed them a moment ago.

In the street, none of the passing traffic had jumped a curb, crashed into a utility pole, or rear-ended another vehicle. Judging by the reaction of motorists, none of them had seen three people blink into existence out of thin air.

No one inside the coffee shop rushed out to gape in amazement, either, which probably meant that no one had happened to be looking toward the entrance when Jilly, Dylan, and Shepherd had traded motel carpet for this concrete walkway in front of the main doors.

Dylan surveyed the scene, no doubt making the same calculations that Jilly made, and when his eyes met hers, he said, 'All things considered, I'd rather have walked.'

'Hell, I'd even rather have been dragged behind a horse.'

'Buddy,' Dylan said, 'I thought we had an understanding about this.'

'Cheez-Its.'

The young man from the pickup tipped his hat as he walked past them – 'Howdy, folks' – and entered the coffee shop.

'Buddy, you can't make a habit of this.'

'Shep is hungry.'

'I know, that's my fault, I should have gotten you breakfast as soon as we were showered. But you can't fold yourself to a restaurant anytime you want. That's bad, Shep. That's real bad. That's the worst kind of bad behavior.'

Shoulders slumped, head hung, saying nothing, Shep looked more hangdog than a sick basset hound. Clearly, being scolded by his brother made him miserable.

Jilly wanted to hug him. But she worried that he would fold the two of them to a better restaurant, leaving Dylan behind, and she hadn't brought her purse.

She also sympathized with Dylan. To explain the intricacies of their situation and to convey an effective warning that performing the miracle of folding from here to there in public would be exposing them to great danger, he needed Shepherd to be more focused and more communicative than Shepherd seemed capable of being.

Consequently, to establish that public folding was taboo, Dylan chose not to explain anything. Instead, he attempted to establish by blunt assertion that being seen folding out of one place or folding into another was a shameful thing.

'Shep,' said Dylan, 'you wouldn't go to the bathroom right out in public, would you?'

Shepherd didn't respond.

'Would you? You wouldn't just pee right here on the sidewalk where the whole world could watch. Would you? I'm starting to think maybe you would.'

Visibly cringing at the concept of making his toilet in a public place, Shepherd nevertheless failed to defend himself against this accusation. A bead of sweat dripped off the tip of his nose and left a dark spot on the concrete between his feet.

'Am I to take your silence to mean you *would* do your business right here on the sidewalk? Is that the kind of person you are, Shep? Is it? Shep? Is it?'

Considering Shepherd's pathological shyness and his obsession with cleanliness, Jilly figured that he would rather curl up on the pavement, in the blazing desert sun, and die of dehydration before relieving himself in public.

'Shep,' Dylan continued, unrelenting, 'if you can't answer me, then I have to assume you *would* pee in public, that you'd just pee anywhere you wanted to pee.'

Shepherd shuffled his feet. Another drop of perspiration slipped off the tip of his nose. Perhaps the fierce summer heat was to blame, but this seemed more like nervous sweat.

'Some sweet little old lady came walking by here, you might up and pee on her shoes with no warning,' Dylan said. 'Is that what I have to worry about, Shep? Shep? Talk to me, Shep.'

After nearly sixteen hours of intense association with the O'Conner brothers, Jilly understood why sometimes Dylan had to pursue an issue with firm – even obstinate – persistence in order to capture Shepherd's attention and to make the desired impression. Admirable perseverance in the mentoring of an autistic brother could, however, sometimes look uncomfortably like badgering, even like mean-spirited hectoring.

'Some sweet little old lady *and a priest* come walking by here, and before I know what's happened, you pee on their shoes. Is that the kind of thing you're going to do now, Shep? Are you, buddy? Are you?'

Judging by Dylan's demeanor, this haranguing took as a high a toll from him as it levied on his brother. As his voice grew harder and more insistent, his face tightened not with an expression of impatience or anger, but with pain. A spirit of remorse or perhaps even pity haunted his eyes.

'Are you, Shep? Have you suddenly decided to do disgusting and gross things? Have you, Shep? Have you? Shep? Shepherd? Have you?'

'N-no,' Shep at last replied.

'What did you say? Did you say no, Shep?'

'No. Shep said no.'

'You aren't going to start peeing on old ladies' shoes?'

'No.'

'You aren't going to do disgusting things in public?'

'No.'

'I'm glad to hear that, Shep. Because I've always thought you're a good kid, one of the best. I'm glad to know you're not going bad on me. That would break my heart, kid. See, lots of people are offended if you fold in or out of a public place in front of them. They're just as offended by folding as if you were to pee on their shoes.'

'Really?' Shep said.

'Yes. Really. They're disgusted.'

'Really?'

'Yes.'

'Why?'

'Well, why are you disgusted by those little cheese Goldfish?' Dylan asked.

Shep didn't reply. He frowned at the sidewalk, as though this abrupt conversational switch to the subject of Goldfish confused him.

The sky blazed too hot for birds. As sun flared off the windows of passing traffic and rippled liquidly along painted surfaces, those vehicles glided past like mercurial shapes of unknown nature in a dream. On the far side of the street, behind heat snakes wriggling up from the pavement, another motel and a service station shimmered as though they were as semitransparent as structures in a mirage.

Jilly had only moments ago *folded* miraculously from one place to another, and now here they stood in this surreal landscape, facing a future certain to be so bizarre at times as to seem like a stubborn hallucination, and yet they were talking about something as mundane as Goldfish cheese crackers. Maybe absurdity was the quality of any experience that proved you were alive, that you weren't dreaming or dead, because dreams were filled with enigma or terror, not with Abbott and Costello absurdity, and the afterlife wouldn't be as chockful of incongruity and absurdity as life, either, because if it were, there wouldn't be any reason to *have* an afterlife.

'Why are you disgusted by those little cheese Goldfish?' Dylan asked again. 'Is it because they're sort of round?'

'Shapey,' said Shepherd.

'They're round and shapey, and that disgusts you.'

'Shapey.'

'But lots of people like Goldfish, Shep. Lots of people eat them every day.'

Shep shuddered at the thought of dedicated Goldfish fanciers.

'Would you want to be forced to watch people eating Goldfish crackers right in front of you, Shep?'

Tilting her head down to get a better look at his face, Jilly saw Shepherd's frown deepen into a scowl.

Dylan pressed on: 'Even if you closed your eyes so you couldn't see, would you like to sit between a couple people eating Goldfish and have to listen to all the crunchy, squishy sounds?'

Apparently in genuine revulsion, Shepherd gagged.

'I like Goldfish, Shep. But because they disgust you, I don't eat them. I eat Cheez-Its instead. Would you like it if I started eating Goldfish all the time, leaving them out where you could see them, where you could come across them when you weren't expecting to? Would that be all right with you, Shep?'

Shepherd shook his head violently.

'Would that be all right, Shep? Would it? Shep?'

'No.'

'Some things that don't offend us may offend other people, so we have to be respectful of other people's feelings if we want them to be respectful of ours.'

'I know.'

'Good! So we don't eat Goldfish in front of certain people—'

'No Goldfish.'

'—and we don't pee in public—'

'No pee.'

'—and we don't fold in or out of public places.'

'No fold.'

'No Goldfish, no pee, no fold,' Dylan said.

'No Goldfish, no pee, no fold,' Shep repeated.

Although the pained expression still clenched his face, Dylan spoke in a softer and more affectionate tone of voice, and with apparent relief: 'I'm proud of you, Shep.'

'No Goldfish, no pee, no fold.'

'I'm very proud of you. And I love you, Shep. Do you know that? I love you, buddy.' Dylan's voice thickened, and he turned from his brother. He didn't look at Jilly, perhaps because he couldn't look at her and keep his composure. He solemnly studied his big hands, as if he'd done something with them that shamed him. He took several deep breaths, slow and deep, and into Shepherd's embarrassed silence, he said again, 'Do you know that I love you very much?'

'Okay,' Shep said quietly.

'Okay,' Dylan said. 'Okay then.'

Shepherd mopped his sweaty face with one hand, blotted the hand on his jeans. 'Okay.'

When Dylan at last met Jilly's eyes, she saw how difficult part of that conversation with Shep had been for him, the bullying part, and her voice, too, thickened with emotion. 'Now . . . now what?'

He checked for his wallet, found it. 'Now we have lunch.'

'We left the computer running back in the room.'

'It'll be all right. And the room's locked. There's a Do Not Disturb sign on the door.'

Traffic still passing in liquid ripples of sunlight. The far side of the street shimmering like a phantasm.

She expected to hear the silvery laughter of children, to smell incense, to see a woman wearing a mantilla and sitting on a pew in the parking lot, to feel the rush of wings as a river of white birds poured out of the previously birdless sky.

Then, without raising his head, Shepherd unexpectedly reached out to take her hand, and the moment became too real for visions.

They went inside. She helped Shep find his way, so he would not have to look up and risk eye contact with strangers.

Compared to the day outside, the air in the restaurant seemed to have been piped directly from the arctic. Jilly was not chilled.

For Dylan, the thought of hundreds of thousands or millions of microscopic machines swarming through his brain was such an appetite-killing consideration that he ate, ironically, almost as though he were a machine refueling itself, with no pleasure in the food.

Presented with the perfect entree – a grilled-cheese sandwich made with square bread lacking an arched crust, cut into four square pieces – complimented by rectangular steak fries with blunt ends, dill pickles that Dylan trimmed into rectangular sticks, and thick slices of beefsteak tomatoes that had also been trimmed into squares, Shep ate contentedly.

Although Shep used his fingers to pick up not just the sandwich, fries, and pickles, but also the remodeled tomatoes, Dylan made no effort to remind him of the rules of fork usage. There were proper times and places to reinforce table manners, and there was *this* time and place, where it made sense just to be thankful that they were alive and together and able to share a meal in peace.

They occupied a booth by a window, though Shep disliked sitting where he could be 'looked at by people inside *and* people out.' These plate-glass windows were so heavily tinted against the glare of the desert sun that from the outside, in daylight, little of the interior could be seen.

Besides, the only booths in the establishment were along the windows, and the regular tables were so closely set that Shep would have quickly become agitated when the growing lunch crowd pressed in around him. The booth offered structural barriers that provided a welcome degree of privacy, and following his recent chastisement, Shep was in a flexible mood.

Psychic imprints on menus and utensils squirmed under Dylan's touch, but he discovered that he continued to get better at being able to suppress his awareness of them.

Dylan and Jilly chatted inanely about inconsequential things, like favorite movies, as though Hollywood-produced entertainments could possibly have serious relevance to them now that they had been set apart from the rest of humanity and were most likely by the hour traveling further beyond ordinary human experience.

Soon, when movie talk began to seem not merely insignificant but bizarre, evidence of epic denial, Jilly started to bring them back to their dilemma. Referring to the convoluted chain of logic with which Dylan had gotten his brother to accept that folding out of or into a public place was as taboo as peeing on old ladies' shoes, she said, 'That was brilliant out there.'

'Brilliant?' He shook his head in disagreement. 'It was mean.'

'No. Don't beat yourself up.'

'In part it was mean. I hate that, but I've gotten pretty good at it when I have to be.'

'The point needed to be made,' she said. 'And quickly.'

'Don't make excuses for me. I might enjoy it too much, and start making them for myself.'

'Grim doesn't look good on you, O'Conner. I like you better when you're irrationally optimistic.'

He smiled. 'I like me better that way, too.'

After finishing the last bite of a club sandwich and washing it down with a swallow of Coors, she sighed and said, 'Nanomachines, nanocomputers . . . if all those little buggers are busy making me so much smarter, why do I still have trouble getting my mind around the whole concept?'

'They aren't necessarily making us smarter. Just different. Not all change is for the better. By the way, Proctor found it awkward to keep talking about nanomachines controlled by nanocomputers, so he invented a new word to describe those two things when they're combined. Nanobots. A combination of *nano* and *robots*.'

'A cute name doesn't make them any less scary.' She frowned, rubbed the back of her neck as if working a chill out of it. 'Déjà vu all over again. Nanobots. That rings a bell. And back in the room, you seemed to expect me to know more about this. Why?'

'The piece I called up for you to read on the laptop, the one I condensed for you instead . . . it was a transcript of an hour-long interview that Proctor did on your favorite radio program.'

'Parish Lantern?'

'Proctor's been on the show three times in five years, the third time for two hours. It figures you might've heard him once, anyway.'

Jilly brooded about this development for a moment and clearly didn't like the implications. 'Maybe I'd better start worrying more about Earth's magnetic pole shifting, and about brain leeches from an alternate reality, for that matter.'

Outside, a vehicle pulled off the street, into the parking lot, and raced past the restaurant at such imprudent speed that Dylan's attention was drawn by the roar of its engine and by the flash of its passage. A black Suburban. The rack of four spotlights fixed to the roof above the windshield didn't come as a standard accessory with every Suburban sold.

Jilly saw it, too. 'No. How could they find us?'

'Maybe we should've changed plates again after what happened at the restaurant in Safford.'

The SUV braked to a stop in front of the motel office, next door to the coffee shop.

'Maybe that little weasel, Skipper, at the service station suspected something.'

'Maybe a hundred things.'

Dylan faced the motel, but Jilly was sitting with her back to the action. Or to some of it. She pointed, tapping one index finger against the window. 'Dylan. Across the street.'

Through the tinted window, through the heat snakes writhing up from the sun-baked pavement, he saw another black Suburban in front of the motel that stood on the far side of the street.

Finishing the last bite of his lunch, Shep said, 'Shep wants cake.'

From his angle of view, even with his face close to the window, Dylan wasn't able to see the entire Suburban now that it had parked in front of the registration office. Half the vehicle remained in his line of sight, however, and he watched two men get out of the driver's side. Dressed in lightweight, light-colored clothes suitable for a desert resort, they looked like golfers headed for an afternoon on the links: unusually big golfers; unusually big, tough-looking golfers.

'Please,' Shep remembered to say. 'Cake please.'

30

Dylan was accustomed to being one of the biggest guys in just about any room, but the two hulks who got out of the driver's side of the Suburban looked as if they had spent the morning in a rodeo ring, tossing cowboys in the air and goring them. They disappeared around the car, heading toward the motel office.

'Let's go,' he said, sliding out of the booth, rising to his feet.

Jilly got up at once, but Shep didn't move. Head bowed, staring at his clean plate, he said, 'Cake please.'

Even if served in a wedge instead of a square, the single curved end of a piece of cake could be flattened easily. Otherwise, a wedge was satisfyingly angular, not curvy, not shapey. Shep loved cake.

'We'll get cake,' Dylan lied. 'But first we're going to the men's room, buddy.'

'Pee?' Shep asked.

'Pee,' Dylan confirmed quietly, determined to avoid making a scene.

'Shep doesn't need to pee.'

Fire laws and a need to receive deliveries guaranteed the existence of a back door; but no doubt they would have to go through the kitchen to reach it, a route that would assure too much commotion even if they were permitted to take it. They dared not leave by the front door, for fear of being spotted by the faux golfers. Only one exit remained.

'You may not get another chance for a while, buddy. Better go now,' Dylan explained.

'No pee.'

Their waitress arrived. 'Will that be everything?'

'Cake,' said Shep.

'Could we have menus to look at the desserts?' Dylan asked.

'Cake.'

'I thought you were leaving,' the waitress said.

'Just going to the men's room,' Jilly assured her. When the waitress frowned, Jilly added, 'The men's and the ladies'.'

'Cake.'

Withdrawing their lunch ticket from a pocket of her apron, the waitress said, 'We have some wonderful cakes.' She extracted a pencil from her elaborately piled and pinned red hair. 'Toasted-coconut, Black Forest, lemon, and lemon-walnut.'

'We don't all want cake,' Dylan said. 'We'll need menus.'

'Cake,' said Shepherd.

As the waitress went to get menus, Dylan said, 'Come on, Shep.'

'Cake. Toasted-coconut—'

'Pee first, Shep.'

'—Black Forest—'

By now the men in the Suburban would be at the registration desk in the motel office.

'—lemon—'

If they were carrying law-enforcement credentials, they would be presenting them to the desk clerk.

'—and lemon-walnut.'

If they had no credentials, they would be using intimidation to get the information they wanted.

'No pee,' Dylan quietly informed Shep, 'no cake.'

Licking his lips in anticipation of the cake, Shep considered this ultimatum.

'Dylan,' Jilly said softly but urgently. 'The window.'

The second black Suburban had crossed the street from the other motel. It parked behind the SUV that already stood in front of the registration office next door to the coffee shop.

Unless given absolutely no other option, Dylan didn't want to seize his brother by the arm and haul him out of the booth. In that event, the kid would probably come, although his cooperation was not a certainty. He wouldn't resist violently, but if he set his mind to it, he could become as immovable as a stubborn octopus.

Carrying menus, the waitress began the return trip from the hostess station.

'No pee, no cake?' Shepherd asked.

'No pee, no cake.'

'Pee, then cake?' Shep asked.

'Pee, then cake,' Dylan agreed.

Shepherd slid out of the booth.

Arriving with the menus just as Shepherd stood up, dropping them on the table, the waitress asked, 'Can I get you coffee?'

Dylan saw the front door open. Sun glared on that moving glass panel, and from this oblique angle, he couldn't see who might be entering until they stepped inside.

'Two coffees,' Jilly said.

An elderly couple crossed the threshold. They were probably in their eighties. Not stooped, spry enough, but surely not assassins.

'Milk,' Shep mumbled.

'Two coffees and one milk,' Dylan told the waitress.

The glass that the milk came in would have a round mouth; but the milk itself wasn't round. It wasn't shapey, but shapeless, and Shepherd never harbored a prejudice against any food solely because of the design of the container in which it might be served.

'Cake,' Shepherd said as, head down, he followed Dylan between the tables, with Jilly at the end of their procession. 'Cake. Pee, then cake. Pee, then cake.'

The restrooms lay off a hall at the back of the coffee shop.

Ahead of Dylan, a burly bearded man in a tank-top shirt sported enough colorful tattoos just on his exposed arms and neck, and on his bald head, to qualify as an attraction in a sideshow. He went into the men's room.

As they gathered in the hallway, still in the line of sight of some of the diners in the restaurant, Dylan said to Jilly, 'Check the women's room.'

She stepped into the lavatory and returned before the door had time to fall shut behind her. 'Nobody's in here.'

Dylan urged his brother to step into the women's restroom with Jilly, and followed close behind him.

The doors stood open on each of two stalls. The outer door between the lav and the hallway could not be locked. Someone might walk in on them at any moment.

The only window appeared to be painted shut, and in any event, it was too small to provide escape.

Dylan said, 'Buddy, I need you to do something for me.'

'Cake.'

'Shep, I need you to fold us out of here and back to our room in the motel.'

'But they'll be going to our room,' Jilly objected.

'They won't be there yet. We left the computer running, with the Proctor interview. We don't want them to see that. I don't know where we'll be going from here, but wherever it is, they'll have a better chance of staying on our heels if they realize how much we know and can try to anticipate our moves.'

'Toasted-coconut cake.'

'Besides,' Dylan added, 'there's an envelope of cash in my shaving kit, almost five hundred bucks, and right now all we have is what's in my wallet.' He put one hand under Shep's chin, raised his head. 'Shep, you've got to do this for me.'

Shep closed his eyes. 'Don't pee in public.'

'I'm not asking you to pee, Shep. Just fold us back to our room. Now. Right now, Shep.'

'No Goldfish, no pee, no fold.'

'This is different, Shep.'

'No Goldfish, no pee, no fold.'

'That rule doesn't apply, buddy. We're not in public now.'

Shepherd wasn't buying that line of argument. After all, this was called a *public* restroom, and he knew it. 'No Goldfish, no pee, no fold.'

'Listen, buddy, you've seen a lot of movies, you know what bad guys are.'

'Pee in public.'

'Worse bad guys than that. Bad guys with guns. Killers like in the movies. We've got some bad guys looking for us, Shep.'

'Hannibal Lecter.'

'I don't know. Maybe they're that bad. I don't know. But if you don't help me here, if you don't fold us when I ask you to, then for sure things are going to get gooey-bloody.'

The kid's eyes were active behind his lids, an indication of the degree of his agitation. 'Gooey-bloody is bad.'

'Gooey-bloody is very bad. And it's going to get very gooey and very bloody if we don't fold back to our room *right now*.'

'Shep is scared.'

'Don't be scared.'

'Shep is scared.'

Dylan admonished himself not to lose his temper as he had lost it on the hilltop in California. He must never speak to Shep that way again, never, no matter how desperate the situation became. But he was left with no tactic but to plead. 'Buddy, for God's sake, *please*.'

'Sh-shep is s-s-scared.'

When Dylan checked his Timex, the sweep-motion second hand seemed to be *spinning* around the watch face.

Moving to Shepherd's side, Jilly said, 'Sweetie, last night when I was in my bed and you were in your bed, and Dylan was asleep and snoring, do you remember the little conversation we had?'

Dylan had no idea what she was talking about. She hadn't told him about a conversation with Shep. And he was certain that he didn't snore.

'Sweetie, I woke up and heard you whispering, remember? You said you were scared. And what did I say?'

Shepherd's hyperactive eyes stopped moving behind his closed lids, but he didn't respond to her.

'Do you remember, honey?' When she put an arm around Shepherd's shoulders, he didn't cringe from contact or even flinch. 'Sweetie, remember, you said, "Shep is scared," and I said, "Shep is brave."'

Dylan heard noises in the hallway, glanced at the door. No one came in, but the coffee shop had a big lunch crowd; this privacy wouldn't last much longer.

Jilly said, 'And you are brave, Shep. You're one of the bravest people I've ever known. The world is a scary place. And I know it's scarier for you than it is for us. So much noise, so much brightness and color, so many people, strangers, always talking at you, and then germs everywhere, nothing neat like it ought to be, nothing simple like you want it so much to be, everything shapey, and so much that's disgusting. You can put a puzzle together and make it right, and you can read *Great Expectations* like twenty times, a hundred times, and every time it'll be exactly like you expect it to be, exactly right. But you can't make life come together like a puzzle, and you can't make it be the same every day – and yet you get up every morning, and you *try*. That's very brave, sweetie. If I were you, if I were the way you are, I don't think I could be as brave as you, Shepherd. I know I couldn't. Every day, *trying* so hard – that is as brave as anything any hero ever did in any movie.'

Listening to Jilly, Dylan eventually stopped glancing worriedly at the door, stopped consulting his wristwatch, and discovered that this woman's face and melodious voice were more compelling even than the thought of professional killers closing in from all sides.

'Honey, you have to be as brave as I know you can be. You have to not worry about bad guys, not worry about gooey-bloody, just do what needs to be done, like you get up every morning and shower and do what needs to be done to make the world as neat and as simple as you can make it. Sweetie, you have to be brave and fold us back to our room.'

'Shep is brave?'

'Yes. Shep is brave.'

'No Goldfish, no pee, no fold,' said Shep, but his eyes remained still behind his closed lids, which suggested that even the issue of the impropriety of public folding did not trouble him as much as it had a minute ago.

Jilly said, 'Actually, folding in public isn't quite like peeing in public, sweetie. It's more like spitting in public. It's still not something that polite people do. But while you *never* pee in public, no matter what, sometimes you just have to spit in public, like when a bug flies in your mouth, and that's okay. These bad guys are like a bug that flies in your mouth, and folding away from them is no worse than spitting out a bug, Shep. Do it now, sweetie. Do it quickly.'

Shepherd reached up and pinched a scrap of nothing between his thumb and forefinger.

Beside him, Jilly put the palm of her left hand against the back of Shepherd's right.

Shep opened his eyes, turned his head to meet Jilly's gaze. 'You feel how it is?'

'Do it, sweetie. Hurry. *Now.*'

Dylan stepped in closer, afraid of being left behind. He saw the air crimp where Shepherd's fingers met, and he watched in wonder as wrinkles formed outward from the crimp.

Shep plucked the fabric of reality. The women's restroom folded away, and a new place folded toward them.

31

As he himself folded or as the women's restroom folded around him, whichever in fact was happening, Dylan panicked, convinced that Shep would kink-and-pleat them to someplace other than their room in the motel, that they might arrive instead in another motel where they had stayed two nights ago or three, or ten, that when they unfolded they might find themselves helplessly flailing in midair, a thousand feet above the ground, and plummet to their deaths, that they might travel from the lavatory to the lightless bottom of an oceanic abyss, where they would be crushed instantly by the hideous pressure of the miles of sea above them, even before they sucked in a first drowning breath of water. The Shepherd whom Dylan knew from twenty years of brotherhood and from ten years of daily caregiving was childlike, perhaps with all his faculties intact, but lacking the competency to apply them in any consistent fashion. Although they had folded back alive from the hilltop in California and had traveled safely from their motel room to the front doors of the coffee shop, Dylan could not trust in this new Shepherd O'Conner, this overnight genius of physics, this maven of applied quantum mechanics – or whatever he was applying – this sudden sorcerer who *still* reasoned like a young child, who could manipulate time and space, but who would not eat 'shapey' food, referred to himself in the third person, and avoided direct eye contact. If he had been foolish enough to give Shepherd a loaded gun, he would not have expected anything other than darkest tragedy; and surely the potential for disastrous consequences in this herethere *folding* must be immeasurably greater than the damage that could be wrought even by a submachine gun. Though transit time proved all but instantaneous, Dylan considered enough dire possibilities to keep fans of gooey-bloody cinema supplied with trashy films full of pukey moments for at least a generation, and then the last of the lavatory folded away and a new place entirely unfolded into existence around them.

The metaphorical loaded gun had not gone off. They were in their motel bedroom: drapes closed, light provided for the most part by a single lamp, standing in front of the desk, the laptop.

Behind them, Shep had closed the gateway to the women's lavatory as they came through it. Good. They couldn't safely go back, anyway. And they didn't need a freaked-out visitor to the restroom shrieking for witnesses.

They were safe. Or so it seemed for an instant.

In fact, they were whole, physically and mentally intact, but they were *not* safe. In the breathless moment of arrival, before any of them inhaled or exhaled, Dylan heard the click of a passkey in a lock and then the scrape of the deadbolt being disengaged in a slow and cautious fashion meant to make as little noise as feasible.

The barbarians had arrived at the gate, and no cauldrons of boiling oil had been set upon the parapets to drive them back with a rain of terror.

Beneath the deadbolt was a simpler lock to which the passkey would next be applied. The security chain remained engaged, but it would not hold against even one good kick from a brute who knew just where to place his boot.

Even as the deadbolt retracted, Dylan grabbed one of the three straight-backed chairs that still stood before the desk. He crossed the room in long strides, tipped the chair backward under the knob, and braced the door shut as the passkey turned the second lock.

As short of time as he was of money, he dared not wait to see if the bracing chair kept the door tightly shut or instead allowed a dangerous degree of play. Forced to trust the makeshift barricade as he had needed to trust Shep's wizardry at folding, Dylan raced into the bathroom, snatched the envelope of cash from his shaving kit, and shoved it into a pants pocket.

Returning to the bedroom, he saw that the door was indeed closed tight, the chair wedged firmly in place, as the knob worked back and forth and wood creaked under steady pressure.

For precious seconds, the men outside might believe that the resistance they encountered could be attributed to a problem with one of the locks. He couldn't count on them being stupid, however, or even gullible, and considering how aggressively they drove their black Suburbans, he couldn't expect them to be patient, either.

Already, Jilly had unplugged, closed, and secured the laptop. She slung her purse over one shoulder, turned to Dylan as he approached, and pointed at the ceiling, for some reason reminding him of Mary Poppins, but a Mary Poppins who had never been rinsed pale by England's bad weather, clearly intending by her gesture to say *Up and away!*

A cessation of the creaking-wood sounds and the resumption of the stealthy clicking of a key in the lock suggested that the pumped-up golfers were still bamboozled.

Shep stood in the classic Shep pose, a portrait of defeat at the hands of cruel Nature, looking nothing whatsoever like a wizard.

'Okay, buddy,' Dylan whispered, 'do your thing and fold us out of here.'

Arms hanging slack at his sides, Shepherd made no move to tweak the three of them to safety.

'Now, kiddo. Now. *Let's go.*'

'It's no more wrong than spitting out a bug,' Jilly reminded Shepherd.

The faint *click-click* of key in keyhole gave way again to the protest of hinge screws biting in the jamb and to the quiet creaking of the straight-backed chair responding to a relentless pressure on the door.

'No fold, no cake,' Dylan whispered urgently, for cake and Road Runner cartoons were more motivating to Shep than fame and fortune would have been to most men.

At the mention of cake, Jilly gasped and said, 'Don't take us back to the coffee shop, Shep!'

Her admonition drew from Shepherd a question that explained his hesitation: 'Where?'

Outside, the killers lost patience with the stealthy approach and resorted to the lust for drama that seemed to be their most reliable characteristic. A shoulder or a boot heel struck the door, which shuddered, and the bracing chair shrieked like a tramped cat.

'Where?' Jilly demanded of Dylan. 'Where?'

Battered again, the door boomed a timpani note, and something in the structure of the chair cracked, but held.

In transit from the women's restroom, he had imagined numerous unintended destinations that would have proved disastrous, but now he could not think of a single place in this world where they might wisely seek sanctuary.

The crash of determined meat against resistant wood came again, and the meat grunted not with pain or anger, but as if a perverse pleasure had been taken from this punishment.

Immediately following the grunt came another crash, but this time it was the brittle percussion of shattering glass. The closed drapes stirred at one of the windows as fragments of the broken pane rapped off the back of the fabric.

'Home,' Dylan told Shepherd. 'Take us home, Shep. Take us home real quick.'

'Home,' Shepherd echoed, but he seemed unsure of precisely the place to which the word referred.

Whoever had broken the window raked with some instrument at the remaining sharp shards in the frame, clearing the way for entrance.

'Our house in California,' Dylan said, '*California* – one hundred something thousand square miles—'

Shep raised his right hand as if to swear fealty to the state of California.

'—population thirty something million something thousand—'

Whatever genetic cousin to a bull was charging the door charged it again, and the chair cracked, sagged.

Frowning as though still unsure of himself, Shepherd pinched the air between the thumb and forefinger of his raised hand.

'—state tree,' Dylan said, but then fumbled for the species.

'The redwood!' Jilly said.

The drapes billowed as one of the assassins began to climb in from outside.

'State flower, the golden poppy,' Dylan continued.

Persistence paid. On the fifth blow, the door shuddered inward and the bracing chair collapsed.

The first man across the threshold, kicking at the fragments of the chair, was wearing pale-yellow pants, a pink-and-yellow polo shirt, and a murderous expression. He had a pistol, and as he rushed forward, he raised it with the clear intention of squeezing off a shot.

'Eureka,' Shep said, and tweaked.

Dylan thanked God that he heard no gunfire as the motel room folded away from him, but he *did* hear his name – 'O'Conner!' – shouted by the would-be shooter.

This time while in kaleidoscopic transit, he had something entirely new to fear: that the thug in golf togs had gotten too near to them before they escaped the motel room, and that Shep had folded a well-armed killer with them to California.

32

Abundant slabs of shadow and a few shards of pale light unfolded through the receding motel bedroom, and one split second before Dylan recognized the new room that fell into place around him, he smelled the lingering savor of a cinnamon-pecan-raisin cake baked according to his mother's cherished recipe, its delicious aroma unmistakable.

Shep, Jilly, and Dylan himself arrived unscathed, but the killer in the polo shirt didn't have a ticket to ride, after all. Not even the echo of his shouted *O'Conner!* followed them out of Arizona.

In spite of the comforting aroma and the gladdening absence of a door-busting assassin, Dylan enjoyed no sense of relief. Something was wrong. He couldn't at once identify the source of his current uneasiness, but he felt it too strongly to discount it as bad nerves.

The gloom in the kitchen of their California house was relieved only slightly by a soft butterscotch-yellow light seeping across the threshold of the open door to the dining room, and even less by the illuminated clock set into the belly of a smiling ceramic pig that hung on the wall to the right of the sink. On the counter under the clock, revealed by that timely light, a sheet-cake pan containing the fresh cinnamon-pecan-raisin delight cooled on a wire rack.

Vonetta Beesley – their once-a-week Harley-riding housekeeper – sometimes cooked for them, using their late mother's best recipes. But as they weren't scheduled to return from their art-festival tour until late October, she must have prepared this treat for herself.

Following the momentary disorientation of being folded, Dylan realized why a sense of *wrongness* could not be dispelled. They had departed eastern Arizona, which lay in the Mountain time zone, before one o'clock Saturday afternoon. In California, in the Pacific time zone, the day should have waned one hour less than it had back in Holbrook. Shortly before one'clock in Holbrook translated to shortly before noon on the shores of the Pacific, yet the black of night pressed at the kitchen windows.

Darkness at noon?

'Where are we?' Jilly whispered.

'Home,' Dylan said.

He consulted the luminous hands of his wristwatch, which he had set to Mountain time days ago, before the arts festival in Tucson. The watch showed four minutes till one o'clock, about what he had expected and surely correct.

Here in the land of the golden poppy and the redwood tree, the time ought to be four minutes till noon, not four till midnight.

'Why's it dark?' Jilly asked.

In the belly of the pig, the illuminated clock showed 9:26.

During the previous trips via folding, either no time elapsed in transit – or at most a few seconds. Dylan had not been aware of any significant period of time passing on this occasion, either.

If they truly had arrived at 9:26 in the evening, Vonetta should have left hours ago. She worked from nine o'clock until five. If she had gone, however, she would have taken the cake with her.

Likewise, she wouldn't have forgotten to turn off the light in the dining room. Vonetta Beesley had always been as reliable as the atomic clock at Greenwich, by which all the nations of the world set their timepieces.

The house stood in a funereal condition, hung with cerements of silence, draped in shrouds of stillness.

The *wrongness* involved something more than the darkness peering in at the windows, involved the house itself and something within the house. He could hear no evil breathing, no demon on the prowl, but he sensed that *nothing* here was right.

Jilly must have been alarmed by the same queer perception. She stood precisely on the spot where she had been unfolded, as though afraid to move, and her body language was so clearly written that her tension could easily be read even in these shadows.

The quality of light issuing from the dining room wasn't as it should be. The chandelier over the table, which Dylan couldn't see from this angle, was controlled by a switch with a dimming feature, but even at this low level of brightness, the glow had far too rich a butterscotch color and too moody an aspect to have been thrown off by the brass-and-crystal fixture. Besides, the light didn't originate from chandelier height; the ceiling in the next room was troweled in shadow, and the light appeared to fall to the floor from a point not far above the top of the table.

'Shep, buddy, what's happening here?' Dylan whispered.

Having been promised cake, Shep might have been expected to go directly to the cinnamon glory cooling in a pan under the clock, for it was his nature to be single-minded in all things, and not least of all in the matter of cake. Instead, he took one step toward the door to the dining room, hesitated, and said, 'Shep is brave,' although he sounded more fearful than Dylan had ever before heard him.

Dylan wanted to avoid venturing deeper into the house until he gained a better sense of their situation. He needed a good weapon, as well. The knife drawer offered a trove of wicked cutlery; but he'd had enough of knives lately. He longed for a baseball bat.

'Shep is brave,' Shep said, with even a greater tremor in his voice and with less confidence than before. Yet his head was raised to face the dining-room door rather than the floor at his feet, and as though defying an inner counsel that always advised him to retreat from any challenge, he shuffled forward.

Dylan quickly moved to his brother's side and placed one hand on his shoulder, intending to restrain him, but Shep shrugged it off and continued slowly but determinedly toward the dining room.

Jilly looked to Dylan for guidance. Her dark eyes shone with reflected clock light.

In a stubborn mood, Shep could be an inspiration for any mule; and Dylan detected here an infrequently seen but familiar obstinacy that experience had taught him could not be dealt with easily and certainly not quietly. Shep would do in this matter what he wanted to do, leaving Dylan no option but to follow him warily.

He surveyed the shadowy kitchen for a weapon but saw nothing immediately at hand.

At the threshold, in the burnt-ocher light, Shepherd hesitated, but only briefly, before stepping out of the kitchen. He turned left to face the dining-room table.

When Dylan and Jilly entered the dining room behind Shepherd, they found a boy sitting at the table. He appeared to be ten years old.

The boy did not look up at them, but remained focused on the large basket filled with adorable golden-retriever puppies, which lay before him. Much of the basket was complete, but many of the puppies lacked portions of their bodies and heads. The boy's hands flew, flew from the box of loose puzzle pieces to empty areas of the picture that waited to be filled.

Jilly might not have recognized the young puzzle worker, but Dylan knew him well. The boy was Shepherd O'Conner.

33

Dylan remembered this puzzle, which possessed a significance so special that he could have painted it from memory with a considerable degree of accuracy. And now he recognized the source of the burnt-ocher light: a pharmacy-style lamp that usually stood on a desk in the study. The lamp featured a deep-yellow glass shade.

On those occasions when Shepherd's autism expressed itself in a particular sensitivity to bright lights, he could not simply work a jigsaw puzzle in the reduced glare made possible by a dimmer switch. Although virtually inaudible to everyone else, the faint buzz of resistance produced by the restraint of electrical current in the rheostat shrieked through his skull as if it were a high-speed bone saw. Therefore, he resorted to the desk lamp with the heavily tinted shade, in which the regular bulb had been replaced with one of lower wattage.

Shepherd hadn't worked a puzzle in the dining room in the past ten years, having moved instead to the table in the kitchen. This basketful of puppies had been the last jigsaw that he had finished in this room.

'Shep is brave,' the standing Shepherd said, but the younger Shepherd at the table didn't look up.

Nothing that had happened heretofore had filled Dylan with a dread as terrible as the anxious fear that now seemed to shrink his heart. This time what lay ahead of him in the next few minutes was not unknown, as had been the case with all that had come before this, but in fact was known too well. He felt himself being swept toward that known horror as surely as a man in a small rowboat, on the brink of Niagara, would be helpless to avoid the falls.

From Jilly: *'Dylan!'*

When he turned to her, she pointed at the floor.

Under them lay a Persian-style carpet. Around each foot, the Persian pattern had been blotted out by a glimmering blackness, as though their shoes rested in pools of ink. This blackness rippled subtly but continually. When he moved one foot, the inky puddle moved with it, and the portion of the rug that had seemed to be stained at once reappeared unmarred.

A dining-room chair stood near Dylan, and upon touching it, he saw another inklike stain at once spread out from his hand across the upholstery, larger than his palm and fingers but conforming to their shape. He slid his hand back and forth, and the surrounding black blot slid with it, leaving the fabric immaculate.

Dylan could feel the chair under his hand, but when he tried to grip it firmly, the upholstery didn't dimple. Applying greater force, he attempted to jerk it away from the table – and his hand passed through the chair as if it were an illusion.

Or as if he were a ghost with no material substance.

Aware of Jilly's shock and continuing confusion, Dylan put one hand on her arm to show her that this inky phenomenon didn't occur between them, only when they attempted to have an influence upon their surroundings.

'The boy at the table,' he told her, 'is Shepherd when he was ten years old.'

She seemed to have worked that much out for herself, for she showed no surprise at this revelation. 'This isn't . . . some vision Shep's sharing with us.'

'No.'

Her understanding came as a statement rather than a question, as though she had begun to put the clues together before Dylan revealed the young puzzle worker's identity: 'We folded not just to California but also to sometime in the past.'

'Not just sometime.' His heart sank in dismay, though it wasn't weighted by an overwhelming peril, for he was reasonably sure that nothing in this past place could harm them, just as they were unable to influence anything here; instead, his heart was weighed down with sorrow, and it sank in a familiar sea of loss. 'Not just sometime. One night in particular. One awful night.'

More for Jilly's benefit than to confirm his own perception of their situation, Dylan stepped to the dining-room table and swept one arm across it with the intent of spilling the jigsaw puzzle to the floor. He was unable to disrupt a single piece of the picture.

Ten-year-old Shepherd, wrapped in the insulation of autism and focused intently on a puzzle, might not have reacted to their voices even if he had heard them. He would have flinched or at least blinked in surprise, however, at the sight of a man sweeping an arm across the table, attempting to undo his work. He reacted not at all.

'We're essentially invisible here,' Dylan said. 'We can see but not be seen. We can hear sounds, but we can't be heard. We can smell the cake. We can feel the warm air coming out of the heating vent and breathe it, feel the surfaces of objects, but we can't have an effect on anything.'

'Are you saying that's how Shepherd wants it?'

Shepherd continued to watch his younger self give feet to lame puppies and eyes to those that had been blind.

'Considering what night this is,' Dylan said, 'that's the last thing Shepherd would want. He doesn't set the rules. This must be how *Nature* wants it, just how it is.'

Apparently Shepherd could fold them into the past, but only to walk through it as they would walk through a museum.

'The past is the past. It can't be undone,' Dylan said, but he ardently wished that this were not true.

'Last night,' Jilly reminded him, 'Shepherd suddenly began to reel off all those synonyms for feces – but he did it long after I'd told you to clean up your language 'cause you sounded like my old man.'

'You didn't say I sounded like your old man.'

'Well, that's why trash talk bothers me. He was a garbage mouth. Anyway, you said Shep's sense of time isn't like yours and mine.'

'His sense of just about anything isn't like ours.'

'You said the past and present and future aren't as clearly separated for him as for us.'

'And here we are. February, 1992, more than ten years ago, before everything went to hell.'

From the adjacent living room, through an open door, came voices, argumentative but not loud.

Dylan and Jilly looked toward that door, beyond which glowed more and brighter lights than the single pharmacy lamp in the dining room. Younger Shep continued filling the holes in the puppies while older Shep watched him with an anxious expression.

On the battlefields of mind and heart, an imperative curiosity warred with Dylan's dread. If so much horror wouldn't have attended the satisfaction of his curiosity, then curiosity might have won. Or if he could have affected the outcome of this long-ago night, he would at once have been able to overcome his all but paralyzing anticipation of evil. But if he could make no difference – and he could not – then he didn't want to be a useless witness to what he had not seen ten years ago.

The voices in the living room grew louder, angrier.

'Buddy,' he urged the older Shepherd, 'fold us out of here. Fold us home, but to our own time. Do you understand me, Shep? Fold us out of the past *now*.'

The younger Shep was deaf to Dylan, to Jilly, and to his older self. Although the older Shep heard every word his brother spoke, he reacted as though he, too, were of this earlier time and were stone deaf to the voices of those who weren't. Clearly, judging by the intensity with which he watched his younger self, he didn't want to fold anywhere just yet, and he couldn't be forced to work his magic.

When the angry exchange in the living room escalated, ten-year-old Shep's fleet hands dropped to the table, each with an unplaced piece of the puzzle. He looked toward the open door.

'Oh,' Dylan said, as a chilling realization came to him. 'Oh, buddy, no, no.'

'What?' Jilly asked. 'What's wrong?'

At the table, younger Shep put down the puzzle pieces and got up from his chair.

'The poor damn kid. He saw,' Dylan said miserably. 'We never knew he saw.'

'Saw what?'

Here on the evening of February 12, 1992, ten-year-old Shepherd O'Conner rounded the dining-room table, shuffling toward the door to the living room.

Twenty-year-old Shepherd stepped forward, reached out, tried to stop his younger self from going farther. His hands passed through that Shepherd of a far February as if through a spirit, without the slightest hindering effect.

Staring at his hands, the older Shep said, 'Shep is brave,' in a voice that shook with fear. 'Shep is brave.' He seemed not to be speaking admiringly of ten-year-old Shepherd O'Conner, but to be encouraging himself to face the horror that he knew lay ahead.

'Fold us out of here,' Dylan persisted.

Shepherd made eye contact, and even though he was eye to eye with his brother, not with a stranger, this intimacy always cost him. Tonight, in these circumstances, the cost was especially high. His gaze revealed a terrible vulnerability, a sensitivity for which he didn't possess the usual compensating human armor: ego, self-esteem, an instinct for psychological self-preservation. 'Come. Come see.'

'No.'

'Come see. You have to see.'

The younger Shepherd stepped out of the dining room, into the living room.

Breaking eye contact with Dylan, the older Shepherd insisted, 'Shep is brave, brave,' and trailed after himself, man-child in the wake of child, out of the dining room, the inky puddles under his feet moving with him as he shuffled off the Persian carpet onto the blond maple tongue-and-groove floor.

Dylan followed, Jilly followed, into the living room as it had been on February 12, 1992.

Younger Shepherd stopped two steps past the doorway, but older Shepherd walked around him and deeper into the momentous scene.

The sight of his mother, Blair, not yet dead and therefore seeming to be once more alive, rocked Dylan worse even than he had expected it would. Barbed-wire grief fenced his heart, which seemed to swell to test itself upon the sharpest points.

Blair O'Conner had been forty-four, so young.

He remembered her as gentle, as kind, as patient, with a beauty of the mind equal to her lovely face.

Here, now, however, she revealed her fiery side: green eyes by anger brightened, face by anger sharpened, stalking back and forth as she talked, with a mother-panther threat in every movement, in every pause.

She had never been angry without good cause, and never *this* angry in Dylan's experience.

The man who'd struck these sparks of anger from her flinty sense of right and wrong stood at one of the living-room windows, his back to her, to all of them gathered here from this time and from across time.

Her ghostly audience unseen, not yet even aware of ten-year-old Shep watching from just this side of the dining-room doorway, Blair said, 'I told you they don't exist. And even if they did exist, I'd never give them to *you*.'

'And if they did exist, who *would* you give them to?' the man at the window asked, turning to face her.

Slimmer in 1992 than in 2002, with more hair than he would have in a decade, Lincoln Proctor, alias Frankenstein, was nonetheless at once recognizable.

34

Jilly had once described it as an 'evil-dreamy smile,' and so it appeared to Dylan now. The man's faded-denim eyes had earlier seemed to be the lusterless lamps of a meek soul, but on this second encounter, he saw windows of ice looking out from a cold kingdom.

His mother had known Proctor. Proctor had been in their house all those years ago.

This discovery shocked Dylan so profoundly that for a moment he forgot to what dark resolution this encounter must progress, and he stood in semiparalytic fascination, a rapt listener.

'Damn it, the diskettes don't exist!' his mother declared. 'Jack never mentioned any such thing. There's no point discussing this.'

Jack had been Dylan's father, dead now fifteen years, dead five years on the February night of this confrontation.

'He took delivery of them the day he died,' said Proctor. 'You wouldn't have known.'

'If they ever existed,' Blair said, 'which I doubt, then they're gone with Jack.'

'If they *did* exist,' Proctor pressed, 'would you give them to the unfortunate investors who lost money—'

'Don't prettify it. You *cheated* them out of their money. People who trusted Jack, trusted you – and you *swindled* it from them. Set up companies for projects you never intended to develop, funneled the money out of them into your stupid robot research—'

'Nanobots. And it's not stupid. I'm not proud of swindling people, you know. I'm ashamed of it. But nanomachine research takes a lot more money than anyone wants to invest in it. I had to find additional sources of funds. There were—'

Defiant, Dylan's mother said, 'If I had these diskettes you're talking about, I'd have given them to the police. And there's your proof that Jack never had them, either. If he'd had that kind of evidence, he would never have killed himself. He'd have seen some hope. He'd have gone to the authorities, fought for the investors.'

Proctor nodded, smiled. 'Not the kind of man you expected to swallow a bottle of pills and suck an exhaust hose, was he?'

Some fire went out of Blair O'Conner, doused by emotions more raw than anger. 'He was depressed. Not just over his own losses. He felt he'd failed the good people who relied on him. Friends, family. He was despondent. . . .' Belatedly she read a more ominous meaning in Proctor's question. Her eyes widened. 'What're you saying?'

From inside his leather coat, Proctor drew a pistol.

Jilly gripped Dylan's arm. 'What *is* this?'

Numbly, he said, 'We thought an intruder killed her, a stranger. Some passing psychopath just off the highway. It was never solved.'

For a moment Dylan's mother and Proctor regarded each other in silence, as she absorbed the truth of her husband's death.

Then Proctor said, 'Jack was my size. I'm a thinker, not a fighter. I admit I'm a coward in that regard. But I thought I might overcome him with surprise and chloroform, and I did.'

At the mention of chloroform, Jilly's hand tightened on Dylan's arm.

'Then while he was unconscious, gastric intubation was an easy matter. All I needed was a laryngoscope to be sure I got the tube down the esophagus, not the trachea. Flushed the Nembutal capsules down with water, straight into the stomach. Pulled out the tube, kept him sedated with chloroform till the Nembutal overdose kicked in.'

Dylan's shock gave way to anger, but not entirely a personal anger arising from what this monstrous man had done to their family. Indignation was a part of it, too, a wrath directed not merely at Lincoln Proctor but at evil itself, at the fact of its existence. All of humanity might be fallen from grace, but far too many among humankind eagerly embraced darkness, sowed the earth with cruelty and fed on the misery of others, falling farther still, down and down, *thrilled* by the plummet.

'I assure you,' Proctor told Blair O'Conner, 'your husband felt no pain. Though he was unconscious, I took great care not to force the intubation.'

Dylan had felt this way on finding Travis chained to that bed on Eucalyptus Avenue: sympathy for all the victims of violence and a pure poignant rage on their behalf. Storming through him were emotions no less overblown than those of the characters in an opera, which he found as strange as anything else that had happened to him, as strange as his new sixth sense, as strange as being folded.

'I'm not at all a good man,' Proctor said, indulging in the smarmy self-deprecation that had been his style the previous night, when he injected Dylan. 'Not a good man by any standard. I know my faults, and I've got plenty. But as bad as I am, I'm not capable of inflicting pain thoughtlessly or when it isn't absolutely necessary.'

As though Jilly shared Dylan's operatic wrath and painfully affecting pity for the weak, the victimized, she went to the older Shepherd, on whom her compassion could have an effect not possible on the untouchable boy of this earlier era. She put an arm around Shep, gently turned him away from Lincoln Proctor, from his mother, so that he would not witness again what he had seen ten years ago.

'By the time I rigged the hose from the exhaust pipe,' Proctor said, 'Jack was so deeply asleep that he never knew he was dying. He had no sense of suffocation, no fear. I regret what I did, it eats at me, even though I had no choice, no option. Anyway, I feel better that I've had the chance to let you know your husband didn't abandon you and your children, after all. I regret misleading you till now.'

To Proctor's self-justification and to the realization that her own death was imminent, Blair O'Conner reacted with a defiance that stirred Dylan. 'You're a parasite,' she told Proctor, 'a stinking ugly worm of a man.'

Nodding as he slowly crossed the room toward her, Proctor said, 'I'm all that and worse. I have no scruples, no morals. One thing and one alone matters to me. My work, my science, my vision. I'm a sick and despicable man, but I have a mission and I will see it through.'

Although the past would surely remain immutable, as unchangeable as the iron hearts of madmen, Dylan found himself moving between his mother and Proctor, with the irrational hope that the gods of time would in this one instance relax their cruel laws and allow him to stop the bullet that had ten years ago killed Blair O'Conner.

'When I took those diskettes off Jack's body,' Proctor said, 'I didn't know he'd been given two sets. I thought I had them all. I've only recently learned differently. The set I took from him – he had intended to turn those over to the authorities. The others must be here. If they'd been found, I'd already be in jail, wouldn't I?'

'I don't have them,' Blair insisted.

His back to his mother, Dylan faced Proctor and the muzzle of the handgun.

Proctor looked through him, unaware that a visitor through time stood in his way. 'Five years is a long time. But in Jack's line of work, tax-law considerations are damn important.'

Trembling with emotion, Dylan approached Proctor. Reached out. Put his right hand on the pistol.

'The federal statute of limitations in tax matters,' Proctor said, 'is seven years.'

Dylan could feel the shape of the handgun. The chill of steel.

Clearly, Proctor failed to sense any pressure from Dylan's hand upon the weapon. 'Jack would have been in the habit of saving all his records at least that long. If ever they're found, I'm through.'

When Dylan tried to close his hand around the pistol, to pull it from the killer's grip, his fingers passed through the steel and folded into an empty fist.

'You're not a stupid woman, Mrs. O'Conner. You know about the seven years. You've kept his business records. I'm sure that's where the diskettes will be. You might not have realized they existed. But now that you do . . . you'll search them out, and you'll go to the police with them. I wish this . . . this unpleasantness weren't necessary.'

In a fit of useless fury, Dylan swung his clenched fist at Proctor – and saw it pass, with an ink-black comet's tail, through the bastard's face, without eliciting so much as a flinch.

'I'd have preferred your assistance,' Proctor said, 'but I can conduct the search myself. I'd have had to kill you either way.

This is a vicious, wicked thing I'm doing, a terrible thing, and if there were a Hell, I'd deserve eternal pain, eternal torture.'

'Don't hurt my son.' Blair O'Conner spoke calmly, refusing to beg or cower before her murderer, aware that she couldn't humiliate herself enough to win his mercy, making her argument for Shepherd's life in a level voice, with logic instead of emotion. 'He's autistic. He doesn't know who you are. He couldn't be a witness against you even if he knew your name. He can barely communicate.'

Sluggish with dread, Dylan backed away from Proctor, toward his mother, desperately assuring himself that somehow he would have more influence on the trajectory of the bullet if he was nearer to her.

Proctor said, 'I know about Shepherd. What a burden he must've been all these years.'

'He's never been a burden,' Blair O'Conner said in a voice as tight as a garroting wire. 'You don't know anything.'

'I'm unscrupulous and brutal when I need to be, but I'm not needlessly cruel.' Proctor glanced at ten-year-old Shepherd. 'He's no threat to me.'

'Oh, my God,' Dylan's mother said, for she had been standing with her back to Shepherd and had not realized until now that he'd abandoned his puzzle and that he waited just this side of the doorway to the dining room. 'Don't. Don't do it in front of the boy. Don't make him watch . . . *this*.'

'He won't be shattered, Mrs. O'Conner. It'll roll right off him, don't you think?'

'No. Nothing rolls off him. He's not you.'

'After all, he's got the emotional capacity of – what? – a toad?' Proctor asked, disproving his contention that he was never needlessly cruel.

'He's gentle,' Blair said. 'He's sweet. So special.' These words were not aimed at Proctor. They were a good-bye to her afflicted son. 'In his own way, he sparkles.'

'As much sparkle as mud,' Proctor said ruefully, as though he possessed the emotional capacity to be saddened by Shep's condition. 'But I promise you this – when I've achieved what I know I surely will achieve one day, when I stand in the company of Nobel laureates and dine with kings, I won't forget your damaged boy. My work will make it possible to transform him from a toad into an intellectual titan.'

'You pompous ass,' Blair O'Conner said bitterly. 'You're no scientist. You're a monster. Science shines light into darkness. But you are the darkness. Monster. You do *your* work by the light of the moon.'

Almost as though watching from a distance, Dylan saw himself raise one arm, saw himself hold up one hand as if to stop not just the bullet but also the merciless march of time.

The *crack!* of the shot was louder than he had expected it to be, as loud as Heaven splitting open to bring forth judgment on the Day.

35

Perhaps he imagined that he felt the bullet passing through him, but when he turned in horror toward his beloved mother, he could have described in intimate detail the shape, texture, weight, and heat of the round that killed her. And he felt bullet-punched, pierced, not when the slug hissed through him, but when he saw her falling, and saw her face clenched in shock, in pain.

Dylan knelt before her, desperate with the need to hold her, to comfort his mother in her last seconds of life, but here in her time, he had less substance than a ghost of a ghost.

From where she lay, she gazed directly *through* Dylan toward ten-year-old Shep. Fifteen feet away, the boy stood slump-shouldered, his head half bowed. Though he didn't approach his mother, he met her gaze with a rare directness.

By the look of him, this younger Shep either didn't understand fully what he had just seen or understood too well and was in shock. He stood motionless. He said nothing, nor did he cry.

Over near Blair's favorite armchair, Jilly embraced the older Shepherd, who did not shrink from the hug as usually he would have done. She kept him turned away from the sight of his mother, but she regarded Dylan with an anguish and a sympathy that proved she had ceased to be a stranger and had become, in less than twenty-four hours, part of their family.

Staring through Dylan at young Shep, their mother said, 'It's okay, sweetheart. You're not alone. Never alone. Dylan will always take care of you.'

In the story of her life, Death placed his comma, and she was gone.

'I love you,' Dylan said to her, the doubly dead, speaking across the river of the past ten years and across that other river that has an even more distant shore than the banks of time.

Although he'd been shaken to his deepest foundations by bearing witness to her death, he had been equally shaken by her final words: *You're not alone. Never alone. Dylan will always take care of you.*

He was deeply moved to hear her express such confidence in his character as a brother and as a man.

Yet he trembled when he thought of the nights he had lain awake, emotionally exhausted from a difficult day with Shepherd, stewing in self-pity. Discouragement – at worst, despondency – had been as close as he'd ever gotten to despair; but in those darker moments, he'd argued with himself that Shep would be better off in what the masters of euphemism called 'a loving, professional-care environment.'

He knew there would have been no shame in finding a first-rate facility for Shep, and knew also that his commitment to his brother came at a cost to his own happiness that psychologists would declare indicative of an emotional disorder. In truth he regretted this life of service at some point every day, and he supposed that in his old age he might feel bitterly that he had wasted too many years.

Yet such a life had its special rewards – not the least of which was this discovery that he had fulfilled his mother's faith in him. His perseverance with Shepherd, all these years, suddenly seemed to have an uncanny dimension, as if he'd somehow known about the pledge his dying mother had made in his name, although Shepherd had never mentioned it. He could almost believe that she had come to him in dreams, which he did not remember, and in his sleep had spoken to him of her love for him and of her confidence in his sense of duty.

For ten years, if not longer, Dylan had thought he understood the frustrations with which Shepherd lived, had thought he fully grasped the chronic sense of helplessness in the face of overwhelming forces with which an autistic person daily struggled. Until now, however, his understanding had been woefully incomplete. Not until he had been required to stand by helplessly and watch his mother shot, had tried to hold her in her dying moment and could not, had longed to speak with her before she passed but couldn't make himself heard – not until this terrible moment had he felt a powerlessness like that with which his brother had always lived. Kneeling beside his mother, riveted by her glazed eyes, Dylan shook with humiliation, with fear, with a rage that could not be vented because it had no single and no easy object, a rage at his weakness and at *the way things were and always would be*. A scream of anger built in him, but he didn't let it out because, displaced in time, his shout would go largely unheard – and also because this scream, once begun, would be difficult to stop.

Not much blood. Be thankful for that.

And she didn't linger. Suffered little.

Then he realized what ghastly spectacle must come next. 'No.'

$\approx \quad \approx \quad \approx$

Holding Shepherd close, looking over his shoulder, Jilly watched Lincoln Proctor with a loathing that heretofore she had been able to work up only for her father at his meanest. And it didn't matter that ten years hence, Proctor would be a smoking carcass in the ruins of her Coupe DeVille: She loathed him bitterly and none the less.

Shot fired, he returned the pistol to the shoulder holster under his leather jacket. He appeared to be confident of his marksmanship.

From a coat pocket he removed a pair of latex gloves and worked his hands into them, all the while watching ten-year-old Shep.

Even to Jilly, who knew how to read the subtleties of expression in Shepherd's guarded face, the boy appeared to be unmoved by his mother's death. This couldn't be the case, for ten years later he had brought them back in time to bear witness; in his older incarnation, he'd come to this scene with palpable dread, repeating *Shep is brave*.

Features slack, no tremor at the mouth, without tears, the boy turned from his mother's body. He walked to the nearest corner, where he stood staring at the meeting of the walls.

Overwhelmed by traumatic experience, he reduced his world to a narrow space, where he felt safer. Likewise, he dealt with grief.

Flexing his latex-sheathed hands, Proctor went to the boy and stood over him, watching.

Rocking slowly back and forth, young Shepherd began to murmur a rhythmic series of words that Jilly could not quite hear.

Dylan still knelt at his mother's side, his head bowed as though in prayer. He wasn't ready to leave her yet.

Satisfied that corner-focused Shepherd would serve diligently as the warden of his own imprisonment, Proctor walked out of the living room, crossed the entrance hall, and opened the door to another room.

If they weren't going to fold out of here immediately, then it made sense to follow Proctor and learn what he was doing.

With an affectionate squeeze, she released Shep. 'Let's see what the bastard is up to. Will you come with me, sweetie?'

Leaving Shep alone wasn't an option. Still scared and grieving, he needed companionship. Besides, though Jilly doubted that he would fold out of here without her and Dylan, she dared not chance it.

'Will you come with me, Shepherd?'

'Rat, Mole, Mr. Toad.'

'What does that mean, Shep? What do you want?'

'Rat, Mole, Mr. Toad. Rat, Mole, Mr. Toad.'

By the third time he recited this mantra, he had synchronized his words to those of ten-year-old Shepherd in the corner, and the resonance between them revealed the words that the younger Shep was murmuring as he rocked. 'Rat, Mole, Mr. Toad.'

Jilly didn't know the meaning of this, and she didn't have the time to get involved in one of those long, circuitous conversations with Shepherd. 'Rat, Mole, Mr. Toad. We'll talk about that later, sweetie. Right now, just come with me. Come along with me.'

Somewhat to her surprise, without hesitation, Shep followed her out of the living room.

As they entered the study, Proctor used the computer keyboard to smash the monitor. He shoved the entire machine off the desk, onto the floor. He exhibited no glee, even winced at the mess he'd made.

Drawer by drawer, he quickly searched for diskettes. He found a few, stacked them aside. He tossed the other contents of the drawers on the floor, scattering them widely, evidently hoping to create the impression that the person or persons responsible for the death of Dylan's mother had been ordinary thieves and vandals.

File cabinets in the bottom of the study closet contained only paper records. He dismissed these at once.

Atop the file cabinets were double-wide diskette-storage boxes: three of them, each capable of holding perhaps a hundred diskettes.

Proctor snatched diskettes out of the boxes, tossing them aside in handfuls without reading labels. In the third box, he found four diskettes different from the others, in canary-yellow paper sleeves.

'Bingo,' Proctor said, bringing these four to the desk.

Holding Shep's hand, Jilly moved close to Proctor, expecting him to cry out as if he'd seen a ghost. His breath smelled of peanuts.

The yellow sleeve of each diskette blazed with the word WARNING! printed in red. The rest of the printing was in black: legalistic prose stating that these diskettes contained private files protected by lawyer-client privilege, that criminal and civil prosecution would be undertaken against anyone in wrongful possession of same, and that anyone not in the employment of the below-referenced law firm would automatically be in wrongful possession.

Proctor slid one diskette out of its sleeve to read the label. Satisfied, he tucked all four into an inner jacket pocket.

Now that he had what he'd come for, Proctor played vandal once more, pulling books off the study shelves and slinging them across the room. With flapping pages, the volumes flew through Jilly and Shepherd, dropping like dead birds to the floor.

$\approx \quad \approx \quad \approx$

When the computer crashed off the study desk, Dylan remembered the mess in which parts of the house had been found that February night long ago. Thus far he had remained at his mother's side with the irrational hope that even though he had been unable to save her from the bullet, he would somehow spare her from the indignity yet to come. The racket in the study forced him to accept that in this matter, he was indeed as helpless as his brother.

His mother was gone, ten years gone, and all that had followed her death remained immutable. His concern now must be for the living.

He didn't care to watch Proctor engaged in set-dressing. He knew what the ultimate look of the scene would be.

Instead, he went to the corner where ten-year-old Shep rocked back and forth, murmuring. 'Rat, Mole, Mr. Toad.'

This was not what Dylan might have expected to hear his brother chanting, but it did not mystify him.

After the complete works of Dr. Seuss and others, the first story for older children that their mother read to Shep was Kenneth Grahame's *The Wind in the Willows*. Shep had so adored the tale of Rat, Mole, Toad, Badger, and the other colorful characters of the Wild Wood that he had insisted she read it to him again and again during the year that followed. By the time he was ten, he'd read it at least twenty times on his own.

He wanted the company of Rat, Mole, and Mr. Toad, the story of friendship and hope, the dream of life in warm and secure burrows, in deep lamplit warrens, in sheltered glades, wanted the reassurance that after fearful adventures, after chaos, there would be always the circle of friends, the firelit hearth, quiet evenings when the world shrank to the size of a family and when no heart beat in a stranger.

Dylan couldn't give him that. In fact, if such a life could be lived in this world, the likelihood was that it could be enjoyed only by characters in books.

In the downstairs hall, the mirror by the front door shattered. If memory served, it had been broken with the vase that had stood on the small entry table.

From the living-room doorway, Jilly called to Dylan, 'He's going upstairs!'

'Let him go. I know what he does. Sacks the master bedroom and steals Mom's jewelry . . . I guess to make it look like a robbery. Her purse is up there. He empties it, takes the money from her wallet.'

Jilly and Shepherd joined him, gathering behind the long-ago Shepherd in the long-ago corner.

This was not where Shep had been found on the night of February 12, 1992. Dylan wanted to remain in this time until he knew if Shep had been spared bearing witness to what was yet to come.

From upstairs echoed the hard crashes of drawers being pulled out of the bureau and thrown against the walls.

'Rat, Mole, Mr. Toad,' said the younger Shepherd, and the older Shep, armoring himself against a scary world and perhaps speaking also to his ten-year-old self, said, 'Shep is brave, Shep is brave.'

After a minute, the noises of destruction ceased upstairs. Proctor had probably found the purse. Or he was loading his pockets with her jewelry, none of which had great value.

Head bowed in his posture of eternal supplication, the younger Shep moved out of the corner and shuffled to the dining-room door, and the older Shep closely followed him. Like processional monks, they were, in a brotherhood of the genteel estranged.

Relieved, Dylan would have followed them anyway, but when he heard Proctor's footsteps thundering as hard as knocking hooves on the stairs, he stepped after his brother more quickly, pulling Jilly with him, out of the living room.

Ten-year-old Shep rounded the table and returned to his chair. He sat and stared at his puzzle.

The golden-retriever puppies in the basket revealed a moment of peace and charm that couldn't possibly exist in this violent fallen world, that must instead represent a glimpse into a burrow in the Wild Wood.

Shepherd stood across the table from his younger self, flanked by Jilly and Dylan, watching.

In the living room, Proctor began to overturn furniture, tear paintings from the walls, and smash bibelots, further developing the scenario that would lead the police away from any consideration that the intruder might have been other than a common drug-pumped thug.

Younger Shep selected a piece of the jigsaw from the puzzle box. He scanned the incomplete picture. He tried the fragment in a wrong hole, another wrong hole, but inserted it correctly on his third try. The next piece he placed at once. And the next, faster.

After the loudest of the crashes, the living room grew quiet.

Dylan tried to focus on the gracefulness with which ten-year-old Shep turned chaos into puppies and a basket. He hoped to block from his mind images of the final bit of scene setting in which Proctor must be now engaged.

Inevitably, he failed.

To suggest that the initial intentions of the murderous intruder had included rape as well as robbery, Proctor would tear open Blair O'Conner's blouse, popping the buttons from throat to belt line. To suggest that the victim had fought back before she could be sexually assaulted, and that she'd been shot accidentally during a struggle or on purpose by a man enraged when rejected, Proctor would tear at her bra, snapping one shoulder strap, jerking the cups below her breasts.

With these indignities committed, he came into the dining room, flushed from his exertions.

If ever Dylan had been capable of murder, this was the moment. He had the will, but he did not have the way. His fists were less than smoke to Proctor here. Even if he'd come with a revolver from his own time, the bullet would drill Proctor without shredding one filament of flesh.

Stopping just inside the doorway, the killer watched ten-year-old Shep at the table, oblivious of his audience. He blotted his brow with a handkerchief. 'Boy, do you smell my sweat?'

Fingers plucked, hands darted, unfinished puppies were made whole, but Shepherd did not answer the question.

'I stink of worse than sweat, don't I? Treachery. I've stunk of that for five years, and I always will.'

The man's self-dramatization and self-flagellation infuriated Dylan, for just as in the motel room the previous night, it wasn't a fraction as sincere as Proctor might believe it was, but allowed the creep to indulge in self-pity while calling it courageous self-analysis.

'And now I stink of *this*.' He watched as the young puzzler puzzled, and then said, 'What a wretched little life. One day, I'll be your redemption, boy, and maybe you'll be mine.'

Proctor stepped from the room, left the house, went out into the night of February 12, 1992, beginning his journey toward his so-called redemption and his fiery death in Arizona more than ten years later.

The puzzle-working Shepherd's face had acquired a glaze of tears as silently as dew forms from the air.

'Let's get out of here,' Jilly said.

'Shep?' Dylan asked.

The older puzzler, who shook with emotion but did not cry, stood watching his younger self. He didn't immediately reply, but after his brother spoke to him twice more, he said, 'Wait. No gooey-bloody Mr. David Cronenberg movie. Wait.'

Although they supposedly weren't engaging in teleportation, per se, and although the mechanism of their travel still mystified him, Dylan could imagine lots of errors in transport almost as unpleasant as those portrayed in *The Fly*. Accidentally folding onto a highway, in the path of a hurtling Peterbilt, could be a quashing experience.

To Jilly, he said, 'Let's wait till Shep's confident of doing it right.'

Here a bit of golden fur, there the tip of a black snout, and here a quizzical eye: Although time seemed to crawl, the boy's hands flew rapidly toward a full solution.

After a few minutes, older Shepherd said, 'Okay.'

'Okay – we can go?' Dylan asked.

'Okay. We can go, but we can't leave.'

Baffled, Dylan said, 'We can go, but we can't leave?'

'Something,' Shep added.

Interestingly, Jilly was the first to understand. 'We can go, but we can't leave something. If we don't have everything we brought, he's not able to fold us out of the past. I left my purse and the laptop in the kitchen.'

They retreated from the dining room, leaving younger Shep to his tears and to the final pieces of his puzzle.

Although he could have felt the light switch if he'd touched it, Dylan knew he couldn't turn on the fluorescents any more than he had been able to stop a bullet. In the kitchen gloom, he couldn't see if the purse and the laptop, which Jilly had put on the table, rested in the inky blots that traveled under their feet and that spread between them and everything they touched here in the past, but he assumed the black puddles were there.

Slinging the purse over her shoulder, grabbing the laptop, Jilly said, 'Got 'em. Let's go.'

The back door opened, and she whirled toward it as if certain that the door-busting, window-bashing, steroid-chugging crowd from Holbrook, Arizona, had folded themselves back to this California yesteryear in hot pursuit.

Dylan was not surprised to see a younger version of himself step through the door.

On February 12, 1992, he had been attending an evening class at the University of California Santa Barbara. He'd ridden to and from class with a friend who had dropped him off at the end of the long driveway less than two minutes ago.

What *did* surprise Dylan was how soon after the murder he had arrived home. He checked his watch, then looked at the pig-belly clock. That February night, if he had arrived home five minutes sooner, he would have encountered Lincoln Proctor as the killer left the house. If he'd arrived all of sixteen minutes earlier, he might have been shot dead – but he might have prevented his mother's murder.

Sixteen minutes.

He refused to think about what might have been. Dared not.

Nineteen-year-old Dylan O'Conner closed the door behind him, without bothering to switch on the lights, walked through a startled Jilly Jackson. He put a couple books on the kitchen table and headed toward the dining room.

'Fold us out of here, Shep,' Dylan said.

In the dining room, the younger Dylan spoke to the younger Shepherd: 'Hey, buddy, smells like we have cake tonight.'

'Fold us home, Shep. Our own time.'

In the adjacent room, the other Dylan said, 'Buddy, are you crying? Hey, what's wrong?'

Hearing his own tortured wail when he found his mother's body would be the camel-crippling straw. 'Shep, get us to hell out of here now, *now*.'

The dark kitchen folded away. A bright place folded toward them. Crazily, Dylan wondered if Shepherd's fantastic trick of travel might not be limited merely to journeys through space and time, but if it might extend to dimensions unknown to the living. Perhaps it had been a mistake to say 'to hell' just before they left 1992.

36

The kaleidoscope tweaked. Around Jilly the sunlit kitchen folded in through the outgoing night kitchen, and fell into place in every bright detail.

No delicious smell of freshly baked cake. No shimmering black energy underfoot.

The smiling ceramic pig on the wall clasped its front hooves around the clock in its belly, which read 1:20, twenty-four minutes after they had folded out of the besieged motel room in Arizona. The present had progressed equal to the amount of time that they had spent in the past.

No open gateway loomed behind them, giving a view of the dark kitchen in 1992, nor a radiant tunnel. She had the feeling that the tunnel had been a travel technique that Shepherd didn't need to use anymore, that it was crude compared to his current method, by which he moved them from place to place without maintaining a tether to the location that they had departed.

Impressed by her own aplomb, as though she had just stepped out of a conveyance no more extraordinary than a common elevator, Jilly put the laptop on the kitchen table. 'You didn't change the place much, did you? Looks the same.'

Dylan shushed her, cocked his head, listening intently.

A pool of stillness flooded the house until the refrigerator motor kicked on.

'What's wrong?' Jilly asked.

'I'm going to have to explain this to Vonetta. Our housekeeper. That's her Harley in front of the garage.'

Looking out the kitchen windows, Jilly saw the garage at the end of the backyard, but no motorcycle. 'What Harley?'

'There.' Dylan turned, pointing through a window to a place

where no Harley stood. 'Huh. She must've gone to the store for something. Maybe we can get in and out of here before she's back.'

Shepherd opened the refrigerator. Perhaps he was looking for a consoling piece of cake.

Still assimilating their journey into the past, unconcerned about the housekeeper, Jilly said, 'While Proctor's enemies, whoever they are, were closing in on him, he was tracking down you and Shep.'

'Last night when he had me strapped in that chair, he said he was so eaten away with remorse that he was empty inside, but it didn't make sense to me then.'

'The creep's always been empty inside,' Jilly said. 'From day one, from the cradle, if you ask me.'

'The remorse is bullshit. He's got this self-deprecation shtick that makes him feel good about himself. Sorry, Jilly.'

'That's okay. After what we've been through, you've got every right not to say diaper dump.'

She almost got a laugh out of him, but 1992 was still too much in their minds for Dylan to manage more than a smile. 'No. I mean, I'm sorry you got caught up in this because of me. Me and Shep.'

'Proctor just had an extra dose of his hell juice, he needed someone to screw over, and there I was, out for a root beer.'

Standing at the open refrigerator, Shepherd said, 'Cold.'

'But Proctor wouldn't have been there,' Dylan said, 'if Shep and I hadn't been there.'

'Yeah, and I wouldn't have been there if I hadn't spent all of my relatively short, so-called adult life trying to be a standup joke jockey, telling myself that performing is not just a meaningful life but the only life. Hell, I don't have to worry about my ass getting big, 'cause I'm already a big ass. So don't *you* start with your own remorse shtick. It happened, we're here, and even with the nanobots supposedly building the New Jerusalem inside our skulls, being here and alive is – so far, anyway – better than being dead. So what now?'

'What now is we pack up some gear, and quick. Clothes for Shep and me, some money I've got in a lockbox upstairs, and a gun.'

'You've got a gun?'

'Bought it after what happened to my mother. They never caught the killer. I thought he might come back.'

'You know how to use it?'

'I'm no Little Annie Oakley,' he said. 'But I can point the damn thing and squeeze the trigger if I have to.'

She was dubious. 'Maybe we should buy a baseball bat.'

'Cold,' said Shepherd.

'Clothes, money, gun – then we hit the road,' Dylan said.

'You think those guys who trailed us to the motel in Holbrook might show up here?'

He nodded. 'If they have law-enforcement connections or any kind of national reach, yeah, they'll come.'

Jilly said, 'We can't keep folding everywhere we go. It's too weird, it's too full of surprises, and it might wear Shep out and leave us stuck somewhere – or something worse than stuck.'

'I've got a Chevy in the garage.'

'Cold.'

Jilly shook her head. 'They'll probably know you've got the Chevy. They come here, find it missing, they'll be looking for it.'

'Cold.'

'Maybe we'll dump the plates,' Dylan suggested, 'steal a set from another car.'

'Now you're an experienced fugitive?'

'Maybe I better learn to be.'

Peering into the open refrigerator, Shep said, 'Cold.'

Dylan went to his brother's side. 'What're you looking for, buddy?'

'Cake.'

'We don't have any cake in there.'

'Cake.'

'We're all out of cake, buddy.'

'No cake?'

'No cake.'

'Cold.'

Dylan closed the refrigerator door. 'Still cold?'

'Better,' said Shep.

'I've got a bad feeling,' Jilly said, and she did, but her deep uneasiness lacked a specific focus.

'What?' Dylan asked.

'I don't know.' The ceramic pig's smile now seemed more like a wicked grin. 'Just . . . a not-good feeling.'

'Let's grab that lockbox first. Even with the envelope I got out of my shaving kit, we're short of money.'

'We'd better stay together,' Jilly said. 'Close together.'

'Cold.' Shepherd had opened the refrigerator door again. 'Cold.'

'Buddy, there's no cake.'

Wickedly jagged and gleaming, appearing from behind Jilly, gliding past the right side of her face in slow motion, six or eight inches from her, accompanied by no shattering sound, came a shard of glass about the size of her hand, sailing past her as majestically as an iceberg on a glassy sea.

'Cold.'

'We'll get some cake later, buddy.'

Then she noticed something moving a few inches in front of the gravity-defying piece of glass, a much smaller object, and darker: a bullet. Tunneling lazily through the air, the bullet spun languidly as it advanced across the kitchen.

'Close the fridge, Shep. There's no cake.'

If the bullet traveled in true slow motion, the glass followed in *super* slow-mo.

And here came additional spears and flinders of glass behind the first, sliding brightly through the air, slow and easy.

'Cold,' Shep said, 'we're cold.'

She realized that the glass and the bullet were no more real than the red votive candles in the desert or the shoals of white birds. This wasn't current destruction, but a vision of violence to come.

'You're cold, I'm not,' Dylan told Shepherd.

She sensed these new clairvoyant images were not associated with those that she had received previously. This glass wasn't church glass, and it would be bullet-shattered in a place different from the church.

'We're all cold,' Shep insisted.

When Jilly turned her head toward the brothers, she saw still more fragments of windowpanes – this must be what they were – to the left of her, a galaxy of glittering splinters and larger wedges leisurely tumbling-flying past.

'We're all cold.'

Looking through this deconstructed puzzle of a windowpane,

Jilly saw Shepherd step back from the refrigerator, allowing Dylan to close the door again. The brothers moved at normal speed.

The racing of her heart indicated that she, too, was out of phase with the slow-motion glass. She reached for a passing fragment, but it had no substance. The shard slid slowly between her pinched fingers without cutting her.

Her attempt to interact with the vision seemed to break its spell, and the glass faded from view as a flotilla of ghost ships might appear real at first sight, all sails rigged and searching for a wind, and yet dissolve into tatters of mist a moment later.

Turning to face the windows that offered a view of the backyard, she confirmed that of course the panes remained intact.

Recognizing that Jilly was distracted as in past clairvoyant episodes, Dylan said, 'Hey, are you all right?'

Most likely these were not the windows in her vision. She'd been receiving images of the bloodbath in the church since the previous evening, and that event had not yet transpired. She had no reason to believe that this other violent incident would occur here rather than elsewhere or sooner rather than later.

Dylan approached her. 'What's wrong?'

'I'm not sure.'

She glanced at the clock, the grinning pig.

She knew the porcine smile hadn't changed in the least. The lips were fixed in their expression under the ceramic glaze. The smile remained as benign as she'd first seen it less than half an hour ago, ten years in the past. Nevertheless, a malevolent energy *seethed* off the pig, off the clock.

'Jilly?'

In fact not just the pig but the entire kitchen seemed to be alive with an evil presence, as though a dark spirit had come upon them and, unable to manifest itself in the traditional ectoplasmic apparition, took residence in the furnishings and in the surfaces of the room itself. Every edge of every counter appeared to gleam with a lacerating sharpness.

Shepherd opened the refrigerator door again, and peering into it, he said, 'Cold. We're all cold.'

The black glass oven doors watched, watched like hooded eyes.

Dark bottles in a wine rack seemed to have Molotov potential.

Flesh crawled, fine hairs quivered, a chill settled on the nape of her neck when she imagined the steel teeth gnashing silently in the throat of the garbage disposal.

No. Absurd. No spirit possessed the room. She didn't need an exorcist.

Her sense of alarm – actually a presentiment of death, she realized – was so powerful and growing so rapidly that she desperately needed to discover a cause for it. She superstitiously projected her fear onto inanimate objects – pig clock, oven doors, garbage-disposal blades – when the real threat lay elsewhere.

'We're all cold,' said Shep at the open refrigerator.

This time, Jilly heard those three words differently from the way she had heard them before. She remembered Shepherd's talent for reeling off synonyms, and now she realized that they might have the same meaning as *We're all dead*. Cold as a corpse. Cold as the grave. Cold and dead.

'Let's get out of here now, fast,' she urged.

Dylan said, 'I've got to get the money in the lockbox.'

'Forget the money. We'll die trying to get the money.'

'That's what you see?'

'That's what I *know*.'

'Okay, all right.'

'Let's fold, let's go, *hurry!*'

'We're all *cold*,' said Shep.

37

Tick-tock, pig clock. Gleaming little eyes squinting out of folds of pink fat. That knowing leer.

Forget the damn clock. The pig clock isn't a threat. Focus.

Dylan returned to his brother, closed the refrigerator door for the third time, and drew Shep toward Jilly. 'We've got to go, buddy.'

'Where's all the ice?' Shep asked, deeper into this obsession than Jilly had seen him in any other. 'Where's all the ice?'

'What ice?' Dylan asked.

This clairvoyance, this foreshadowing talent was still new to Jilly, as frightening as it was new, as *unwanted* as it was new, and she had not been channeling it properly.

'Where's all the ice?' Shepherd persisted.

'We don't need ice,' Dylan told him. 'Buddy, you're starting to scare me here. Don't freeze up on me.'

'Where's all the ice?'

'Shep, be with me now. Listen to me, hear me, stay with me.'

By struggling to identify the cause of her alarm, letting her suspicion hop from object to object, place to place, she had not been allowing the alarm to direct the compass needle of her intuition. She needed to relax, to trust this strange precognition and let it show her precisely what to fear.

'Where's all the ice?'

'Forget about the ice. We don't need ice, buddy. We need to get out of here, all right?'

'Nothing but ice.'

Inevitably, Jilly's attention was drawn toward the windows, and the deep backyard beyond the windows. The green grass, the garage, the golden meadow behind the garage.

'Nothing but ice.'

Dylan said, 'He's fixated on this ice thing.'

'Get him off it.'

'Nothing but ice,' said Shepherd. 'Where's all the ice?'

'You know Shep by now. There's no getting him off it until he *wants* to get off. The thing keeps . . . ricocheting around in his head. And this seems worse than usual.'

'Sweetie,' she said, her gaze riveted on the windows, 'we have to fold. We can get you some ice after we fold.'

'Where's all the ice?'

Dylan put a hand under his brother's tucked chin, raised his head. 'Shep, this is crucial now. You understand crucial? I know you do, buddy. It's crucial that we fold out of here.'

'Where's all the ice?'

Glancing at Shepherd, she saw that he refused to relate to his brother. Behind his closed lids, his eyes moved ceaselessly.

When Jilly returned her attention to the backyard, a man knelt on one knee at the northwest corner of the garage. He sheltered in shadows. She almost didn't spot him, but she was sure he hadn't been there a moment ago.

Another man ran in a crouch from the cover of the meadow to the *south*west corner of the garage.

'They're here,' she told Dylan.

Neither of these men wore desert-resort pastels, but they were of a type with the faux golfers in Arizona. They were big, they were purposeful, and they weren't going door to door to preach salvation through Jesus.

'Where's all the ice?'

As far as Jilly was concerned, the scariest thing about them was the headset that each man wore. Not just earpieces but also extension arms that placed penny-size microphones at their mouths. This high degree of coordination argued that the assault force had to be larger than two men, and further suggested that these weren't just your ordinary knee-breaking, contract-kill thugs, but thugs with a keen sense of organization.

'Where's all the ice?'

The second man had covered the ground between meadow and garage. He crouched at the southwest corner, half concealed by a shrub.

She expected them to come well-armed, so their guns were only the *second* scariest thing about them. Big weapons. Sort of futuristic looking. Probably what were called assault rifles. She didn't know much about firearms, didn't need to know much to be a comedian, even in front of the most unruly audience, but she figured that these guns were capable of firing a gazillion rounds before they needed to be reloaded.

'Where's all the ice?'

She and Dylan had to buy time until Shepherd could be persuaded that the way to get cake *and* ice would be to fold the three of them someplace that offered both.

'Get away from the windows,' Jilly warned, retreating from those that faced the backyard. 'Windows are . . . windows are death.'

'Every room has windows,' Dylan worried. 'Lots of windows.'

'Basement?'

'Isn't one. California. Slab construction.'

Shep asked, 'Where's all the ice?'

Jilly said, 'They know we're here.'

'How could they know? We didn't come in from outside.'

'Maybe a listening device, planted in the house earlier,' she suggested. 'Or they spotted us with binoculars through the windows.'

'They sent Vonetta home,' he realized.

'Let's hope that's all they did to her.'

'Where's all the ice?'

The thought of harm having come to his housekeeper cast an ashen pallor over Dylan's face as the recognition of his own mortal danger had not. 'But we only folded out of Holbrook half an hour ago.'

'So?'

'We must have surprised the hell out of the guy in the motel room, the one who saw us go.'

'He probably needed clean underwear,' she agreed.

'So how could they have even figured out what folding *was* in just half an hour, let alone alerted people here in California?'

'These guys didn't come here on an alert sent out half an hour ago. They staked out this house when they didn't know where we were, before the Arizona goons confirmed we were in Holbrook, hours before they went into the motel after us.'

'So they connected you to the Coupe DeVille and me to you last night, pretty quick,' Dylan said. 'We've always been just a few hours ahead of them.'

'They didn't *know* we'd come back here soon or ever. They were just here waiting, hoping.'

'Nobody was running surveillance on the house this morning when Shep and I folded onto that hilltop back there.'

'They must've gotten here not long after that.'

'Ice,' said Shep, 'ice, ice, ice, ice.'

The guy on one knee in the shadows, the other guy half hidden by the shrub, talking on their headsets, were probably not talking just to each other, but were chatting with a cozy knitting circle of like-minded assassins surrounding the house, exchanging tips on weapons maintenance, garroting-wire techniques, and recipes for nerve poison, while synchronizing their watches and coordinating their murderous attack.

Jilly could have tapped her veins for the ice Shep wanted. She felt defenseless. She felt naked. Naked in the hands of fate.

'Ice, ice, ice, ice, ice.'

In her mind's eye, she considered the slowly drifting shards of glass, the bullet crawling through the air. She said, 'But *by now* this team has talked to the team in Arizona, bet your ass, talked to them sometime in the past fifteen or twenty minutes, so they know we can do the old herethere boogie.'

Dylan's mind was spinning as fast as hers: 'In fact, maybe one of Proctor's previous experimental subjects pulled the same trick, so they *have* seen folding before.'

'The idea of a bunch of nano-whacked ginks running around with superpowers scares the hell out of them.'

'Who can blame 'em? Scares the hell out of me,' Dylan said, 'even when the ginks are us.'

'Ice, ice, ice.'

Jilly said, 'So when they come, they're going to come in fast and blast the crap out of the house, hoping to kill us before we know they're here and can do our folding routine.'

'This is what you think or what you know?'

She knew it, felt it, *saw* it. 'They're using armor-piercing rounds that'll punch straight through the walls, through masonry, through anydamnthing.'

'Ice, ice, ice.'

'And worse than armor-piercing rounds,' she continued. 'Lots worse. Stuff like . . . explosive rounds that throw off cyanide-coated shrapnel.'

She had never read about such hideous weapons, had never heard about them, but thanks to the new nanobot-engineered connections in her brain, she foresaw their use here. She heard ghost voices in her head, men's voices talking about details of the attack at some point in the future, perhaps policemen sifting through the ruins of the house later today or tomorrow, perhaps the killers themselves engaged in a little nostalgic reminiscence about bloody destruction conducted with perfect timing and homicidal flair.

'Cyanide shrapnel, and God knows what else,' she continued, and shuddered. 'When they're finished with us, what Janet Reno did to the Branch Davidians will seem like a friendly Christian taffy pull.'

'Ice, ice, ice.'

With a new urgency, Dylan confronted Shep. 'Open your eyes, buddy, get out of that hole, out of the ice, Shep.'

Shepherd kept his eyes closed.

'If you ever want cake again, Shep, open your eyes.'

'Ice, ice, ice.'

'He's not close to coming around yet,' Dylan told Jilly. 'He's lost in there.'

'Upstairs,' she said. 'It's not going to be a picnic up there, but the downstairs is going to get chopped to pieces.'

Out at the garage, the guy stood up from the shadows, and the other guy stood up from the masking shrub. They started toward the house. They were coming at a run.

38

Jilly said, 'Upstairs!' and Dylan said, 'Go!' and Shepherd said, 'Ice, ice, ice,' and a kink in Dylan's mental wiring brought to mind that old dance-party hit 'Hot, Hot, Hot,' by Buster Poindexter, which might have struck him as funny under more congenial circumstances and if the idea of 'Hot, Hot, Hot' as suitable death-throe music had not been so ghastly.

The stairs were at the front of the house, and two doors led out of the kitchen, one into the dining room, one into the lower hall. The second route would have been the safer of the two, less exposed to windows.

Jilly didn't realize the hall option existed because that door was closed. She probably thought it was a pantry. She hurried out of the kitchen, into the dining room, before Dylan thought to direct her the other way.

He was afraid to take the hallway because he figured she might look back, fail to see him following her, and return here in search of him and Shep, or at least falter in her flight. A lost second might mean the difference between life and death.

Urging, pushing, all but lifting his brother, Dylan harried him forward. Shep shuffled, of course, but faster than he was accustomed to shuffling, still fretting about ice, ice, ice, the repetitions coming in threes, and he sounded more aggrieved with every step, unhappy about being driven like a wayward sheep.

Jilly had already reached the living room by the time Dylan and Shep got out of the kitchen. Shepherd balked slightly at the door, but he allowed himself to be herded forward.

Entering the dining room, Dylan half expected to see ten-year-old Shep working a puppy puzzle. As much as he had wanted to get out of that hateful night in the past, it seemed preferable to the present, which offered only the most fragile of bridges to any future whatsoever.

Shep protested his brother's insistent prodding – 'Ice, don't, ice, don't, ice, don't' – and after crossing the dining room, he grabbed at the next doorjamb with both hands.

Before Shepherd could get a firm grip, before he could spread his legs and wedge his shoes against the jamb, Dylan shoved him into the living room. The kid stumbled and dropped to his hands and knees, which proved to be a fortuitous fall, for in that instant the gunmen opened fire.

The woodpecker-fast rapping of submachine guns – even noisier than they were in movies, as hard and loud as jackhammers knocking steel chisels through high-density concrete – shattered the stillness, shattered the kitchen windows, the dining-room windows. More than two submachine guns, perhaps three, maybe four. Underlying this extreme rapid fire came the lower-pitched, more reverberant, and slower-paced reports of what might have been a heavier-caliber rifle, something that sounded as though it had enough punch to knock the shooter on his ass with recoil.

At the first rattle of gunfire, Dylan pitched forward onto the living-room floor. He knocked Shepherd's arms out from under him, dropping the kid off his hands and knees, flat on the tongue-and-groove maple.

'Where's all the ice?' Shepherd asked, as though unaware of the ceaseless fusillades pumping into the house.

Following the shattering of the windows, following the ringing cascades of glass, wood splintered, plaster cracked, bullet-rapped pipes sang *plonk-plonk-plonk* in the walls.

Dylan's heart raced rabbit-fast, and he knew what small game animals must feel like when their pastoral fields became killing grounds on the first day of hunting season.

The gunfire seemed to come from two directions only. Out of the east, toward the rear of the house. And out of the south.

If assassins were on all four sides of the structure – and he was sure they were – then to the west and north, they were lying low. They were too professional to establish a crossfire that might kill them or their comrades.

'Belly-crawl with me, Shep.' He raised his voice above the cacophony. 'Belly-crawl, come on, *let's scoot!*'

Shepherd hugged the floor, head turned toward Dylan but eyes closed. 'Ice.'

The living room featured two south-facing windows, and four that presented a view to the west. The glass in the south wall had dissolved in the first instant of the barrage, but the west windows remained intact, untouched even by ricochets.

'Make like a snake,' Dylan urged.

Shep remained frozen: 'Ice, ice, ice.'

Relentless raking volleys punched the south wall, penetrated to the living room, chopping wooden furniture into kindling, smashing lamps, vases. Scores of rounds punched upholstered furniture, each with a thick flat slap that unnerved Dylan, maybe because this might be what flesh sounded like when a bullet tore into it.

Although his face was inches from Shep's face, Dylan shouted, partly to be sure he was heard above the din of gunfire, partly in the hope of stirring Shep to action, partly because he was angry with his brother, but mostly because he seethed again with that righteous rage he had first felt in the house on Eucalyptus Avenue, furious about the bastards who always had their way by force, who resorted to violence, first, second, last, and always. 'Damn it, Shep, are you going to let them kill us the way they killed Mom? Cut us down and leave us here to rot? Are you going to let them get away with it *again*? Are you, Shep, damn you, Shep, *are you*?'

Lincoln Proctor had killed their mother, and these gunmen were opposed to Proctor and to his life's work, but as far as Dylan was concerned, Proctor and these thugs were on the same team. They just wore different unit patches in the army of darkness.

Stirred either by Dylan's passion and anger, or perhaps by the delayed realization that they were besieged, Shep stopped chanting ice. His eyes popped open. Terror had found him.

Dylan's heart double-clutched, shifting first into neutral when it skipped a beat or two, then shifting into higher gear, because he thought Shep would fold them, right here and now, without Jilly, who had reached the front hall.

Instead, Shepherd decided to make like a snake. He polished the floor with his belly as he squirmed from the dining-room doorway into the downstairs hall, angling across the northeast quadrant of the living room.

Raised on his forearms, locomoting on his elbows and on the toes of his shoes, the kid moved so fast that Dylan had trouble keeping up with him.

Chips of plaster, splinters of wood, chunks of foam padding, and other debris rained on them as they crawled. Between them and the south wall, a reassuring bulk of furniture absorbed or deflected the lower incoming rounds, while the rest passed over them.

Bullets whistled overhead, the sound of fate sucking air through its teeth, but Dylan didn't yet hear any shrieking shards of whirling shrapnel, neither cyanide nor any other flavor.

A thin haze of plaster dust cast a dream pall over the room, and pillow feathers floated in the air, as thick as in a henhouse roiled by a fox.

Shep snaked into the hallway and might have kept going into the study if Jilly had not been lying prone at the foot of the stairs. She wriggled backward, blocked him, grabbed him by the loose seat of his jeans, and redirected him to the steps.

When not stopped by furniture or otherwise deflected, bullets penetrated the front hall through the open door to the living room. They also slammed into the south wall of the hallway, which was also the north wall of the living room. Impact with this second mass of wood and plaster stopped some rounds, but others punched through with plenty of killing force left.

Wheezing with fear more than with exertion, grimacing at the alkaline taste of plaster dust, gazing up from the floor, Dylan saw scores of holes in that wall. Some were no larger than a quarter, but a few were as big as his fist.

Bullets had hacked chips and chunks out of the handrail. They hacked another and another as he watched.

Several balusters had been notched. Two were shattered.

Those rounds that made it through the wall and past the stair railing were finally stopped by the north wall of hallway, which became the stairwell wall. Therein, the powerful rounds had spent the last of their energy, leaving the plaster as pocked and drilled as the backstop to a firing squad.

Even if Jilly and the brothers O'Conner, like a family of snake-imitating sideshow freaks, ascended the steps with a profile as low as that of a descending Slinky toy, they weren't going to be able to reach the first landing unscathed. Maybe one of them would make it alive and whole. Maybe even two, which would be irrefutable proof of guardian angels. If miracles came in threes, however, they wouldn't be miracles anymore; they would be common experience. Jilly or Shep, or Dylan himself, would be killed or gravely wounded in the attempt. They were trapped here, flat on the floor, inhaling plaster dust with a gasp, exhaling it with a wheeze, without options, without hope.

Then the gunfire abated and, within just three or four seconds, stopped altogether.

With the first phase of the assault completed in no more than two minutes, the assassins to the east and south of the house were falling back. Taking cover to avoid being wounded by crossfire.

Simultaneously, to the west and north of the house, other gunmen would be approaching at a run. Phase two.

The front door, in the west wall of the house, lay immediately behind Dylan, flanked by stained-glass sidelights. The study was to their left as they faced the first landing, just beyond the stairwell wall, and the study had three windows.

In phase two, the hallway would be riddled with such a storm of bullets that everything heretofore would seem, by comparison, like a mere tantrum thrown by belligerent children.

Taunting Death had granted them a mere handful of seconds in which to save themselves, and his skeletal fingers were spread wide to facilitate the sifting of time.

These same lightning calculations must have flashed through Jilly's mind, for even as the echo of the last barrage still boomed through the house, she bolted to her feet in concert with Dylan. Without pause for even one word of strategic planning, they both reached down, grabbed Shep by his belt, and hauled him to his feet between them.

With the superhuman strength of adrenaline-flushed mothers lifting overturned automobiles off their trapped babies, they pulled Shep onto tiptoe and muscled him up the steps, against which his feet rapped, tapped, scraped, and occasionally even landed on a tread in such a way as to modestly advance the cause and assist them with a little upward thrust.

'Where's all the ice?' Shep asked.

'Upstairs,' Jilly gasped.

'Where's all the ice?'

'Damn it, buddy!'

'We're almost there,' Jilly encouraged them.

'Where's all the ice?'

The first landing loomed.

Shep hooked the toe of one foot under a tread.

They maneuvered him over it, onward, up.

'Where's all the ice?'

The stained-glass sidelights dissolved in a roar of gunfire, and many sharp bony knuckles knocked fiercely against the front door, as if a score of determined demons with death warrants were demanding admission, splitting the wood, punching holes, and vibrations passed through the staircase underfoot as round after round smashed into the risers between the lower treads.

39

Once they reached the landing and started to climb the second flight, Dylan felt safer, but his relief immediately proved to be premature. A bullet cracked up through a tread three steps *ahead* of them, and slammed into the stairwell ceiling.

He realized that the underside of this second flight of stairs faced the front door. Essentially, beneath their feet lay the back wall of a shooting gallery.

Proceeding was dangerous, retreating made no sense whatsoever, and halting in midflight meant certain death later if not sooner. So they hauled more aggressively on Shepherd's belt, Jilly with both hands, Dylan with one, dragged-heaved-bounced him up the second set of stairs, and this time 'Where's all the ice?' squeaked from him in a semifalsetto.

Dylan expected to be shot through the soles of his feet, in an arm, through the bottom of his chin, or all of the above. When they arrived in the upper hall without any of them yet resembling a morgue photo in a forensic-pathology textbook, he let go of his brother and leaned with one hand on the newel post to catch his breath.

Evidently, Vonetta Beesley, their housekeeper, had put her hand on the newel cap earlier in the day, for when Dylan made contact with her psychic trace, images of the woman flared through his mind. He felt compelled to seek her out at once.

If this had occurred the previous evening, if he hadn't learned to control his response to such stimuli, he might have plunged down the stairs, into the maelstrom below, as he had raced recklessly to Marjorie's house on Eucalyptus Avenue. Instead, he snatched his hand off the post and dialed down his sensitivity to the spoor.

Already Jilly had pulled Shepherd farther into the hall, away from the head of the stairs. Raising her voice to compete with the explosive tumult below, she pleaded with him to fold them out of here.

Joining them, Dylan saw that his brother remained icebound. The issue of ice continued to bounce around inside Shep's head to the exclusion of virtually everything else.

No formula existed to determine how long Shepherd would take to extract himself from the tar pit of this latest obsession, but wise money would have to take short odds on a long period of distraction. He was more likely to awaken to the world around him in an hour than in two minutes.

Focusing tightly on one narrow question or area of interest was, after all, another way to insulate himself when the inflow of sensory stimuli became overwhelming. In the midst of gunfire, he couldn't choose a safe corner and turn his back to the chaos behind him, but he could flee to a symbolic corner in a dark room deep in the castle of his mind, a corner that contained nothing to consider except ice, ice, ice.

'Where's all the ice?'

'When they're done downstairs,' Jilly asked, 'what's next?'

'They blast the second floor. Maybe come up on the porch roofs to do it.'

'Maybe they come inside,' she said.

'Ice, ice, ice.'

'We've got to get him off this ice,' Jilly worried.

'That'll only happen with time and quiet.'

'We're screwed.'

'We're not screwed.'

'Screwed.'

'Not screwed.'

'You got a plan?' she demanded.

Dylan's only plan, which Jilly in fact suggested, had been to get above the gunfire. Now he realized that the gunfire would come to them wherever they went, not to mention the gunmen.

The ferocious clatter-bang downstairs, the fear of a stray bullet finding its way up the stairwell or even through the ceiling of the lower hall and the floor of the upper hall: All this made concentrating on tactics and strategy no easier than lassoing snakes. Once again, circumstances thrust upon Dylan a deeper understanding of how his brother must feel when overwhelmed by life, which in Shep's case was nearly all the time.

Okay, forget about the money he kept in a lockbox. The Beatles had been right: Money can't buy you love. Or stop a bullet.

Forget about the 9-mm pistol that he'd bought after his mother's murder. Against these assailants' artillery, the handgun might as well have been a stick.

'Ice, ice, ice.'

Jilly coaxed Shepherd to skate out of the ice and rejoin them, so he could fold them to someplace safe, but with his eyes closed and thought processes frozen, he remained resistant to sweet talk.

Time and quiet. Although they couldn't buy much time, every minute gained might be the minute during which Shep would come back to them. Deep quiet was beyond attainment during this jihad, but any reduction in the bang and clangor would help the kid find a way out of that corner of ice.

Dylan crossed the hallway and threw open the door to the guest bedroom. 'In here.'

Jilly seemed to be able to tug Shepherd along in a reasonably fast shuffle.

The impact of the fierce barrage sent shudders upward through the walls of the house. The second-floor windowpanes rattled in their frames.

Moving ahead of Jilly and Shep, Dylan hurried into the bedroom, to a walk-in closet. He switched on the light.

A cord dangled from a pull-down trapdoor in the closet ceiling. He yanked on the cord, lowering the trap.

Downstairs, the deafening volume of gunfire, which had sounded like the fiercest moment during the Nazi siege of Leningrad, as Dylan had once seen it portrayed on the History Channel, abruptly grew louder.

He wondered how many major splintering hits the wall studs could sustain before structural damage became critical and one or another corner of the house sagged.

'Ice, ice, ice.'

Arriving at the closet door with Shep, referring to the ungodly racket on the lower floor, Jilly said, 'We got a double scoop of Apocalypse now.'

'With sprinkles.' A ladder in three folded segments was mounted to the back of the trapdoor. Dylan lowered it.

'Some of Proctor's experimental subjects must've developed weird talents a lot scarier than ours.'

'What do you mean?'

'These guys don't know what we can do, but they're so wet-pants scared of what it *might* be, they want us seriously dead, faster than fast.'

Dylan hadn't thought about that. He didn't *like* thinking about it. Before them, Proctor's nanobots had evidently produced monsters. Everyone expected him and Jilly and Shep to be monsters, too.

'What?' Jilly asked disbelievingly. 'You want us to go up that freakin' ladder?'

'Yeah.'

'That's death.'

'It's the attic.'

'The attic is death, a dead end.'

'Everywhere we can go is a dead end. This is the only way we can buy some time for Shep.'

'They'll look in the attic.'

'Not right away.'

'I hate this,' she declared.

'You don't see me dancing.'

'Ice, ice, ice.'

Dylan said to Jilly, 'You go first.'

'Why me?'

'You can coax Shep from the top while I push from below.'

The gunfire ceased, but the memory of it still rang in Dylan's ears.

'They're coming.'

Jilly said, 'Crap.'

'Go.'

'Crap.'

'Up.'

'Crap.'

'Now, Jilly.'

40

The attic limited their options, put them in the position of trapped rats, offered them nothing but gloom and dust and spiders, but Jilly ascended the sloped ladder because the attic was the only place they could go.

As she climbed, her shoulder-slung purse banged against her hip and briefly got hooked on the long scissoring hinges from which the ladder was hung. She had lost the Coupe DeVille, all her luggage, her laptop, her career as a comedian, even her significant other – dear adorable green Fred – but she was damned if she'd give up her purse under any circumstances. It contained only a few dollars, breath mints, Kleenex, lipstick, compact, a hairbrush, nothing that would change her life if kept or destroy it if lost, but supposing that she miraculously survived this visit to Casa O'Conner, she looked forward to freshening her lipstick and brushing her hair because at this dire moment, anyway, having the leisure to primp a little appealed to her as a delicious luxury on a par with limousines, presidential suites in five-star hotels, and Beluga caviar.

Besides, if she had to die far too young with a brain full of nanomachines, *because* of a brain full of nanomachines, she wanted to leave as pretty a corpse as possible – assuming that she didn't take a head shot that left her face as distorted as a portrait by Picasso.

Negative Jackson, vortex of pessimism, reached the top of the ladder and discovered that the attic was high enough to allow her to stand. Through a few screened vents in the eaves, filtered sunlight penetrated this high redoubt, but with insufficient power to banish many shadows. Raw rafters, board walls, and a plywood floor enclosed a double score of cardboard boxes, three old trunks, assorted junk, and considerable empty space.

The hot, dry air smelled faintly of ancient roofing tar and

strongly of uncountable varieties of dust. Here and there, a few cocoons were fixed to the sloped planks of the ceiling, little sacs of insect industry vaguely phosphorescent in the murk. Nearer, just above her head, an elaborate spider web spanned the junction of two rafters; though its architect had either perished or gone traveling, the web was grimly festooned with four moths, their gray wings spread in the memory of flight, their body shells sucked empty by the absent arachnid.

'We're doomed,' she murmured as she turned to the open trap door, dropped to her knees, and peered down the ladder.

Shep stood on the bottom rung. He gripped a higher rung with both hands. Head bowed as if this were some kind of prayer ladder, he appeared reluctant to climb farther.

Behind Shep, Dylan glanced through the open closet door, into the guest bedroom, no doubt expecting to see men on the porch roof beyond the windows.

'Ice,' said Shep.

To Jilly, Dylan said, 'Coax him up.'

'What if there's a fire?'

'That's damn poor coaxing.'

'Ice.'

'It's a tinderbox up here. What if there's a fire?'

'What if Earth's magnetic pole shifts?' he asked sarcastically.

'*That* I've got plans for. Can't you push him?'

'I can sort of encourage him, but it's pretty much impossible to *push* someone up a ladder.'

'It's not against the laws of physics.'

'What're you, an engineer?'

'Ice.'

'I've got bags and bags of ice up here, sweetie,' she lied. 'Push him, Dylan.'

'I'm trying.'

'Ice.'

'Plenty of ice up here, Shep. Come on up here with me.'

Shep wouldn't move his hands. He clung stubbornly to his perch.

Jilly couldn't see Shepherd's face, only the top of his bowed head.

From below, Dylan lifted his brother's right foot and moved it to the next rung.

'Ice.'

Unable to get the image of the dead moths out of her head, and growing desperate, Jilly gave up on the idea of coaxing Shep to the attic, and instead hoped to break through to him by transforming his monologue on ice into a dialogue.

'Ice,' he said.

She said, 'Frozen water.'

Dylan lifted Shepherd's left foot onto the higher rung to which he'd already transferred the right, but still Shepherd wouldn't move his hands.

'Ice.'

'Sleet,' Jilly said

Far down in the house, on the ground floor, someone kicked in a door. Considering that the volleys of gunfire must have reduced the outer doors to dust or to lacy curtains of splinters, the only doors requiring a solid kick would probably be inside the house. A search had begun.

'Ice.'

'Hail.'

'Ice.'

'Floe,' Jilly said.

Another crash downstairs: This one reverberated all the way up through the house, trembling the floor under Jilly's knees.

Below, Dylan closed the closet door, and their situation seemed markedly more claustrophobic.

'Ice.'

'Glacier.'

Just when she suspected that Shepherd was about to respond to her, Jilly exhausted her supply of synonyms for ice and words for types of ice. She decided to change the nature of the game, adding a word to Shepherd's ice as if to complete a thought.

Shep said, 'Ice.'

'Berg,' said Jilly.

'Ice.'

'Cube.'

All this talk of ice made the attic hotter, hotter. Dust on the rafters, dust on the floor, dust drifting in the air seemed about to combust.

'Ice.'

'Rink.'

'Ice.'

'Skater.'

'Ice.'

'Hockey. You ought to be embarrassed, sweetie, taking the easy half of the game, always the same word.'

Shepherd had raised his bowed head. He stared at the section of the ladder rung exposed between his clenched hands.

Downstairs: more crashing, more breaking, a quick nervous burst of gunfire.

'Ice.'

'Cream. Shep, how much fun would it be to work a puzzle that only had one piece?'

'Ice.'

'Pick.'

'Ice.'

'Tongs.'

As she slipped new words into his head, ice no longer ricocheted around in there all by itself. A subtle change occurred in his face, a softening, suggesting a relaxation of this obsession. She felt sure she wasn't imagining it. Pretty sure.

'Ice.'

'Bucket.'

'Ice.'

'Age. You know what, sweetie? Even if I've got the harder half of this game, it's a bunch more fun than listening to synonyms for *feces*.'

A faint smile found his lips, but almost at once he breathed it away with a trembling exhalation.

'Ice.'

'Cold.'

Shepherd shifted his right hand to a higher rung, then his left. Then to a still higher rung. 'Ice.'

'Bag.'

Shepherd moved his feet without assistance from his brother.

Downstairs the doorbell rang. Even in a squad of professional killers, there had to be a bonehead joker.

'Ice.'

'Box.'

Shepherd climbed, climbed. 'Ice.'

'Show.'

'Ice.'

'Storm.'

'Ice.'

'Tea, ax, breaker, man, chest, water,' Jilly said, talking him up the last rungs and into the attic.

She helped him off the ladder, to his feet, away from the trapdoor. She hugged him and told him he was terrific, and Shep didn't resist, though he did say, 'Where's all the ice?'

Down in the closet, Dylan switched off the light. He climbed quickly in the darkness. 'Good work, Jackson.'

'*De nada*, O'Conner.'

On his knees in the gloom, Dylan folded the accordion ladder upward, as quietly as possible reloading it onto the back of the trapdoor, which he would then pull shut. 'If they aren't upstairs yet, they're coming,' he whispered. 'Take Shep over there, the southwest corner, behind those boxes.'

'Where's all the ice?' Shepherd asked too loudly.

Jilly hushed him as she guided him across the shadow-choked attic. He wasn't tall enough to rap the lowest rafters with his forehead, but his big brother would have to duck.

In lower realms the wrecking crew crashed into another room.

A man shouted something unintelligible. Another man returned his shout with a curse, and someone barked with laughter.

A hardness, a roughness, a swagger of presumption in these voices made them sound less like men to Jilly, more like the never quite defined shapes in a nightmare chase, which pursued sometimes on two feet, sometimes on four, alternately howling like men and crying like beasts.

She wondered when the cops would come. *If* they would come. Dylan had said the nearest town was miles away. The closest neighbor lived half a mile south of here. But surely somebody had heard the gunfire.

Of course the assault had started just five minutes ago, maybe six, and no rural police force would be able to answer such a remote call sooner than another five minutes, more likely ten.

'Where's all the ice?' Shepherd asked as loudly as before.

Instead of hushing him again, Jilly answered in a soft voice with which she hoped to set an example: 'In the refrigerator, honey. That's where all the ice is.'

Behind stacked boxes in the southwest corner, Jilly encouraged Shep to sit beside her on the dusty floor.

Filtered through a screened fresh-air vent, a blush of daylight revealed a long-dead bird – a sparrow, perhaps – reduced by time to papery bones. Beneath the bones were trapped a few feathers that drafts had not stirred to other corners of the attic.

The bird must have stolen in here on a chilly day, through some chink in the eaves, and must have been unable to find its way out. Perhaps having broken a wing battering against rafters, certainly exhausted and hungry, it had waited for death by the screened vent, where it could see the sky.

'Where's all the ice?' Shepherd asked, this time lowering his voice to a whisper.

Worried that the kid had not come as far out of his ice corner as she had thought when he climbed the ladder, or that he was sliding into it once more, Jilly pressed forward with her new game, seeking dialogue. 'There's ice in a margarita, isn't there, sweetie? All slushy and nice. Man, I could use one now.'

'Where's all the ice?'

'In a picnic chest, there'd be ice.'

'Where's all the ice?'

'Christmas in New England, there'd be ice. And snow.'

Moving gracefully and quietly for such a large man, Dylan loomed out of the deeper darkness swaddling the center of the attic, into the bird light that dimly illuminated their refuge, and sat next to his brother. 'Still the ice?' he asked worriedly.

'We're going somewhere,' Jilly assured him with more confidence than she felt.

'Where's all the ice?' Shep whispered.

'Lots of ice in a skating rink.'

'Where's all the ice?'

'Nothing but ice in an *icemaker*.'

Boots met doors on the second floor. Rooms were breached with crash and clatter.

Whispering yet more discreetly, Shepherd said, 'Where's all the ice?'

'I see champagne in a silver bucket,' Jilly said, matching his quiet tones, 'crushed ice packed around the bottle.'

'Where's all the ice?'

'North Pole has a lot of ice.'

'Ahhh,' Shepherd said, and for the moment he said no more.

Jilly listened tensely as voices in rooms below replaced the boom and crack of violent search. Mummified conspirators in pyramidal tombs, speaking through their grave wrappings, could not have been less clear, and nothing said below was intelligible up here.

'Ahhh,' Shep breathed.

'We have to move along, buddy,' Dylan said. 'It's way past time to fold.'

Under them the ravaged house sank into silence, and after half a minute, the disquieting hush grew more ominous than anything that had preceded it.

'Buddy,' Dylan said, but made no further plea, as if he sensed that Shep would respond better to this silence, this stillness, than to additional pressure.

In her mind's eye, Jilly saw the kitchen clock, the pig grinning as the second hand swept around the numbers on its belly.

Even in memory, that porcine smile disturbed her, but when she wiped the image from her mind, she saw instead, equally unbidden, the Minute Minder with which Shep timed his showers. This image shook her worse than she'd been shaken by the pig, for the Minute Minder looked remarkably like a bomb clock.

Gunmen opened fire on the ceilings below, and geysers of bullets erupted through the attic floor.

41

Starting at opposite ends of the house but moving toward each other, gunmen fired bursts of heavy-caliber, penetrant rounds into the ceiling of the second-floor hallway. Bullets cracked through the plywood attic floor, spitting sprays of wood chips, admitting narrow shafts of pale light from below, establishing a six-foot-wide zone of death the length of this upper space. Slugs slammed into rafters. Other rounds punched through the roof and carved blue stars of summer sky in the dark vault of the attic ceiling.

Jilly realized why Dylan wanted to be in a corner, back pressed against an outer wall. The structure between them and the lower floor would be denser along the perimeter, more likely to stop at least some of the rounds from penetrating into the attic.

Her legs were straight out in front of her. She drew her knees in toward her chest, making as small a target of herself as possible, but not small enough.

The bastards kept changing magazines down below, reloading in rotation, so the assault remained continuous. The rattle-crack-boom of gunfire numbed the mind to all feeling except terror, precluded all thought except thoughts of death.

No shortage of ammunition in this operation. No reconsideration of the recklessness or the immorality of cold-blooded murder. Just the relentless, savage execution of the plan.

In the thin wash of daylight from the screened vent in the eave, Jilly saw that Shepherd's face was animated by a succession of tics, squints, and flinches, but that behind his closed lids, his eyes were not twitching as they so often did. The thunder of gunfire disturbed him, but he seemed less scared to distraction than focused intently on some enthralling thought.

The gunfire stopped.

The house popped and creaked with settling ruination.

In this certain to be brief cease-fire, Dylan dared to motivate Shepherd with the threat of what was coming: 'Gooey-bloody, Shep. Coming fast, gooey-bloody.'

Having moved out of the upstairs hall, into rooms on both sides of the house, the gunmen opened fire again.

The killers were not yet in the room immediately below the attic corner in which Jilly, Dylan, and Shep huddled. But they would visit it in a minute. Maybe sooner.

Although the brutally pounding fusillades were concentrated in two widely separate areas, the entire attic floor vibrated from the impact of scores of heavy rounds.

Wood cracked, wood groaned, bullet-struck nails and in-wall pipes twanged and clanked and pinged.

A mist of dust shook down from rafters.

On the floor the bird bones trembled as if an animating spirit had returned to them.

Freed, one of the few remaining feathers spiraled up through the descending dust.

Jilly wanted to scream, dared not, could not: throat clenched as tight as a fist, breath imprisoned.

Rapid-fire weaponry rattled directly below them, and in front of their eyes, swarms of bullets ripped through stacked storage boxes. Cardboard puckered, buckled, shredded.

As his eyes popped wide open, Shepherd thrust off the floor, stood upright, pressing back against the wall.

With an explosive exhalation, Jilly bolted to her feet, Dylan too, and it seemed the house would come apart around them, would be blown to pieces by the cyclone of *noise* if not first blasted and shaken into rubble by the shattering passage of this storm of lead, of steel-jacketed rounds.

Two feet in front of them, the plywood floor ruptured, ruptured, ruptured, bullets punching through from below.

Something stung Jilly's forehead, and as she raised her right hand, something bit her palm, too, before she could press it to the higher wound, causing her to cry out in pain, in shock.

Even in this dusty dimness, she saw the first drops of blood flung from her fingertips when she convulsively shook them. Droplets spattered darkly against the cardboard boxes in a pattern that no doubt foretold her future.

From her stung brow, curling down her right temple, a fat bead of blood found the corner of that eye.

One, three, five, and more rounds smashed up through the floor, closer than the first cluster.

Shepherd grabbed Jilly's uninjured hand.

She didn't see him pinch or tweak, but the attic folded away from them, and brightness folded in.

Low rafters flared into high bright sky. Knee-caressing golden grass slid firmly underfoot as attic flooring slipped away.

Sounding as brittle and juiceless as things long dead, clicking flitters of startled grasshoppers shot everywhichway through the grass.

Jilly stood with Shep and Dylan on a hilltop in the sun. Far to the west, the sea seemed to wear a skin of dragon scales, green spangled with gold.

She could still hear steady gunfire, but muffled by distance and by the walls of the O'Conner house, which she saw now for the first time from the outside. At this distance, the structure appeared less damaged than she knew it must be.

'Shep, this isn't good enough, not far enough,' Dylan worried.

Shepherd let go of Jilly and stood transfixed by the sight of blood dripping from the thumb and first two fingers of her right hand.

Two inches long, roughly a quarter of an inch wide, a splinter had pierced the meaty part of her palm.

Ordinarily the sight of blood wouldn't have weakened her knees, so perhaps her legs trembled less because of the blood than because she realized this wound could have been – *should* have been – far worse.

Dylan slipped a supporting hand under her arm, examined her forehead. 'It's just a shallow laceration. Probably from another splinter, but it didn't stick. More blood than damage.'

Below the hill, beyond the meadow, in the yards surrounding the house, three armed men stood sentinel to prevent their quarry from somehow escaping through battlefield barrages and through the cordon of killers that searched the bullet-riddled rooms. None of the three appeared to be looking toward the hilltop, but this bit of luck would not hold.

While Jilly was distracted, Dylan pinched the splinter in her hand and plucked it free with one sharp pull that made her hiss with pain.

'We'll clean it out later,' he said.

'Later where?' she asked. 'If you don't tell Shepherd where to fold us, he's liable to take us on a trip somewhere we don't dare go, like back to the motel in Holbrook, where you can bet they're waiting for us – or maybe even back into the house.'

'But where *is* safe?' Dylan wondered, momentarily blank.

Maybe the blood on her hand and on her face reminded her of the desert vision in which she'd been splashed by a wave of white wings and worse. Into the hard reality of this desperate day, the dreamy portents of imminent evil suddenly intruded.

Rising out of the wheatlike smell of dry grass came the sweet spicy fragrance of incense.

At the house, the muffled popping of gunfire rapidly declined, ceased altogether, while here on the hilltop arose the silvery laughter of children.

By one tell or another, Dylan recognized her condition, knew that she was surfing a swell of paranormal perception, and said,'What's happening, what do you see?'

Turning toward the mirthful music of the children's voices, she found not those who made the laughter, but saw instead a marble font of the kind that held holy water in any Catholic church, abandoned here on the grassy hilltop, canted like a tombstone in an ancient graveyard.

Movement beyond Shep caught her attention, and when she shifted her focus from the font, Jilly discovered a little girl, blond and blue-eyed, perhaps five or six years old, wearing a lacy white dress, white ribbons in her hair, holding a nosegay of flowers, solemn with purpose. As the unseen children laughed, the girl turned as though in search of them, and as she rotated away from Jilly, she faded out of existence—

'Jilly?'

—but turning *into* existence and toward her, precisely where the little girl had been standing, appeared a fifty-something woman in a pale yellow dress, wearing yellow gloves and a hat with flowers, her eyes rolled so far back in her head that only the whites showed, her torso pocked by three hideous bullet wounds, one between the breasts. Although dead, the woman walked toward Jilly, an apparition as real in blazing summer sunlight as any that had ever haunted beneath a moon, reaching out with her right hand as she approached, as though seeking aid.

No more able to move than if she had been rooted to the ground, Jilly shrank from the ghostly touch, thrust out her bleeding hand to ward off contact, but when the dead woman's fingers touched her hand – with a sense of pressure, coldness – the apparition vanished.

'It's going to happen today,' she said miserably. 'Soon.'

'Happen? What?' Dylan asked.

Far away a man shouted, and another man answered in a shout.

'They've seen us,' Dylan said.

The vast aviary of the sky contained just one bird, a circling hawk gliding silently on currents high above, and no birds erupted into flight from the grass around them, yet she heard wings, at first a whispery flutter, then a more insistent rustle.

'They're coming,' Dylan warned, speaking not of birds but of assassins.

'Wings,' Jilly said, as the whisking thrum of invisible doves rapidly grew more turbulent. 'Wings.'

'Wings,' said Shepherd, touching the bloody hand with which she had tried to fend off the dead woman, and which she still held out before her.

The *chop-chop-chop* of automatic gunfire, real to this place and time, was answered by the more deliberate crack of high-powered rifles that only she could hear, by shots fired in another place and in a time yet to come – but coming fast.

'Jilly,' said Shepherd, startling her by the use of her name, which he had never before spoken.

She met his lotus-green eyes, which weren't in the least dreamy, nor at all evasive as they had been in the past, but clear and direct and sharp with alarm.

'Church,' said Shepherd.

'Church,' she agreed.

'Shep!' Dylan urged, as bullets kicked up plumes of dirt and torn grass from the hillside less than twenty feet below them.

Shepherd O'Conner brought here to there, folded the sunshine, the golden grass, the flying bullets, and unfolded a cool vaulted space with stained-glass windows like giant puzzles fully solved.

42

The nave of this Spanish baroque church, huge and old and lovely – currently undergoing a little restoration – featured a long central barrel vault, deep groin vaults on two sides, and a long center-aisle colonnade of massive thirty-foot columns that stood on ornately sculpted six-foot pedestals.

The crowd in the church, perhaps three hundred, was dwarfed by the space and by the dimensions of the architectural elements. Even dressed in finery, they could not compete with the colorific cascades of light flung down upon them by the backlit western windows.

The pipework of the scaffolding – erected for the restoration of the painted-plaster frieze that enhanced three walls of the nave – blocked little of the jewel-bright glory of the windows. Incoming sunlight pierced sapphire, ruby, emerald, amethyst, and adamantine-yellow shapes of glass, scattering gems of light across half the nave and dappling portions of the center aisle.

Within ten racing heartbeats of arrival, Dylan swept the great church with his absorbent gaze, and knew a thousand details of its ornamentation, form, and function. As testament to the depth of the baroque design, knowledge of a thousand details left him as ignorant of the structure as an Egyptologist would be ignorant of a newfound pyramid if he studied nothing more than the six feet of its pinnacle not buried in Sahara sands.

Following a quick survey of the church, he lowered his attention to the pigtailed girl, perhaps nine years old, who had been exploring the shadowy back corner of the massive nave into which Shepherd had folded them. She gasped, she blinked, she gaped, spun around on one patent-leather shoe, and ran to rejoin her parents in their pew, no doubt to tell them that either saints or witches had arrived.

Although redolent of incense, as in Jilly's visions, the air shivered neither with music nor with a tumult of wings. The hundreds here assembled spoke in murmurs, and their voices traveled as softly as the fragrance of incense through these columned spaces.

Most of those in the pews sat in the front half of the church, facing the sanctuary. If any had been turned in their seats to talk with people in the rows behind them, they must not have glimpsed the infolding witchery, for no one stood to get a better look or called out in surprise.

Nearer, tuxedoed young men escorted late arrivals down the center aisle to their seats. The escorts were too busy – and arriving guests were too caught up in anticipation of the pending event – to take notice of a miraculous materialization in one far, shadowy corner.

'A wedding,' Jilly whispered.

'This is the place?'

'Los Angeles. My church,' she said, and sounded stunned.

'Yours?'

'Where I sang in the choir when I was a girl.'

'When does it happen?'

'Soon,' she said.

'How?'

'Shot.'

'More damn guns.'

'Sixty-seven shot . . . forty dead.'

'Sixty-seven?' he asked, staggered by the number. 'Then there can't be one lone gunman.'

'More than one,' she whispered. 'More than one.'

'How many?'

Her gaze sought answers in the heavenward-curving voussoirs of the serried vaults, but then slid down the polished marble columns to the life-size sculptures of saints that formed the dados of the pedestals.

'At least two,' she said. 'Maybe three.'

'Shep is scared.'

'We're all scared, buddy,' Dylan replied, which at the moment was the best that he could do by way of reassurance.

Jilly seemed to study the friends and family of bride, of groom, as though by sixth sense she could deduce, from the backs of their heads, whether any of them had come here with violent intentions.

'Surely the gunmen wouldn't be wedding guests,' Dylan said.

'No . . . I think . . . no. . . .'

She took a few steps toward the back of the unoccupied pews in the last row, her interest rising from the assembled guests to the sanctuary beyond the distant chancel railing.

An arc of columns separated the nave from the sanctuary and also supported a series of transverse arches. Beyond the columns lay the choir enclosure and the high altar, with pyx and tabernacle, behind which towered a monumental downlighted crucifix.

Moving to Jilly's side, Dylan said, 'Maybe they'll come in after the wedding begins, come in shooting.'

'No,' she disagreed. 'They're here already.'

Her words were ice to the back of his neck.

She turned slowly, searching, searching.

At the pipe organ in the sanctuary, the organist struck the first notes of the welcoming hymn.

Evidently, workmen involved in the restoration of the painted plaster frieze had left windows or doors open, thereby admitting some temporary tenants to high apartments. Frightened from roosts in the ribs of the vaults and from carved-marble perches on the ornate capitals of the columns, doves swooped down into the nave, not the multitudes that Jilly had foreseen, but eight or ten, a dozen at most, arising from different points overhead but joining at once into a flock this side of the chancel railing.

The wedding guests exclaimed at this white-winged spectacle, as though it must be a planned performance preceding the nuptials, and from several delighted children arose a singular silvery laughter.

'It's starting,' Jilly declared, and a sculpting terror wrought her blood-streaked face.

In gyres the flock flew through the church, from bride's family to groom's to bride's again, progressing toward the back of the nave even as they explored both sides of it.

A quick-witted usher raced down the aisle to the back of the nave, under the scaffolding, through the open doors into the narthex, no doubt intending to prop open a pair of entry doors to provide the winged intruders with an unobstructed exit.

As though synchronized to the hymn, the birds soared, dived, and swooped in their blessing circles from the chancel to the rear of the nave. Drawn toward the draft caused by the open door, charmed toward a glimpse of sunlight not filtered through stained glass, they went where the usher had induced them, out and away, leaving only a few luminous white feathers adrift in the air.

At first transfixed by a feather rising on a thermal current, Jilly's gaze abruptly flew to the scaffolding in the aisle on the west side of the nave, then to the scaffolding in the east aisle. *'Up there.'*

The apex of each arched window lay about twenty feet above the church floor. The top of the scaffolding thrust two feet higher, to service the three-foot-tall band of carved and painted plaster that began at approximately the twenty-four-foot mark.

That work platform, where on weekdays craftsmen and artisans conducted restoration, was perhaps five feet wide, nearly as wide as the aisle below it, constructed of sheets of plywood secured to the horizontal ribs of pipe that formed the scaffold cap. The height, combined with the gloom that prevailed in the vaulted upper reaches of the church, where the work lights were not aglow, prevented them from seeing who lurked in those cloistered elevations.

The back wall of the nave lacked windows; however, the frieze continued there, as did the scaffolding. Ten feet away, just to the right of Shepherd, a ladder was built into the scaffold: rungs of pipe coated with fine-grooved rubber.

Dylan went to the ladder, touched a rung above his head, and felt at once, like a scorpion sting, the psychic spoor of evil men.

Having hurried with him to the ladder, Jilly must have seen a dire shift in his expression, in his eyes, for she said, 'Oh, God, what?'

'Three men,' he told her, taking his hand off the ladder rung, repeatedly flexing and clenching it to work out the dark energy that had leeched into him. 'Bigots. Haters. They want to kill the entire wedding party, the priest, as many of the guests as they can get.'

Jilly turned toward the front of the church. 'Dylan!'

He followed her stare and saw that the priest and two altar boys were already in the sanctuary, descending the ambulatory from the high altar to the chancel railing.

From a side door at the front, two young men in tuxedoes entered the nave, crossed toward the center aisle. The groom, the best man.

'We've got to warn them,' Jilly said.

'No. If we start shouting, they won't know who we are, might not understand what we're saying. They won't react right away – but the gunmen will. They'll open fire. They won't get the bride, but they'll cut down the groom and lots of guests.'

'Then we've got to go up,' she said, gripping the ladder as if to climb.

He stayed her with a hand on her arm. 'No. Vibrations. The whole scaffold will shake. They'll feel us climbing. They'll know we're coming.'

Shepherd stood in a most unusual posture for him, not bowed and slumped and floor-gazing, but with his head tipped back, watching a floating feather.

Stepping between his brother and the feather, Dylan met him eye to eye. 'Shep, I love you. I love you . . . and I need you to be *here*.'

Refocusing his vision from the more distant feather to Dylan, Shep said, 'The North Pole.'

Dylan stood in bafflement for a moment before he realized that Shep was repeating one of Jilly's answers to his monotonous question *Where's all the ice?*

'No, buddy, forget the North Pole. Be *here* with me.'

Shep blinked, blinked as if with puzzlement.

Afraid that his brother would close his eyes and retreat into one mental corner or another, Dylan said, 'Quick, right now, take us from here to there, Shep.' He pointed to the floor at their feet. 'From here.' Then he pointed toward the top of the scaffolding along the back wall of the nave, and with his other hand, he turned Shep's head toward where he pointed. 'To that platform up there. Here to there, Shep. Here to there.'

The welcoming hymn concluded. The final notes of the pipe organ reverberated hollowly through the vaults and colonnades.

'Here?' Shep asked, pointing at the floor between them.

'Yes.'

'There?' Shep asked, pointing to the work platform above them.

'Yes, here to there.'

'Here to there?' Shep asked through a puzzled frown.

'Here to there, buddy.'

'Not far,' said Shep.

'No, sweetie,' Jilly agreed, 'it's not far, and we know you can do much bigger things, much longer folds, but right now all we need is here to there.'

Seconds after the final notes of the hymn had quivered into silence in the farthest corners of the church, the organist struck up 'Here Comes the Bride.'

Dylan looked toward the center aisle, perhaps eighty feet away, and saw a pretty young woman step out of the narthex, escorted by a handsome young man in a tuxedo, through a passage in the scaffolding, past the holy-water font, into the nave. She wore a blue dress with blue gloves and carried a small bouquet of flowers. A bridesmaid on the arm of a groomsman. Concentrating solemnly on her timing, they walked in that classic halting rhythm of bridal processions.

'Herethere?' asked Shep.

'Herethere,' Dylan urged, *'Herethere!'*

The assembled guests had risen from their seats and turned to witness the entrance of the bride. Their interest would be captured so entirely by the wedding party that it was unlikely a one of them, except perhaps a certain pigtailed girl, would notice three figures vanish from a far, shadowy corner.

With fingers still wet with Jilly's blood from when he'd touched her on the hilltop, Shepherd reached once more for her wounded hand. 'Feel how it works, the round and round of all that is.'

'Here to there,' Jilly reminded him.

As a second bridesmaid with escort followed the first out of the narthex, everything in Dylan's view folded away from him.

43

With the carved frieze to Dylan's right and a neck-breaking drop to his left, the work platform atop the scaffold unfolded under their feet, creaked, and trembled with the assumption of their weight.

The first of the three gunmen – a bearded specimen with unruly hair and a big head on a scrawny neck – sat only a few feet from them, his back against the nave wall. An assault rifle lay at his side, and six spare magazines of ammunition.

Although the processional music had begun, the bigot hadn't yet assumed firing position. At his side lay *Entertainment Weekly*, with which he'd apparently been passing time. Only an instant ago, he'd extracted a thick circlet of chocolate from a roll of candies.

Surprised by the shudder that passed through the scaffolding, the gunman turned to his left. He looked up in amazement at Dylan looming no more than four feet away.

As far as the candy might be concerned, the guy was on automatic pilot. Even as his eyes widened in astonishment, he flicked his right thumb and popped the chocolate morsel off his index finger, directly into his open mouth.

Dylan chased the candy with a kick to the chin, perhaps knocking not only the chocolate but also a few teeth down the bastard's throat.

The chocolate-lover's head snapped back, rapping the plaster frieze. His eyes rolled up, his head sagged on a limp neck, and he slid onto his side, unconscious.

The kick unbalanced Dylan. He swayed, clutched the frieze with one hand, and avoided a fall.

≈ ≈ ≈

On the work platform, Dylan arrived nearest the gunman, with Shep behind him.

Still feeling how it worked, the round and round of all that is, Jilly unfolded third in line and released Shep's hand. *'Uh!'* she said explosively because she knew no adequate words to express what she'd come to understand – more intuitively than intellectually – about the architecture of reality. *'Uh!'*

Under more benign circumstances, she might have sat down for an hour to brood, an hour or a year, and she probably would have sucked on her thumb and periodically asked for Mommy. They had folded not merely from the church floor to the top of the scaffold, however, but into the shadow of Death, and she didn't have the leisure to indulge in the comfort of thumb sugar.

If Dylan wasn't able to handle the human rodent with the gun, she could do nothing to help from her position, in which case they were doomed to death by gunfire, after all. Consequently, even as Dylan kicked, Jilly looked at once into the church, searching for the other two killers.

Twenty-two feet below, the wedding guests watched as the maid of honor followed bridesmaids along the main aisle. They were more than halfway to the altar. The height of the platform and the shadows gave cover to Dylan kicking, Jilly scouting, and Shepherd shepping.

Below, the bride had not yet appeared.

Step by thoughtful step, a little boy, serving as ring bearer, followed the maid of honor. Behind him came a pretty blond girl of five or six; she wore a lacy white dress, white gloves, white ribbons in her hair, and carried a small container of rose petals, which she scattered on the floor in advance of the bride.

The organist, with nothing but the chords of the wedding march, blasted promises of marital bliss to the high vaults, and in a rage of joy at the prospect of the pending vows, seemed to want to shake down the roof-lifting columns.

Jilly spotted the second gunman on the west-wall scaffold, above the colorful windows, far forward in the nave, where he would have a clean shot down through the chancel colonnade and under the high transverse arches, into the sanctuary. He lay on the platform, angled toward the waiting groom and the best man.

As far as she could tell, given the poor light at this height, the killer didn't turn to watch the processional, but coolly prepared for slaughter, scoping targets and calculating lines of fire.

Holding an assault rifle by the barrel, Dylan joined Jilly and Shep. 'Do you see them?'

She pointed at the west scaffold. 'That one, but not the third.'

Their angle of view toward the east scaffold was not ideal. Too many intervening columns hid sections of the work platform from them.

Dylan asked Shepherd to fold them off this south-wall scaffold, but with an exquisite precision that would bring them to the side of the prone gunman on the west platform, with Dylan in the lead, where he could administer a little justice to the second killer with the butt of the assault rifle that he had taken from the first.

'Not far again,' said Shep.

'No. Just a short trip,' Dylan agreed.

'Shep can do far.'

'Yeah, buddy, I know, but we need short.'

'Shep can do very far.'

'Just here to there, buddy.'

On the arm of her father, the bride appeared in the nave below.

'Now, sweetie,' Jilly urged. 'We need to go now. Okay?'

'Okay,' said Shep.

They remained on the south-wall platform.

'Sweetie?' Jilly prodded.

'Okay.'

'Here Comes the Bride,' the pipe organ boomed, but from their perspective, the bride had already passed. She proceeded toward the chancel railing where her groom waited.

'Buddy, what's wrong, why aren't we out of here already?'

'Okay.'

'Buddy, are you listening to me, really listening?'

'Thinking,' said Shep.

'Don't think, for God's sake, just do it.'

'Thinking.'

'Just fold us out of here!'

'Okay.'

The groom, the best man, the bridesmaids, the groomsmen, the maid of honor, the ring bearer, the flower girl, the father of the bride, the bride: The entire wedding party had moved within the field of fire enjoyed by the killer on the west scaffold, and most likely had presented themselves, as well, to the third gunman who had not yet been located.

'Okay.'

Shep reached behind the world we see, behind what we detect with our five senses, and pinched the matrix of reality, which seemed to be the thinnest film, as simple as anything in creation, and yet was comprised of eleven dimensions. He tweaked that pinch, inducing time and space to conform to his will, and folded the three of them from the south-wall platform to the west-wall platform, or more accurately folded the south away from them and the west in to them, although the distinction was entirely technical and the effect identical.

As the west scaffold became their reality, Jilly saw Dylan raise the assault rifle over his head with the intention of using the butt as a club.

Prone on the platform, the second gunman was raised slightly on his left forearm, squinting across the church at the east wall, when they arrived. A tether ran from his belt to a piton that, like a mountain climber on a rock face, he had secured in the wall, most likely to counter the effects of recoil and provide stability if he decided to shoot from a standing position.

Sporting beard stubble instead of a full beard like the first man, wearing Dockers and a T-shirt emblazoned with that universal symbol of American patriotism – a Budweiser label – on the back, he would nevertheless have failed to be passed through the U.S. Customs Station east of Akela, New Mexico, where even poor shady Fred in his suspicious pot had been regarded warily.

The gunman had raised up on his left arm, the better to signal someone with his right hand.

The someone proved to be the third killer.

Directly opposite the Budweiser fan, the last gunman – a sharp-edged shadow among otherwise soft shapeless shadows – had risen to his feet. Probably tethered to the church wall, he held a compact weapon that in this poor light appeared to be an assault rifle, one of those compact killing machines with a collapsible stock.

Shepherd said, 'Shep wants cake,' as if he had just realized they were at a wedding, and Dylan hammered the butt of the assault rifle down at the second gunman's head, and Jilly realized that they were in deep trouble, sure to be shot along with the wedding party and numerous guests.

The third killer, having witnessed their miraculous arrival, even now watching as his comrade was clubbed unconscious, would open fire on them in seconds, long before Shepherd could be persuaded that another short trip was required.

In fact, even as with satisfying force the rifle butt met the skull of the second gunman, the third began to raise his rifle toward the west scaffold.

'Here, there,' Jilly said. 'Here, there.'

Desperately hoping that she remembered the eleven-dimension-matrix-round-and-round-of-all-that-is with the same certainty that she remembered 118 jokes about big butts, Jilly let her purse slide off her shoulder and drop to the platform at her feet. She pinched, tweaked, and folded away from the west wall, to the east platform, hoping that surprise would give her sufficient advantage to wrench the rifle out of the killer's hands before he squeezed the trigger. She folded herself and only herself because at the last instant, as pinch turned to tweak, she thought of *The Fly*, and she didn't want to be responsible for Dylan's nose being displaced forever in Shepherd's left armpit.

She almost made it from platform to platform.

She arrived no more than eight or ten feet short of her goal.

One instant she stood beside Shep atop the west scaffold, and halfway through that same instant, she unfolded in midair, twenty-two feet above the floor of the church.

Although what she had done, even in this imperfect fold, had to be judged a fantastic achievement by any standard, and though the busy horde of nanomachines and nanocomputers in her brain had within less than a day cursed her with amazing powers, Jillian Jackson could not fly. She materialized close enough to the third gunman to see his expression of absolute, unalloyed, goggle-eyed astonishment, and she seemed to hang in the air for a second, but then she dropped like a 110-pound stone.

The terrorist disguised in the Budweiser T-shirt most likely had a fine hard head, considering that imperviousness to new ideas and to truth was a prerequisite for those who wished to dedicate their lives to senseless brutality. The rifle butt, however, proved to be harder.

Especially for a man with the sensitive soul of an artist, Dylan took a disturbing amount of pleasure in the sound of club meeting skull, and he might have taken a second whack at the guy if he hadn't heard Jilly say, 'Here, there.' The note of extreme anxiety in her voice alarmed him.

Just as he looked at her, she folded into an asterisk of pencil-thin lines, which themselves at once folded into a dot the size of a period, and vanished. Dylan's racing heart beat once, beat twice – call it a second, maybe less – before Jilly reappeared in midair, high above the wedding guests.

For two of Dylan's explosive heartbeats, she hung out there in defiance of gravity, as though supported by the upsurge of pipe-organ music, and then a few wedding guests screamed in shock at the sight of her suspended above them. After a missed heartbeat followed by a hard knock that indicated a resumption of his circulation, he saw Jilly plummet into a rising chorus of screams.

She vanished during the fall.

44

Tough audiences had sometimes greeted her material with silence, and on rare occasion they had even booed her, but never before had an audience *screamed* at her. Jilly might have screamed back at them as she plunged into their midst, but she was too busy pinching-tweaking-folding out of the yawning maw of Death and back up to the top of the east scaffold, which had been her intended destination when she had left Dylan clubbing the second gunman.

Ruby and sapphire beams of stained-glass light, carved-marble columns, ranks of wooden pews, upturned faces wrenched in horror – all folded away from her. Judging by the percentage of blue-and-white brightness in the kaleidoscopic pattern that rapidly folded toward her, however, the new place appeared too well lighted to be the work platform atop the east scaffold.

She arrived, of course, standing high on the roof of the church, having dramatically overshot her target this time instead of coming up ten feet short of it. Azure-blue sky, white puffy clouds, golden sunshine.

Black slate.

The black slate roof had a fearsomely steep pitch.

Peering down the slope toward the street, she suffered an attack of vertigo. When she looked up at the bell tower looming three stories above the roof, her vertigo only grew worse.

She would have folded off the church roof instantly upon arrival – except that she clutched, lost her nerve, afraid of making a still bigger mistake. Maybe this time she would unfold with half her body inside one of the marble columns down in the nave, and half her body out of it, limbs flapping in death throes, most of her internal organs mingled with stone.

In fact, now that she had thought of such a gruesome turn of events, it would almost certainly come to pass. She wouldn't be able to banish the mental image of herself half wedded to stone, and when she folded herethere, *there* would prove to be the heart of a column, leaving her more completely involved with the church than ever she had been when she'd sung in the choir.

She might have stood on the roof for a couple minutes, until she calmed herself and regained her confidence; but she didn't have that option. Three seconds, four maximum, after her arrival, she began to slide.

Maybe the slate had been black when first installed, but maybe it had been mostly gray or green, or pink, for all she knew. Right now, here in the heart of a rainless summer, these shingles appeared smooth and black because a fine powder of soot had settled upon them from the oily air of smoggy days.

This soot proved to be as fine as powdered graphite. Powdered graphite is an excellent lubricant. So was this.

Fortunately Jilly started near the peak of the roof; therefore, she didn't at once slide all the way off and drop to whatever expanse of bone-breaking concrete or impaling iron fence, or pack of savage pit bulls, might be waiting for her below. She glided about ten feet, regained traction too abruptly, almost pitched forward, but stayed upright.

Then she slid again. Skiing down black slate. Big jump coming up. Building momentum for an Olympic-qualifying distance.

Jilly wore athletic shoes, and she was pretty athletic herself, but she couldn't arrest her slide. Although she waved her arms like a lumberjack in a log-rolling contest, she teetered on the brink of losing her balance, teetered, and then one foot flew out from under her. As she started to go down, realizing that she was going to smack slate with her tailbone, she wished she had a fat butt instead of a skinny little ass, but all the years of doughnut denial had at last caught up to her, and here came the void.

Like hell. She refused to die a Negative Jackson death. She had the willpower to *make* her destiny, rather than be a victim of fate.

The round and round of all that is, beautiful in its eleven-dimensional simplicity, folded to her command, and she left the roof, the soot, left the slide to death unfinished.

≈ ≈ ≈

Falling toward the floor of the church, Jilly vanished, and with her disappearance, the screams of the wedding guests spiked, causing the organist to abandon the keyboard. The many screams broke off as one in a collective gasp of astonishment.

Gazing down on the spectacle, Shepherd said, 'Wow.'

Dylan snapped his attention toward the work platform on the east scaffold, where the gunman with the rifle stood. Perhaps too stunned to act on his original intentions, the killer hadn't yet opened fire. His hesitation wouldn't last long; in mere seconds, his hatred would prove powerful enough to purge the wonder of having witnessed an apparent miracle.

'Buddy, here to there.'

'Wow.'

'Take us over there, buddy. To the bad man.'

'Thinking.'

'Don't think, buddy. Just go. Here to there.'

Down on the floor of the church, the majority of the wedding guests, who hadn't been looking up during Jilly's midair appearance and subsequent plunging disappearance, turned in bewilderment to those who had seen it all. A woman started to cry, and the piping voice of a child – no doubt a certain pigtailed girl – said, 'I told you so, I told you so!'

'Buddy—'

'Thinking.'

'For God's sake—'

'Wow.'

Inevitably, one of the wedding guests – a woman in a pink suit and a pink feathered hat – spotted the third killer, who stood at the edge of the work platform atop the east-wall scaffold, leaning out, looking down, restrained from falling by a tether that anchored him to the wall. The pink-suited woman must have seen the rifle, too, for she pointed and screamed.

Nothing could have been better calculated than this cry of alarm to snap the gunman out of his merciful hesitation.

≈ ≈ ≈

Sooty roof to scaffold platform, Jilly folded in to the church with the expectation of finding the third gunman and kicking him in the head, the gut, the gonads, or any other kickable surface that might be presented to her. She found herself facing a long run of deserted platform, with the painted-plaster frieze to her left, and with the massive marble columns rising through the open church to her right.

Instead of a multitude of screams, as there had been when she'd folded in midfall to the roof, only one rose from below. Looking down, she saw a woman in a pink suit attempting to alert the other guests to the danger – 'Up there, up there!' – pointing not at Jilly, but some distance past her.

Realizing that she faced the back of the nave, not the altar, Jilly turned and saw the third killer, twenty feet away, tethered to the wall, balancing on the edge of the platform, peering down at the crowd. He held the rifle with the muzzle up, aimed at the vaulted ceiling – but he began to react to the woman in pink.

Jilly ran. Twenty-four hours ago, she would have run away from a man with a gun, but now she ran toward him.

Even with her heart lodged in her throat and pounding as loud as a circus drum, with fear twisting like a snake through the entire length of her entrails, she possessed sufficient presence of mind to wonder if she had found a fine new courage in herself or instead had lost her sanity. Maybe a little of both.

She sensed also that her compulsion to go after the gunman might be related to the fact that the nanogadgets busily at work in her brain were making profound changes in her, changes more fundamental and even more important than the granting of supernatural powers. This was not a good thought.

The twenty feet between her and the would-be bride killer were as long as a marathon. The plywood seemed to move under her, foiling her advance, as if it were a treadmill. Nonetheless, she preferred to sprint rather than to trust once more in her as yet unpolished talent for folding.

The hard *boom-boom-boom* of running feet on the platform and the vibrations shuddering through the scaffolding distracted the gunman from the wedding guests. As he turned his head toward Jilly, she slammed into him, rocking him sideways, grabbing the rifle.

On impact, she tried to wrench the gun away from the killer. His hands remained locked to it, but she held tight, as well, even when she lost her footing and fell off the scaffold.

Her grip on the weapon spared her from another plunge. The garlic-reeking gunman's tether prevented him from being dragged immediately off the platform with her.

Dangling in space, looking up into the bigot's eyes – such black pools of festering hatred – Jilly found in herself an intensity of anger that she had never known before. Anger became a rage stoked by the thought of all the sons of Cain crawling the hills and cities of this world, all like this man, motivated by innumerable social causes and visions of utopia, but also by personal fevers, forever craving violence, thirsting for blood and mad with dreams of power.

With Jilly's entire weight suspended from the rifle, the killer didn't have the strength to shake the weapon out of her hands. He began instead to twist it left and right, back and forth, thereby torquing her body and putting stress on her wrists. As the torsion built, twist by twist, the laws of physics required rotation, which would tear her hands off the gun as her body obeyed the law.

The pain in her tortured wrist joints and tendons rapidly became intolerable, worse than the still tender spot in her hand where the splinter had punctured her. If she let go, she could fold to safety during her fall, but then she would be leaving him with the rifle. And before she could return, he'd pump hundreds of rounds into the crowd, which was so transfixed by the contest above it that no one had yet thought to flee the church.

Her rage flared into *fury*, fueled by a fierce sense of injustice and by pity for the innocent who were always the targets of men like this, for the mothers and babies blown to pieces by suicide bombers, for the ordinary citizens who often found themselves between street-gang thugs and their rivals in drive-by shootings, for the merchants murdered for the few dollars in their tills – for one young bride and a loving groom and a flower girl who might be shredded by hollow-point bullets on what should have been a day of joy.

Empowered by her fury, Jilly attempted to counter the killer's torquing motion by swinging her legs forward, back, forward, like an acrobat hanging from a trapeze bar. The more successfully she swung to and fro, the more difficult he found it to keep twisting the rifle from side to side.

Her wrists ached, throbbed, *burned*; but his arms must have felt as though they would pull out of his shoulder sockets. The longer she held on, the greater the chance that he would let go of the weapon first. Then he would be not a potential killer anymore, but merely a madman on a high scaffold with spare magazines of ammunition that he couldn't use.

'*Jillian?*' Someone down on the floor of the church called her name in astonishment. '*Jillian?*' She was reasonably certain that it was Father Francorelli, the priest who had heard her confessions and given her the sacrament for most of her life, but she didn't turn her head to look.

Sweat was her biggest problem. The killer's perspiration dripped off his face, onto Jilly, which disgusted her, but she remained more concerned about her own sweat. Her hands were slick. By the second, her grip on the weapon became more tenuous.

Resolving her dilemma, the gunman's tether snapped, or the piton pulled out of the wall, unable to support both his weight and hers.

Falling, he let go of the gun.

'*Jillian!*'

Falling, Jilly folded.

≈   ≈   ≈

The words *astonishment* and *amazement* both describe the momentary overwhelming of the mind by something beyond expectation, although astonishment more specifically affects the emotions, while amazement especially affects the intellect. The less-used word *awe* expresses a more intense and profound – and rare – experience, in which the mind is overwhelmed by something almost inexpressibly grand in character or formidable in power.

Awe-stricken, Dylan watched from atop the west scaffold as Jilly raced full-tilt along the east-scaffold platform, slammed violently into the gunman, plunged over the brink, hung from the assault rifle, and performed a credible audition for a job with the Flying Wallendas of circus fame.

'Wow,' said Shepherd as the tether snapped with a sound like the crack of a giant whip, dropping Jilly and the killer toward the church floor.

Penned in by the pews, the squealing wedding guests tried to scatter and duck.

Jilly and the gun vanished about four feet short of impact, but the hapless villain fell all the way. He struck the back of a pew with his throat, broke his neck, somersaulted into the next row, and in a tangle of limbs, he crashed to a stop, big-time dead, between a distinguished gray-haired gentleman in a navy-blue pinstripe suit and a matronly woman wearing an expensive beige knit suit and a lovely feathered hat with a wide brim.

When Jilly appeared at Shep's side, the dead man was already dead but still flopping and thudding into the final dramatic pose in which the police photographer would want to immortalize him. She put down the assault rifle and said, 'I'm pissed.'

'I could tell,' Dylan said.

'Wow,' said Shepherd. 'Wow.'

Cries flew up from the wedding guests when the gunman caromed off the back of one pew into the next row and stayed down dead, his head askew and one arm akimbo. Then a man in a gray suit spotted Jilly standing with Dylan and Shep atop the west-wall scaffold, and pointed her out to the others. In a moment, the entire congregation stood with heads tipped back, gazing up at her. Evidently because they were in a state of shock, every one of them had fallen silent, so the hush in the church grew as deep as the quiet in a tomb.

When the silence held until it became eerie, Dylan explained to Jilly: 'They're awe-stricken.'

Jilly saw a young woman wearing a mantilla in the crowd below. Perhaps the same woman in the desert vision.

Before the crowd's shock could wear off and panic set in, Dylan raised his voice to reassure them. 'Everything's okay. It's over now. You're safe.' He pointed to the cadaver crumpled among the pews. 'Two accomplices of that man are up here, out of commission, but in need of medical attention. Someone should call nine-one-one.'

Only two in the crowd moved: The woman in the mantilla went

to the votive rack to light a candle and say a prayer, while a wedding photographer began shooting pictures of Dylan, Jilly, and Shep.

Looking down on these hundreds, sixty-seven of whom would have been shot, forty of whom would have perished, if she and Dylan and Shep hadn't gotten here in time, Jilly was overcome by emotions so powerful, so exalting, and simultaneously so humbling, that no matter how long she lived, she would never forget her feelings at this incredible moment or be able to describe adequately the intensity of them.

From the platform at her feet, she picked up her purse, which contained what little she still owned in this world: wallet, compact, lipstick. . . . She wouldn't have sold these pathetic possessions at any price, for they were the only tangible proof she had that she'd once lived an ordinary existence, and they seemed like talismans by which she might recover that lost life.

'Shep,' she whispered, her voice tremulous with emotion, 'I don't trust myself to fold three of us out of here. You'll have to do it.'

'Somewhere private,' Dylan warned, 'somewhere lonely.'

While everyone around her still stood immobile, the bride moved in the center aisle, weaving among her guests, stopping only when she arrived directly before Jilly. She was a beautiful woman, radiant, graceful in a stunning dress that would have been much talked about at the reception if the guests hadn't had plenty of murder, mayhem, and derring-do to discuss instead.

Below, looking up at Jilly, at Dylan, at Shep, the radiant young woman in the fabulous white dress raised the bridal bouquet in her right hand, as though in tribute, in thanks, and the flowers blazed like the flames in a white-hot torch.

Perhaps the bride had been about to say something, but Jilly spoke first, with genuine sympathy. 'Honey, I'm *so* sorry about your wedding.'

Dylan said, 'Let's go.'

'Okay,' said Shep, and he folded them.

45

Here lay a true desert so seldom washed by rain that even the few small cactuses were stunted by an enduring thirst. The widely scattered and thinly grown bunch-grass colonies would be a seared blackish green in the winter; here in the summer, they were silver-brown and as crisp as parchment.

The landscape offered considerably more sand than vegetation, and significantly more rock than sand.

They stood on the western slope of a hill that terraced gently in serried layers of charred-brown and rust-red rock. Before them, in the near distance and at least to the midpoint of a wide plain, curious natural rock formations rose like remnants of a vast ancient fortress: here, three sort-of columns thirty feet in diameter and a hundred high, perhaps part of a might-have-been entry portico; there, the hundred-foot-long, eighty-foot-high, crumbling crenelated ruins of use-your-imagination battlements from which skilled bowmen might have defended the castle keep with rains of arrows; here, turreted towers; there, ramparts, bastions, a half-collapsed barbican.

Men had never lived in this hostile land, of course, but Nature had created a vista that encouraged fantasy.

'New Mexico,' Dylan told Jilly. 'I came here with Shep, painted this scene. October, four years ago this autumn, when the weather was friendlier. There's a dirt road just the other side of this hill, and a paved highway four miles back. Not that we'll need it.'

Currently this rockscape was a glowing forge where the white sun hammered into shape horseshoes of fire for those ghost riders in the sky that supposedly haunted these desert realms by night.

'If we get in the shade,' Dylan said, 'we can endure the heat long enough to gather our wits and figure out what the hell we're going to do next.'

Painted in dazzling shades of red, orange, purple, pink, and brown, the castellated formations were at this hour east of the sun, which had descended well past its apex. Their refreshing shadows, reaching toward this hillside, were the color of ripe plums.

Dylan led Jilly and Shepherd down the slope, then two hundred feet across flat land, to the base of an almost-could-be turreted tower suitable for an Arthurian tale. They sat side by side on a low bench of weather-smoothed stone, their backs to the tower.

The shade, the windless silence, the stillness of lifeless plain and birdless sky were such a relief that for a few minutes, none of them spoke.

Finally, Dylan raised what seemed to him to be if not the most immediate issue before them, then certainly the most important. 'Back there after he fell into the pews, when you said you were pissed, you meant it like you've never meant it before in your life – didn't you?'

She breathed the stillness for a while, gradually quelling the tumult within. Then: 'I don't know what you mean.'

'You know.'

'Not really.'

'You know,' he insisted quietly.

She closed her eyes under the weight of the shade, tipped her head back against the tower wall, and tried to hold fast to her tiny piece of property in the great state of denial.

Eventually she said, 'Such a rage, such a white-hot fury, but not consuming, not stupid-making like anger can be, not negative . . . It was . . . it was . . .'

'A cleansing, exhilarating, *righteous* anger,' he suggested.

She opened her eyes. She looked at him. A bloodied demigod-dess resting in the shade of the palace of Zeus.

Clearly, she didn't want to talk about this. She might even be *afraid* to talk about it.

She could no more avoid this subject, however, than she could go back to the comedy-club life that she had been leading less than one day ago. 'I wasn't just furious at those three evil bastards. . . . I was . . .'

When she reached for words and didn't at once find them,

Dylan finished her thought, for he'd been the first of them to experience this righteous rage, all the way back on Eucalyptus Avenue, where Travis had been shackled and Kenny had hoped to put his collection of knives to bloody use; therefore, he'd been given more time to analyze it. 'You were not just furious at those evil bastards . . . but at evil itself, at the fact that evil exists, infuriated by the very idea of evil allowed to go unresisted, unchecked.'

'Good God, you've been inside my head, or I've been in yours.'

'Neither,' Dylan said. 'But tell me this . . . In the church, you understood the danger?'

'Oh, yeah.'

'You knew that you might be shot, crippled for life, killed – but you did what had to be done.'

'There was nothing else to do.'

'There's always something else to do,' he disagreed. 'Run, for one thing. Give up, go away. Did you think about doing that?'

'Of course.'

'But was there one moment, even one brief moment in the church, when you *could* have run?'

'Oh, man,' she said, and shuddered as she began to recognize the burden coming, the weight that they would never be able to put down until they were in the grave. 'Yeah, I could've run. Hell, yeah, I could've. I almost did.'

'All right, so maybe you could've. Maybe we still can run. But here's the thing. . . . Was there one moment, even one brief moment, when you could have turned your back on your responsibility to save those people – *and still lived with yourself?*'

She stared at him.

He met her stare.

Finally she said, 'This sucks.'

'Well, it does and it doesn't.'

She thought about that for a moment, smiled shakily, and agreed: 'It does and it doesn't.'

'The new connections, the new neural pathways engineered by the nanomachines, have given us some clairvoyance, an imperfect talent for premonitions, the folding. But those aren't the only changes we've gone through.'

'Sort of wish they were the only changes.'

'Me too. But this righteous anger seems always to lead to an irresistible compulsion to act.'

'Irresistible,' she agreed. 'Compulsion, obsession, or something we don't have a term for.'

'And not merely a compulsion to act, but . . .'

He hesitated to add the last five words, which would express the truth that would shape the course of their lives.

'Okay,' said Shep.

'Okay, buddy?'

Gazing out of the tower shade toward the blazing land, the kid said, 'Okay. Shep isn't afraid.'

'Okay then. Dylan isn't afraid, either.' He took a deep breath and finished what must be said: 'The righteous anger always leads to an all but irresistible compulsion to act regardless of the risks, and not merely a compulsion to act, but *to do the right thing*. We can exercise free will and turn away – but only at a cost in self-respect that's intolerable.'

'That couldn't have been what Lincoln Proctor expected,' Jilly said. 'The last thing a man like him would want was to be the father of a generation of do-gooders.'

'You'll get no argument from me. The man was slime. His visions were of an amoral master race that might make a more orderly world by cracking the whip on the rest of humanity.'

'Then why have we become . . . what we've become?'

'Maybe when we're born, all of us, our brains are already wired to *know* the right thing, to know always what we *ought* to do.'

'That's sure what my mama taught me,' Jilly said.

'So maybe the nanomachines just made some improvements in that existing circuit, redesigned it for less resistance, until now we're wired to do the right thing no matter what our preferences, no matter what our desires, regardless of the consequences to us, *at any cost*.'

Working her mind through it, formulating a final understanding of the code by which she was henceforth fated to live, Jilly said, 'From here on, every time I get a vision of violence or disaster—'

'And every time a psychic spoor reveals to me that someone is in trouble or up to no good—'

'—we'll be compelled—'

'—to save the day,' he finished, putting it in those words because he thought they might wring another smile from her, even if a feeble one.

He needed to see her smile.

Maybe her expression was what a smile might look like in the twisting influence of a funhouse mirror, but the sight of it didn't cheer him.

'I can't stop the visions,' she said. 'But you can wear gloves.'

He shook his head. 'Oh, I imagine I could go so far as to buy a pair. But putting them on to avoid learning about the plans of evil people or the troubles of good people? That would be the *wrong* thing to do, wouldn't it? I suppose I could buy the gloves, but I don't think I'd be able to put them on.'

'Wow,' said Shepherd, perhaps as a comment about all that they had said, perhaps as a comment on the desert heat, or maybe just in reaction to some event that had transpired on Shepworld, the planet of the high-functioning autistic, on which he had spent more of his life than he had spent on their common Earth. 'Wow.'

They had a great deal more to discuss, plans to make, but for the time being, none of them was able to summon the nerve or energy to continue. Shep couldn't even squeeze another *wow* out of himself.

The shade. The heat. The iron and silicate and ashy scents of superheated rock and sand.

Dylan imagined that the three of them might sit exactly where they were now, dreaming contentedly of good deeds already done at any cost, but never venturing forth to take new risks or to face new terrors, dreaming on and on until they petrified upon this rock bench like the trees in the Petrified Forest National Park in neighboring Arizona, thereafter to spend eons as three peacefully reclining stone figures here in the shade until discovered by archaeologists in the next millennium.

Eventually, Jilly said, 'What must I look like?'

'Lovely,' he assured her, and meant what he said.

'Yeah, right. My face feels stiff with dried blood.'

'The cut on your forehead is crusted shut. Just some grisly crusty stuff, some dried blood, but otherwise lovely. How's your hand?'

'Throbbing. But I'll live, which I guess is a plus.' She opened her purse, withdrew a compact, and examined her face in the small round mirror. 'Find me the Black Lagoon, I need to go home.'

'Nonsense. A little washup is all you need, and you'll be ready for the royal ball.'

'Hose me down or run me through a car wash.'

She searched her purse again and came up with a foil packet containing a moist towelette. She extracted the lemon-scented paper wash cloth and carefully cleaned her face using the compact mirror for guidance.

Dylan settled back into his reverie of petrification.

Judging by his stillness, silence, and unblinking stare, Shep had a head start on this turning-into-stone business.

Moist towelettes were designed for freshening your hands after eating a Big Mac in the car. A single cloth proved insufficient to swab up a significant amount of dried blood.

'You should buy the extra-large, serial-killer-size towelettes,' Dylan said.

Jilly rummaged in her purse. 'I'm sure I have at least one more.' She unzipped one small interior side compartment, poked around, opened another side compartment. 'Oh. I forgot about these.'

She produced a bag of peanuts of the size dispensed by vending machines.

Dylan said, 'Shep would probably like some Cheez-Its if you have any, and I'm a little-chocolate-doughnut sort of guy.'

'These belonged to Proctor.'

Dylan grimaced. 'Probably laced with cyanide.'

'He dropped them in the parking lot outside my room. I picked them up just before I met you and Shep.'

Interrupting his effort at petrification, but continuing to stare into the hard radiation of sun-nuked stone and sand, Shepherd said, 'Cake?'

'No cake,' Dylan said. 'Peanuts.'

'Cake?'

'Peanuts, buddy.'

'Cake?'

'We'll get cake soon.'

'Cake?'

'Peanuts, Shep, and you know what peanuts are like – all round and shapey and disgusting. Here, look.' He took the bag of nuts from Jilly, intending to hold them in front of Shepherd's face, but the psychic spoor on the cellophane packet, under the pleasant trace left by Jilly, was still fresh enough to bring into his mind an image of Proctor's dreamy, evil smile. The smile came to him, but much more: an electrical, crackling, pandemoniacal, whirling shadow show of images and impressions.

He didn't realize he'd gotten up from the rock bench until he was on his feet and moving away from Jilly and Shep. He halted, swung toward them, and said, 'Lake Tahoe.'

'Nevada?' Jilly asked.

'Yeah. No. That Lake Tahoe, yes, but the north shore, on the California side.'

'What about it?'

Every nerve in his body seemed to be twitching. He had been seized by an irresistible compulsion to *get moving*. 'We've got to go there.'

'Why?'

'Right now.'

'Why?'

'I don't know. But it's the right thing to do.'

'Damn, that makes me nervous.'

He returned to Jilly, drew her to her feet, and placed her uninjured hand over the hand in which he held the bag of peanuts.

'Can you feel it, what I feel, where it is?'

'Where what is?'

'The house. I see a house. This sort of Frank Lloyd Wright place overlooking the lake. Dramatic floating roofs, stacked-stone walls, lots of big windows. Nestled in among huge old pine trees. Do you feel where it is?'

'That's not my talent, it's yours,' she reminded him.

'You learned how to fold.'

'Yeah, started to learn, but I haven't learned this,' she said, withdrawing her hand.

Shepherd had risen from the rock bench. He put his right hand on the bag of peanuts, on Dylan's hand. 'House.'

'Yes, a house,' Dylan replied impatiently, his compulsion to act growing more powerful by the second. He danced from foot to foot like a child overcome by an urgent need to go to the bathroom. 'I see a house.'

'I see a house,' said Shep.

'I see a big house overlooking the lake.'

'I see a big house overlooking the lake,' said Shep.

'What're you doing, buddy?'

Instead of repeating *What are you doing, buddy*, as Dylan expected, the kid said, 'I see a big house overlooking the lake.'

'Huh? You see a house? You see it, too?'

'Cake?'

'Peanuts, Shep, peanuts.'

'Cake?'

'You've got your hand on it, you're looking right at it, Shep. You can see it's a bag of peanuts.'

'Tahoe cake?'

'Oh. Yeah, maybe. They probably have cake at this place in Tahoe. Lots of cake. All kinds of cake. Chocolate cake, lemon cake, spice cake, carrot cake—'

'Shep doesn't like carrot cake.'

'No, I didn't mean that, I was wrong about that, they don't have any carrot cake, Shep, just every other kind of friggin' cake in the world.'

'Cake,' said Shepherd, and the New Mexico desert folded away as a cool green place folded toward them.

46

Great pines, both conical and spreading varieties, many standing over two hundred feet tall, built sublimely scented palaces on the slopes around the lake, green rooms of perpetual Christmas ornamented with cones as small as apricots and others as large as pineapples.

The famous lake, seen through felicitous frames of time-worked branches, fulfilled its reputation as the most colorful body of water in the world. From a central depth greater than fifteen hundred feet to shoreline shallows, it shimmered iridescently in countless shades of green, blue, and purple.

Folding from the magnificent barrenness of the desert to the glory of Tahoe, Jilly exhaled the possibility of scorpions and cactus moths, inhaled air stirred by butterflies and by brown darting birds.

Shepherd had conveyed them to a flagstone footpath that wound through the forest, through a softness of feathery pine shadows and woodland ferns. At the end of the path stood the house: Wrightian, stone and silvered cedar, enormous yet in exquisite harmony with its natural setting, featuring deeply cantilevered roofs and many tall windows.

'I know this house,' Jilly said.

'You've been here?'

'No. Never. But I've seen pictures of it somewhere. Probably in a magazine.'

'It's definitely an *Architectural Digest* sort of place.'

Broad flagstone steps led up to an entry terrace overhung by a cedar-soffited, cantilevered roof.

Ascending to the terrace between Dylan and Shepherd, Jilly said, 'This place is connected to Lincoln Proctor?'

'Yeah. I don't know how, but from the spoor, I know he was here at least once, maybe more than once, and it was an important place to him.'

'Could it be *his* house?'

Dylan shook his head. 'I don't think so.'

The front door and flanking sidelights doubled as sculpture: an Art Deco geometric masterpiece half bronze and half stained glass.

'What if it's a trap?' she worried.

'No one knows we're coming. It can't be a trap. Besides . . . it doesn't feel that way.'

'Maybe we should run a little surveillance on the joint for a while, watch it from the trees, till we see who comes and goes.'

'My instinct says go for it. Hell, I don't have a choice. The compulsion to keep moving is like . . . a thousand hands shoving on my back. I've *got* to ring that doorbell.'

He rang it.

Although Jilly considered sprinting away through the trees, she remained at Dylan's side. She in her changefulness no longer had any refuge in the ordinary world where she could claim to belong, and her only place, if she indeed had one at all, must be with the O'Conner brothers, as their only place must be now with her.

The man who opened the door was tall, handsome, with prematurely snow-white hair and extraordinary gray eyes the shade of tarnished silver. Those piercing eyes surely had the capacity to appear steely and intimidating, but at the moment, they were as warm and as without threat as the gray skeins of a gentle spring rain.

His voice, which Jilly had always assumed must be electronically enhanced during his broadcasts, possessed precisely the reverberant timbre and the smoky quality familiar from radio, and was instantly recognizable. Parish Lantern said, 'Jillian, Dylan, Shepherd, I've been expecting you. Please come in. My house is your house.'

Apparently as stunned as Jilly, Dylan said, 'You? I mean . . . really? *You?*'

'I am certainly me, yes, at least the last time I looked in the mirror. Come in, come in. We've much to talk about, much to do.'

The spacious reception hall had a limestone floor, honey-tone wood paneling, a pair of rosewood Chinese chairs with emerald-green cushions, and a central table holding a large red-bronze jardiniere filled with dozens of fresh yellow, red, and orange tulips.

Jilly felt surprisingly welcome, almost as if she had found her way as sometimes a dog, lost during its family's move from one city to another, can travel by instinct across great distances to a new home it has never seen.

Closing the front door, Parish Lantern said, 'Later, you can freshen up, change clothes. When I knew you'd be coming and in what condition, without luggage, I took the liberty of having my houseboy, Ling, purchase fresh clothes for all of you, of the style I believe you prefer. Finding Wile E. Coyote T-shirts on such short notice proved to be something of a challenge. Ling had to catch a flight to Los Angeles on Wednesday, where he obtained a dozen in Shepherd's size at the souvenir shop on the Warner Brothers Studio lot.'

'Wednesday?' Dylan asked, with a trowel's worth of bewilderment plastered on his face.

'I didn't even meet Dylan and Shepherd until last night,' Jilly said. 'Friday night. Less than eighteen hours ago.'

Smiling, nodding, Lantern said, 'And it's been quite a thrilling eighteen hours, hasn't it? I'll want to hear all about it. But first things first.'

'Cake,' said Shep.

'Yes,' Lantern assured him, 'I've got cake for you, Shepherd. But first things first.'

'Cake.'

'You're a determined young man, aren't you?' Lantern said. 'Good. I approve of determination.'

'Cake.'

'Good heavens, lad, one might suspect that you're possessed by a cake-loving brain leech from an alternate reality. If there were such things as brain leeches from an alternate reality, of course.'

'I never believed there were,' Jilly assured him.

'Millions do, my dear,' said Lantern.

'Cake.'

'We'll get you a big square of cake,' Lantern promised Shep, 'in just a little while. But first things first. Please come with me.'

As the three of them followed the talk-show host out of the reception hall and through a library that contained more books than did the libraries of most small cities, Dylan said to Jilly, 'Did you know about all this?'

Amazed by the question, she said, 'How would I know about this?'

'Well, you're the Parish Lantern fan. Big Foot, extraterrestrial conspiracy theories, all that stuff.'

'I doubt that Big Foot has anything to do with this. And I'm not an extraterrestrial conspirator.'

'That's exactly what an extraterrestrial conspirator would say.'

'For God's sake, I'm not an extraterrestrial conspirator. I'm a standup comedian.'

'Extraterrestrial conspirators and standup comedians aren't mutually exclusive,' he said.

'Cake,' Shep insisted.

At the end of the library, Lantern halted, turned to them, and said, 'You've no reason to be afraid here.'

'No, no,' Dylan explained, 'we were just goofing, a private joke sort of thing that goes back a long way with us.'

'Almost eighteen hours,' Jilly said.

'Just remember at all times,' Lantern said cryptically yet with the warmth of a loving uncle, 'regardless of what happens, you've no reason to be afraid here.'

'Cake.'

'In due time, lad.'

Lantern led them out of the library into an enormous living room furnished with contemporary sofas and armchairs upholstered in pale-gold silks, enlivened by an eclectic but pleasing mix of Art Deco decorative objects and Chinese antiquities.

Formed almost entirely of six enormous windows, the south wall provided a magnificent panoramic view of the colorful lake between the graceful framing branches of two giant sugar pines.

The vista was so spectacular that Jilly spontaneously exclaimed – 'Gorgeous!' – before she realized that Lincoln Proctor stood in the room, awaiting them, holding a pistol in his right hand.

47

This Lincoln Proctor wasn't a charred slab of meat and shattered bones, although Dylan hoped to reduce him to that or worse if given a chance. Not one singed patch of hair, not the smallest smudge of ash remained to suggest that he had burned to death in Jilly's Coupe DeVille. Even his dreamy smile remained intact.

'Sit down,' Proctor said, 'and let's talk about this.'

Jilly responded with a rudeness, and Dylan topped her suggestion with one even ruder.

'Yes, you've good reason to hate me,' Proctor said remorsefully. 'I've done terrible things to you, unpardonable things. I'm not going to make any attempt to justify myself. But we *are* in this together.'

'We're not in anything with you,' Dylan said fiercely. 'We're not your friends or associates, or even just your guinea pigs. We're your victims, your enemies, and we'll gut you if we get a chance.'

'Would anyone like a drink?' asked Parish Lantern.

'I owe you an explanation at least, at the very least,' Proctor said. 'And I'm sure once you hear me out, you'll see that we have a mutual interest that *does* make us allies, even if uneasy allies.'

'Cocktail, brandy, beer, wine, soft drink?' Lantern offered.

'Who burned up in my car?' Jilly demanded.

'An unlucky motel guest who crossed my path,' said Proctor. 'He was about my size. After I killed him, I put my ID on him, my watch, other items. Since going on the run a week ago, I'd carried with me a briefcase bomb – small explosive charge, but mostly jellied gasoline – for just that purpose. I detonated it with a remote control.'

'If no one cares for a drink,' said Lantern, 'I'll just sit down and finish mine.'

He went to an armchair from which he could watch them, and he picked up a glass of white wine from a small table beside the chair.

The rest of them remained on their feet.

To Proctor, Jilly said, 'An autopsy would prove the poor son of a bitch wasn't you.'

He shrugged. 'Of course. But when the gentlemen in the black Suburbans were closing in on me, the big boom distracted them, didn't it? The diversion bought me a few hours, a chance to slip away. Oh, despicable, I know, to sacrifice an innocent man's life to gain a few hours or days for myself, but I've done worse in my life. I've—'

Interrupting Proctor's wearisome self-accusatory patter, Jilly said, 'Who *are* those guys in the Suburbans?'

'Mercenaries. Some former Russian Spetznaz, some American Delta Force members gone bad, all former special-forces soldiers from one country or another. They hire out to the highest bidder.'

'Who're they working for now?'

'My business partners,' Proctor said.

From his armchair, Parish Lantern said, 'When a man is so badly wanted that an entire army has been put together to kill him, that's quite an achievement.'

'My partners are extremely wealthy individuals, billionaires, who control several major banks and corporations. When I started to have some success with experimental subjects, my partners suddenly realized that their personal fortunes and those of their companies might be at risk from endless liability suits, billions in potential settlements when . . . things went wrong. Settlements that would have dwarfed the billions squeezed from the tobacco industry. They wanted to shut everything down, destroy my research.'

'What things went wrong?' Dylan asked tightly.

'Don't go through the whole dreary list like you did with me. Just tell them about Manuel,' Lantern suggested.

'A fat angry sociopath,' said Proctor. 'I should never have accepted him as a subject. Within hours of injection, he developed the ability to start fires with the power of his mind. Unfortunately, he enjoyed burning things too much. Things and people. He did a lot of damage before he could be put down.'

Dylan felt queasy, almost moved to a chair, but then remembered his mother and stayed on his feet.

'Where in the name of God do you get subjects for experiments like this?' Jilly wondered.

The dreamy smile kinked up at one corner. 'Volunteers.'

'What kind of morons would *volunteer* to have their brains pumped full of nanomachines?'

'I see you've done some research. What you couldn't have learned is that we progressed secretly to human experimentation at a facility in Mexico. Officials are still easily bribed there.'

'More cheaply than our best senators,' Lantern added dryly.

Proctor sat on the edge of a chair, but he kept the pistol aimed at them. He looked exhausted. He must have come directly here from Arizona the previous night, with little or no rest. His usually pink face was gray and drawn. 'The volunteers were felons, lifers. The worst of the worst. If you were condemned to spend the rest of your days in a stinking Mexican prison, but you could earn money for luxuries and maybe even time off your sentence, you'd volunteer for just about anything. They were hardened criminals, but this was an inhumane thing I did to them—'

'A wicked, wicked thing,' Lantern said, as though admonishing a naughty child.

'Yes, it was. I admit it. A wicked thing. I was—'

'So,' said Dylan impatiently, 'when some of these prisoners dropped sixty IQ points, like you said, your partners started having nightmares about hordes of attorneys thick as cockroaches.'

'No. Those who collapsed intellectually or self-destructed in some other manner – they weren't of concern to us. Prison officials just filled in false information on their death certificates, and no one could link them to us.'

'Another wicked, wicked thing,' said Lantern, and clucked his tongue in disapproval. 'The wicked, wicked things just never stop.'

'But if someone like Manuel, our firestarter, ever got loose and burned his way through customs at the border, got into San Diego and went nuts there, destroying whole blocks of the city, hundreds if not thousands of people . . . then maybe we couldn't distance ourselves from him. Maybe he'd talk about us to someone. Then . . . liability suits from here to the end of the century.'

'This is an excellent Chardonnay,' Lantern declared, 'if anyone would like to reconsider. No? You're just leaving more for me. And now we come to the sad part of the tale. The sad and frustrating part. An almost tragic revelation. Tell them the sad part, Lincoln.'

Proctor's unnerving dreamy smile had faded and brightened and faded. Now it vanished. 'Just before they shut down my labs and tried to eliminate me, I'd developed a new generation of nanobots.'

'New and improved,' Lantern said, 'like new Coke or like adding a new color to the M&M spectrum.'

'Yes, much improved,' Proctor agreed, either missing his host's sarcasm or choosing to ignore it. 'I've worked the bugs out of it. As I've proved with you, Dylan, with you, Ms. Jackson. And with you, as well, Shepherd? With you, as well?'

Shep stood with his head bowed, saying nothing.

'I'm eager to hear what the effects have been with all of you,' said Lincoln Proctor, finding his smile once more. 'This time the quality of the subjects is what it should always have been. You are much better clay. Working with those criminal personalities, disaster was inevitable. I should've understood that from the start. My fault. My stupidity. But now, how have you been lifted up? I'm desperately interested to hear. What has been the effect?'

Instead of answering Proctor, Jilly said to Parish Lantern, 'And how do you fit into this? Were you one of his investors?'

'I'm neither a billionaire nor an idiot,' Lantern assured her. 'I had him on my program a few times because I thought he was an entertaining egomaniacal nutball.'

Proctor's smile froze. If glares could have scorched, Proctor would have reduced Parish Lantern to a cinder as readily as the late Manuel had apparently done to others.

Lantern said, 'I was never rude to him or let on what I thought of this insanity of forced evolution of the human brain. That's not my style. If a guest is a genius, I let him win friends and influence people on his own, and if he's a lunatic, I'm happy to let him make a fool of himself without my assistance.'

Although color flooded into Proctor's face at this offense, he looked no healthier. He rose from the chair and pointed the pistol at Lantern instead of at Dylan. 'I've always thought you were a man of vision. That's why I came to you first, with the new generation. And this is how I'm repaid?'

Parish Lantern sipped the last of the Chardonnay in his glass, savored it, swallowed. Ignoring Proctor, he spoke to Dylan and Jilly: 'I'd never met the good doctor face to face. I'd always interviewed him live by telephone. He showed up on my doorstep five days ago, and I was too polite to kick his ass into the street. He said he wished to discuss something of importance that would serve as a segment for my show. I was kind enough to invite him into my study for a brief meeting. He repaid this kindness with chloroform and a hideous . . . horse syringe.'

'We're familiar with it,' Dylan said.

Putting aside his empty wineglass, Lantern rose from his chair. 'Then he left me with the warning that his partners, half-crazed with the prospect of litigation, were intent on killing him and anyone he injected, so I'd better not try to report him to the police. Within hours I was going through some terrifying changes. Precognition was the first curse.'

'We call them curses, too,' Jilly said.

'By Wednesday, I began to foresee some of what would happen here today. That our Frankenstein would return to learn how I was doing, to receive my praise, my gratitude. The clueless fool expected me to feel indebted to him, to receive him as a hero and shelter him here.'

Proctor's faded-denim eyes were as hard and icy as on the night that he had killed Dylan's mother in 1992. 'I'm a man of many faults, grievous faults. But I've never been gratuitously insulting to people who have meant well toward me. I can't understand your attitude.'

'When I told him I'd foreseen your visit here on this same day,' Lantern continued, 'he became terribly excited. He expected all of us to kneel and kiss his ring.'

'You knew we'd come here even before he'd connected with us in Arizona and given us the injections,' Jilly marveled.

'Yes, even though I didn't quite know who you were at first. I can't easily explain to you how all this could be,' Lantern acknowledged. 'But there's a certain harmony to things—'

'The round and round of all that is,' Jilly said.

Parish Lantern raised his eyebrows. 'Yes. That's one way to put it. There are things that might happen, things that must happen, and by feeling the round and round of all that is, you can know at least a little of what will occur. If you're cursed with vision, that is.'

'Cake,' said Shepherd.

'In a little while, lad. First, we have to decide what we must do with this reeking bag of shit.'

'Poopoo, kaka, crap.'

'Yes, lad,' said the maven of planetary pole shifts and alien conspiracies, 'all that, too,' and he moved toward Lincoln Proctor.

The scientist thrust the gun more aggressively at Lantern. 'You stay away from me.'

'I told you that precognition was the extent of my new talents,' Lantern said as he continued to cross the living room toward Proctor, 'but I lied.'

Perhaps remembering Manuel the firestarter, Proctor fired point-blank at his adversary, but Lantern didn't flinch from the sound of the shot let alone from the impact of the slug. As if the round had ricocheted off their host's chest, it lodged – with a *crack!* – in the living-room ceiling.

Desperately, Proctor fired twice more as Lantern approached him, and these two rounds were also deflected into the ceiling, forming a perfect triangular grouping with the first slug.

Dylan had become so accustomed to miracles that he observed this dazzling performance in a state better described as amazement, short of genuine awe.

For Parish Lantern, taking the gun from the stunned scientist's hand required no struggle. Proctor's eyes swam as if he'd been poleaxed, but he didn't collapse.

Dylan, Jilly, and shuffling Shep moved to Lantern's side, like a jury gathering to pass judgment.

'He's got another full syringe,' Lantern said. 'If he likes what the new generation of nanogunk has done to us, he intends to work up the courage to inject himself. You think that's a good idea, Dylan?'

'No.'

'What about you, Jilly? Do you think that's a good idea?'

'Hell, no,' she said. 'He's definitely not better clay. It'll be Manuel all over again.'

'You ungrateful bitch,' said Proctor.

When Dylan took a step toward Proctor, reaching for him, Jilly grabbed a fistful of his shirt. 'I've been called worse.'

'Any ideas about how we deal with him?' Lantern asked.

'We don't dare turn him over to the police,' said Jilly.

'Or his business partners,' Dylan added.

'Cake.'

'You are admirably persistent, lad. But first we deal with him, and then we have the cake.'

'Ice,' said Shep, and folded here to there.

48

All the way back in the kitchen of the house on the lonely coast well north of Santa Barbara, when peering into the refrigerator, Shep might not have been expressing a desire for a cold drink, but might have had a prescient awareness of their final encounter with Lincoln Proctor. In fact, Jilly remembered now that Shepherd didn't like ice in his soft drinks.

Where's all the ice? he'd asked, trying to identify a landscape of which he'd had a foretelling glimpse.

North Pole has a lot of ice, Jilly had told him.

And it sure did.

Under a lowering sky that appeared to be as hard as the lid of an iron kettle, from horizon to horizon, somber white plains receded into a semitwilight and a gray haze. The only points of elevation were the jagged pressure ridges, and the slabs of ice – some as large as caskets, some bigger than entire funeral homes – that had cracked out of the icecap and stood on end like grave markers in some strange alien cemetery.

Cold, Shepherd had said.

And it sure was.

They weren't dressed for the top of the world, and even though the infamous polar winds had gone to bed, the air bit with wolfish teeth. The shock of the abrupt temperature change tripped Jilly's heart into painful stutters and nearly dropped her to her knees.

Clearly stunned to find himself out of Lake Tahoe and in this hostile realm of grim adventure stories and Christmas legends, Parish Lantern nevertheless adjusted with remarkable aplomb. 'Impressive.'

Only Proctor reeled in panic, staggering in a circle, flailing his arms as though this panorama of ice were an illusion that he could tear away to reveal Tahoe in its warm green summer. He might have been trying to scream, but the leeching cold stole most of his voice and left him with only a shrill wheeze.

'Shepherd,' Jilly said, discovering that the cold air burned in her throat and made her lungs ache, 'why here?'

'Cake,' said Shepherd.

As the biting cold steadily chewed Proctor's panic into numb bewilderment, Parish Lantern pulled Dylan and Jilly into a tight huddle with Shep, sharing body heat, their heads touching, their faces bathed in one another's warm exhalations. 'This is killing cold. We can't take much of it.'

'Why here?' Dylan asked Shep.

'Cake.'

'I think the lad means we leave the bastard here, then go have our cake.'

'Can't,' Dylan said.

'Can,' said Shep.

'No,' Jilly said. 'It's not the right thing to do.'

Lantern expressed no surprise to hear her say such a thing, and she knew he must share their nanomachine-engineered compulsion to do what was right. His usually commanding voice quaked from the cold: 'But if we did it, a lot of problems would be solved. There'd be no body for the police to find.'

'No risk of him leading his business partners to us,' Jilly said.

'No chance of him getting his hands on a syringe for himself,' Dylan added.

'He wouldn't suffer long,' Lantern argued. 'In ten minutes, he'd be too numb to feel pain. It's almost merciful.'

Alarmed when, with her tongue, she felt a skin of ice on her teeth, Jilly said, 'But if we did it, we'd be torn up by it for a long time to come, 'cause it's not the right thing.'

'Is,' Shep said.

'Not.'

'Is.'

'Buddy,' Dylan said, 'it's really not.'

'Cold.'

'Let's take Proctor back with us, buddy.'

'Cold.'

'Take us all back to Tahoe.'

'Cake.'

Proctor snared a fistful of Jilly's hair, jerked her head back, pulled her out of the huddle, and locked one arm around her neck.

She grabbed his arm, clawed his hand, realized he was going to tighten his chokehold until she couldn't breathe, until she blacked out. She had to get away from Proctor, get away fast, which meant folding.

Her screw-ups at the church were fresh in her mind. If the government had issued learners' permits for folding, she would have been required to have one. She didn't want to fold herself out of the chokehold and discover that she'd left her head behind, but as her vision clouded, as darkness flooded in at the corners of her eyes, she went here—there, *there* being a few feet behind Proctor's back.

Arriving with her head on her shoulders where it belonged, she found herself in a perfect position to boot Proctor in the ass, which she'd wanted to do since she'd been in a chloroform haze the previous evening, in the motel.

Before Jilly could wind up to deliver a solid kick, Dylan body-checked the scientist. Proctor slipped, went down hard, and rapped his head on the ice. Curling into a fetal ball, shuddering with cold, he sought their mercy through his usual rap, wheezily declaring himself to be a weak man, a bad man, a wicked man.

Although her vision cleared, the arctic cold stung Jilly's eyes, drew a flood of tears, froze the tears on her lashes. 'Sweetie,' she said to Shepherd, 'we have to get out of here. Take us all back to Tahoe.'

Shep shuffled to Proctor, crouched at his side – and the two of them folded away.

'Buddy!' Dylan shouted, as if he could call his brother back.

The shout didn't echo across the vast iciness, but fell away into it as if into a muffling pillow.

'Now *this* worries me,' said Parish Lantern, stamping his feet to encourage circulation, hugging himself, surveying the icecap as though it held more terrors than any alternate reality inhabited by brain leeches.

The subzero air caused Dylan's sinuses to run, and a miniature icicle of nasal drippings formed from the rim of his left nostril.

Mere seconds after folding elsewhere, Shep returned, sans the scientist. 'Cake.'

'Where'd you take him, sweetie?'

'Cake.'

'Somewhere else out here on the ice?'

'Cake.'

Dylan said, 'He'll freeze to death, buddy.'

'Cake.'

Jilly said, 'We've got to do the right thing, sweetie.'

'Not Shep,' said Shepherd.

'You too, sweetie. The right thing.'

Shepherd shook his head and said, 'Shep can be a little bad.'

'No, I don't think you can be, buddy. Not without a lot of torment later.'

'No cake?' Shep asked.

'It's not an issue of cake, sweetie.'

'Shep can be just a little bad.'

Jilly exchanged a look with Dylan. To Shep, she said, 'Can you be bad, sweetie?'

'Just a little.'

'Just a little?'

'Just a little.'

Lantern's eyelashes were crusted with frozen tears. His eyes streamed, but nevertheless Jilly could read the guilt in them when he said, 'A little would be useful. In fact sometimes, when the evil is big enough, the *right* thing to do is act decisively to end it.'

'Okay,' said Shep.

They shared a silence.

'Okay?' Shep asked.

'Thinking,' Dylan said.

Out of the still sky sifted snow. This was like no snow Jilly had ever seen before. Not fluffy flakes. Needle-sharp white granules, flecks of ice.

'Too much,' Shep said.

'Too much what, sweetie?'

'Too much.'

'Too much what?'

'Thinking,' Shepherd said. Then he declared, 'Cold,' and folded them back to Tahoe, without Proctor.

49

Chocolate-cherry cake with dark chocolate icing, eaten while everyone stood around the island in the center of Parish Lantern's kitchen, was solace and reward, but to Jilly it also seemed to be the bread of a strange communion. They ate in silence, staring at their plates, all conforming to the table etiquette of Shepherd O'Conner.

This, she supposed, was as it should be.

The house proved to be even larger than it had appeared from the outside. When Parish escorted them into the expansive guest wing, to the two bedrooms that he had prepared for their use, she thought that he might have been able to accommodate a score of visitors on a moment's notice.

Although Jilly had been exhausted on returning from the North Pole and had expected to nap away the remaining afternoon and early evening, she felt awake, alert, and energetic after the cake. She wondered if the changes that she was going through might ultimately leave her with less of a need to sleep.

Each bedroom featured a large and sumptuously appointed bath with marble floors and walls and counters, gold-plated fixtures, both a shower and a large tub designed for leisurely soaking, plus heated racks to ensure the small but welcome comfort of warm towels. She took a long, luxurious shower, and with the lazy self-absorption of a cat, she found bliss in grooming and prettifying herself.

Parish had tried to foresee her preferences in everything from shampoo and bar soap to makeup and eyeliner. Sometimes he'd made the right choice, sometimes not, but he'd hit the mark more often than he missed. His consideration charmed her.

Refreshed and remade, in clean clothes, she found her way from the guest wing to the living room. During this ramble, she was more than ever convinced that the warm style and the coziness of the house distracted most visitors from clearly perceiving its true immensity. Beneath its softened and romanticized Wrightian lines, in spite of its open embrace of nature with windows and courtyards, the structure was deeply mysterious, cloistered when it appeared not to be, keeping secrets precisely when it seemed most to expose itself.

This, too, was as it should be.

From the living room, she stepped out onto the cantilevered deck that the architect had magically suspended high among the fragrant pine trees to provide a breathtaking view of the fabled lake.

Within moments, Dylan joined her at the railing. They stood in silence together, enchanted by the panorama, which had the luminous vibrancy of a Maxfield Parrish painting in this late-afternoon light. The time for talking had both passed and not yet arrived.

Parish had apologized in advance for not being able to provide them with the usual level of service that he offered to his guests. When he'd first realized that the injection of nanomachines would change him profoundly, he had given four members of his household staff a week's vacation so that he could endure the metamorphosis in private.

Only Ling, the majordomo, remained. Dylan had been at the deck railing with Jilly no more than two minutes when this man arrived. He brought cocktails on a small black-lacquered serving tray featuring a lily-pad design formed by inlaid mother-of-pearl. A pair of perfect dry martinis – stirred, not shaken.

Slender but well conditioned, moving with the grace of a *maitre de ballet* and with the quiet self-assurance of one who most likely had earned a black belt in tae kwon do, Ling might have been thirty-five years old, but in his ebony-black eyes could be glimpsed the wisdom of the ancients well distilled. As Jilly took her martini from the lily-pad tray, and again as Dylan accepted his, Ling bowed his head slightly and with a kind smile spoke one word of Chinese to each of them, the same word twice, which Jilly somehow knew was both a welcome and a wish for their good fortune. Then Ling departed almost as discreetly as a ghost dematerializing; had this been winter and had the deck been dusted with snow, he might have left no footprints either coming or going.

This, too, was *uncannily* as it should be.

While Jilly and Dylan enjoyed the perfect martinis and the view, Shepherd remained in the living room behind them. He'd found a corner to his liking, where he might stand for an hour or two, sensory input limited to the contemplation of wall meeting wall.

The French have a saying – *Plus ça change, plus c'est le même chose* – which means 'The more things change, the more they remain the same.' Shepherd, as he stood now in the corner, embodied the comedy and the tragedy of that truth. He represented both the frustration and the graceful acceptance that it suggested, but defined as well the melancholy beauty in those words.

Considering that Parish's nationally syndicated radio program was heard on over five hundred stations six nights a week, Monday through Saturday, he would ordinarily have been at work as twilight cast its purple veils across the lake. In a state-of-the-art studio in the basement of the house, he could take calls from some of his ten million listeners and from his interview subjects, and with the assistance of Ling and an engineer, he could conduct his show. The actual production facility remained in San Francisco, where call-ins were screened and patched through to him, and where the combined audio feeds were filtered and enhanced for all-but-instantaneous rebroadcast.

This Saturday night, however, as on the first night following injection with Proctor's *stuff*, Parish would forego the usual live broadcast and run instead a best-of program from his archives.

Shortly before they were expected to join their host for dinner, Jilly said to Dylan, 'I'm going to call my mom. I'll be right back.'

Leaving her empty martini glass on the deck railing, she folded to a shadowy corner of the gardens at the back of the Peninsula hotel in Beverly Hills. Her arrival went unnoticed.

She could have folded anywhere to make the call, but she liked the Peninsula. This hotel was the five-star quality she had hoped one day to be able to afford if her career as a comedian had taken off.

At a pay phone inside, she fed change to the slot and keyed in the familiar number.

Her mother answered on the third ring. Recognizing Jilly's voice, she blurted: 'Are you all right, baby girl, are you hurt, what's happened to you, sugar – Sweet Jesus keep you safe – where are you?'

'Relax, Mom. I'm fine. I wanted to let you know that I'm not going to be able to see you for a week or two, but I'll figure out a way for us to get together soon.'

'Jilly girl, since the church, people been here from the TV, from the newspapers, all of them as rude as any welfare bureaucrat on a dry-cracker diet. Fact is, they're out in the street right now, with all their noise and satellite trucks, littering with their filthy cigarettes and their granola-bar wrappers. Rude, rude, rude.'

'Don't talk to any of them, Mom. As far as you know, I'm dead.'

'Don't you say such a terrible thing!'

'Just don't tell anyone you've heard from me. I'll explain all this later. Listen, Mom, some big, tough-looking dudes are going to come around soon. They'll say they're with the FBI or somesuch, but they'll be lying. You just play dumb. Be nice as pie with them, pretend to be worried sick about me, but don't give them a clue.'

'Well, I'm just a one-eyed, two-cane, poor-as-dirt, ignorant, big-assed simpleton, after all. Who could *expect* me to know anything about anything?'

'Love you to pieces, Mom. One more thing. I'm sure your phone isn't tapped already, but eventually they might find a way. So when I come to see you, I won't call first.'

'Baby girl, I'm scared like I haven't had to be scared since your hateful father was good enough to get himself shot dead.'

'Don't be scared, Mom. I'll be all right. And so will you. You're in for some surprises.'

'Father Francorelli is here with me. He wants to talk to you. He's all excited about what *happened* at the wedding. Jilly girl, what happened at the wedding? I mean, I know, sure, I been told, but none of it makes a lick of sense.'

'I don't want to talk to Father Francorelli, Mom. Just tell him I'm so sorry I ruined the ceremony.'

'Ruined? You *saved* them. You saved them all.'

'Well, I could have been more discreet about it. Hey, Mom, when we get together in a couple weeks, would you like to have dinner in Paris?'

'Paris, France? What in the world would I eat in Paris?'

'Or maybe Rome? Or Venice? Or Hong Kong?'

'Baby girl, I know you wouldn't do drugs in a million years, but you got me worried now.'

Jilly laughed. 'How about Venice? Some five-star restaurant. I know you like Italian food.'

'I do have a passion for lasagne. How are you going to afford five stars, let alone in Venice, Italy?'

'You just wait and see. And Mom . . .'

'What is it, child?'

'I wouldn't have been able to save my own ass, not to mention all those people, if I hadn't grown up with you to show me how not to let the fear eat me alive.'

'God bless you, baby girl. I love you so much.'

When Jilly hung up, she took a moment to recover her composure. Then she used a ransom of quarters to place a long-distance call to a number that Dylan had given her. A woman answered the first ring, and Jilly said, 'I'd like to speak to Vonetta Beesley please.'

'You're speakin' to her. What can I do you for?'

'Dylan O'Conner asked me to call and make sure you're okay.'

'What could anyone do to me that Nature won't eventually do worse? You tell Dylan I'm fine. And it's good to know he's alive. He's not hurt?'

'Not a scratch.'

'And little Shep?'

'He's standing in a corner right now, but he had a nice piece of cake earlier, and he'll be fine by dinner.'

'He's a love.'

'That he is,' Jilly said. 'And Dylan wanted me to tell you they won't be needing a housekeeper anymore.'

'From what I hear happened up at their place, you couldn't clean it up with anything less than a bulldozer, anyway. Tell me something, doll. You think you can take good care of them?'

'I think so,' Jilly said.

'They deserve good care.'

'They do,' she agreed.

Finished with the second call, she would have liked to erupt from the phone booth in cape and tights, leaping into flight with great drama. She didn't have a cape and tights, of course, and she couldn't actually fly. Instead, she looked both ways to be sure the pay-phone hallway was deserted, and then without trumpets, without flourishes, she folded herself to the deck overlooking the lake, where Dylan waited in the last of the Tahoe twilight.

The moon had risen long before the late summer sunset. In the west, the night kissed the last rouge off the cheek of the day, and in the east the full moon hung high, the lamp of romance.

Precisely at nightfall, Ling reappeared to lead them, and Shep, down through previously unseen passages and chambers, and finally out of the house to the dock. The ordinary dock lights had been turned off. The path was charmingly illuminated by a series of tapered candles floating in midair, eight feet above the planking.

Apparently, Parish enjoyed finding other uses for the power with which he had deflected and then redirected speeding bullets.

The great house stood on ten wooded acres, fenced against the uninvited, and the trees guaranteed seclusion. Even from far across the lake, with binoculars trained on the candles, no curious soul would quite know what he was seeing. The lark seemed worth the risk.

As though he himself were drifting a fraction of an inch off the dock planks, Ling led them through the lambent candlelight, under the levitated tapers, along the dock and down the gangway. The sound made by water lapping at the pilings might almost have been music.

Ling gave no indication that he found the levitating candles to be remarkable. By all appearances, nothing could disturb either his mental calm or his balletic equilibrium. Evidently, his discretion and his loyalty to his employer were beyond question, to a degree that seemed almost supernatural.

This, too, was as it should be.

At the bottom of the gangway, in the slip, rested a forty-five-foot cabin cruiser from an age when pleasure boats were not made from plastic, aluminum, and fiberglass. White painted wood, decks and trim of polished mahogany, and bracelets and necklaces of sparkling brass brightwork made this not merely a cabin cruiser, but a vessel that had sailed out of a dream.

When all were aboard, the candles on the dock were extinguished one by one and allowed to drop to the planking.

Parish piloted the boat out of the slip and into the lake. The waters would have been everywhere as black as aniline if the generous moon had not scattered silver coins across the wavelets. He dropped anchor far from shore, relying on the amber-paned ship's lanterns to warn other night travelers of their presence.

The spacious afterdeck of the cruiser allowed a table for four and sufficient room for Ling to serve a candlelight dinner. The wild-mushroom ravioli, as an appetizer, were nicely square. On the entree plate, the zucchini had been cubed before it had been sauteed; the serving of potato-onion casserole was presented in a neat block; and the medallions of veal had been thoughtfully trimmed into squares not merely for Shepherd, but for everyone, so as to ensure that the young Mr. O'Conner would not feel that he had in any way been set apart from his companions.

Nevertheless, Ling stood ready in the galley to make a grilled-cheese sandwich if necessary.

Every course proved to be delicious. The accompanying Cabernet Sauvignon rated exceptional by any standard. The cold glass of Coke without ice cubes satisfied as fully as could any cold glass of Coke in the world. And the conversation, of course, was fascinating, even though Shepherd limited most of his contributions to one or two words and made excessive use of the adjective *tasty*.

'You will have a wing of the house for your own,' Parish said. 'And in time, if you'd like, a second house can be constructed on the property.'

'You're very generous,' Jilly said.

'Nonsense. My radio program is a money cow. I've never married, have no children. Of course, you'll have to live here secretly. Your whereabouts must never be known. The media, authorities, the whole of humanity would hound you ceaselessly, more and more as the years go by. I may have to make a couple staff changes to ensure our secret will be kept, but Ling has brothers, sisters.'

'Funny,' Dylan said, 'how we sit here planning, on the same page from the start. We all know what must be done and how.'

'We're of different generations,' Jilly said, 'but we're all children of the same culture. We're marinated in the same mythology.'

'Exactly,' said Parish. 'Now, next week I'll change my will to make all of you my heirs, though this will have to be done through Swiss attorneys and a chain of offshore accounts, with ID numbers rather than names. Your names are already too well known nationally, and in the years ahead, you'll be ever more famous. Should anything happen to me, or to any of us, the others can go on without tax or financial problems.'

Putting down his knife and fork, clearly moved by their host's easy generosity, Dylan said, 'There aren't words to properly thank you for all this. You are . . . an exceptional man.'

'No more gratitude,' Parish said firmly. 'I don't need to hear it. You are exceptional, as well, Dylan. And you, Jilly. And you, Shepherd.'

'Tasty.'

'We are all different from other men and women, and we'll never be like them again. Not better, but very different. There is nowhere in the world where any of us truly belongs anymore except here, with one another. Our task from this day forward – a task at which we must not fail – is to make absolutely certain that we use our difference to *make* a difference.'

'We must go wherever we're needed,' Dylan agreed. 'No gloves, no hesitation, no fear.'

'Plenty of fear,' Jilly disagreed. 'But we can't ever surrender to it.'

'That's better said,' Dylan complimented her.

As Ling poured more Cabernet, an airliner crossed Tahoe at high altitude, perhaps en route to the airport in Reno. If night on the lake had not been silent except for the knocking of the moon coins against the hull, they might have failed to hear the faint exhalation of the jet engines. Looking up, Jilly saw a tiny winged silhouette cross the lunar face.

'One thing I'm grateful for,' said Parish. 'We won't have all the trouble of designing, building, and maintaining a damn Batplane or Batmobile.'

Laughter felt good.

'Being tragic figures with the world on our shoulders might not be so bad,' Dylan decided, 'if we can have some *fun* at it.'

'Great fun,' Parish declared. 'Oh, I insist upon it. I'd rather we didn't give ourselves silly names with heroic flair, since I've already done damage of that kind to myself, but I'm up for anything else that comes to mind.'

Jilly hesitated as she was about to sip her wine. 'You mean Parish Lantern isn't your real name?'

'Would it be anyone's? It's my legal name now, but I was born Horace Bloogernud.'

'Good lord,' said Dylan. 'You were something of a tragic figure from day one.'

'As a teenager, I wanted to go into radio, and I knew the kind of show I hoped to create. A late-night program concerned mostly with strange and spooky stuff. It seemed that Parish Lantern would serve me well, since it's an old English term for the moon, for moonlight.'

'You do your work by the light of the moon,' Shepherd said, but without the anguish that had wrenched his voice when he had spoken these words previously, as if they meant something new to him now.

'Indeed I do,' Parish told Shep. 'And in a way, we'll all be doing our great work by the light of the moon, in the sense that we will try to do as much of it as possible with discretion and a sense of secrecy. Which brings me to the subject of disguises.'

'Disguises?' Jilly asked.

'Fortunately,' said Parish, 'the fact that I've been cursed like you isn't known to anyone but us. As long as I can do what must be done and enjoy my share of derring-do, while keeping my secret, I can be the interface between our little group and the world. But you three – your faces are widely known, and no matter what care we take to operate discreetly, your images will become more universally recognized as time passes. Therefore you will have to become—'

'Masters of disguise!' Dylan said with delight.

This, too, Jilly decided, was as it should be.

'When all is said and done,' Parish continued, 'about all we'll be lacking are silly heroic names, cumbersome vehicles full of absurd gadgets, spandex costumes, and an archvillain to worry about between all the ordinary rescues and good deeds.'

'Ice,' said Shepherd.

Ling at once approached the table, but with a few Chinese words, Parish assured him that no ice was needed. 'Shepherd is correct.

We did in fact have an archvillain for a little while, but now he's just a block of ice.'

'Ice.'

Later, over lemon cake and coffee, Jilly said, 'If we don't call ourselves something, the media will give us a name, and it's sure to be stupid.'

'You're right,' Dylan said. 'They aren't imaginative. And then we'll have to live with something that makes us grind our teeth. But why don't we use a collective name, something that applies to all of us as a group?'

'Yeah,' Jilly agreed. 'And let's be as sneaky-clever as Horace Bloogernud was in his day. Let's use *moonlight* in the name.'

'The Moonlight Gang,' Dylan suggested. 'Has the right tabloid ring, doesn't it?'

'I don't like the *gang* part,' said Parish. 'Too many negative connotations with that one.'

'The Moonlight . . . something,' Jilly brooded.

Although half his cake remained on his plate, Shepherd put down his fork. Staring at this treat postponed, he said, 'Squad, crew, band, ring, society—'

'Here we go,' Dylan said.

'—guild, alliance, association, team, coalition, clan, outfit, league, club—'

'The Moonlight Club.' Jilly played the three words across her tongue. 'The Moonlight Club. That's not half bad.'

'—fellowship, company, troop, posse, family—'

'I assume this will take a while,' said Parish, and indicated to Ling that the time had come to remove three of the four dessert plates and to uncork another bottle of wine.

'—travelers, voyagers, riders—'

Listening with one ear to the good Shepherd's cascade of words, Jilly dared to think about their future, about destiny and free will, about mythology and truth, about dependency and responsibility, about the certainty of death and the desperate need to live with purpose, about love and duty, and hope.

The sky is deep. The stars lie far away. The moon is nearer than Mars but still distant. The lake is a lustrous black, enlivened by the mercurial light of the parish lantern. The vessel rocks gently at anchor. The Moonlight Club, or whatever it eventually will be called, conducts its first meeting with serious intent, laughter, and cake, beginning what all its members hope will be a long exploration of the round and round of all that is.